Land of Wolves
Revelations

Invi Wright

Copyright © 2026 by Invi Wright

All rights reserved.

No part of this book may be reproduced or used in any manner without the prior written permission of the copyright owner, except for the use of brief quotations in a book review.

This is a work of fiction. Names, characters, plots, and incidents either are the product of the author's imagination or are used fictitiously, and any resemblance to actual persons, living or dead, business establishments, events, or locales is entirely coincidental.

Editing by: Amy McNulty

Cover Design by: Krafigs Design

Interior Artwork by: Invi Wright

❀ Formatted with Vellum

Thank You

The largest thank you possible to my husband. You gave me the confidence and support to pursue writing, and none of this would be possible without you.

Also, to my Patreon subscribers. Your support is the sole reason I'm able to do this, and I can't properly convey in words just how much you mean to me. I hope you enjoy this story.

Completed Works

THE FEMALE SERIES

The Female is a why choose demon romance with a dark dystopian setting, declining fertility rates, captured women, and three irresistible men.

The Female | Her Males | Their War

Chev's Mate

Queens

THE CURSED KINGDOM SERIES

The Cursed Kingdom is a slow burning, why choose romance with a mystical faerie realm, two infuriatingly attractive princes, and high conflict between the faerie and shifter kingdoms.

The Cursed Kingdom

The Shattered Kingdom

LAND OF WOLVES DUOLOGY

Land of Wolves is a high intensity shifter romance with fated mates, government indoctrination that leads to painful betrayal, and impending war between the shifters and humans.

Land of Wolves: Revelations

Land of Wolves: Retribution (Coming June 2026)

STANDALONES

The Nanny | A Nanny/Single Father Romance

Lord of Dread | An Arranged Marriage Historical Romance

Aine | A Dark Shifter Romance

Upcoming Works

STANDALONES

His Assignment | A Bodyguard Mafia Romance (Release Date TBD)

The Dragon's Agreement | A Dragon Fantasy Romance (Release Date TBD)

ONGOING SERIES

Fates | Book Six of *The Female* Series (Release Date TBD)

The Hidden Kingdom | Book Three of *The Cursed Kingdom* Series (Release date TBD)

TRIGGER WARNINGS CAN BE FOUND ON:

inviwright.com

STAY CONNECTED

SOCIAL MEDIA

Follow Invi Wright on social media to stay up to date on her newest releases, listen to her gab about romance & fantasy books, get regular book recs, and join a fun community of romance lovers!

TikTok & Instagram: @inviwright

EXCLUSIVE CONTENT & CHARACTER ART

Subscribe to **@inviwright** on Patreon for:

- Exclusive access to ongoing novellas
- Exclusive audio chapters
- SFW and NSFW character art
- Partake in polls (help decide what book she'll write next!)
- A free ebook copy of every book she publishes

*For those who never outgrew 2013 Wattpad.
Long live 1D fanfics, shifters, and Y/N inserts.*

Chapter One

I was never foolish enough to believe starvation would be fun, but I sure didn't anticipate it being this damn hard.

My mouth waters as I eye the food in Daniel's hands, the ache in my abdomen growing. He said this would be challenging, but I thought he was exaggerating. I've broken too many bones to keep track of, have sprained and torn more muscles than I can count, and was even stabbed once. I survived.

But this hunger has me questioning my sanity.

Daniel frowns, his full, graying eyebrows pulling inward. Concern looks out of place on his otherwise severe face. Daniel has been working for HPAW longer than I've been alive, and the years here have hardened him. He may be almost fifty, but he's more frightening than most of the combat-ready thirty-year-olds who work here.

He looks me up and down, his frown deepening. He pities me. I'm so hungry, I'm beginning to pity myself.

"I know you're hungry, Evelyn," he starts, "but this is a necessary evil."

I clear my throat, sitting up in bed. "I understand."

My thin, government-issued sheets don't offer much warmth, but I run hot, so it doesn't bother me. The air vent directly above my bed does, though. It blows frigid air against me all night long, keeping me awake. My metal bedframe is firmly anchored to the ground, too, so there's no hope of escaping the vent.

Daniel steps inside my room, letting the heavy, metal door swing shut behind him. It slams, and there's a faint click as the lock engages. He'll have to swipe his keycard to leave.

I toss my legs over the side of the bed, planting my sock-covered feet against the cement ground. I eye my sleep pants, absentmindedly flicking away a stray dark hair. I had it chopped just above my shoulders for this mission. The shorter length is easier to deal with.

Daniel gifted me a rug for my fourteenth birthday, and I drag my toes over the deep-purple fibers as I meet his gray eyes.

This is a necessary evil. I understand that, but I'm still teetering on the edge of starvation-induced madness. I'm milliseconds away from lunging for Daniel, taking him to the ground and snatching that food from his hands.

Tucked underneath his arm is a thin manila folder. Nothing positive ever comes from those folders.

"What is it this time?" I ask, gesturing toward it.

Daniel exhales, adjusting his stance and freeing up a hand so he can toss the folder at me. It lands on the end of my bed, just out of reach. My bones feel like they're rubbing together as I lean sideways, snatching it up.

I skim the first few pages. "Shit." I sigh, wincing. Another family murdered. There are several photographs, all of them graphic. Two adults, two children. Each of them violently ripped apart by the shifters.

Along with the images is a detailed medical report. I don't read it. I don't need to. The victims are torn to shreds. Their cause of death isn't much of a mystery.

"I assume they lived on the border," I say.

Daniel hums an affirmative.

"Has this been shared?" I continue. "Surely, this is enough proof of violence for other leaders to take action."

Daniel sucks his cheeks into his mouth, shaking his head. "They don't wish to get involved."

I don't understand why. America may be the only country that shares a land border with the shifters, but shifters are a threat to *all* humans. We need help. The shifters have been infringing on our lands, pushing and pushing. They want us gone.

This murdered family is proof enough of what happens when we get in their way.

I set the folder aside, my stomach grumbling. Daniel cracks a rare sympathetic smile.

"It won't be long now," he says. He's been saying that for days. "Our timing is everything."

I nod, absentmindedly stroking the marking on the back of my hand. The color has darkened with age, the once intricate white design now a deep red. I hate it, and I hate even more what the mark stands for.

I was told as a child to keep it hidden. My parents insisted that the marking was dangerous, and they constantly hid it underneath a second-skin covering. The flesh-covered bandage was seamless, hiding all evidence of my curse.

Then I saw it on the news.

The way the delicate floral design travels up my middle two fingers before spreading across the back of my right hand is impossible to mistake. The people on the television had an exact drawing of it.

Only shifters have these markings. Usually. I'm an unfortunate exception. Shifters typically revere their markings, cherishing the connection to their fated mate. HPAW managed to get their hands on a drawing of a future shifter alpha's marking. A child with a wolf so dominant that he's set to lead the largest pack once he comes of age. The future Alpha Knox.

His marking was being shared amongst the smaller shifter packs. They were looking for his match. *Me*. I draw in an even breath, digging my thumbnail into my flesh. I wish I could cut the marking off. I'm so fucking unlucky.

Seven-year-old me was entranced with the idea of having a fated mate. *How utterly romantic.* I was an idiot.

Daniel finally hands over the single warmed potato he's been cleared to give me. Potatoes are the only food I've been permitted to eat, and I've very quickly grown sick of them. I shove the bland vegetable into my mouth in the blink of an eye.

It's a miracle HPAW intercepted me before I found my way into the shifter domain, my childhood delusions of true love urging me to sneak into the empty, forested lands separating our territories. I thought I'd find my mate. Most likely, I would've been eaten alive.

The shifters retreated into Canada after outing their true nature, officially separating themselves from humankind. It didn't take long for the Canadian government to fall, the once-proud country deteriorated into nothing.

The territories have since been divided into packs, each one led by an alpha.

The Human Protection Against Wolves organization was quick to form. They protect our borders, ensuring humans are safe from the vicious predators. They saved my life. They gave me purpose.

I pick at my marking. My job is to infiltrate and dismantle the shifter organization from within. It's said that the shifters cherish their mates, but I'm human. There's no telling how my mate and his pack will react to me.

Exposing myself to them is a risk I'm willing to take, though.

I swallow, my throat dry. "Will you leave my ribs alone?"

Daniel grimaces, the action answer enough.

I understand why my injuries need to be real, but injured ribs take forever to heal. I've been training for this day as long as I can remember, and I've never gotten used to the painful snap of a rib cracking.

HPAW has taught me how to fight and defend myself, but I need to appear weak.

It should be easy enough to do. I've always had a lean frame, and HPAW's decision to periodically starve me over the past several months has given me a borderline gaunt look. It's all part of the plan.

My muscles have deteriorated, removing all evidence of the years of combat training I've undergone. I won't need it. Even at peak physical form, I don't stand a chance against the shifters.

The alpha, *my mate*, must think I'm a victim, captured and tortured by a group of misfit humans because of my marking. He'll feel inclined to believe me because I'm his mate, and once I've gathered all the necessary information regarding him and his pack, I'll slit his throat. It's the easiest way to kill a shifter.

I'll kill the alpha just as his people killed my parents, ripping them to shreds when they traveled into the shifter territory searching for me.

Daniel doesn't like it when I say this, but I'm glad they're dead. My parents were shifter sympathizers, and I suspect they were eventually planning to deliver me to the violent beasts. There's no other reason for them to have kept my mark hidden, forcing me to wear bandages over the stained skin.

"Approval came through for your sedation," Daniel says. "I had to pull some strings, but they agreed to drug you for transport. They're going to sprain your shoulder, bruise your ribs, and break your collarbone. The blood we've been collecting from you has been soaked into the dress, and we'll mat the hair along the left side of your head."

Daniel speaks through a clenched jaw as he describes the extent of the injuries I'll sustain.

I'm too relieved that leadership approved my sedation to care. They want me to experience the trauma firsthand, making my story that much more believable. Daniel's been working hard to change their minds. He has been my primary caretaker since I arrived at the HPAW facility, and he has grown protective over the years.

"You'll be tied to the bed in the cabin, your marked hand facing outward," Daniel continues. "The shifters should be arriving that night. The pair has been visiting the cabin every month. They don't deviate. We'll make sure to have your mark be the first thing they see, though, lest they decide to kill first and ask questions later."

My lip curls at the mention of my marking. I hate acknowledging its existence.

I blow out a slow breath. "And I'll tell the shifters I've been hiding my mark out of fear of being judged, but somebody must've noticed the second skin. I was grabbed on my way home from work, and I woke up alone in the cabin. I don't know how or who brought me there."

I've memorized every detail of our plan. I won't disappoint.

We've been perfecting my lies for years, to the point that I can confidently pass a lie detector test. Daniel insists it won't come to that, the shifters foolish in their blind trust of mates, but you can never be too prepared.

"I'm so proud of you, Evelyn," Daniel says, leaning against the locked door.

I hold back a smile. This isn't easy, but it's a small price to pay to save the lives of millions of humans. The shifters are natural predators, and it's only a matter of time before they attack. HPAW suspects it's coming soon. The frequency of border attacks has ratcheted up significantly, and while we don't have much insight into what's happening on shifter lands, HPAW has spotted movement. The alphas are relocating soldiers, preparing for war.

It doesn't matter that the shifters often walk around in forms identical to humans. Their human traits will never outweigh their animal ones. They're bloodthirsty.

I glance at my hand. "I hope we aren't putting too much faith in the mate bond."

HPAW believes the alpha will fall in love with me, the bond bringing us together in ways I can't even begin to conceptualize. It's a romantic idea, but I'm not sure how much I believe it.

"The mate bond is everything to shifters," Daniel says. "Alpha

Knox will bend over backward for you, and I doubt it'll be long before he's willingly and openly sharing with you every bit of information we need to bring his pack down." Daniel grins, his teeth on full display. "We'll have armed men at the meeting spot twenty-four-seven, but there's no rush. Wait until you have everything you need."

I nod, swallowing the last of my food and lying back on my bed. My head aches, likely due to dehydration. I'm being given water, but not enough.

I'm our best chance of bringing down the shifters. I won't disappoint.

Chapter Two

Explosive pain travels up my ribcage, stealing my breath and forcing my muscles into a tense rigidness. *Son of a bitch.* My hands are tied above my head, and when I twist my wrists, the skin rubs painfully against rope. It throbs, pulsating with every beat of my heart.

It's nothing compared to the flare of pain in my right shoulder. It must be broken, or at the very least dislocated. I don't need to see it to know. I can feel that I'm in a bloody dress, too, the damp fabric bunched at my thighs.

It begins.

My vision is blurred, and I blink several times to clear it before scanning the small cabin HPAW scouted out. I knew they didn't intend to give me much warning before setting our plan into motion, but I thought I'd get *some* sort of heads-up.

It's beyond disorienting to wake up in a bed and a building different than the one you fell asleep in. The cabin is old, but it's well cared for. The bed I'm tied to is comfortable, and the brown flannel sheets twisted around my ankles are thick and clean. There's a small kitchenette near the door and a cozy sitting area on my right.

Everything is covered in a thick layer of dust.

This cabin is deep in what used to be Ontario before the shifters claimed the land as their own. HPAW has been monitoring it for years. There are two shifters, a man and a woman, who visit this place every month. Assuming the couple hasn't strayed from tradition, they should be arriving today.

I gulp, my throat burning.

Daniel wasn't exaggerating when he said the medical team would bruise my ribs, and I worry they've gone as far as to break one. Every breath is torturous. They promised not to do anything that would cause permanent damage—excluding leaving a small handful of cuts that will likely lead to nasty-looking scars.

A slight tinge of fear I work hard to ignore travels down my spine, and I bring my knees to my chest before scooting back against the dark wooden headboard I'm restrained to. The slight movement is enough to have sweat dotting my forehead, and I rest my chin against my knees to prevent myself from passing out.

This is really happening.

The shifters should be able to smell the blood on my dress, the metallic scent acting as a beacon. If that doesn't get their attention, my ragged breathing surely will. The shifters are known to have impeccable hearing.

I have to hope it's enough. This cabin is deep within the shifter lands, and it was a risk to bring me here. HPAW won't come back to check that I've been found. If the couple doesn't come and the shifters don't find me, I'll die chained to this bed.

My gaze travels to my arms. My wrists are swollen, and I was indeed positioned in a way that has my mark on full display. That's a relief. I don't trust the shifters not to attack the second they scent me, and I'm hoping the sight of my marking brings them pause. Will they recognize it as the match to their alpha?

I chew at my bottom lip as I take in the mangled skin below my wrists. Sometimes I think HPAW's doctors are rougher than they need to be. Their hatred for the shifters extends to me...as if I had any say in being mated to an alpha.

I scan the room once more, wishing I were in a position to see out the window near the door. This cabin is isolated—the perfect place to bring a young woman you intend to torture. Nobody is around to hear my screams and pleas for help.

Something snaps outside. It sounds like a twig, and unease climbs up my throat.

The shifters are here.

The front door to the cabin is slammed open and a large, feral wolf comes barreling inside a heartbeat later. It practically fills the doorframe, its dark-brown fur brushing against each end. The animal snarls, revealing a drooling mouth filled with sharp, white teeth.

I've never seen a shifter in person, and pure adrenaline courses through my system as I take in its sheer size. Nothing could have prepared me for this. It's fucking huge.

I open my mouth, a scream tearing from my throat. This has been rehearsed, but it feels real enough.

A smaller, light-brown wolf comes running inside behind the larger one.

This must be the couple.

The animals exchange a look before shifting into their skin forms. The sight is gruesome, their limbs twisting at unnatural angles that would have most humans wishing for death. It's a quick transformation, though, and at the end of it stand two human-looking creatures.

A man and a woman. Both naked as the day they were born.

I keep my attention on the man. He's the larger of the two—the bigger threat. His brown eyes flicker from injury to injury, lingering on my shoulder before finally settling on my wrists. Every muscle in his body grows taut as he notices my marking.

What does he think of it? He's either going to kill me or save me. I'm at his mercy.

He curses, dragging a hand through his messy, dark hair before running it down his face. He has thick facial hair, but it's kept short. He's rugged, every bit of him screaming *wilderness*. It's precisely how I pictured a shifter male to look.

The man extends one muscular arm to the side, covering his female's torso. He's trying to tuck her behind him. She doesn't move. Her brown eyes are blown wide, and when she roughly shoves her long, dark hair out of her heavily freckled face, I notice her hand is shaking. Why? The man beside her shows no outward expression.

I glance between the two of them, not needing to pretend my fear is real. It ratchets up as the man steps forward, rapidly closing the distance between us. I'm supposed to be pleading for help. It's what I rehearsed with HPAW, but my jaw remains clamped shut. I work it from side to side, trying and failing to find the courage to speak.

The man takes my wrist, his touch feather-light as he runs his fingers over my dark-red marking. He's trying to smudge it. Luckily for him, it's real.

"Sash…" His voice is surprisingly hoarse. "Get Knox."

The woman vanishes. I pay her no mind, too occupied by the man as he begins untying my wrists. Instinct takes over as I kick at him, harsh breaths slipping from my throat as I put a little distance between us.

"Shit," the man curses. "You're okay. I'm not going to hurt you."

I curl my arms around myself the second my hands are freed, protectively cradling my front. My shoulder aches with the movement, as does my ribcage and collarbone.

The man scans me with poorly concealed panic. The medical team did a number on me.

I begin counting.

Shifters are fast. They can sprint up to fifty or so miles an hour, and the time it takes the woman to return will reveal a lot about the location of the nearest pack. HPAW doesn't have much visibility beyond this cabin. I'm most interested in how long it takes the alpha to reach me. We know he resides in this general area, but we haven't been able to pinpoint a specific location.

"How did you get here?" The man scratches at his thick, short beard. "It doesn't matter. We need to move you. The cabin reeks of gas."

Gas? I wasn't told anything about gasoline. *Assholes*.

The man reaches for me, then hesitates, his hands hovering over my shoulders.

"Where are you hurt?" he asks.

It takes me a moment to respond. I shake my head, jostling myself into clarity. I need to focus. I'm scared, in pain, and a little nauseous, but I have a mission to complete. *Focus*.

"I—" I cough, my ribs screaming. "Everywhere."

The man grimaces. "Well, I'm sorry in advance."

His hands close around my shoulder, and before I have the opportunity to react, he's popping it back into place. I hiss through my teeth, sweat dotting along my forehead as I throw my head back and curse every god, star, and world wonder known to man. *Son of a bitch*.

The man grabs my waist. The shriek I release as he lifts me out of bed is very much real, and I resist the urge to bite off his ear as he takes me into his arms.

My instinct is to fight, but I suppress those urges. They're useless, anyway. I'm a trained fighter, but I know my limits. I stand no chance against an adult shifter male. Besides, attempting to defend myself would only raise questions.

I'm playing a part, and I can't let anything real slip. I'm to be just an ordinary young woman—one who has lived her life hiding the marking she's so ashamed of. She's scared of the shifters, the rumors of them widespread and vicious, but she's desperate to be loved.

If the alpha is kind, she'll fall in love with him in no time. If he's not... I'll figure something else out. I'll beg him for information under the guise of wanting to get to know him better.

The shifter carries me outside. The blast of cold air that smacks me in the face as he kicks open the cabin door sends me momentarily reeling. I don't spend much, if any, time outside.

HPAW doesn't allow it. The facility where I was raised has a small courtyard I had access to, but it's not well-maintained.

Once I've completed my work and the shifters are no longer a concern, I'll get to enjoy the outside. I won't have to fear humans recognizing my mark—not when the man it links me to is dead. I'll finally get to live as a normal human.

The shifter is surprisingly gentle as he carries me outside, but every step still sends a flare of agony throughout my body. Pain licks up my ribcage, rendering it nearly impossible to breathe, and my arm hangs limply by my side.

I continue counting, refusing to lose focus. The pain is temporary, and my injuries aren't fatal. HPAW would never allow that. I'm too big an asset.

The man crouches, setting me on the ground. I scamper away from him, my feet kicking at the ground until my back hits a tree. I prop myself against it, refusing to take my eyes off the shifter. HPAW warned me to remain vigilant, not that I need their warning. The shifters are terrifying creatures.

The man clears his throat. "Sash is getting Caleb. He'll be here soon."

I blink, overwhelmed by my pain. I knew this would hurt, but *fuck*.

"Who?" I croak out.

The shifter licks his lips, sitting back on his heels. I'm painfully aware that he's naked, his bits dangling openly between his thighs. I avoid looking, but I wish he'd turn away.

"Sash, my mate," he starts. "She's getting Knox. *Caleb*. He's..." He points to my mark. "Well, he's yours."

My mate. Caleb. The alpha's name is Caleb.

We know him as 'Alpha Knox.' That's also how the other countries refer to him. His first name has always remained an unknown. I've been in the presence of these shifters for less than five minutes, and already, I have valuable information.

The shifter rises, standing to his full height.

He's still looking at me, probably taking a mental tally of my injuries, but he makes no moves to touch me. I take this moment to eye him, too. Every muscle on his tanned frame ripples as he shifts his weight from his left to his right foot. He stands several feet away, his hands clasped behind his back and his shoulders rolled forward.

It looks like he's trying to make himself appear smaller, probably for my benefit.

A part of me I'll never admit to appreciates it. Shifters have a natural physical advantage over humans. I've always taken pride in being strong and athletic by human standards, but I can't do much of anything with my injuries.

It will take weeks, if not months, for me to regain my strength. It's going to be an agonizing wait, and I'm impatient. I don't enjoy being vulnerable.

I raise my good arm and wipe at my face. My palm comes back wet.

"Who are you?" I finally ask.

I spare a glance at my hand. My palm is red, covered in blood. I didn't realize I was bleeding, and I wince as I feel along a deep cut near my hairline. That's going to scar.

The man crouches again, his muscular frame folding until he's eye level with me. He bounces on the balls of his feet, his forearms resting on his thighs.

"I'm Logan," he says. He cocks his head to the side, his lips turning down at the corners. "Do you know what that marking on your hand means?"

I nod, forcing myself to look at the dark-red lines. The color seems even more pronounced than the last time I examined it, but maybe that's just my mind playing tricks on me. I've lost a lot of blood.

Logan remains silent as I touch my mark, tracing the vine-like lines on my knuckles.

"I do," I admit. I draw in a deep breath. "Are you going to kill me?"

I'm reasonably certain they aren't going to. Logan carried me outside because the cabin smells of gasoline, and HPAW is confident that shifters revere their mate bonds. I don't want to seem too knowledgeable about the shifters, though.

Most humans are rightfully terrified of them.

Logan frowns. "No. Never." He clears his throat. "How did you get here? Do you know who did this to you, or where they went?"

I shake my head. "No."

Logan touches his face. I spot his marking, the harsh lines traveling from his knuckles to his wrist. We don't know much about the marks or how they work, but each is unique. Mine is delicate, almost floral. Logan's is rough.

His is also the white color mine used to be. I wonder if time or distance has anything to do with the changing of mine, the dark color deepening with each passing year.

Will my mate's be a dark red as well?

Logan falls silent, ending the conversation. I appreciate it, mainly because speaking is hard with my bruised ribs. Every breath hurts, and I rest my head against the tree trunk as I focus on counting how long the female shifter is gone for.

I estimate that a little over an hour passes before Logan's head snaps to the right. She's back. The nearest pack is about twenty-five miles away, then. That's closer than I would've guessed. Good to know.

Logan squints at the trees before scrambling to his feet. I shift, eager to see, but I grow rigid when Logan places a hand on my shoulder.

"Stay," he orders.

He removes his hand and steps forward, his shoulders relaxing and chest deflating with breath. He's relieved.

I don't share that emotion.

Chapter Three

A loud, low noise vibrates out from the trees. It faintly reminds me of a dog's bark, but it's evident it comes from a much larger creature. It sends a shudder down my spine, and my heart skips a beat as Logan obediently lowers his head.

I've heard audio recordings of the shifters, but it's nothing compared to the real-life sound. It's terrifying, and I curl my hands into my fists as I wait.

Despite my training, I'm scared. What's going to happen when the shifters reach us? Pairings between shifters and humans are rare, practically unheard of. For all I know, the alpha could take one look at me and decide to tear out my throat. I'd be helpless to stop him.

The shifters near. Sweat trails down my spine.

I've waited my entire life for this, but now that it's here, I feel entirely unprepared. I never wanted this for myself. I never wanted a mate. I hate the shifters.

Four wolves enter my line of sight. My gaze immediately lands on the one in front. He's fucking huge, easily as tall as me despite being on all fours, and his head and paws are massive. I would *never* stand a chance against him. His dark, chestnut-brown fur is suspiciously the same color as my hair, and he's larger and faster than the two shifters who have arrived with him.

This is Alpha Knox. Caleb. My mate.

Bile rises up my throat. I push it down, refusing to react to the sight of him.

He shifts into his skin form mid-run and drops to his knees beside me. I feel an unmistakable pull to him, an intense urge to literally *crawl* in his direction. I hate it.

Caleb is the most beautiful man I've ever seen. He's naked, too. I look.

A muscular torso, narrow hips, a flaccid cock I force myself to skim over, and thick thighs. All shifters are tall and muscular, the picture of physical perfection. Caleb is no different, albeit slightly larger.

His hair is the same color as his fur, and he has the dark-brown eyes all shifters seem to share. He's freshly shaven, with a slight hint of stubble just beginning to appear along his jaw. When he gulps, his throat bobbing, my gaze travels to his neck.

Someday soon, I'm going to slit his throat.

His fingertips graze my cheek, and it takes everything in me not to recoil. My pulse threatens to race again, but his touch soothes the quick pattering. My hands unclench. It's an automatic reaction, one I have no control over. I don't like that.

Alpha Knox feels like home—or at least the distant memory I have of home. The shifters took that from me when they murdered my parents, and the HPAW facility I was raised in sure wasn't an adequate replacement.

The alpha's gaze darkens as he looks down, taking in my injuries.

"I don't..." He works his jaw from side to side. "Where are you hurt?"

His voice is too soothing, the low pitch drawing me in more than I'd care to admit. I knew the bond would be intense, but I wasn't expecting this. *This man was made for me.* The nagging thought lingers at the back of my mind, but I shove it away. I have a job to do.

I choose HPAW and the humans over the idea of a mate.

"My ribs are the worst," I choke out.

Logan speaks up. "Her shoulder was dislocated. I already reset it."

The three shifters that came with Caleb circle me, but I keep my focus on the alpha. He grabs my wrist, his touch soft as he turns my hand over. I expect him to examine my mark, making sure it's a match, but his focus goes instead to my shoulder.

Two of the shifters transform into their human form. The first is the freckled woman who found me—Logan's mate. She clears her throat and moves to stand beside Logan, her fingertips grazing his inner arm.

The second is somebody new. He's an older man, maybe in his early sixties, and his hair is beginning to gray. I keep him in my sight as he approaches from the right.

"Hello." He offers what I assume he believes to be a friendly smile as he crouches beside me. "You sound like you're having trouble breathing."

I eye him, then give a curt nod. I wish HPAW had given me a weapon, but that wouldn't fit with my victim narrative.

"I'm a doctor," he continues. "I'm going to take a look at your ribs, okay?"

He waits for my permission, which I give with another curt nod. Then he looks to Alpha Knox, waiting for my mate to give him permission as well. When the alpha nods, the doctor rips open my dress, exposing my bare skin.

I'm surprised they asked for my approval. It's not what I expected from a shifter.

The third shifter who arrived with Caleb finally transforms. It's a woman. She has dark skin and wide eyes, and she tucks her long, spiraled hair behind her ear as she kneels beside me.

"I'm a nurse," she says, her voice hushed. "My name is June."

I'm surrounded, and I don't like it.

The alpha introduces himself. "I'm Caleb." He reaches for my face, his palms open, before he winces and pulls away. *Smart choice.* "You're safe now."

The doctor examining my ribs sucks on his teeth, the sound screaming displeasure, before turning and mumbling something to Nurse June. I don't pay much attention to his evaluation, already knowing exactly what's wrong with me.

Caleb seems to be hanging on to every word. His eyes dart between me and the doctor, and the anger he's clearly trying to hide begins to appear. At first, it's a twitch of the lips and a scrunch of the nose, but it quickly transforms into a full snarl.

He's upset by my injuries. That's a good sign.

I'm surprised I'm not being hammered with questions, but I'm sure they're coming. These people will want every detail about who I am and how I got here. It's only a matter of time before they demand answers.

I look at Caleb's right hand.

His marking is identical to mine, minus the color. His remains white. Why is mine the only one that has darkened? I assumed we'd match. Without thinking, I touch the back of his hand. Caleb sucks in a sharp breath, but he doesn't pull away as I run my fingertips along the length of his mark.

Every brush of our skin is electrifying, and I hope Caleb feels something similar. Getting information from him will be easier if he feels drawn to me.

I ignore the metallic tang of blood as I lick my lips.

"Mine doesn't look like that," I say.

Caleb stills, his gaze finally settling on my hand. I turn it toward him, showing my marking. The action hurts, pain spreading through my wrist, but I ignore it.

There's a moment of tense quiet before Caleb shakes his head and grabs my hand, flipping it over so my mark isn't in his sight. *Interesting reaction.* That's not what I expected, but a sharp pain shooting up my side pulls my focus.

The doctor grunts. "Well, this isn't ideal."

He leans closer and brushes his thumb back over the spot he just touched. I just barely resist the urge to smack at his hands as I hiss and jerk away. What the hell is he doing?

Caleb darts forward, batting the doctor's hand away. "Enough."

He pulls me into his arms a second later. The movement should hurt, but all I feel is relief as my face is pressed against his bare chest. Our bond is going to be a problem.

The doctor frowns. "I don't believe anything is broken, but I'm not certain. We should get her to the hospital." He pushes off his knees and rises. "Can you carry her?"

His question isn't met with a verbal response.

Caleb loops one arm around my back and another under my knees, then stands. My body does *not* like this, and I bite back a cry as I'm lifted and held against his chest. He turns, spinning me toward Logan and his freckled mate.

Nurse June is still crouched, and she purses her full lips as she bounces to her feet. Her white mark stands out against her deep-brown skin. It's floral like mine, and it curls from the inside of her wrist toward her pinky finger. It stops just before reaching the digit.

Her hand disappears from my line of sight. She tucks it behind her back, and when I meet her eye, I realize she's upset. Should I not have looked? Maybe the marks are private.

"You two stay here," Caleb orders Logan and the freckled woman. The freckled one is staring at the ground, her skin unnaturally pale. She looks sick. Caleb turns toward Nurse June. "Run ahead and alert the hospital staff." The doctor is the last to receive orders. "You stay with me."

Logan shakes his head. "Sash can monitor the cabin herself. I'll follow the trail."

Sash. That's the freckled woman's name. Logan told me earlier, but I didn't remember. I commit it to memory now.

Caleb makes a quiet noise in the back of his throat, then approves Logan's revision with a curt jerk of his head. Logan is quick to transform into his wolf form and disappear. He can follow the trail all he wants. It won't lead him anywhere. HPAW knows how to cover their tracks.

Caleb peers at me. I force myself to meet his gaze.

"You're my mate..." he mumbles.

Is he asking or telling me? I can't quite tell, and I run my tongue over my dry, cracked lips before giving another nod. His questions will come soon. I have carefully crafted answers for all of them.

I'll tell him that I've always known I was his mate, but I'm scared of the shifters and have gone through great efforts to stay away. I've heard the horror stories, and I never wanted to take the risk of finding out whether or not they were true.

"Are you going to kill me?" I ask, putting an extra tremor in my voice.

"Kill you?" Caleb shakes his head and begins walking, carrying me into the forest. His movements are even and steady, which I appreciate. "Never. I'll never hurt you. My pack lands are close. We'll get you fixed up there, and then I'll answer all your questions. I promise."

Those words are music to my ears. I have *many* questions.

My eyes slip shut in a long blink before I force them open. I need to keep tabs on the direction we're going. A glance at the sun tells me we're heading north, which I suspected.

I shift, wrapping my good arm around Caleb's neck. The other one rests on my stomach.

"How far is your pack?" I ask.

If I counted Sash's absence correctly, it's twenty-five miles away from this location, which I wouldn't necessarily consider close. I suppose the shifters have a different perception of distance, though. It makes sense considering they can shift and run faster than most animals. Must be nice.

"It's several hours on foot." Caleb grimaces before continuing. "And the roads here are too overgrown for vehicles. I'll carry you. Don't worry."

I nod, frustration rising. It slipped my mind that shifters don't use vehicles, the creatures preferring to travel in their wolf forms. They spurned most human forms of transportation after taking over these lands.

They let nature ruin what used to be sprawling cities and carefully cultivated land. Canada as we once knew it is long gone. I've seen images in history books, but they were taken *before*.

It's been three generations since the shifters exposed themselves, revealing their true nature and retreating into Canada. Their mass exodus is well documented. HPAW made sure I was aware of every detail.

Neighbors, friends, celebrities, and even politicians were there one day and gone the next. Humans had had no idea they'd been living among such animals, and the fact that the shifters had been able to keep their true selves a secret for so long is horrifying. The deception is nauseating. *What else are they capable of?* The unknown has kept humans on edge for decades.

I let my head rest against Caleb's chest. He seems to enjoy my touch, and I'm going to milk that for all it's worth. I have to. I have no other options.

He smells good, and I gently tilt my chin so more of his scent reaches my nose. I'm aiming for subtlety, but it's obvious Caleb notices by the way his chest rumbles against my cheek. HPAW suspects the shifters have two consciousnesses, the 'human' and the 'wolf.'

They know nothing for certain, though.

I clear my throat. "What do—"

The doctor speaks up from behind. "You should refrain from speaking until we've had the opportunity to examine your lungs."

Caleb nods, quickly agreeing. "We'll talk later. I promise."

Patience has never been a virtue of mine, and I struggle to remain quiet as Caleb carries me through the woods and onto what clearly used to be a road. It's overgrown, the pavement falling victim to nature's persistent claiming. I'll never admit to finding the sight beautiful. It's probably because I've spent most of my life locked up in an HPAW facility—staring at cement walls and concrete floors.

Every muscle in my body aches, making the minutes pass agonizingly slowly. I'm waiting for the moment Caleb grows tired and asks me to walk, but it doesn't come. The hours pass, and Caleb shows no sign of fatigue.

He carries me with terrifying ease.

Exactly how strong are the shifters? Is Caleb an exception?

Eventually, the road clears up, and to my complete surprise, a black SUV is waiting for us. I don't know much about vehicles, but I can tell this one is old. Rust covers the back bumper, and the paint is dulled and chipping.

There's a shifter standing beside the trunk, a slim, young man no older than twenty, and he rushes to open the back door as Caleb nears. I assume Nurse June is to thank for the transportation.

I grind my teeth, a pained grunt slipping from my throat as Caleb lays me across the back seats. He crawls in behind me, squeezing his long limbs in the small space between the front and back seats.

It's almost comical how uncomfortable he looks trying to fit his large body into the gap, but he voices no complaint as the doctor takes the front passenger seat and the newcomer begins driving.

"Shifters drive?" I ask.

Caleb frowns, pushing my sweaty hair out of my face. The strands have been stuck to me for a while, and I let out a sigh as they're removed.

"We can," he says. "But we prefer not to."

The SUV jolts to life, and electric pain explodes along my ribcage.

"Shit." Caleb jumps into action, pinning my shoulder and thigh against the seat to keep me in place. "I'm so sorry. This road leads straight to the pack. We'll be there soon."

We resume driving. There are so many potholes, and I break

out into a cold sweat. I'm going to vomit. Or faint. I'm not sure which.

Caleb continues to hold my shoulder and thigh, trying his best to prevent me from jostling with the SUV's damn near-continuous jerks.

"I'm so sorry," he repeats. "You're safe now, my mate."

"It's Evelyn."

He blinks, his mouth silently forming around the word.

"Evelyn," he repeats, this time with volume. "We're almost there, Evelyn."

I hate the way my name feels flowing off his tongue. It's smooth. Addicting. I want him to say it again.

Caleb frowns, then quickly tugs down the bottom of my dress, covering my exposed thighs. I wasn't bothered by it. My need for privacy was lost during my time within the HPAW facility. I was watched through cameras every second of every day, including while I showered and used the restroom.

Shame isn't something I possess.

I force my lips into a small smile, though, pretending to be thankful for Caleb's attempt at keeping me modest. The average human woman cares deeply about it, and most other women would have been flattered by his actions.

"Thank you," I whisper.

Caleb's eyes light up. "You're welcome."

By the time we reach the pack, I'm ready for the sweet relief of death.

My thoughts fall to the wayside as I take in the city where Caleb's pack resides. It's stunning. This place must have been around before the exodus. The streets are narrow, lined on both sides with tall, brick buildings. There are shops, apartment buildings, and I even spot a park off in the distance. This place is surprisingly quaint.

And there are shifters everywhere.

Hundreds of them. They walk through the streets—men, women, children. So many children. They squeal and scream, weaving through legs with wild abandon. I'm not sure what I expected, but it sure wasn't this.

Several of the children sprint toward the SUV the moment they notice it, but they slow when they see me peering out the window. Then they grow weary, almost even afraid, as they glance between me and Caleb.

Parents usher them away with hushed whispers, their gazes averted.

We drive through the busy streets, continuing until we reach a hospital. The circular parking lot is empty, *shocker*, and the driver pulls into the spot closest to the entrance. Caleb doesn't hesitate to jump out and scoop me into his arms.

The hospital's front doors slide open as we approach. Everything I've seen of the pack feels rustic, but this place is sleek. Small, but sleek.

The interior is sterile, every surface shiny and spotless. On the right is a long reception desk, and on the left are several open rooms. The crisp, white curtains are pulled back, revealing an empty bed in the center of each room.

The woman from the forest is here, already waiting with two others. The doctor rushes ahead of us, barking orders with every step.

I've done it.

I'm in the heart of a shifter pack, and the alpha seems to care deeply about my health. I suspect he believes in the bond. It's actually happening. I'm going to save the humans.

Chapter Four

Caleb squeezes my hand as the doctor—Greg, I've learned his name is—stands at the end of my bed scanning my charts, double-checking his work. I don't like how Caleb's handholding makes me feel, and I especially dislike how the heart monitor reflects it. It's practically blasting my inner emotions to the entire room, screaming that the shifter standing on my right affects me.

These past three hours have been a whirlwind. I've been put through examination after examination, every injury from head to toe meticulously cataloged. Caleb has been beside me almost the entire time.

The nurses have given him a few sideways glances and Doctor Greg has outright asked him to leave and give me privacy, but the alpha has refused.

The medication I was given is finally taking effect, the pain relief allowing my thoughts to sharpen. I'm no longer debilitated by my injuries. It's a relief.

Caleb's gaze darts toward the heart monitor, his lips twitching as he runs his thumb along the back of my hand, directly over my mark. The heart monitor blares, alerting the room that my pulse has increased.

Caleb's lips curl into a full grin. He's sure enjoying this, and it takes all my resolve not to rip my hand out of his. His touch is disgusting. I just wish my body were getting that memo.

If things go according to plan, I won't have to endure his touch for too long. I was anticipating Caleb to be a hardened leader. Surely, the feared Alpha Knox would be intimidating and frightening. Caleb seems softer than I expected, and I hope that means I'm able to secure all the information I need from him sooner rather than later.

This just might be *too* easy.

Doctor Greg sets down my chart. "I want to see you once a week," he says. "We need to monitor your ribs." He points to the cast on my right arm. "I'll remove *that* the next time I see you."

I sure fucking hope so. My wrist is only sprained. I don't need a cast, but Caleb insisted. It's overdramatic. A splint would suffice, and it's significantly less constricting.

It seems Doctor Greg's assumption about my ribcage was correct, though. Nothing is broken, but it sure fucking hurts. The doctor contemplated putting me on oxygen but ultimately decided against it.

Caleb nods. "Of course. What else?"

"Keep an eye on her," Doctor Greg says. "I trust you to monitor her symptoms and pain levels. Bring her in if you notice anything concerning."

Doctor Greg begins removing the IV from my left hand.

I gulp, glancing at the doctor before shifting my attention back to Caleb.

"I want to go home," I say.

Caleb's weary smile falls, which I expected. I already know he plans to keep me here, but it would be odd not to ask about my home. I should want to return to my life, not stay here with the shifters I'm terrified of.

Caleb visibly hesitates, the muscles of his jaw tightening. I doubt he ever anticipated having a human mate, let alone one who wants to leave him. The shifters are cocky like that. Caleb probably thought his female would fall to her knees and beg for his affection.

"You're my mate, Evelyn," he finally says. "Your place is with me, by my side." He shifts, dragging his fingers through his hair. "The human lands aren't safe for you, not with your marking."

I don't respond, mildly nervous that if I push too hard, he'll agree to let me leave. I'd never forgive myself if I ruined this before even beginning.

"I don't know..." I pause, sucking in what I hope looks like a contemplative breath. "I don't know."

"I hate to interrupt," Doctor Greg chimes in. "But I'm sure you're eager to get out of here, and I have a spiel."

He begins explaining how to care for my wounds, nothing I'm unfamiliar with. These aren't my first injuries. Still, I stare at him with wide eyes, pretending to soak in every word he says.

He's well educated, that's for sure. What do the shifters do for higher education? They have their own pharmaceuticals. The stuff they gave me is fantastic. It's erased my pain, but my mind remains clear. Pain medication usually makes me hazy and disoriented, but not this stuff.

The doctor hands Caleb a large bottle of capsules. I intend to steal and deliver some of the capsules to HPAW. They'll want to examine them.

Caleb stuffs the bottle into the pocket of the scrubs the doctors forced him into. They're small on him, the dusty-blue fabric stretched comically across his shoulders and chest. The bottoms are no better, his muscular thighs at risk of popping the stitching.

There are a handful of women here, but none have looked twice at Caleb. They're respectful, maintaining a polite distance. Still, I find myself reading into every interaction. Has Caleb been with these women?

I'm sure, as their leader, he has access to any woman he wants.

The thought fills me with burning jealousy, which is absolutely ridiculous. I don't want a mate, and I have no reason to care who finds Caleb attractive. He's going to be dead soon, anyway.

"You're free to leave," Doctor Greg says, pulling the damned heartrate monitor off my finger. He levels Caleb with a sharp look. "Don't forget to bring her in."

Caleb's responding glare is pure ice. Doctor Greg immediately lowers his head, dropping his gaze to the floor, before he spins on his heel and darts from the room.

What kind of leader is Caleb? I can't quite decide. He seems friendly enough, but the way Doctor Greg scurried out of sight says otherwise. Perhaps Caleb prefers to keep his true nature behind closed doors.

I suppose I'll find out soon enough. I'm prepared for anything.

"What now?" I ask, pretending not to have noticed the interaction between him and the doctor. "Are you... Am I a prisoner here?"

Caleb straightens up. The weight of his gaze is intense, but I refuse to look away.

"You're my mate," he starts. "I can't... Well..." He rubs the back of his neck. "If you truly wish to leave, I won't force you to stay, but you're my mate. I'd *like* you to stay. Do you have family to return to? A job? I'm sure we can figure something out."

I glance at my arm, examining my cast. Then I eye the marking on the back of my right hand. "No and not really. I've spent my entire life avoiding the shifters, and other humans. Can't exactly risk somebody seeing my marking."

Caleb is silent. I continue. "People say you're violent."

Caleb is quick to shake his head, dismissing my statement. "That's not true. Americans are afraid of us, and that fear has bred contempt. We are good people. I'm good people. Stay. Give me the chance to prove it."

When I don't immediately answer, Caleb points to my cast. "Shifters didn't do that to you. Humans did."

I chew at my bottom lip, contemplating Caleb's proposal, the way Daniel and I practiced, before giving in with a jerky nod. "Fine. I'll stay. For now."

Caleb pushes his shoulders back, straightening up. "Thank you, Evelyn."

He's scooping me into his arms a moment later, carrying me the same careful way he did earlier. I'd prefer to walk, and I bite my tongue as my side is pressed against his chest.

"It's a bit of a drive to my home," he says, "but I had a van readied for us. It's the best I can do on such short notice." He smiles. "I wasn't expecting to find my mate today, nor for her to be human. I'm a bit unprepared."

Caleb has a dimple on his right cheek. It's not hugely prominent, but it occasionally peeks through when he speaks. It's endearing, and I find my attention continually darting toward it. If he notices, he says nothing. I'm sure he's noticed.

I've always prided myself on my ability to notice details, and I fear I may have met my match. Caleb is always paying attention, always locked in. The realization hit me when he noticed Nurse June mispronouncing my name. It was a slight mistake, but it didn't go unnoticed. He quirked a brow. Then he promptly corrected her.

The fact that he had been in the middle of an entirely different conversation when it happened is what caught my interest.

Caleb carries me outside, his gaze never once straying from mine. He acts like I'm the first woman he's ever seen, constantly staring at me with open amazement. It's intense, and I'm unsure how to feel about it.

The van Caleb mentioned is parked outside the front doors. It's in similar shape to the SUV, and the back door creaks as it's pulled open.

I raise a brow. The back has been converted into a bed. A mattress fills the entire space, and it's even topped with sheets and pillows. It looks surprisingly comfortable, and I chew at the inside of my cheek as Caleb helps me get adjusted.

It's indeed comfortable—significantly better than my bed back at the HPAW facility. I lie back with a quiet sigh. Fuck, that feels good.

"It's not perfect," Caleb says. He messes with the pillows surrounding me, fluffing and rearranging them until I'm covered on every side. "But it's the best we could do on such short notice. I'll drive slowly, but let me know if you're in any pain. We can take as many breaks as you need."

He's fretting over me. The realization has my cheeks warming.

I knew the bond would be intense, but I never imagined it would have me flushing around the alpha within mere hours of meeting him. I figured I'd be attracted to him, but this is so much more.

My heart is pounding, and my fingers twitch with the need to reach forward and yank him into the back of the van with me.

It's a relief that HPAW found me when they did. Had I wandered any deeper into the woods and stumbled upon the shifters, there's no telling how my life would have turned out. I was an impressionable little girl, and it would have been easy for the shifters to convince me that their way of life was the right one.

I would've fallen in love with Caleb—I'm sure of it. I'd have no knowledge of the torture they inflict on humans. I'd be living in painful ignorance.

But HPAW *did* find me, and I *do* know. It doesn't matter how charming this man is. My mission takes precedence over my personal feelings. It has always been, and it will always be. The humans are relying on me.

"You did this for me?" I dart forward and snatch Caleb's marked hand before he shuts the door.

He stills, his eyes going comically wide as I pull his hand toward me and press a chaste kiss to his mark. I maintain eye contact, getting a direct view of his dilating pupils. We've observed mated pairs doing this. It's a sign of affection between the shifters, one Caleb clearly enjoys.

His rough hands find my face. He cups my cheeks, the pads of his thumbs stroking over my cheekbones. He's kissing me a second later, his lips meeting mine in an innocent, soft kiss that's over with just as quickly as it began.

It leaves me breathless. Odd. With the way my heart is pounding, this might as well be my first kiss. How embarrassing.

Caleb releases me. I clear my throat.

Shifters are intimate creatures. Caleb will expect me to have sex with him or, at the very least, crave him. The knowledge that I'll have to sleep with a shifter has always filled me with disgust, and to my immense shame, I now feel a slight thread of excitement.

I'm fighting the urge to lean in and steal another kiss. I can't fathom how sex will feel. It'll ruin me. *It's a small price to pay.*

Caleb peers at me for a long moment, practically staring into my soul, before he finally retreats. The door shuts with a quiet click, and I collect myself as he walks around the van and climbs into the driver's seat.

I feel marginally better as he starts the engine.

"I won't force you to talk," he starts, glancing at me through the rearview mirror. "But I'd love to know how you ended up in those woods."

I grimace, throwing my arm over my eyes to hide most of my face. I suspect Caleb is going to be closely monitoring my expressions, and this feels like a natural way to hide them.

"It all happened so fast," I start. "I was walking home from work—I'm a server at the Chickie Dickies in Dell Rapids—and… I'm not sure. I keep my mark covered, but a customer must've noticed it. Humans don't care much for shifters, y'know? I was grabbed from behind, and I don't really know what happened or how I was brought here. Everything was fuzzy. I know they beat me, and I think they gave me something to keep me drowsy. I woke up tied to that bed just a few hours before those shifters found me."

Caleb turns, peering at me over his shoulder. His brown eyes are piercing, full of poorly concealed anger. I don't think it's directed at me, but it still has my hackles rising. Caleb is frightening, and I don't intend to get on his bad side.

"What did they look like?" he asks. "Did you catch their names, or anything identifying?"

I shake my head. "I'm sorry."

Caleb's eyes slip shut for a brief moment before returning to the road. "You have nothing to apologize for. Logan has a unit of shifters tracking your scent. They'll find whoever hurt you. I promise."

No, he won't. We thought through every detail, and the HPAW soldiers should already be long gone. It's an almost six-hour drive to the cabin from the border, and HPAW was meticulous in their planning.

"Do you have any family we should reach out to?" Caleb asks, returning to his earlier questioning. "Is there somebody looking for you? Friends? Coworkers?"

I shake my head again. "No. My parents are dead, and I was an only child. I don't really..." I give a dramatic pause. "I don't have any close friends. I don't think anybody is looking for me."

That's the first honest thing I've told Caleb. It's depressing to admit.

"So..." I start, wanting to change the subject. "You're Alpha Knox?"

"I am."

I wait for him to continue, to elaborate, but he doesn't. He's not offering up much, which I suppose is to be expected. I'm human. His kind hate mine, and mine hate his. There's no trust.

"How did you come about this...job?"

Caleb cocks his head to the side. "I forget how little humans know about us." He takes a minute to think. "I was born into this pack, and my title was decided when my wolf showed his dominance. My father was the alpha before me, but that was a coincidence. The position isn't a birthright. It's given to the most dominant wolf, regardless of bloodline."

It isn't a birthright? HPAW will be quite interested in that detail.

"And you—" I pause, coughing.

Caleb meets my gaze in the rearview mirror. "Rest, Evelyn. I'll answer your questions later."

He falls silent. I don't push. I could try to engage in conversation, but it's probably best I don't. I might encourage Caleb to ask questions in return, and lies can be complicated to keep track of. I have rehearsed answers, but I should avoid giving them when I'm injured and dazed.

Caleb seems like the type of person to notice inconsistencies, and I can't draw any more attention to myself.

Chapter Five

I wake with a jolt, pain just beginning to rear its ugly head as the van comes to a stop. How long was the drive? I fell asleep, which wasn't planned. It must be the medication.

I thought being surrounded by shifters would make it hard to relax, but Caleb's presence has the opposite effect. It's calming, soothing my mind in a way I didn't think was possible.

I push myself into a sitting position as Caleb kills the engine. He's pulling open the back door a heartbeat later.

"Let me help you," he says, once again lifting me into his arms. My heart flutters.

I'm sick of being carried, annoyed with my body's reaction to his proximity, but it's only temporary. Caleb can't possibly carry me around forever. I'm sure he'll stop as I begin to heal. He has to.

I flinch as he tucks me up against his chest.

"Are you in pain?" he asks.

"A little."

"I'll give you more medication once we get inside." He jerks his head to the side. I follow his gaze. *Holy fuck.*

I didn't have a good view out of the van window, leaving our surroundings a mystery. The house we've pulled up to is positively stunning. It's secluded, the house nestled within a massive clearing surrounded by dense forest. The driveway we stand on is long and winding, eventually disappearing into a set of trees. I imagine the main road is just beyond them.

I turn back to the house.

Floor-to-ceiling windows span the entire exterior, the glass reflecting an image of the clearing and surrounding woods. There's a decently sized front porch, complete with a cozy sitting area.

"Is this your house?" I whisper.

"Ours." Caleb chews on his bottom lip. "It's *our* house."

He carries me across the porch and pushes open the front door.

It takes several long moments to absorb the sight before me. I've spent a long time thinking about what Alpha Knox's house would look like. My suspicions have ranged from a dilapidated cabin to a high-tech loft—and everything in between. Or, at least, I *thought* I'd considered everything in between.

Caleb's home is exactly that... a home. The place is neat and spacious, but it's cozy. A small foyer opens up into the living room. A giant, deep-gray sectional fills the space, the furniture large enough to comfortably fit several people. It's covered in pillows, and there's a throw blanket crumpled up in one corner.

Does Caleb curl up underneath it? It's an impossible image to conjure.

A wooden coffee table sits in the center, the surface cluttered with paperback books, two candles, and a decorative bowl. Behind the couch are more windows. Sheer beige curtains are pulled open to reveal the side and back yard. There's nothing but grass and trees.

We're truly secluded.

Along the side wall are shelves filled with more books, pottery, and plants. Framed art fills the rest of the wall. It's curated.

I chew on my bottom lip. "Do you live with a woman?"

My question is met with a short, booming laugh. Caleb

shakes his head. "No, but I did ask the females in the pack to help me decorate shortly after moving in. You're welcome to change anything you don't like."

I point to the flowers on the coffee table. They can't be more than a week old.

Caleb shrugs. "I like flowers." He shoots me a sly, almost teasing look. "That's not a crime, Evelyn." A moment of silence, then a quiet, "Do you like it?"

"Yes. It's beautiful." It's the truth.

Caleb sucks his cheeks into his mouth, his gaze darting to the ground. Is he blushing?

"I asked the females to decorate for my mate, for you," he admits. "I spent a lot of time reviewing styles until one felt right. The pack teased me about it for weeks, but I think the place turned out well."

Oh, fuck me.

Is Caleb a nice guy?

He's proven to be a monster to humans, but is he kind to his people? *It doesn't matter.* This bond is killing me. It's making me question things I shouldn't be questioning. I don't care if Caleb treats his people well. The shifters are the least of my concerns.

Caleb turns, beginning to carry me up a set of stairs on the right. He pauses as we reach the top landing.

"I'm bringing you to my room," he says. "There's a spare room, but I'd rather you be in mine. It's more comfortable. I'll sleep in the spare until you're ready to share."

I'd rather die than share a bed with Caleb, but a woman who was abducted would probably be terrified to sleep alone. She would want her big, strong mate by her side.

"Can you..." I start, curling my fingers into the fabric of his shirt. "You don't have to stay in the spare room."

Caleb hesitates. "Are you sure?"

"Yes."

His chest seems to vibrate underneath my hand, and a low, barely audible purr pours from his throat. Shifters fucking purr, too? I wasn't warned about this, so I assume HPAW doesn't know.

"You purr?" I ask.

The noise stops. "We prefer to call it a *murmur*. It's a sound that shifters make when happy. Content. We don't have much control over it."

"Is it intimate?"

It feels so.

Caleb chews on his bottom lip. "Yes. It's typically only made around family, specifically mates and young children."

Maybe I won't tell HPAW about it. The information doesn't benefit them.

Caleb walks forward, carrying me into the first bedroom on the left. It's as cozy as his living room, maybe even more so. A large bed takes up the center of the room, the olive-green comforter standing out against the crisp, white sheets and pillows.

Above the headboard are several paintings in thick, wooden frames, all portraying varying landscapes. Did the women of his pack decorate this room, too? I assume so.

The thought sends a pang of annoyance down my spine.

I push it away as Caleb carries me to the bed, setting me carefully down in the center. I don't think he's intending to seduce me tonight, but I'm still acutely aware that this is where he sleeps. If we *were* to have sex, this is where we would do it.

The sheets smell like him. It's pleasant, so very pleasant, and I suspect I only notice it because of the mate bond. It's woodsy, reminiscent of the sandalwood candles my mother used to own.

Caleb doesn't say anything about how I continue to cling to him, my fist curled tightly around the fabric of his shirt. I release him the moment I notice, my cheeks flushing. Pretending to be enamored by him is going to be easier than I thought. It's coming naturally.

"Stay here," he orders. "I'll be right back."

He's gone a moment later, retreating from the room.

I relax into the sheets the second I'm alone, my tense muscles truly softening for the first time in hours. My exhaustion is bone deep, and I need rest.

I can't do my job injured. HPAW knows this. They had to injure me to make my story of abduction and torture believable, but they went too far. There was no reason to so badly bruise my ribs or sprain my wrist. That wasn't discussed.

My anger mounts, and I force myself to take a deep, calming breath. I can be angry later.

I look around Caleb's room. I intend to go through his things, but not today. It's too soon, and the risk of getting caught is too high.

My hand shakes as I run my fingers through my hair, loosening one of the tangled knots, and I stare up at the ceiling before turning and peering into the ensuite bathroom. The door has been left open, but I can't see much more than the sink from this angle.

Ten minutes pass before I start to feel impatient. Where is Caleb? My pain medication is wearing off, and this endless waiting is a form of torture all on its own.

I rise into a sitting position, wincing as I adjust so that my back is pushed up against the headboard. I'm still in my hospital gown, and it's uncomfortable. Everything is uncomfortable.

I trace my collarbone, flinching when my fingers graze the swollen skin surrounding the break. There isn't much to be done about it. Doctor Greg said the bone is relatively useless, and while he can reset it, it's a lot of work for something that won't have much of an effect on my life.

It's going to heal like this—a permanent reminder of my time here.

The floor outside the bedroom door creaks, and I drop my hands back into my lap as Caleb steps into the room. He's holding a tray. On it is a bowl I can't see inside, a glass of water, and my bottle of pills. Whatever is in the bowl smells so fucking good.

"Sorry for the delay," he says. "I thought you might be hungry."

All I can manage is a jerky nod. I'm starving, have been for weeks.

Caleb climbs onto the bed. I stare into the bowl. Potato soup.

I could cry. I'm so sick of potatoes. I never want to look at one again, and I bite my tongue as Caleb settles beside me.

"Greg said to start you off with something light," he says. Can he see my disappointment? "I don't want to upset your stomach."

The bottle of pills is sitting on the edge of the tray, the cap removed, and I grab it the second it's within reach. Caleb busies himself getting the tray situated on my lap, overly cautious not to spill any of the soup.

I can feel his calculated gaze on me, though, as I dump two pills into my palm and throw them back with a large gulp of water. Is he monitoring my intake? Probably. Doctor Greg gave explicit dosage instructions, and Caleb was hanging on to his every word.

Caleb takes the bottle from me and replaces the cap, and I shift my attention to the soup. *Fucking potatoes.* The world is out to get me. Still, I don't voice my complaint as I grab the spoon. My good arm is in a cast, rendering it useless, so I use my left to eat.

I don't even need this cast. Doctor Greg chose not to argue with Caleb, but I could tell by his expression that he felt the cast was overkill.

"Do you need help?" Caleb eventually asks.

I shake my head. "No." My answer is curt, so I make my following words softer. "Thank you."

Caleb falls silent. The only sounds are my spoon clanking against the bowl and my slurping. It's uncomfortable. I don't like people watching me eat.

Caleb eventually touches my kneecap, tracing the old scar that travels across it. "What happened here?"

I frown, trying to remember. It's an old injury, from before HPAW found me.

"A trampoline accident," I finally say. "I was doing flips, and I accidentally launched myself into a tree."

Caleb clears his throat. "Launched yourself?"

"Unfortunately." I use my hands to imitate myself flying through the air. "It wasn't a fun time."

Caleb snorts, his lips curling. A deep laugh bubbles up out of his mouth a second later. The noise is loud and shocking, and I stare dumbfounded when his eyes light up as if I've just told the funniest joke.

I should compliment him. It's an easy way to earn his affection.

"You're beautiful," I say.

Caleb quiets, his smile softening.

"You said your title was decided when you were born and your wolf showed his dominance," I say, bringing up our earlier conversation. This is valuable information. "How did your wolf show his dominance? Is there a test?"

Caleb gestures for me to continue eating. "No test. It's something we sense in one another. It's instinctual."

I continue to pry. "When did you take over? Are your parents alive?" I can't believe he's sharing this information with me. It's too easy. It feels almost wrong.

Caleb's gaze darts to my soup. I shove a soft potato into my mouth.

"I stepped into the position when my parents passed away. I was seventeen."

I hum. "What if somebody stronger than you comes along?"

"Then I'll no longer be the alpha." Caleb says it like it's the simplest thing on the planet. I don't believe it.

"You would just hand over your title..." I snap my fingers. "Just like that?"

Caleb nods. "I wouldn't have a choice. Wolves submit to

those who are more dominant than them. It's biology. There's no controlling it."

I suck my cheeks into my mouth, debating what to ask next. I don't want to push my luck and make Caleb suspicious, but it's hard not to pry when he's being this open.

"Why are you telling me this?" I ask.

"You're my mate." He shrugs, like that answers everything. "Finish eating, and I'll help you wash up. You're covered in blood, and you smell like Logan and Greg."

Help me? The mental image of Caleb helping me bathe excites me more than I care to admit. I shove the emotion aside. I'm getting good at doing so.

I gave myself a rough cleaning at the hospital, but I still feel disgusting. I need a real shower, or bath, with soap and shampoo. I'm excited for *that*—not Caleb's help. That's what I'm telling myself.

Chapter Six

I hand Caleb my empty bowl. The soup, despite being filled with potatoes, was precisely what I needed. The pain medication has finally kicked in, too, replacing my sharp aches with comforting nothingness.

Caleb collects the empty dish with slow, gentle movements. "Let's get you cleaned up."

Despite my best attempts to avoid it, my cheeks warm. I'm comfortable with nudity, but knowing Caleb is about to help me bathe has my heart pounding. I'd insist on cleaning myself if I thought I could, but we both know I'm incapable.

The medicine numbs the pain, but I'm still incredibly injured. I shouldn't push myself.

Caleb helps me off his bed, his strong arms steady as he practically carries me into his ensuite bathroom. It's nice in here, everything pristine. *Does Caleb clean it himself, or does he hire someone to do it for him?* There's a large tub in front of an even larger floor-to-ceiling window, and beside it is a walk-in shower. Caleb brings me to the tub.

"We could do a shower, but a bath will be easier," he says, turning the faucet.

Water splutters into the tub, and Caleb urges me to sit on the edge as he collects several bottles from the shower. His eyes are continually darting toward me, and when he fumbles with one of the bottles, I snort.

It's a short, curt noise I hurry to cut off, but Caleb still reacts.

He shoots me a dirty look, but I can tell there's no real malice behind it. "It's not funny."

I shrug, not responding. I don't know why I laughed. It's not funny. *He's* not funny.

The bath fills, every inch mounting my nerves. If Caleb notices, he doesn't say anything about it. The air between us grows quiet, and when the bath is filled and Caleb shuts off the water, it becomes tense.

I can't remove my clothing, not with my sprained arm and bruised ribs.

Caleb clears his throat. "Are you okay with this? I can find a woman to help if you'd prefer."

I'm surprised it took him this long to ask. I'd consider taking him up on the offer if he were making this sexual, but I can tell that's not his intention. Some part of me intuitively trusts Caleb. I'm sure it's the bond.

"It's fine," I say.

I want to be clean, and I trust Caleb more than some random shifter woman.

Caleb nods, his throat bobbing, before reaching for the hem of my dress. I'm on edge, but Caleb's eyes remain locked on mine as he pulls my dress over my head. His gaze never strays, not even as he kneels before me and tugs the thin hospital socks off my feet.

I'm naked. Vulnerable beyond belief. Caleb knows it. I know it.

Caleb rises, and then he's helping me step into the tub. He holds my bicep, his grip tight enough to offer support but not enough to seem threatening. He doesn't need to physically harm me to seem threatening, though. His sheer size, and the fact that he's a shifter, are threats enough.

I let out a near-silent sigh as I sink into the warm water. This feels amazing. HPAW didn't have baths. They had lukewarm, painfully sterile showers I hated using.

I can't help but relax, resting the back of my head against the tub's edge.

"Good?" Caleb asks.

I nod, my eyes growing heavy as he scoops water into his hands and pours it over my exposed shoulders. The water is clear. If he looks down, he'll see everything. I'm surprised he doesn't.

"So good," I admit.

"I'm happy to hear that." A beat of silence, then, "Do you need help washing?"

Probably not. HPAW injured my dominant arm, but I can make do with my left.

"Yes." The lie slips off my tongue without much thought.

Caleb's throat bobs once more, and he nods slightly before dropping to his knees beside the tub. I debate correcting my lie and insisting on washing myself, but those thoughts vanish as Caleb readies a washcloth. His eyes go comically wide as they land on my exposed skin. Caleb looks *amazed*, his eyes full of wonder.

He clears his throat, rushing to avert his gaze. "Sorry." He shakes his head. "I've never seen a naked woman, and, well, it's distracting. *You're* distracting."

His confession takes me by surprise. It's rumored that shifters are prudish, avoiding intimacy until they find their mate, but I never anticipated Alpha Knox falling into this category. He's almost thirty. That's a long time to wait, especially considering his title. I'm sure there are more than a few women eager to jump into his bed.

"You've never seen a naked woman?" I ask. "Ever?"

Caleb's shoulders rise and fall in a quick, jerky motion. "Nudity is common amongst shifters. We're exposed when transitioning between our wolf and skin forms, but it's common decency to avert your gaze. I don't look."

"Are you a virgin?" I blurt out.

Caleb recoils. He looks offended. "Yes." He scoffs, as if the mere idea of him being anything other than a virgin is absolutely ridiculous. "Of course I am."

He says it with such conviction, such pride, that I'm left entirely speechless. A part of me wants to sink into the tub and drown myself. I might attempt it if I didn't already know that Caleb would immediately haul me right back up.

HPAW encouraged me to have sex. They know how addicting the bond can be, and they felt that my having prior sexual experience would help me fight the pull. They never forced anything on me, but they made it abundantly clear that promiscuity was welcome.

They placed young guards outside my quarters, and they never batted an eye when those men slipped into my bed in the middle of the night. I welcomed them. Anything to help the cause.

Now, though, I'm feeling a very distinct feeling of shame. I don't enjoy it.

Caleb watches emotions filter across my face, but his expression gives away nothing. Does he expect me to be a virgin, too? If so, he'll find himself sorely disappointed.

"I'm aware that humans have different views about sex," he finally says. "I don't expect you to be...*inexperienced*."

He rolls the word *inexperienced* around his tongue, testing it. It doesn't sound like he particularly enjoys the flavor of it, but he isn't showing the telltale signs of anger. The HPAW facility was filled with men, most of whom blamed the world for their less-than-perfect lives.

I learned how to tell when a man is angry.

Caleb isn't angry.

I clear my throat. "You can look at me. I don't mind."

He won't be the first, and I highly doubt he'll be the last. Besides, I want his eyes on me. He's never seen a woman, and a sick, twisted piece of me takes pleasure in being the first. He'll never forget this—not that he's going to be alive for much longer to do so.

Caleb's cheeks turn an impressive shade of red, and his tongue darts out to wet his bottom lip as his gaze travels to my body. I can practically feel everywhere his eyes land. They start on my stomach, a safe spot, before traveling toward my chest.

Most of my hard-earned muscle has vanished thanks to HPAW's decision to starve me, but I remain lean. My body is taut, my breasts perky. I'm proud of the way I look, and I preen underneath Caleb's gaze.

"Are you going to wash me?" I ask. My voice is low.

Caleb shuts his eyes and sucks in a slow breath. "Yes."

He brings the soapy washcloth to my exposed shoulders, running the soft fabric over each one before carefully cleaning around the cast on my right arm. We should probably put a bag over it, but I'm not too concerned about the moisture. The cast is coming off next week, anyway.

Caleb's gentle as he sets my arm back on the tub's edge.

Then he sticks his hand into the water, lifting my good arm out of the tub and wiping the dirt off. He's thorough, cleaning every inch of my skin. This has no business feeling as good as it does.

When he finishes with my arm, I lift my leg, resting my ankle against the lip of the tub. My ribs scream in protest, but I ignore them. He cleans both my legs, starting at my toes and ending just above my knee. He avoids my thighs—especially the sensitive flesh between them. He doesn't even look, much to my annoyance.

I want him to look. I want to see his expression when he sees a woman's sex for the first time. He's expressive, and the pull I feel to him is possessive.

"Do you—" he starts.

"I want you to do it."

He grimaces. "In the cabin... Did..."

I know where this is going. Doctor Greg kicked Caleb out of the room before gently prodding the subject, then offering to bring in a female doctor to complete a cervical check and STD screening. I rejected both. The HPAW soldiers didn't assault me, and I'm regularly tested.

Caleb wasn't in the room, but I assumed Doctor Greg would've shared the information with him. I suppose not.

"They didn't rape me—or do anything sexual," I say. "I want you to clean me, Caleb."

He curses, the word whispered lowly under his breath, before he runs the washcloth over my breasts. He's careful not to touch my bare skin, but his warmth is felt even through the washcloth.

When he drags the fabric over my nipples, I tense. It feels good, like a bolt of lightning shooting straight between my thighs. I want more, my injuries be damned. I'm not sure what's gotten into me, but the bond between us screams, pulls, and aches. I've never felt anything like this. It's otherworldly.

It's going to be a problem.

Does Caleb feel the same way? Is he suffering with the intoxicating pull, too? Is it stronger because he's a shifter? I can't imagine. This must be absolute torture for him. It's even more of a reason to encourage this. It'll make winning him over and earning his trust so much easier.

He makes brief eye contact with me, double-checking that everything's okay, before trailing the washcloth down my torso. He skims over my ribcage, applying almost no pressure, but the weight of his hand presses into me as he reaches the trimmed hair between my legs.

I spread my thighs. It's a clear invitation.

One he takes.

The washcloth travels between my thighs, ghosting over my clit.

I practically choke. "*Oh.*"

Caleb pants into the air between us. His breathing is just as uneven as mine, if not more. I'd give anything to know what he's thinking.

He slides his hand lower, over my entrance. I don't *really* need to be cleaned here. The outside skin, sure, but it doesn't need much more than a swipe. Vaginas are self-cleaning.

Caleb runs the washcloth along the length of me again, lightly wiping. I curl my fingers around the tub's edge, holding it for dear life as I fight the need to roll my hips into the touch. This feels amazing, better than anything I've ever experienced. It's the damned bond. It must be. Caleb isn't trying to get me off, but this is going to get me there.

I give in and roll my hips, losing the battle with myself. The medication keeps my pain at bay, but I know I'm going to regret this later. I don't really care about that right now. I need Caleb to run that damned washcloth over my clit about twenty more times. I estimate that's all it will take.

Caleb, thank the fucking heavens, is on the same page as me. He presses his fingers against the washcloth, directly over my clit, and circles.

I grit my teeth and throw my head back. *Fuck.*

Caleb chuckles. "Greg would be pissed if he knew I was working you like this so soon into your recovery."

A low groan pours from my throat. "I don't give a fuck what Doctor Greg thinks."

I want Caleb's hands on me. I want him to make me cum.

HPAW would be proud of how successfully I'm earning the attention of Alpha Knox. They'd be upset to know how much I'm enjoying doing so, but I suppose it's not a huge concern, as long as I keep my mission at the forefront of my mind.

I can enjoy Caleb—specifically his touch—but that's as far as it goes. Once he's given me what I need, I'll slit his throat. It's as simple as that.

I'm desperate to feel Caleb's bare skin on mine. He has big, thick, masculine fingers. I want them inside me. I want to see the mark on the back of his hand flex as he fucks his fingers into me.

My eyes squeeze shut, but they spring back open as Caleb groans. His left hand is below the tub, out of my line of sight, but his shoulder is moving. It's jerking forward and back.

"Are you touching yourself?" I ask. God. I hope so.

Caleb nods, lingers, then rises to his knees. He's hard, pressing against the seam of his pants. My breath hitches as he squeezes himself, his hand molding around the rough fabric of his pants.

"Show me," I order.

Caleb grunts. "That's not—"

"Please," I practically beg. "I want to see it."

Caleb gives himself another squeeze before tugging on his pants, shoving them down his waist. When I finally lay eyes on his cock, I send a prayer to the gods. I'm going to die, and I mean that in the best way possible.

I'm not sure what, exactly, I was expecting—I haven't had a lot of time to fantasize about Caleb—but the sight of his fingers curled around his cock does me in. He's thick, thicker than anybody I've ever taken before, and impossibly long. He slides his hand up his length before twisting at the end.

My orgasm slams into me. It's damn near explosive, and it takes even me by surprise.

Caleb's moan is the only sound that registers as I clamp my thighs around his wrist, holding him captive between my legs. His moan is deep and husky, easily the most erotic thing I've ever heard.

I drop my chin to my chest, fighting to keep my breathing as even as possible. My ribs are aching despite the medication, the pain only confirming what I already know to be true. I took it too far, and my body is pissed.

It was worth it. That was the best orgasm I've ever had, my body wracked with pleasurable aftershocks even now. I shiver as he removes the washcloth from between my thighs.

His bare hands are on my shoulders a second later, easing me back against the tub and straightening my sitting position.

"Are you okay?" His question is quiet, tinged with worry.

"I'm okay," I force myself to say. "That was good. Thank you."

I never thought I'd be thanking a shifter. The words are bitter on my tongue. My connection to Caleb doesn't change my opinion on the shifters, only complicates it.

He adds more soap to the washcloth. "Lean forward. I'm going to wash your back."

Is he not going to finish? His cock looked angry—swollen, red, and leaking at the tip. It wanted to cum. I have half a mind to offer my help, but I don't want to appear too eager. I want Caleb to believe the mate bond is working, pulling me toward him, but not too quickly.

He begins washing my back. I peer over the tub's edge, surprised to see his dick has been put away and his pants are buttoned up. I'm not imagining things. He was stroking himself just a minute ago. When did he put it away and do up his pants? How did he do it without me noticing? I'm clocked into his every move.

"How'd you do that so fast?" I ask, gesturing to his waist.

Caleb frowns, looking down. That's when I notice it. There's cum on the floor between his knees. He finished? So quickly? It must have been at the same time as me. That realization brings a sickening satisfaction.

Caleb's frown deepens. "You came quite quickly, too."

"No, not that." I snort. "How'd you get your pants back up so quickly? I didn't notice."

"Oh." The lines between Caleb's eyebrows disappear as his face softens. "Shifters are fast, I suppose. Our reflexes are quickest in our skin form, and you had a particularly long orgasm."

He says the last bit with pride.

Their reflexes are faster when they're in their skin form? I would've never guessed. HPAW surely doesn't know. I'll file this away for them.

"We should sleep." Caleb looks out the bathroom window. It's gotten dark. "This has been a long day. I've let the pack know that I'll be preoccupied for the next few days, so we won't be interrupted."

He helps me dress, putting me in his own clothing. It's several sizes too big, practically hanging off my frame. It's warm and comfortable, though, and I don't put up a fuss as he helps me into bed. Then he lingers.

"You can sleep with me," I repeat. I hesitate, then continue. "For an alpha, you're awfully skittish."

I'm testing the waters. How will he react when I insult him?

Caleb snorts. "You're my mate, and you've been abducted and brutalized. I'm going out of my way to be accommodating, Evelyn."

"Is this not what you're truly like, then?"

Caleb flicks off the bedroom light, then slides underneath the sheets beside me. "You are my mate," he finally says. "This is how I will be *with you*."

He kisses my forehead, not-so-subtly signaling that this particular conversation is over. I grind my teeth, debating pushing further, before deciding against it. I have time. I don't need to rush into anything.

Chapter Seven

Caleb sleeps, his slow, even breaths filling the silence. I lie awake, mentally cataloging everything I've learned.

Alpha Knox's pack is roughly twenty-five miles from the cabin HPAW scouted. Judging by the clustered buildings and roads, it's in what once must have been a populated human city. I'll see if I can get the name of it out of Caleb.

There appears to be only one pack doctor. There were several nurses, but Doctor Greg was the only one I encountered. Everybody there was clearly trained, though. There must be universities here. The shifters aren't nearly as wild as I assumed them to be. They've scorned several facets of the human society that once made up this land, namely vehicles and democracy, but they remain civilized.

The alpha title isn't passed through the bloodline.

Shifter reflexes are quickest in their skin form. That's a particularly interesting revelation. I was under the impression their wolf forms were the most threatening, but perhaps not. I'll need to learn more about the differences between the skin and fur forms.

How many packs are there? We know Caleb leads the largest one, and we've heard rumors of a few others that rival its size, but nothing has been confirmed. Alpha Knox, and apparently his father before him, has always been the main point of contact between the humans and shifters.

Who are Caleb's direct reports? I'll kill Caleb before returning to HPAW, but I should know who is next in line before doing so.

Something heavy lands on my ribcage. I exhale, shock and pain rendering me silent.

Still, something must alert the shifter sleeping beside me. Caleb jolts awake, removing the arm he threw across me as he sits upright. So, he's a light sleeper, then. Not ideal.

"Evelyn?" he asks. "What's happened?"

I take a moment to catch my breath. "You threw your arm over my ribs."

There's some shuffling as he slides out of bed, and then the overhead light flickers on. I wince, my eyes adjusting. Caleb stands by the door, staring. Always staring.

"What?" I snap, then I force myself to calm. "What are you doing?"

He raises a brow, the corners of his lips twitching. "I'm listening to your breathing. Give me a big inhale and slow exhale."

I gulp, doing just that. Caleb nods. "Good. Again."

I do it again.

"Good." He flicks off the light. "I'll be sleeping in the guest bedroom until you're healed."

"What?" I sit up, my arms shaking. "Why?"

"You're vulnerable, and I'm too big. Don't worry. I'll just be in the next room over."

He leaves, and I carefully lower myself back down. I suppose I should be relieved. I don't want to share a bed with a shifter, anyway. Fucking disgusting.

I wake up to Caleb carrying in a tray of food.

I rub my eyes, unable to do much else. My pain medication has all but worn off, and every movement hurts. Even breathing is agonizing, which Caleb seems to recognize as he sets the tray on the edge of the bed and plucks two pills off it.

He brings them to my mouth. "Open."

He doesn't need to tell me twice. I'm reasonably certain he's not going to poison me, and I greedily swallow down the pills. It takes almost twenty minutes for them to kick in. Caleb spends that time beside me, patiently waiting until I give him the go-ahead to help me sit up.

I look at the breakfast tray. Oatmeal. I'm tired of soft food, and I'm going to lose my mind if I don't get a crunch soon.

"You said you were a server at the Chickie Dickies in Dell Rapids," Caleb says, handing over the tray of food.

I nod.

"There's no Chickie Dickie in Dell Rapids."

Well, fuck. There *was* one six months ago. HPAW crafted my entire backstory, and Daniel and I have been rehearsing the contents of the file they gave him over the summer.

I roll my shoulders, refusing to panic. I've trained for this.

"You don't believe me?"

"That's not it." Caleb shakes his head. "I thought your co-workers might appreciate knowing that you're alive. I had someone reach out to the restaurant, but I was informed this morning that it shut down almost two months ago."

I shrug. "Okay. So I'm unemployed and embarrassed. Is that what you'd like me to say? I've been trying to find work, but it's a small town and there aren't many opportunities. I was on my way home from a failed job interview when I was abducted, okay?"

Caleb stares at me, his expression blank, before he purses his lips and gestures to my right hand.

"Is it hard to find work with a mate marking on your hand?"

He's offered me an excuse on a silver platter.

I look away, then awkwardly nod. "I wouldn't say it's been easy. I cover it with a second skin, but sometimes it's noticed. People don't know the design of it, so they don't know *you're* my mate, but just knowing that I have a shifter mate is enough to make people uncomfortable."

Caleb clears his throat. I continue. "I don't care to talk about myself. My family is dead. I don't have friends. I didn't graduate from high school. I'm between jobs. I just…I'm not proud of it, and I don't want to talk about it."

I shove food into my mouth. I don't bother chewing. I don't need to. It's oatmeal, and I swallow it whole before scooping in more.

Caleb says nothing, but I feel his gaze on the side of my head.

Only once I've finished eating does he speak up. "Would you like a tour of the house?"

"Yes."

He holds my elbow, helping me hobble out of bed. I'm happy he isn't trying to carry me, but we move slowly out of the bedroom. He shows me the spare room where he slept first. It's bland, a bed filling the center of the space but not much more in terms of furniture.

There's a small third room that's been converted into an office. A large desk takes up a good chunk of the room, a monitor resting in the center. There's a computer here. Perfect. Several wooden filing cabinets sit behind the desk, practically calling to me. I need unmonitored access to this room. I can only imagine the information stored in here.

Caleb leads me downstairs. I saw the living room last night, but today, I notice a television.

"Shifters watch TV?" I ask.

"Sometimes," Caleb admits. "It's not a big pastime for us, but I like sports."

"You…" I pause, struggling to wrap my mind around this. It feels entirely too human. "You like sports?"

Caleb nods. "Shifters aren't primitive, my mate. We have different customs, but we live in the same modern world."

He guides me into the small dining room, then into the kitchen. Everything is so normal. It's not what I was expecting.

"Your house is modest," I say.

Caleb chuckles. "Is that meant to be an insult?"

"No." It's the truth, and I hate to admit that I respect Caleb more for it. He's not living in excess. "I'm just surprised, is all. Most people assume you live in a sprawling, gaudy mansion with a large pool and dozens of concubines."

"*Concubines?*"

I shrug. "Humans think you're a whore."

"Of course." Caleb turns, facing me directly. "You understand that I'm not, correct? There have been no other women."

It wouldn't bother me either way. At least, that's what I'm telling myself. I'm going to be in and out of here. Collect information, then kill Caleb and get the fuck out of here before the shifters learn who I really am. That's all that matters.

Caleb doesn't pry into my background again. He asks about my favorite colors and the things I enjoy eating, but nothing deep. It's a relief.

The day passes by in a blur of scheduled medication refills, frequent awkward silences, and a shit-ton of wincing.

I learn that Caleb likes the color green. He's twenty-nine years old and stands at six-feet-three-inches. I'm not sure how much he weighs, but I'd estimate about two hundred twenty. He's not big on sweets, but he'll eat a chocolate chip cookie if offered. He also dislikes cats and he hates being likened to a dog.

Fun facts, I suppose, but useless.

He cooks, too, the man surprisingly adept in the kitchen. I'm continually surprised by how self-sufficient Caleb is. I assumed shifters would be waiting on him hand and foot, but he's done everything himself.

I refuse to let a single fact soften my feelings toward him.

Chapter Eight

No more dillydallying. I gave myself yesterday to rest and heal, but it's time to lock in. HPAW is waiting, and every day I procrastinate is a day the shifters have to plan and prepare for an attack.

I slink downstairs, following the sound of shuffling into the kitchen. Caleb stands in front of the sink, his shirt sleeves rolled up his forearms as he scrubs the pan he set aside last night to soak.

He spares me a quick glance as I step into the room. "Morning, Evelyn."

I grunt, taking a seat in the connected dining room. I'm not a fan of mornings.

Caleb smiles, his lips twitching. "Are you hungry?"

"Not yet."

I cock my head to the side, watching him work. I'm trying to appear nonchalant, but I'm interested in his cleaning. I've never had to wash my own dishes. An HPAW soldier would bring me a tray of food during mealtime, and they'd take it from me once I finished eating.

Caleb seems content, and he disappears momentarily beneath the counter as he sets something in the dishwasher. I've never used a dishwasher, either.

"What do you do for fun?" he asks as he pops back up.

Random question. I suspect he has created a checklist of things to ask me. I've done the same, but my questions are less about him and more about his pack's dynamics.

"What do I do for fun?" I repeat his question. I don't have fun. "I enjoy exercise, I suppose."

Caleb hums. He turns off the sink, then kicks the dishwasher shut. I don't miss the way he scans my body, silently evaluating my frame as he leans against the kitchen island separating us.

I do the same to him. It's impossible not to. Caleb is intimidating, and it's no wonder the shifters respect him as their leader. I sure wouldn't want to get on his bad side. He'd crush me like a bug, and no amount of my training would help. I can only imagine how terrifying his wolf form must be.

I caught a glimpse of it when he rescued me from the cabin, but I was in too much pain to truly admire it. I'll need another look before I leave.

Caleb unrolls his sleeves. "You like to exercise?"

I nod. "Yes."

"What kind?"

"Running, primarily." I also enjoy sparring with Daniel, but I intend to keep that to myself. I don't believe it's common for human women to enjoy fighting, and I don't care to draw attention to my years of training. I need Caleb to think I'm weak and defenseless.

Caleb clasps his hands together. "I enjoy running, too."

"You run in…" I pause, gesturing to his body. "This form?"

Caleb nods. "Sometimes. I enjoy exercise in both forms, but I find running to be more challenging in this one. Maybe, when you're healed, we can run together."

I force a smile. "Maybe."

Caleb will be long dead by the time I'm healed. At least, I hope so. It will take weeks for my ribcage to fully recover. I have no interest in being here for that long. In and out. That's the plan.

I should probably ask Caleb a question now. I'm not sure

what to ask. I'm not a great conversationalist, a painful fact I've come to realize about myself. I've never had to be. Daniel is the only person I ever really converse with, but he's not much of a chatterer.

He prefers to communicate through grunts and sharp looks.

The occasional conversations we do have are HPAW related. When I think about it, I don't know anything about that man. He doesn't know anything about me, either.

"What else do you like to do?" Caleb pries, breaking the silence.

I shrug. "There isn't much else. I live a boring life." It isn't a lie. "What do you do for fun?" I ask, turning the conversation around on Caleb.

He purses his lips. "I fear my answer is similar to yours. I work a lot. I'll adjust my schedule now that you're here, of course. Shifters are social creatures, though, so I spend a lot of my free time with my sister and her mate. I occasionally attend the bonfires, too."

"The bonfires?"

"Yeah." Caleb waves a hand, dismissing the topic. "It's a popular recreational activity among the shifters. I'll bring you to one when you're all healed up."

We fall silent. It's not necessarily uncomfortable, but it's noticeable.

I ask the first question that comes to mind. "How many shifters live here?"

"In this town or in my pack?"

"Both."

"There's about a hundred thousand in the area and about eleven million total in my pack."

Eleven million? I must have misheard him. That's so many shifters. *Too many.* When Caleb and the other alphas decide to attack, they'll demolish us. It's a terrifying thought.

Sweat pebbles along my hairline, and I hope Caleb doesn't notice as I tuck several strands behind my ear.

"Where does most everybody live?" I ask.

Caleb shrugs. "The large cities you're probably familiar with still exist. Toronto, Ottawa, Montreal. Most of my pack members live in and around those areas."

"How many shifters are there in total?" I ask.

I'm not sure I want the answer.

"About twenty million."

I'm going to faint. We know the shifters have a healthy population, but twenty million is beyond even my wildest assumptions. Even if I manage to kill Caleb and return to HPAW with useful information, we're in no position to fight twenty million shifters.

I clear my throat. "That's so many."

Caleb beams, visibly proud of his numbers. "It is. The lifestyle we were forced to maintain before the exodus wasn't ideal for shifters, and we've been thriving since separating and forming formal packs."

He meets my gaze, his eyes narrowing. I level my expression, hiding my horror, but it's too late. Caleb saw it flash across my face.

"What is it?" he asks.

My years of training are the sole reason I'm able to remain calm. I can be damn good at lying when the situation calls for it.

"Nothing," I start. "It's just intimidating to learn I'm the mate of a man who leads eleven million people. Why do you live here instead of in one of the big cities?"

Caleb takes a moment to respond, his narrowed eyes flickering all around me before finally relaxing. "The quiet helps me focus," he eventually says. "I travel when needed, but I prefer to conduct my business from here."

I'd love the opportunity to see one of the larger cities, but I'm not going to push the topic. It's ideal that Caleb chooses to live in a less populated area. It will make my future escape easier.

"And what's my role within the pack?" I ask.

"Right now, your only job is to relax, heal up, and acclimate to life here," Caleb says. "I can only imagine how much of a change this is for you. We'll discuss your position within the pack once you're settled."

I won't be here long enough for any of that.

"Are you in any pain?" Caleb changes the subject.

I shrug. "A little."

Caleb opens a cupboard and pulls down my medicine. I wanted to save a few pills for HPAW to analyze, but I'm not sure there will be any left when I'm done with them. I refuse to feel guilty about that. They were excessive with their injuries. This is their fault.

"Here." Caleb hands me a pill and a glass of water.

I down both.

"Can you help me bathe again?" I ask.

Caleb swallows. "Of course."

He follows me upstairs and into the bathroom, and he looks away as he helps remove my clothing. I wouldn't mind him touching me. If anything, I actively want him to. Caleb has never been with a woman, and I'm willing to bet that sex will be a great way to draw him in and earn his trust. I'm not above using my body to get what I want.

Besides, it's not as if it won't be pleasurable. I'm reasonably certain he'll make it good. He seems the type to care deeply about that.

I step into the bathtub, groaning as my cold feet sink into the warm water. Caleb kneels beside me, quiet as I rest my head against the lip of the tub, my eyes fluttering shut as he runs a washcloth over my skin. He folds it several times before quickly dragging it between my thighs.

I'd laugh if I weren't such a professional.

"You can touch me," I say.

Caleb hums. "We'll wait until you're healed."

"It's not as if you haven't touched me already."

"I lost my composure," Caleb admits, "but it won't happen again. I know you were in pain afterward. Your hands were shaking, and you could barely draw in a full breath or walk for the remainder of the night."

"Maybe that's because my orgasm was strong. You left me jelly-legged."

"That's quite a compliment, Evelyn." His lips press against the side of my head. "But my answer remains the same."

He pulls the bathtub plug, letting the water drain as he helps me dry off and redress. By the time he brings me to bed, I'm half-asleep. It's the medicine. It makes me drowsy.

The bond doesn't help. It acts as a warm blanket, keeping me calm and content whenever Caleb is nearby. Still, I refuse to succumb to sleep as I follow Caleb back downstairs. I intend to observe him today.

He does nothing interesting. He meanders around the house, tidying things that don't need to be tidied and making useless small talk with me. It quickly becomes clear that he has no idea what to do with himself when he isn't working.

I'm hoping that means he'll return to work sooner rather than later. I'm eager for some alone time in this house. His home office is too tempting to ignore, and I fully intend to sneak inside the moment he's gone.

Surely there are important files located in there—something, anything I can share with HPAW. I won't risk trying to communicate with them through the computer, let alone try to share files with them digitally, but I have a good memory. I'll memorize any and all important information I find.

Although, if there are truly twenty million shifters, I highly doubt anything I find will change our outcome. Maybe killing Caleb will cause enough of a stir to postpone the shifter's inevitable attack, but I don't believe it will permanently dismantle them. I'm still willing to give it a try, but I'm discouraged.

It's hard to hide my sour mood, but I manage.

Caleb's constant chatter helps. He always has a thought to share or a question to ask. It's overwhelming. He asks questions

I've never been asked before, most of which I don't have an answer to.

HPAW didn't think to help me prepare a list of favorite animals or cooking spices. They deemed it useless information. I did, too.

Caleb evidently doesn't.

I try several times to change the topic, to turn it around on him. I'm usually skilled at doing so. People love talking about themselves. If you ask them just the right questions at just the right time, you can have them talking for hours without realizing they haven't learned a single thing about you.

They leave feeling like they had a wonderful conversation. I leave with the upper hand.

Caleb doesn't take the bait. It's infuriating.

I give up shortly after lunch, choosing instead to mope on the couch. When he offers me another dosage of medication shortly before bed, I jump at the opportunity to take it. He hasn't brought up sharing a room with me again, and I don't offer. I enjoy having my personal space. It's time to think. To plan.

I need it.

Chapter Nine

Somebody is at the front door. Caleb's voice is hushed but unmistakable. I tiptoe toward the top of the stairs, trying to eavesdrop. The second voice is masculine, with a mildly familiar tone. Logan?

It grows in volume. Definitely Logan.

What's he doing here this early? The sun has yet to rise fully, the sky currently cast in a haze of yellows and reds.

I try to make out the words exchanged, but I have no luck. The men are too quiet. I could inch closer, maybe sneak down the stairs, but that's too risky. Their discussion sounds serious, though. Clipped words and the occasional grunt. What are they talking about? Me?

The front door shuts. I slink back into the bedroom and crawl onto the bed.

Caleb emerges a minute later. He crosses his arms over his chest, his shoulder resting against the doorframe.

"I have some bad news," he starts.

About me? I swallow. "What is it?"

"We're having some..." Caleb pauses, thinking through his following words. "We're having some border disputes with

HPAW. I need to leave and meet with a few pack members at my office to discuss."

Border disputes? I was under the impression that HPAW would be lying low for the first week or two of my capture. We don't want Caleb distracted, not while I'm trying to work him over for information.

"You're leaving?" I ask.

Caleb nods. "Unfortunately."

Under normal circumstances, I would be ecstatic. I've had no privacy these past few days, and I'm chomping at the bit to dig through Caleb's things. His home office, in particular, is calling to me. I assume his computer is password-protected, but I'm feeling good about his wooden filing cabinets.

But Caleb is leaving to discuss HPAW. This opportunity might only present itself once.

"Can I join?" I ask.

Caleb frowns. "You want to join me?"

"Yes." I slide to the edge of the bed. "We've been holed up in this house for two full days. I'm ready to get out and explore."

Caleb worries his bottom lip between his teeth. It's not an immediate rejection. I push.

"I'll be quiet. You won't even know I'm there."

"You should be resting," Caleb says. "Greg gave very explicit instructions."

Fuck Doctor Greg.

Caleb steps inside the bedroom. He's wearing only a pair of tight, black underwear, and I try not to stare as he walks around the bed, heading toward his closet.

He has a body that human men would kill for, all long limbs and thick muscle. I've found myself fantasizing about digging my teeth into his shoulders. And his chest. And other parts I don't care to admit to.

He's enticing, and I enjoy being the only woman who gets to see this much of his body. I'm trying hard to repress those feelings, but I'm failing miserably. It seems I'm a possessive woman, even toward men I have no right to claim. I'm here to gather information and, eventually, destroy everything Caleb has ever worked for. And to kill him, I suppose.

Caleb grins, clearly enjoying how he holds my attention as he disappears into his closet. I'm glad we aren't sharing a bed. The space has been good. It's given me time to think—to recoup from my injuries and the shock of our bond. I feel in control again.

"I'd like to learn about your pack," I say. "I'm feeling better. Truly."

Caleb steps out of the closet, now dressed. The weather is cooling—not that it ever gets too warm this far up north—but the cold doesn't affect shifters. Not as much as it does humans. Still, Caleb dresses for it with dark jeans and a long-sleeved shirt.

I refuse to meet his eye as I clamor off the bed. My movements are clunky, thanks to my bruised ribs and arm cast.

"You should rest," Caleb says.

I straighten up and face him. "Take me with you. Fresh air is good for me."

Caleb approaches, closing the distance between us in four easy steps. The proximity makes my pulse race, which I suspect Caleb can hear. Still, he says nothing about it as he stares down at me.

His gaze falls to my shirt. It's his, and two lines form between his eyebrows as he rubs the sleeve with his thumb and pointer finger.

Out of pure desperation, I grab his right hand and kiss his white marking. He seemed to enjoy this the last time I did it.

"Please," I say. "Let me come."

"Evelyn..." Caleb squeezes his eyes shut, then gently pulls his hand away. "Everybody said my mate would be outspoken. Persuasive. They teased that I needed a strong woman to match me. I suspect I'm going to find that in you."

Despite the subtle complaint, he smiles.

I'm not offended. I've been told on more than one occasion that I'm a handful. Some of the crueler HPAW members even went as far as to say they hoped the alpha would crush me. That he'd force me to submit. That he'd break me.

It only made me more determined to succeed.

"Would you rather I be different?" I ask. "Quieter? Meeker?"

Caleb shakes his head. "Of course not." He drags a hand through his morning hair, further mussing it up. "Most women struggle to look me in the eye, which is frustrating. I like the way you are. It's refreshing."

I probably shouldn't really care what he thinks of me. It doesn't matter. Still, my cheeks turn warm, and I clear my throat as I think of a subject change.

I repeat my earlier question. "So, can I come with you?"

Caleb sucks his bottom lip into his mouth, worrying it between his teeth, before giving a tentative nod. "I suppose that would be all right." He rocks his weight from foot to foot, then gestures toward his closet. "I'm sorry I haven't thought to get you any clothing yet. Are you okay wearing something of mine out in public?"

He's always asking if I'm all right with things. If I'm comfortable. HPAW didn't care. I was nothing more than a cog in a machine with them, a means to an end, and Caleb's concern feels foreign. I didn't expect to have this much autonomy with the shifters.

"I'm fine with it," I say.

Caleb finds me a pair of sweatpants, which I have to roll at both the waist and ankles so they don't drag against the ground. I'm already wearing one of his shirts, but I change into a clean one. It falls to my mid-thighs.

I look ridiculous.

Caleb seems to like it, though. He stares down at me with open desire, every heated thought visible in his dark eyes and bobbing throat. I was worried he'd be turned off by my human status, but that's seeming to be a non-issue.

"Are you ready?" I ask.

Caleb licks his lips before dragging his gaze away from me. "Yes."

Joining him at work is an opportunity I didn't fathom I'd get. I can eavesdrop on him, hopefully even during his meetings. He might not let me sit in on them immediately, but perhaps he'll grow lax if I establish myself as a regular presence in his office.

He'll let me overhear. I'll bring every detail back to HPAW.

"The pack is excited to meet you," Caleb admits. "I anticipate we'll have lots of visitors today."

I force myself to smile. I'm not eager to meet the other shifters. I don't care to make friends or acclimate, but I need to pretend. Shifters are social creatures. They thrive in their close communities, and Caleb likely expects his mate to join the fold.

Whatever. I can pretend. Caleb has been forthcoming with details, happily answering my probing questions about his land and the shifter way of life. At this rate, I doubt I'll need to be here for longer than a month or two.

That thought has me feeling two very conflicting emotions, but I shove the newer of the two aside. I have a duty to the humans, and I won't abandon my mission because Caleb isn't the heartless monster I anticipated.

I hold my breath the entire way to the front door, nervous that Caleb is going to change his mind about me joining him. He doesn't. He insists on holding my hand as we walk downstairs, then pauses at the coat closet beside the door.

"A cold spell is coming through," he says, pulling out an oversized, bright-orange winter coat. It's ugly. He wraps it around my shoulders before guiding my arms through, careful with my cast. I almost immediately begin to sweat.

This is overkill, but I keep my complaints to myself as we step outside. There's no snow, but it's only a matter of time before the ground is covered in a thin layer of white. My breath puffs in front of my eyes as we head toward the passenger seat of Caleb's car. The van I was brought here in has been replaced with a sleek, black SUV.

"You got a new car," I say.

Caleb nods. "I usually shift into my wolf form and run into town, but the walk in this form is too long. We'll have to drive."

This is perfect. I'll need a car with which to escape after murdering Caleb, and I was struggling to formulate a plan on how to get one.

"How long of a drive is it?" I ask.

Caleb waits for me to click my seatbelt before answering. "About fifteen minutes."

Good to know. I try not to look too observant as Caleb begins the drive. This place is eerily similar to what I suspect a small human town would look like—minus the wolves moving about.

We drive past two wolves jumping on a young man in his skin form. They're circling him, occasionally nipping at his legs. The young man winces, his knee buckling as one of the wolves lands a particularly hard bite. Are they fighting? Nobody around them looks concerned.

I watch, unable to look away as the two shifters rip out the man's calf. It's sickening, and I rub at my throat as the man falls to the ground with a hoarse cry. Why are the shifters letting this happen?

This is behavior I expected, but my few days alone with Caleb lulled me into a false sense of security. The shifters may be able to walk and talk like humans, but they're animals.

Caleb looks over, following my line of sight.

"The Dawson brothers," he says, acknowledging them. He snorts. "They're at it again."

This is normal. Expected.

"What are they doing?" I ask.

Caleb spares them a glance. "Playing."

"It looks like they're hurting him."

"They are."

I press my lips together. If this is how they treat their own, I can't imagine the damage they will inflict on humans. I'm the best advantage we have.

"Do you lose yourself when you transform?" I ask. I've been looking for an opportunity to bring this up.

Caleb furrows his brows. "No." He pauses, then continues. "We don't have two streams of consciousness. I know some humans believe that, but it's not true. I share a mind with my wolf. He's a part of me. My mind remains the same in both forms."

People are looking at the car. I hope they can't see me through the window tint.

"Your heart is pounding," Caleb says, drawing my focus. "What's wrong?"

I swallow. "You can hear my heart?"

"Yes. I find that listening to your heart brings me comfort."

Caleb's cheeks turn red. I don't focus on that. HPAW knows the shifters have good hearing, but I didn't realize it was strong enough to hear a heartbeat from the opposite side of a car. It's no wonder we have such trouble capturing them. They must hear us coming from miles away.

"How well can you hear my heart?" I ask, prying. "How far can you hear it?"

Caleb shrugs. "From this distance, it's as clear as day. In an unobstructed location, I could probably hear it about a hundred feet away." He presses his lips together. "I can hear it from the room I've been sleeping in."

Well, that's not at all creepy.

"Our hearing is a blessing and a curse," Caleb continues.

That captures my attention. "A curse? How so?"

"My hearing is enhanced in this form, but even more so in my wolf form. High-pitched noises can make it impossible to focus, and they can even block transformations. It can be incredibly painful."

Interesting.

I turn back to the window, watching the buildings fly by. The fighting wolves are far behind us. I try not to think about them.

Despite the public fighting, it's surprising how similar the lives of the shifters are to those of humans. I suppose it shouldn't be. Shifters lived among us for thousands of years, each blending in and acting as if they were one of us.

Life as we knew it was shattered when they exposed themselves. There were more shifters than anybody could have ever guessed, and most of them held positions of power. They were in our government, our military, our technology. Every sector was compromised, and when they retreated into Canada, humans were left to pick up the pieces.

We struggled. We're barely surviving.

Some shifters were living in other countries, but the majority resided in America. We took the biggest hit. The shifters did this to us, and we know they're just waiting to attack. They've already begun.

I drag my hands down my thighs, remembering the images of that innocent family in the file Daniel shared with me. All of them murdered. Men, women, children. Nobody is safe.

Caleb drives up to an unsuspecting, three-story brick building in the center of town. It's nestled between identical-looking buildings and is utterly indistinguishable. Is this where he works? There's no way.

"We're here," Caleb says.

He kills the engine and exits, and my car door is pulled open a heartbeat later. Caleb extends a hand, and I hope he can't feel my tremor as I take it. *Here we go.*

Chapter Ten

I curl my fingers into Caleb's arm, letting him help me up the stone walkway leading to the front entrance. My steps are slow, and fire licks up my ribcage every time I lift my leg, but I'll survive.

Caleb is patient. People are watching us, but he hardly seems to care. Does he not see me as a weakness? He's the infamous Alpha Knox. Surely, having an injured human mate is a liability, something to be ashamed of. He probably hoped to be paired with a shifter woman, one with a wolf dominant enough to match him.

He's good at hiding his disappointment.

Caleb reaches across me to push open the oak exterior door, his earthy scent hitting me in the process. I hate myself for my instinctive, immediate inhale. He smells so good, his scent alone causing my nerve endings to fire.

I'm sure Caleb likes my visible attraction to his scent. It perfectly fits the character I'm playing. I'm a weak, scared human who knows nothing about the shifters other than the rumors I've heard. Caleb is my mate, though, and the pull is impossible to resist. I see him as my savior, as the strong male who saved me from the humans who were torturing me in the woods.

Caleb's lips brush against the hair covering my ear. "My people will be upset with me for taking you out of the house so early in your healing. They worry for you."

I don't know how to respond to that. Thankfully, Caleb doesn't wait for me to as he guides me inside the foyer. This place is cute. The entryway is quaint, with an old wooden staircase immediately on the left and a reception desk directly across from the door.

The brown-haired, tall, clearly shifter woman behind the desk shoots both Caleb and me a wide smile. "Welcome!"

She hurries around her desk, her hand outstretched to grab the ugly, orange coat Caleb already has halfway off my shoulders. I slide my casted arm out of the sleeve, still looking around.

This place feels too normal for my liking. The similarities between the shifters and humans are uncanny. It makes it hard to mentally treat them as violent animals. I expected them to spend most of their time in their wolf form, running through the wilderness with bloodied paws and drooling mouths.

Caleb hands the woman my coat. "Morning, Rosy."

She returns to her desk, hanging my coat on one of the hooks behind her. There's a hallway to her right. It leads to the back of the building, but the lights are shut off. I spot a few cracked-open doors, but I don't get a good look inside the rooms as Caleb guides me to the wooden staircase on our left.

"I'm on the third floor," he says. "I'll carry you."

"Oh. That's not necessary. I—"

I squeak, my words cut short as Caleb scoops me into his arms. He holds me bridal style, the same way he did when he carried me through the woods, and I try not to wiggle as he begins up the stairs. They creak beneath his weight, the wood warped and faded from years of heavy use.

HPAW prefers large, sprawling office buildings. They're cold and sterile, with white walls and cement practically everywhere. This place couldn't be any more different. The walls are a soft beige, and the interior is almost entirely made of dark wood.

"This building is..." I pause, searching for the right words. "It's not what I expected."

Caleb hums. "This used to be a bed and breakfast, but my father had it converted to his office building when I was young. He felt that if he was going to spend most of his time within one building, he might as well make it comfortable."

I agree with that sentiment. The facility was cold. I hated it.

Caleb's grip on me is sturdy, and his face is only inches from mine. I try to avoid looking at him, but it's impossible not to. He's so fucking beautiful. It's no coincidence that I think so. We're fated mates. I'm meant to find him stunning.

Does he find me equally attractive? Judging by the way he touched himself while bathing me, I believe he does.

We reach the third floor, and Caleb carries me into the first office on the right. It faces the front of the building, and large windows overlook the busy street. A desk sits to the right of the door, facing the windows, and full, floor-to-ceiling bookcases line the wall behind it. There's a small couch directly below the windows.

"Was this your dad's office, too?" I ask.

"No. He found the street noise distracting and preferred the office in the back."

Caleb carries me to the couch. He's slow to set me down, lingering with me in his arms. I try my best to remain unaffected, but my heart flutters nonetheless. My butt makes contact with the soft cushion, and my heart only continues to betray me as Caleb brushes a strand of hair behind my ear. I know he can hear it. His ears are built-in heart monitors.

"Are you comfortable?" he asks. "Is there any pain?"

"I'm okay."

My pain is manageable, and I really should save some of the pills for HPAW. The medical team will want to test them. The pills might teach us something about the shifters.

"Well, let me know if the pain becomes too much," he says.

He retreats to his desk. The wooden surface is clean, nothing of interest capturing my attention. A laptop sits in the center, but I assume it's password-protected. My assumption is proven correct as Caleb opens it and types. I can't see his fingers or the screen, but it's obvious he's inputting a password.

I need to get in there. It's only a matter of time before the shifters begin infiltrating the human lands, and we need to know when and how they intend to do it. Surely, Caleb has something useful saved.

The American borders are heavily guarded, but it won't be enough. The wolves are too strong, and they have a natural advantage during the winter months. Their wolf forms are resilient to the cold.

"Would you like to use my computer?" Caleb's question catches me off guard.

I stiffen, resisting the urge to panic and look away. I've done nothing wrong, nothing to feel anxious about.

"Really?" I clear my throat. "You'd let me use it?"

Caleb pulls his eyebrows together. He's confused. *Not ideal.* I count to three and breathe, calming my outward appearance.

"I just didn't think you'd let me use it," I say.

"Why wouldn't I?" He sighs, running a hand through his hair. "You aren't a prisoner, Evelyn. Do you feel trapped? Do you want to go home?"

I shake my head. "I don't feel trapped." How can I salvage this? "I'd love to use it. Thank you."

Caleb wordlessly rises, scooping his computer into his arm as he does so. He's walking around his desk a second later, and I forget how to breathe as he opens the lid, types in a password, and sets his unlocked computer onto my lap.

Holy fuck. I shoot Caleb a small smile, careful not to look too excited.

I can only imagine what's in here. The files, the details. Maybe even medical records. Everything. My heart pounds, blood pumping through my veins. This is unbelievable.

I can't rush into anything nefarious, not until I know Caleb isn't monitoring the device.

"Can I use the internet?" I ask.

"Of course."

I search for and find an online game. Something easy I can play in the browser. Daniel let me play on his devices sometimes, and I've developed a love for solitaire. I want to look up the news, but I don't want Caleb to associate me with politics. I'm staying far away from anything related to HPAW or the American government.

I'll build Caleb's trust, and when the right time comes, I'll go digging.

Caleb clears his throat. "I need to meet with Logan and a few others." He jerks his thumb toward the door. "I'll just be down the hall. Holler if you need me."

Should I ask to join? Probably not. I practically begged him to bring me here, and I can't also beg him to let me sit in on his meeting. Baby steps.

Caleb leaves his office door open, then disappears through a door on the right side of the outside hallway. Logan appears at the top of the stairs two minutes later. He peers into the office, his calculated gaze sweeping the space before settling on me.

"Good morning," he says.

This is the first time I've seen him wearing clothing. No amount of fabric hides his muscular frame. He's a few inches shorter than Caleb, but he more than makes up for it in bulk. He fills the doorway, his shoulders brushing each side.

I force a smile. "Morning."

What is Logan to Caleb? He must be important. He came by the house today, and now he's here to meet privately. Is he the second-in-command?

Logan crosses his arms over his chest. "You're looking better." The corner of his right lip twitches upward. "It's good to see you with some color in your cheeks."

I open my mouth, then shut it. Is he trying to seduce me?

The HPAW soldiers only complimented me with the hopes that I'd invite them into my bedroom, but Logan is mated. He's not flirting with me. He can't be.

Especially not with Caleb just down the hall. Surely, Caleb wouldn't stand for another man trying to bed his mate. He can undoubtedly hear this conversation, too. If he can hear my heartbeat from a bedroom over, there's no way Logan's compliments are going unnoticed.

I drag my fingers over the computer trackpad, not wanting the screen to go dark and lock me out.

"Uh, thank you," I say, finally responding to Logan. "I feel better."

"Glad to hear it." He beams, knocking a knuckle against the doorway and backing up into the hallway. "I'll see you around."

Two more shifters walk upstairs. Both pointedly avoid looking in my direction as they vanish into the room with Caleb and Logan. I'm desperate to know what they're talking about.

I mindlessly play on Caleb's computer. His files are calling to me, a seductress nearly impossible to turn away, but I resist. It's damn hard.

Almost an hour passes before Caleb and the others emerge. Caleb walks ahead. He looks angry, his lips thinned and nostrils flared. The two shifters who avoided looking at me hurry down the stairs, but Logan follows Caleb into his office.

Caleb drops into his chair. He's ignoring Logan. Logan doesn't seem to care.

"Alpha," he starts. "We should—"

Caleb shakes his head. "Leave it."

"But—"

"I said to leave it," Caleb repeats. His gaze meets mine, then returns to Logan. "See to it that the Lockstone pack has all the support they need." He glances at his watch. "Maverick doesn't take kindly to tardiness, even coming from you."

Maverick. The Lockstone pack.

Logan blows out a breath, then storms out of the room, slamming the door shut behind him. Caleb pinches the bridge of his nose.

I wait exactly three seconds before speaking. "Who is Maverick?"

Caleb drops his hands to his desk. "He's the alpha of the Lockstone pack."

Details. Details. Details.

"Where's the Lockstone pack?"

Caleb stares at me for a long moment. His gaze is too intense, too calculating. I swallow, keeping my expression open. Finally, Caleb moves, opening the top drawer of his desk. He pulls out a pen and paper.

"Come here," he orders.

I practically sprint to him, his computer long forgotten as I drop into the chair opposite his desk. Caleb draws a rough outline of the Canadian border, then begins filling in the space.

What was once Ontario and Quebec is now one large territory. The Knox pack. That's about all the detail HPAW knows. Caleb continues drawing. Saskatchewan and Manitoba are now the Lockstone pack.

Alberta remains unchanged. Caleb points to it. "The Aubert pack. King Aubert is the alpha."

I blink. "You have a king?"

"Hardly." Caleb snorts. "King is his first name. He had opportunistic parents, and he was raised accordingly. He's insufferable, but he's a good alpha."

Caleb points to what was once British Columbia. "This is the Allard Pack, led by alpha Everett Allard." He taps the paper with his pen. "These are the main four packs. The other territories are scattered with smaller packs, but they mostly keep to themselves."

I don't know what to say. I review every detail of the map, committing it to memory.

"Why is Logan going to the Lockstone pack?" I ask. "Is it because of the border disputes with HPAW?"

Caleb nods. "Unfortunately. They—"

His sentence is cut short by a knock on the door. Two women come barreling inside a moment later, the pair tripping over one another with loud, giddy laughs. I'm going to fucking kill them.

Chapter Eleven

I recognize the first woman immediately. Her freckles are distinct. She's Logan's mate. I don't recognize the second woman. She looks no different from the typical shifter—tall and muscular, with dark hair and eyes, as well as a friendly smile.

Her gaze trails over me before sliding to Caleb and lingering. The hairs on my arm immediately stand on edge. Something isn't right here. I push back my shoulders, mentally preparing.

Caleb stands. "I should've known you'd be the first to stop by."

He rounds his desk and pulls Sash into a quick hug, but he doesn't acknowledge the second woman. He turns to me. "I wish you two had met under better circumstances, but this is Sash, my sister."

Sash is his sister? Caleb briefly mentioned having one, but I would've never guessed Sash. That makes Logan his brother-in-law. Is that why he has such an esteemed position within the pack? It makes sense.

Sash brings her hands to her mouth, trying and failing to hide her absurd smile. Why is she looking at me like this? She refused to look me in the eye after finding me in the cabin. She seemed petrified, on the verge of vomiting.

I try not to let my budding fear show as she approaches, her movements quick and steady. She cups my cheeks once she's within reach. My lips smoosh together, and I glance between her and Caleb in horror. What the fuck is she doing?

"I'm so excited to formally meet you," she says. "Caleb banished me from visiting the house, but the second I saw his car outside, I just knew you were here. There's no other reason for him to drive."

Sash leans in, pressing her cheek against mine.

HPAW is filled with large personalities. It isn't anything new to me, and if Sash weren't a shifter, I suspect I'd like her. She *is* a shifter, though, and she's currently smooshing her face against mine. I'm not a fan.

When she releases me and steps back, I relax. Caleb is the only wolf I'm at ease around, and that's only because of our damned bond.

Caleb finally gestures to the second woman. "And this is Grace."

He gives her no other introduction, and after an awkward second, she steps forward and presses her cheek to mine just as Sash did.

"It's wonderful to meet you, Evelyn," she says, her voice quiet. "I thought it would be best to wait to meet you, but Sash can be quite persuasive when she wants to be. She practically pulled my arm out of its socket when she saw Knox's car."

Sash presses her lips together with a poorly concealed smile. That smile drops as Caleb leans in and whispers something in her ear. I can't hear his words, but even Grace seems unnerved. She straightens up and steps away from me—as if I were an infectious disease.

Both females look pissed, their eyes narrowed and posture stiff. What's happening?

Sash is pulling Grace out of the room a second later. She slams against Caleb's shoulder as she does so. Caleb doesn't react to the aggressive move, but I imagine it would knock me on my ass.

"What'd you say?" I ask the second they're gone.

Caleb drags his hand through his hair, then drops to his knees at my feet.

What. The. Fuck. Is. Happening?

"I've made a mistake," Caleb admits, placing his hands on my knees. His touch sears me, even through my thick sweatpants.

He draws in a deep breath before leaning forward and pressing his cheek against mine.

"What is this?" I ask. "The cheek thing?"

Caleb hums, his facial hair tickling my skin. "It's a sign of respect to bring your cheek to another. My sister and Grace were placing you above them. Between mates, it's an apology."

I don't like the sound of this. "...And why are you apologizing?"

"When I turned twenty-five and still didn't have a mate, I was expected to pick a female to marry at thirty," he says. My blood grows hot. I know where this is going. "Grace and my sister have been friends since childhood. Grace's mate died many years ago, and since she's kind and already close to my family, I chose her."

Caleb is twenty-nine. He's only months away from his thirtieth birthday. He's been engaged to Grace for almost five years. I can't breathe. Pure, unfiltered jealousy courses through me. I don't want it, but there's no controlling the emotion.

It's beyond my control. It's instinctual. It's the bond.

"For you to meet her without knowing..." Caleb rubs his cheek against mine. I resist the urge to push him away. "It puts you at a disadvantage. I should have told you before we left the house today."

My skin *burns* with emotion. I hate that Caleb was in a relationship before me, that Grace has stolen that experience from us. I grind my teeth. There isn't an *us*. Caleb and I aren't anything. I'm not a shifter, and I don't believe in the mate bond. He's nothing to me.

I have no reason to be upset. I refuse to be. I'm better than that.

"How have you two prepared for marriage?" I ask. Has he touched her? He claims to be a virgin, but that doesn't mean he hasn't been with her in other ways. "What have you two done together?"

Caleb opens his mouth to respond, but he's stopped as his office door bursts open and three giant men come storming inside. They look surprised to see me, and they awkwardly slam to a stop before lining up beside the door and bowing their heads.

Caleb makes no effort to move. Doesn't it bother him that other shifters are seeing him on his knees before a human? We don't know much about shifter culture, but we do know their hierarchy is everything. Alphas are at the top.

The man on the right is the first to speak. "Alpha."

Caleb frowns. "What?"

His voice is stern. Unflinching. I'm not familiar with this side of him.

The man on the right continues. "We found them."

Found who? Caleb is already on his feet. I don't miss how he places himself between the men and me, blocking my view. I lean to the side and peer around his waist. The three wolves are large, with bulging muscles and scarred skin. Soldiers?

They're trying to look at Caleb, but their gazes keep darting toward me. I'm expecting to be met with hostility, but instead, I'm met with raised eyebrows and smirking lips.

"Where are they?" Caleb asks.

He practically growls the words. I curl my hands into fists as the low timbre vibrates through me. I like his voice. I want him to speak to me like this. I want him to ask me hard questions and order me around while he touches me.

The three wolves stiffen, their curious glances at me immediately vanishing. They're looking at Caleb and only Caleb.

"In the square," the one on the right says. "Logan is with them. They're military, an HPAW unit. We haven't gotten any information out of them yet, but they smell of your mate."

HPAW? No. There's no way they found the unit that brought

me to the woods. Our plan was foolproof. They would've left hours before Sash and her mate reached me. They had more than enough time to escape.

Caleb is shaking, his arms quivering. Is he holding back a transformation?

"What's going on?" I ask.

"We've found the men who attacked you." Caleb peers at me over his shoulder. "Do you think you can identify them?"

I pause, pretending to think it over. I *need* to see these men. If Caleb's shifters found the soldiers who brought me here, this has all been for nothing. The shifters will torture them, and somebody will crack. He'll tell them who I really am. He will ruin everything.

"I don't want to talk to them," I say. I attempt to sound scared, and I know I've succeeded as Caleb places himself closer to me. He's protective, and I plan to use that to my advantage. I'm just not quite sure how.

"I would never ask that of you," he promises.

I clear my throat. "Then yes. I can identify them."

My heart is pounding, blood rushing through my veins as Caleb lifts me into his arms and carries me downstairs. He's gentle with me despite his mood, and I try and fail to steady my breathing.

"It's okay," Caleb whispers. He brings his lips to my temple, letting them graze against my clammy skin. "I won't let anybody hurt you. Never again."

He doesn't bother forcing me into the ugly, orange coat as he carries me outside and down the street, but his arms keep me warm enough.

The men from his office follow, their hands clasped behind their backs as they walk in a single-file line behind Caleb. When we reach the busy street three blocks away from Caleb's office, my heart drops. *Fuck me.*

They had more than enough time to reach their vehicles. What went wrong?

Caleb continues kissing my temple, distracting me with his touch. He's trying to comfort me, not realizing the real reason for my anxiety.

Wolves crowd the square. There must be hundreds of them, and they part as we approach. Almost all bow their heads as Caleb walks past, but their focus is on me. Am I really that much of a wonder?

I scan the faces of the HPAW soldiers. The men are worse for wear, their faces bloody and their clothing half torn off. It appears they were dragged, and I notice several frostbitten, blackened fingers.

Shit. This wasn't part of the plan.

Caleb tightens his grip, holding me closer. A low, grumbling noise is pouring from his chest, causing mild vibrations. The sound is frightening, but it's nothing compared to my panic as I lock eyes with the HPAW soldiers before me. It only takes one to ruin this entire operation. I bury my face into Caleb's neck, my breathing harsh. He needs to believe I'm terrified of them.

"It's okay, my mate," he whispers. He shifts to the side, removing the men from my line of sight. "Are these the men who hurt you?"

I take a moment to respond. My answer won't change their outcome. These men are going to die either way. They're HPAW soldiers, and that alone is a death sentence. Perhaps their deaths will be quick if I say I don't recognize them, but their scents are on me. I'll be expected to explain why.

Caleb will know I'm lying.

My bottom lip trembles as I sink my teeth into it. I hate this.

"It's them," I confirm. I swallow, my throat dry. "I recognize that one." I point to the man closest to me, the one I've locked eyes with. His expression doesn't change. He knows what capture means. He understands what I need to do and why. "What are you going to do to them?"

Caleb shifts his stance. "We'll question them. Then we'll kill them."

I shake my head, hoping it comes across as frantic. "No!" I'm proud of the tears I'm able to produce on command. "I want them dead *now*. The things they did to me...." I trail off, pretending my throat is clogged.

My pleading is met with silence.

"Please, Caleb," I beg again. "I just want it to be over."

Caleb cups the back of my head, his fingers sifting through my hair. His hand is enormous, covering almost the entirety of my skull. He nudges me, urging me to face him. I do, refusing to look away. His gaze lingers on the fading bruise above my right eye before traveling to my wet cheeks.

"Please." My voice cracks.

Caleb shuts his eyes. "Okay, Evelyn. Whatever you need."

He walks away from the HPAW soldiers, his footfalls steady. When the soldiers are no longer in our line of sight, he flicks his hand over his head, gesturing lazily toward the men.

"Have at it," he says.

Screaming reaches my ears a second later. It's complemented with the sounds of growls, grunts, and gut-wrenching crunching. I bury my face back against Caleb's neck, hiding from the sound.

I'm not upset that Caleb is killing the men who he believes hurt me. If this situation were real, I would want them killed. They'd deserve it for what they did to me. It's the fact that these are innocent HPAW soldiers that affects me most. They were only following orders.

This wasn't supposed to happen. HPAW soldiers were never supposed to die, but I suppose it's better to be done now than after days of torture.

I know what the shifters do to us. They enjoy tearing our skin from our bodies. They eat us alive. They take a sick pleasure in it, and this is the most humane ending I can give our men. It's the only way to save the mission, too.

Caleb brings me to his car, placing me in the passenger seat. "That's enough for today," he says. "You should be resting."

How did the shifters find the HPAW soldiers? I want to know

every detail, but I keep silent. Truthfully, I don't want to think about them any more than I need to. What's done is done, and I should move on.

That's easier said than done. Their screams echo in my ears. Is that what will happen to me if I'm caught? Will Caleb have me brought before a crowd of shifters? Will he aimlessly flick his fingers with the calm order to attack? Will they rip me apart?

I draw in a shaky breath.

Caleb begins driving. "I believe we were discussing Grace before our interruption," he says.

He's trying to change the subject. I appreciate it. I can't let myself dwell on the risks of this mission, and Caleb is offering the perfect distraction.

"Yes," I say. "We were."

Caleb purses his lips, his fingers tightening around the steering wheel. I pay attention to the roads, wanting to memorize his pack. If he lives here, it's safe to assume other high-ranking wolves do as well.

It's unfortunate that HPAW didn't realize the female shifter they've been watching for the past year is Caleb's sister. Sash is valuable. If they had known, they'd have captured her while they'd had the opportunity. Caleb seems to love her. He'd give anything to get her back.

After I kill Caleb and escape, I'll tell HPAW about Sash and any other siblings I discover.

"You asked what she and I have done together," Caleb starts. "I have never intimately touched a woman, Evelyn, and there were no plans for me to do so. Had the marriage gone through, Grace would've been artificially inseminated and we would've lived together as nothing more than co-parents. She had a mate, and he isn't me. We would never desecrate our bonds."

Is that true? I'm at a loss for words, so I stare out the window as I process that information.

"I would've continued to save myself for you," Caleb continues, "and my marriage to Grace would've been annulled the moment you were discovered. She and the entire pack were aware of that from the start."

Are the shifters truly this beholden to their mate bonds? It's unbelievable.

Caleb makes a quiet noise in the back of his throat, then swerves to the right and pulls the car to the side of the road. I barely have time to react before he's shoving his marked hand in front of my face.

"Do you see how light my mark is?" he asks.

"Yes."

"Marks darken whenever the bond is dishonored, and mine remains white. I've been honest to it, to you."

Is that true? I almost don't want to believe it.

My hand shakes, a slight tremor that's impossible to hide, as I take Caleb's marked hand. He lets me, remaining silent as I trace the path of vines trailing up his middle finger and onto the back of his hand. He twitches as I touch the webbing between his middle and ring fingers, but he otherwise remains still.

"My mark is dark," I say, placing my hand beside his.

"I've noticed."

Where his design is white, mine is a deep red. The color has grown more pronounced over the years, but I assumed the change was due to aging. It began darkening shortly after puberty, which I realize now is the same time HPAW encouraged me to seek out the company of men.

I suppose this explains why Caleb avoids my mark. I've caught him occasionally glancing at it, a slight frown marring his features, before quickly looking away. Does he know what I've done? At the very least, he must wonder.

"I'm sorry," I say.

"Don't be."

He shifts away from me, breaking the tension, and resumes driving. Is he not going to ask what I've done to make my mark so dark? Can I blame it entirely on sex? I'm sure my work with

HPAW has contributed to the discoloration. I'm actively working against Caleb. I'm planning to murder him.

I cast a subtle glance at my mark, trying to gauge whether it's grown darker in these past few days. I can't tell. I've always avoided looking at the marking. I hate what it stands for, and I've grown used to pretending it doesn't exist. I'll need to keep a close eye on it until I complete my mission.

"Are you—" Caleb pauses, clearing his throat. "Are you upset about Grace?" He hesitates, then continues. "It wouldn't be considered indecent if you requested me to relocate her to a different pack, but I'd prefer not to do that. She's been here her entire life, and she's my sister's best friend. She's a kind woman, and I—"

"She can stay." My voice is snappy, and I wince at the sound of it. "I'm not upset."

I'm jealous. It's absurd. I hardly know Caleb, and I'm planning to kill him. Not to mention the fact that he's a fucking shifter. Jealousy is the last thing I should be feeling.

"Thank you, Evelyn." Caleb drops his hand to my thigh, his fingers curling around the muscle. I stare at it, unable to look away from his mark. So fucking white.

"Ev," I correct him.

"Pardon?"

"You can call me Ev." I've never had a nickname, but I've always fantasized about it. Now's as good a time as any to choose one.

Caleb squeezes my thigh, his lips curling into a soft smile. "Ev."

My heart thumps, and I nod.

"I like it," Caleb says. "Ev."

It sounds good rolling off his tongue, and I place my hand on his before relaxing back against my seat. I can do this. Only a few more weeks and I can put all this behind me.

Chapter Twelve

"I am Rapunzel."

Caleb kicks off his shoes and pushes the front door shut behind him. He was only gone for twenty minutes, but he looks stressed. He has been slipping outside to meet with shifters with increasing frequency. I know it's because of HPAW.

Those fuckers promised to lay low for my first few weeks here. I should be getting to know Caleb and winning him over, and they're distracting him. I can't fathom why. Something must have changed.

"Rapunzel?" he asks.

I hold up the book I found on his bookshelf. Twenty minutes isn't enough time to search his upstairs home office, but it was enough to examine his living room. I stumbled upon a children's book. I read about Rapunzel. I resonate with her.

Caleb points to my head. "Your hair is much too short, and she's a blonde."

"She's a woman who has been imprisoned inside a tower by a witch."

That's how I feel. It's been several days since Caleb brought me to his office. Four, to be exact. It's been four long days of doing nothing with Caleb. I'm trapped inside his house, apparently because I need to rest and recover.

"Are you calling me a witch?" Caleb asks.

"Yes."

Caleb shakes his head with a laugh, his eyes crinkling. There's something enjoyable about making him laugh, about knowing I'm the direct cause of it. It's almost satisfying. I've never felt that way with any of the other men I've been with, and I'm choosing to blame the bond. I love blaming the bond.

"We have an appointment with Greg in two hours," Caleb says. "He'll remove your cast and examine your ribs. If everything is looking good, I promise you'll be free to explore the pack lands at your leisure."

Caleb cares too much about what Doctor Greg thinks. I like the man and all, but his warnings have gotten on my nerves. I know my body better than anybody else, and I feel fine. I've sustained injuries worse than this and lived to tell the tale.

"You don't need his permission," I argue.

"Of course not, but I value his opinion."

I'm going to rip out my hair. Caleb has the nerve to laugh.

"I know this week has been challenging for you," he starts, "but I promise you'll have your freedom soon."

I sure fucking hope so. I've learned all I can learn from Caleb in this setting. It's hard to ask probing questions when we're sitting around his house. They seem unnatural and draw suspicion, and I need new excuses to pry. If he brings me outside or to his office, I can use what I observe as reasons to dig deeper into the dynamics of his pack.

If Doctor Greg doesn't clear me today, I'm going to throw a fit.

I raise my arms over my head, loving the stretch. Water pours over my face. That feels incredible, too. I've been limited to baths, and this shower is everything I've ever needed.

Doctor Greg said I'm healing exceptionally well, and he removed my arm cast. My ribs are looking good, too, and the cut on my forehead is a thing of the past. My bruises are almost gone, only hints of yellow remaining. I'm starting to look like me again. It feels good.

"Are you sure you don't need help?" Caleb asks. He's fretting.

He's standing two feet from the shower door, trying his hardest not to peek through the glass. He's pointedly staring at the ground. He hasn't touched me since that first night, not intimately, and it's time to change that.

I intend to win Caleb over with whatever means necessary, and with HPAW making moves in the background, I don't have time to waste. Sex is the easy answer.

"Ev?" Caleb approaches the shower door, his eyes flicking upward to meet mine. "Your heart is racing. Are you dizzy? Faint?"

I turn around, ignoring him.

He groans. "Evelyn."

My lips curl. I like his fretting more than I'd care to admit. It makes me warm and tingly inside, which is dangerous. I shouldn't let myself feel any soft emotions toward Caleb. It will end poorly.

I rinse out my hair, then face Caleb again. He's glaring into the shower, but his expression softens as he takes notice of my teasing smile. I don't try to hide my bare skin from him, and I flush as his gaze momentarily dips. He can't help himself.

"You can look," I assure him.

He hums, the sound barely audible over the running water. "I shouldn't."

"I'd like you to."

This time, he groans. "Evelyn..."

"Look at me, Caleb."

For the first time in days, he does. He lets himself see me, and he lingers. I wish I knew what he was thinking. Even more than that, I wish I could see *him*. I've caught glimpses here and there, a flash of skin while he's changing in his closet or the outline of bare, muscular thighs when he checks in on me in the middle of the night.

He sleeps in only underwear, and he doesn't bother putting on pants when he makes his late-night visits.

I think I overheard him pleasuring himself last night. He sleeps in the room beside mine, and I swear I heard a moan. I only heard it once, and it was quiet, but it was enough to set my skin aflame.

Caleb inches closer to the shower.

I pull open the door. "Would you like to join me?"

"Yes."

I raise a brow. "*Will* you join me?"

"No."

"And why not?" I cross my arms, careful not to apply too much pressure to my ribcage. I'm feeling better, but I'm not fully healed. "We're mates, Caleb. From what I've gathered this past week, that means you should be *jumping* at the opportunity to shower with me."

Doctor Greg yelled at him today. My lips twitch at the memory. Caleb looked like a little boy, his head hung low and his hands clasped behind his back. He should've lied when Doctor Greg asked if I've been engaging in any strenuous activity. I had my clit rubbed while soaking in a bathtub. It was hardly strenuous, and it was several days ago. It wasn't worth mentioning.

Caleb steps back. "I really shouldn't."

I tighten my grip on the door. "The floor is awfully slippery...." I sigh, sliding my foot along the ground. "What if I fall?"

I'm desperate to see Caleb's body and, even more than that, I'm desperate to feel it. I'm pretty sure I might die if I don't get it soon. Maybe I should feel ashamed for how eager I am to be with Caleb, but I'm choosing to blame the bond.

I've never felt this needy.

Caleb smirks. "You can't trick me into showering with you, Ev."

"I'm not lying," I lie, dragging my foot along the shower floor. It squeaks.

Caleb finally wavers, his hands moving to the hem of his shirt. *Yes.* He toys with the fabric, working it between his fingers. He knows I'm lying, but I'm giving him a great excuse to join me in the shower. I know he wants to.

Caleb sighs, then yanks his shirt over his head. I step back, victorious. He hooks his thumbs into his bottoms and shoves them down his legs. His underwear is quick to follow.

Magnificent.

His cock is hard, and it bobs as he steps into the shower. The space is tight, and he places a steadying hand on my waist as he finds a spot for himself. I take this time to admire every inch of him. He's so much more than the other men I've been intimate with.

He's taller. Wider. Stronger. He's just so fucking masculine. I lean in, wanting to be closer. Caleb allows it, bringing his other hand to my waist.

We stand before one another, no words spoken as we look. Is Caleb pleased with my body? It's an intrusive thought I've had several times. Shifters are taller, and they tend to carry more muscle. I don't consider myself weak, but I have a leaner frame. My dark hair and brown eyes are my most significant similarity to the shifters, but that's about it.

"You're not how I thought you'd be," I admit, breaking the silence.

Caleb cocks his head to the side. "What did you expect?"

I shrug. "I thought you'd be violent. I knew mate bonds were important to shifters, but I assumed our relationship would be more—I don't know—unequal. I thought you'd think of me as an object to own. A possession."

"Fucking humans." Caleb practically growls the words. "Your government has done an excellent job villainizing us. They make us out to be aggressors, and it's all lies. We don't harm humans without reason. We never have."

I frown but don't argue. Caleb's lying, but that's not an argument I'm looking to have right now. I've seen firsthand evidence of the shifter attacks. Hundreds, if not thousands, of innocent humans have lost their lives simply because they were in the wrong place at the wrong time.

Shifters are aggressors. They always have been, and they always will be.

Caleb licks his lips. "Do you think we're bad people?"

Water pours down his chest, pouring in thick rivulets toward his waist. He's not as hairy as I anticipated. I feared he'd be covered in it. It would make sense, considering the animal he transforms into, but his body hair is pretty average. There's a smattering across his chest, and a thick trail leading from his belly button to his pubic hair. Are all shifters like this? I suspect Caleb won't be pleased with me asking about the pubic and body hair of other shifters.

"Do you?" Caleb urges. "Do you think we're bad people?"

"I don't think you're a bad person." The words feel suspiciously close to the truth.

Caleb's responding smile is a bit crooked, and it practically oozes relief. It shifts into something softer as he leans in for a kiss, and my eyes slip shut as he finally presses his lips against mine.

For a man who has never kissed a woman, he's sure good at it. He angles his mouth against mine, almost immediately deepening the kiss, and he moans as our tongues meet. I'm dying for more.

I grab Caleb's shoulders, not caring if he can sense my desperation. My fingers curl around his muscles, feeling them before sliding to the back of his neck. Caleb moans again, the sound shifting into a groan as I weave my fingers through the short hairs at the back of his head.

I'm holding his mouth prisoner against mine. Not that he's trying very hard to escape.

"Fuck, Ev." Caleb grunts. "You have no idea how long I've waited for this."

I hum. "About twenty-nine years, I suspect."

Caleb hooks his arm around my waist, pulling me forward. We're so close, and I can't suppress my shiver as his cock presses against my stomach. My body is sensitive to his touch, the mere graze of his fingertips sending lightning down my spine.

"Touch me," I beg.

Caleb shakes his head, then drops his forehead against mine. "You're still healing."

"I feel good."

"Your ribs—"

"They feel great."

I can practically *feel* Caleb's disbelief. I don't blame him. Just this morning, Doctor Greg yelled at him for touching me. He called Caleb irresponsible. He said Caleb should know better. He was being dramatic.

Caleb worries his bottom lip between his teeth. His pupils are fully dilated, only a sliver of dark brown remaining at the edges. They're not normal. I can't quite put my finger on what it is, but something is wrong with them.

I swallow. "Your eyes…"

Caleb blinks. "I told you I share a mind with my wolf. He's quiet most of the time, content with letting me lead." Caleb blinks again, his eyes now appearing normal. "But he's interested in what's happening between us."

HPAW would have a field day with this information.

"What does that mean?" I ask. "Are you going to shift?"

"No." Caleb smirks. "Let's save your questions for later, yeah?" He tightens his grip on my wrists, reminding me that he's holding them. "Don't move."

That's not an easy command to follow. It grows especially hard when he drags his free hand up my torso. My skin pebbles beneath his fingers.

He takes his time feeling me, cupping my breast before

changing course and touching himself. He curls his marked hand around the base of his cock, stroking slowly.

"Spread your legs."

He doesn't need to tell me twice. I widen my stance, trembling as he inches forward and places his length between my thighs, nestling himself against me. Is he going to fuck my thighs?

Caleb taps the outside of my leg. "Close them."

I squeeze my legs together, trapping him between them. His length twitches.

"You're destroying me." He groans. He has no idea how true those words are. "You know I can't say *no* to you. Rub against my cock, Ev. Show me how you'd fuck me."

It's damn near impossible to form words, especially when Caleb rocks himself forward. The head of his cock drags against my clit, and I rest my head against the shower wall as he fucks my thighs.

He moans, low and throaty. "You feel so good."

One slight adjustment and he'd be inside me. That's all it would take. Caleb isn't going to fall prey to that, though. He's not going to fuck me until I'm healed, which is a disappointment.

"You're dripping all over me," Caleb continues. "I've been dreaming of the day I can give myself to you. You have no idea how badly I want to be inside you."

He quickens his pace, his thighs slapping against mine.

"I want you." I shift, angling myself so it's easier for him to slip inside.

I'm so fucking turned on, my arousal covering every inch of him. There won't be any resistance. Despite his size, my body will welcome him right on in. We were made for one another, after all.

Caleb laughs, fucking *laughs*, and presses me against the wall. He avoids applying pressure to my injuries, the heel of his palm pressed below my belly button and his fingers resting just below my ribcage.

I'm flattered by the consideration, but I don't let the emotion burrow too deep in my heart. I'm not here to fall in love.

"Caleb!" I whine.

He chuckles again. "Shifters can be rough. I don't want to hurt you."

"You won't."

Caleb has already proven he won't hurt me, and I'm nervous we won't have time to have sex before I've gotten the information I need from him. It'll be weeks before my ribcage is fully healed. At the rate I'm going, I'll have the information I need long before that.

He'll be dead before sex is even on the table.

"It's not going to happen." Caleb looks down, watching himself disappear between my thighs. "It's not a risk I'm willing to take. You're too important."

I'm tempted to spread my legs and ruin his friction. It's a petty thought, one I already know I won't follow through on.

"Do you like my cock?" Caleb asks.

I can feel him looking at me, but I avert my eyes. I stare down instead, unable to look away as he grabs the base of his shaft and removes himself from between my thighs. He has a nice cock. It's perfect, just like the rest of him.

"Well?" Caleb taunts. "Do you like your mate's cock?"

"You know I do."

"Good." Caleb hums, seeming all too pleased with himself, and presses himself back between my thighs. "Are you going to cum on it?"

"I sure fucking hope so."

His blunt tip rubs against my entrance, just barely catching it with each thrust. Paired with the drag of his shaft against my clit, it all has me steamrolling toward orgasm.

I hold Caleb's shoulders. "Don't stop."

He squeezes his eyes shut, his body tensing. "Wouldn't dream of it."

He's trying to hold back his moans, but he's failing. The deep, fevered grunts are pouring from his throat with every thrust. I love the effect I have on him. I love being the reason he's going to cum.

I'm the only person who can make him feel like this. No other woman will know what he sounds or looks like when he cums.

He's mine.

My needy claim is unexpected, but my orgasm ripping through me overshadows my shock. I dig my nails into his shoulders so hard, I'm sure he'll be left with tiny crescent indents.

Caleb is everywhere, the shifter infiltrating my every sense. He's all I can see, all I can hear, all I can fucking feel and taste. For a brief moment, as my orgasm crests, he's everything.

He steps back as my pleasure subsides, his fist curling once more around the base of his shaft. "Spread your legs," he orders. I don't hesitate to do so. Caleb's demands continue. "Spread your pussy, Evelyn."

He's trying to kill me. Still, I do as he asks without complaint. I act on autopilot, dropping a hand between my thighs and spreading myself. I want to do it. I want to please Caleb.

In this moment, there isn't anything I wouldn't do for him.

Caleb surges forward, notching the tip of his cock at my entrance. He doesn't push inside, and my knees tremble as he strokes himself once and begins to cum. The low groan that tumbles from his throat is forever seared into my mind, along with the image of him finishing inside me.

His cum immediately dribbles back out, gravity working against us.

Caleb strokes until he's fully emptied. I struggle to catch my breath. My ribs hurt, but Doctor Greg told me it's good to breathe deeply. It helps clear mucus and prevent infection.

"We probably shouldn't do that again…" I eventually say, gesturing to the cum.

Caleb shrugs, dragging his fingertips along my thighs before easing the tip of one of his cum-soaked fingers inside me. "You aren't ovulating."

"How do you know that?"

"Shifters can smell the luteinizing hormone."

I pause. "What is that?"

"It's a hormone that surges right before the ovary releases an egg."

My mate is a period tracker.

"We should still be careful," I say. "I'm not ready for a baby."

Caleb blows out a slow, controlled breath, then nods. "I understand. It won't happen again."

That's it? He's not going to push? HPAW told me that shifters are eager to have children. They suggested that if I'm struggling to earn Caleb's trust, I should encourage him to impregnate me. It never occurred to me that Caleb would so readily accept my rejection of the idea.

Caleb continually shocks me.

"Can I sleep in bed with you tonight?" he asks.

He turns off the shower and opens the glass door, letting the heat out. I shiver, goosebumps pebbling up along my exposed skin. Caleb hands me the closest towel, then braves the cold as he walks across the bathroom to grab another from the cabinet.

It's a small action, but one I notice.

"I'll be careful not to crush you." He grimaces. "Again."

Do I want to share a bed with Caleb? The bond screams for me to say *yes*, to invite him to spend every night by my side for the rest of our lives. The rational part of me knows it's a bad idea and a slippery slope. Still, I have a role to play. Caleb needs to believe I'm getting close to him, that I'm falling in love with him.

I was hoping intimacy would draw him in, and it seems my assumption was correct. He's lowered his guard. He wants to be closer to me.

"Yes," I say. "I want to share a bed with you."

Caleb smiles, his expression soft as I dry myself. His smile shifts as he eyes my naked form, the bright bathroom light hiding nothing. I'm covered in hundreds of tiny scars from years of training with HPAW, but I see each white spot and slash as a victory.

I grew stronger every time I was hurt, and my body lives to tell the story.

Caleb traces a longer gash along my hip. "What happened here?"

"I fell out of a tree." I've rehearsed a lie for every single scar.

Caleb doesn't immediately respond, and after a second, I touch one of his scars. It's thin and impossible to notice unless you look closely. The small, white slash is about an inch above his left nipple, and it runs almost to his armpit.

He tenses as I run my finger along it.

"What happened here?" I copy his question.

"I fell out of a tree."

Oh. I drop my hand, forcing an easy smile on my face. Caleb knows I was lying about my scar, and this is his subtle way of letting me know. The silence between us stretches, neither of us seeming particularly keen to be the first to break it.

Caleb isn't pushing for the truth, but it's not a good sign that he could tell I was lying. It was a smooth lie, one that slipped off my tongue with ease. Caleb is learning my tells.

I'm running out of time.

Chapter Thirteen

Caleb is a damned furnace. His arms are wrapped securely around my waist, caging me against his chest. I've never shared a bed with a man, and I always assumed it would be uncomfortable. It's not too bad. I'm sweaty and a little constricted, but I'm finding I enjoy it.

Who would've guessed?

I stare at Caleb's sleeping face. He's a beautiful man, and I take this opportunity to imprint every pore, mark, and eyelash into memory. His lips part to release a soft breath of air, drawing my attention to the lower half of his face. His lips are my favorite feature. They're full and pliable. I want to feel them.

I crane my neck and kiss him, my fingers curling into the soft, fine hair on his chest as he purses his lips, sleepily kissing me back. He's so trusting, and he doesn't flinch even as I trail my fingers up his throat. I feel the muscular column of it, beginning to dread the thought of hurting him.

I'm getting attached. It doesn't change my plan, but it sure makes it harder.

Caleb just seems so nice, but I have no options. I can't spare him. *Take down the alpha. Take down the pack.* That's the only way to succeed. It's the only way to keep the humans safe.

"Evelyn..." Caleb grumbles, his voice heavy with sleep. "Why are you awake? Go back to sleep."

He rolls me onto my back, pinning me to the bed with his thigh. It's thrown over my hips, carefully avoiding my ribs. I lick my dry lips, emotion clogging my throat as he burrows his face into the crook of my neck.

I'm alone the next time I wake.

The bed is empty, and the spot beside me is cold. Caleb must have left a while ago. I refuse to feel disappointed as I crawl out of bed and dress myself. Caleb had several items delivered for me.

It's mostly basics, simple tops and jeans along with plain undergarments and pajamas, but everything is comfortable. There are several color options, too. It's more than HPAW ever gave me. I had five pairs of the same shirt, two pairs of identical black pants that *swished* when I walked, and one pair of sneakers.

I suspect Caleb would be more than happy to take me shopping if I asked. If I were planning to stay here longer, I'd ask.

Where did he go?

I search the entire house before tugging on my ugly, orange coat and stepping outside. A light dusting of white coats the ground, the first snowfall of the season.

The car is here, but that doesn't mean much. Caleb prefers to travel in his wolf form. Has he left for work? There's no way. He wouldn't leave without telling me.

Now could be a good time to rifle through his belongings, but it feels risky when I don't know where he went or when he'll be back.

I hesitate, staring at his vehicle, before grabbing the keys and money Caleb keeps on the entryway table. I want to explore the area, and now's as good a time as any. Caleb hasn't explicitly told me I can't drive the car or leave the house without him. Plus, Doctor Greg gave me clearance to resume normal activity.

If Caleb gets upset, I'll feign ignorance.

Daniel taught me how to drive when I was twenty. He wanted

to teach me years earlier, but he had to get approval from HPAW leadership. They dragged their feet.

My skills are rusty as I drive down the winding driveway and turn onto the main road. I memorized the turns, not that there are many. It's a straight shot into town, and I creep slowly in that direction.

I navigate to the busy main street where Caleb works, painfully aware of the fact that my car is the only one here. Everybody else travels on foot, usually in their animal form. I try not to make eye contact with anybody.

Still, several people watch as I park in front of a small brick building with the name *Le Petit Perchoir* printed across it. I have no idea what the fuck that means, but I can tell it's a coffee shop.

Anxiety threatens to consume me, but I refuse to let it. I have a job to do. I need to learn the pack's dynamics, and that means observing how shifters interact with one another.

I square my shoulders, then step out of the car. I've never been to a coffee shop, but I know they're popular among humans. There's a paper taped to the front door. I briefly scan it. This place is hiring. How fun. I've never had a job, and I've always wondered what it would be like.

When I've completed my work and return to the humans, I'm sure I'll find out.

I shake my head, peering through the glass door. This place is busy. There are several tables inside, and all are full. Four people are waiting to order, and three more are waiting for their orders farther down the counter. My heart pounds as I step inside.

I'm surrounded by shifters, and Caleb isn't here to protect me. While I trust that Caleb has no intention of hurting me, that confidence doesn't extend to his pack members. Nothing is stopping these people from swarming me. I can't realistically defend myself.

I'm a sheep surrounded by wolves. Literally.

Well, literal wolves, at least. I'm not sporting wool or *baaing*, I suppose.

The first person in line—a tall, older man with salt-and-pepper hair and a broad smile—gestures for me to go first. "Go on ahead, Evelyn."

He knows my name. *Fan-fucking-tastic*. I give him what I hope looks like a friendly smile and step up to the counter. The barista bounces on her heels, her dark hair bobbing around her shoulders. I eye the large board behind her. There are dozens of drinks listed, and I know almost none of them.

"Good morning, Alpha!" the barista says.

Is Caleb here? I scan the room, but he's nowhere to be seen. The barista's breezy laugh draws my focus back to her.

"I was talking to you, Evelyn," she explains, wiping her palms down the black apron tied around her waist. "You're our female alpha. Calling you 'Alpha' is a sign of respect. What can I get you to drink?"

I didn't realize being Caleb's mate earned me a title, even if it's only symbolic. I'm shocked a shifter is even willing to call a human such a revered title.

I order the first thing on the menu, hating the way my voice trembles. I spent my entire life training for this, preparing to live among the shifters, but being here still terrifies me. My fear feels like failure.

My exchange with the barista is quick and relatively painless. I give her my money, and after a few minutes, she calls out my name and hands over my drink. A small table near the back of the shop has opened up, and I take the seat with my back facing the wall.

The shifters are sneaking looks at me.

I stare out the window, pretending to be lost in thought as I eavesdrop on their conversations. Three teenage girls on my left are working on a school project and whispering to one another about a boy in their class. They clearly have a shared crush on him, but they avoid saying anything even remotely close to romantic.

They're respectful of the mates they hope to have someday. It's weird.

The young couple on the other side of me is more interesting. They're discussing some spat between the Aubert and Allard packs. They don't go into detail, which is unfortunate. The young couple wonders if Caleb will be forced to intervene.

I wasn't aware there were divisions between the packs, and neither is HPAW. Disputes are a weakness, which opens the possibility for HPAW to form alliances. They could work with the other alphas to take down Caleb's pack. The Knox pack is the largest, and he's the first line of defense for the shifters. With him gone, the shifters as a whole will be weakened.

The couple falls quiet as a bell above the front door chimes, and I mentally prepare as Caleb steps inside. He's wearing a short-sleeved shirt and loose workout shorts. It's not his usual attire, and he's sweaty. Was he running?

His eyes find mine immediately. Will he be upset with me for leaving the house? The teens beside me erupt into giggles and hushed whispers.

I sip my drink and greet Caleb with a slight dip of my chin. He doesn't seem upset, but I can't be too sure. He smiles as he approaches, weaving effortlessly between the tables.

"Good morning, mate." He pulls out the chair opposite me. "Are you getting into trouble?"

I shrug. "How'd you know I was here?"

Am I being watched? I wouldn't be surprised.

"I woke up feeling antsy this morning. I thought a quick run would calm me down." Caleb gestures to the car visible through the front windows. "This place is on my route, and it's hard not to notice the single car in the lot."

The barista approaches with a cup of ice water.

"Alpha," she greets Caleb, setting the cup beside his hand.

Caleb turns, shooting her a grateful smile. "Thanks, Cassie."

I wish he treated her poorly. I wish he were an asshole. It would make this so much easier.

"Why were you antsy?" I ask.

The look Caleb gives me has me regretting my question. He

quirks a brow, and his eyes dart around the room before he leans over the table, bringing his lips to my ear. I'm both excited and terrified to hear what he has to say.

"Because I woke up with my half-naked mate underneath me and my cock so hard, it ached." Caleb kisses my heated cheek and pulls away.

I'm stunned speechless, which Caleb seems to enjoy, if his cocky smirk is anything to go by. He drinks his water, his throat bobbing with each gulp.

I want to lick the sweat off his neck, but I'm not going to tell him that. Especially not here. Shifters have good hearing, and anyone who cares enough to listen can easily overhear us. I'm sure most of the room is listening.

"Caleb!" I shake my head. "You can't say things like that in public."

He shrugs, clearly not caring. "I've waited a long time to find you, and I won't be shy in my desires..." He tilts his head to the side. "I'm hoping to fuck your thighs again tonight."

The teenage girls erupt into poorly stifled laughter.

I choke on my spit, positive my face is beet red. I'm not a timid person, but this public dirty talk is more than I can handle. I thought Caleb was shy. He seemed so bashful the first time he touched me, but his confidence is quickly growing.

"Are you working today?" I ask, desperate to change the subject.

"Unfortunately. I can't avoid it forever."

"Can I come with you?"

"Of course." Caleb rises, and I do the same. "You don't have to ask. You're always welcome."

The people sitting near the door smile at us as we leave. It looks genuine. I'm still in disbelief that they seem to like me.

Caleb tries to take the car keys from me, but when I clutch them possessively to my chest, he wordlessly slides into the passenger seat. *He's truly going to let me drive?* Dangerous threads of excitement course through me as I back out of the parking spot.

I'm having fun with Caleb. I'm having fun in this pack.

Caleb seems to regret his decision as I fly down the road that leads to his home. He clutches the door with one hand, his other gripping the center console.

"Are you okay?" I ask.

"No."

"Don't be so dramatic." I whip into the driveway and slam the brakes. "We made it in one piece."

Caleb's knuckles have gone white. I'm not sure what comes over me, but I burst out in laughter as I leave the car. It makes my ribs ache, but I can't seem to control it. I'm honestly not sure I want to. I enjoy laughing. It feels good. I want more of it.

Caleb is on me within seconds. He scoops me up from behind, hoisting me into the air. It makes me laugh more, my face turning red.

"You naughty, naughty woman," he says, kicking open the front door. "You're lucky you're injured, else I'd throw you on the couch." He carefully sets me on my feet, then snatches the keys from my hand. "You're never driving again."

I wipe my cheeks, surprised to find that they're wet with tears. Why am I crying? From laughing? Is that a thing? Caleb doesn't seem exceptionally concerned, so I suppose that means I'm not dying.

I clear my throat. "Oh, I most definitely am."

Caleb levels me a sharp glare. "*Never*."

We'll see.

I slip off my coat and shoes, then meander into the kitchen to make myself something to eat while Caleb showers. For once, my thoughts don't stray to HPAW. I let myself enjoy this moment, this feeling of normalcy I've always wanted. After everything I've been through, I deserve it.

Chapter Fourteen

I spend the next week learning everything I can. It's not much.
Caleb brings me to work each day, but he leaves his office for all his important meetings. I've asked to join, but he always has an excuse as to why I should stay behind.

I fear it's because he's suspicious of me. Maybe he put two and two together when it was revealed that HPAW soldiers were responsible for my abduction. Maybe my insistence on having them killed without questioning is what clued him in. I'm not sure.

There's also the possibility that he's not suspicious and I'm reading too much into things.

Caleb *has* taken a handful of quick meetings in his office, but they've been about inconsequential topics. A representative from the Allard pack came by to ask for help with polar bears. Fucking polar bears. The representative said they've been infringing on the pack, testing boundaries and attacking the children.

Caleb sent a unit of men back with the representative. I've yet to learn more about these units. How many shifters are in a unit? How many units does Caleb have? How does he train them? Where are they?

Caleb's pack is enormous, but if his warriors cluster in one area, HPAW could take them out in one fell swoop.

I sigh, dragging my mug of steaming tea across the kitchen counter. Today was exhausting. Caleb had back-to-back meetings, and I lost thirty-four solitaire games. I haven't yet found a good opportunity to go through his computer files, not until I'm sure it isn't a trap.

"What're you thinking about?"

I jolt, shocked by the proximity of Caleb's voice. He's too sneaky for his size. Men as large as him shouldn't be able to sneak around a house the way Caleb can. It must be a shifter trait. They're all incredibly agile.

"I'm thinking about how many solitaire games I lost today."

Caleb laughs, leaning against the counter. "I'm sorry to hear that." He taps his fingers against my mug. "I know how to cheer you up, though."

"Is that so?" Genuine enthusiasm flares. "Do tell."

Caleb stalks around the counter, for once looking every bit the predator he is. I'm not afraid. If anything, I'm excited.

Once I'm within reach, Caleb curls his hands underneath my thighs and lifts me onto the kitchen counter. He hasn't touched me like this since our shared shower. I've made the first move several times now, and I'm waiting for him to take charge. I don't want to appear too eager.

Caleb slides his hands down my calves and wraps my legs around his waist.

"The pack is growing antsy to meet you," he admits. "I've been told I'm hoarding you, and one of the elders recently told me that keeping you locked away in my home and office is impolite."

The corners of his lips twitch upwards. "I told him that you likened yourself to Rapunzel last week. He took great enjoyment in the comparison."

I squeeze Caleb's shoulders. "What do you have in mind, then?"

"It's a surprise." Caleb leans in, pressing his lips against mine in a chaste kiss before pulling back and setting me onto the ground. "Go get dressed. Something warm."

This is stupid. Still, I feel almost giddy as I hurry upstairs to change. I don't care about Caleb's pack, and I don't care about meeting them. It doesn't matter that he wants to show me off. Caleb's excitement to introduce me to his people means nothing.

But it does.

Nobody has ever been proud to be seen with me. Nobody has looked or touched me with such softness. I've never been important.

I suppose I'm important to HPAW, but that's different. They're using me. Caleb doesn't have ulterior motives. I'm sure the mate bond is responsible for some of his emotions, but it feels like more than that. Unless Caleb is an exceptional actor, he seems to genuinely like me for who I am.

He laughs at my jokes. He indulges my curiosity. He shivers at my touch.

I speed upstairs, skipping every other step and pushing the limits of what my injured ribs can tolerate. Doctor Greg said deep breathing and light exercise are good for me, though. I'm only following orders.

What does Caleb have in mind? Where is he taking me? I run through a thousand different scenarios as I change into dark pants and a thick sweater. Is this a date? Will it be romantic?

Caleb is waiting for me at the bottom of the stairs, and his gaze slides pointedly down my frame in a way that sets me on fire. I'm not wearing anything alluring. Most of my skin is covered. Still, I love the way he looks at me.

"Here." He pulls open the entryway closet and removes my giant, orange coat, a black hat, and a pair of gloves. "Put these on."

"Why?"

"Because it's been snowing all day and we're going to be outside."

Outside? What the fuck does he have planned? I shoot him a

curious look as I slip the items on, but I hold back my questions. I'm truthfully excited about the surprise, and I don't want to ruin it for myself.

"Can I drive?" I ask. The sun is beginning to set, but it's not yet dark. There's probably another hour or so of sunlight left.

"No."

I let out a dramatic sigh. He's a spoilsport. It's not as if my poor driving is putting anybody at risk. I'm the only one on the road. Shifters prefer to bulldoze through the forest in their animal forms.

I decide not to argue as I climb into the passenger seat, but I do turn all the air vents toward myself and adjust the radio, two things I know Caleb hates but won't say anything about. He rolls his eyes when I settle on a human pop station, but I compromise and keep the volume low.

Caleb has sensitive ears, and I'm not trying to deafen him.

He drops his marked hand to my thigh, his fingers curling around the rough fabric of my jeans. His white mark stands out against his skin, and a pang of something uncomfortable shoots down my spine. I refuse to dwell on it as I place my gloved hand over his.

After almost thirty minutes of driving, he parks in front of a lone, abandoned building. It's falling apart, the metal roof rusted and the pavement cracked and uneven.

"Caleb?"

He grins. "Don't move."

He jumps out of the car and hurries to grab something from the trunk. I hope it's not a shovel he plans to kill and bury me with. Caleb's pulling open my door a second later, his wide frame filling the space as he hands me a pair of thick snow pants and giant, white boots.

I stare at them. "Why?"

"It's cold out."

"We're not in the fucking tundra, Caleb. I'm not wearing

that." I set the items in the driver's seat and exit the car, pushing past Caleb in the process. He huffs but lets me through.

It's chilly, and it *is* snowing, but he's being dramatic. I've come to learn that shifters have an incredible tolerance for cold, and Caleb clearly has no idea how much bundling humans need. The coat, hat, and gloves are more than enough. I'll put on the snow pants and boots in a few months when winter truly settles in.

"Are you sure you don't—"

"Caleb." I level him a sharp glare. "I'm not meeting your pack dressed like the Michelin Man."

"Who is that?"

"I'm not sure," I admit. "He's a big, puffy man who I think sells car tires. He also somehow bestows the most prestigious restaurant recommendations. I don't understand it."

Caleb blinks, looking at a loss for words, before grabbing my hand and dragging me around the side of the abandoned building. It backs up into thick woods, and I'm not the least bit surprised when Caleb leads me into them.

The shifters sure love their forests.

"So, what's—"

My question is cut short as a wolf bursts through the trees and sprints past me, its brown fur brushing against my coat. I still, frozen to my spot as the wolf slams into another, sending them both tumbling to the side.

What the fuck?

Despite the hard impact, both wolves are up and running in a matter of seconds. They're large and muscular, near impossible to tell apart as they run side by side, nipping at one another. Caleb is bringing me here to die. He's figured out who I really am.

Something howls, and I flinch as another wolf sprints past me. It's moving too fast to follow, making me painfully aware that I'm surrounded by predators. I feel like a fucking bunny, and my legs burn with the urge to take off running.

Caleb wraps his arm around my waist, guiding me farther into the forest.

I clear my throat. "What is this?"

"Shifters have a lot of energy, and we get antsy when in our skin forms for too long," Caleb explains. "We take to these woods most nights. It's a time for us to burn through our pent-up energy."

Three wolves collide on my left. Two are off again in a heartbeat, and the third spends a few seconds limping before collecting itself and rejoining the other two.

"Like a doggy play date?" I ask.

One wolf stops in its tracks, its head snapping in my direction. Large, sharp teeth are revealed as the shifter snarls, and fear claws its way up my throat as it takes a step toward me.

Caleb flicks his hand toward the wolf. "Don't."

The wolf's large, brown eyes dart toward Caleb, then it takes off. It takes me several moments to find my voice.

"What was he going to do?"

Caleb shrugs. "I'm not sure. Probably knock you over. He was trying to play with you."

"Play with me?" My voice is high-pitched. I clear my throat before continuing. "I can't play with you. You guys are twice my size."

"Well, I never said it would be a fair fight." Caleb nudges my back, urging me to continue walking. "These nights consist of play-fighting and hunting, mostly for rabbits and deer, and a fair amount of general degeneracy. There's a clearing with a bonfire up ahead. That's where we're going. I thought you'd like to sit with me and watch the chaos."

So he's not planning to kill me tonight. Good to know.

Something about his tone is off, though, and when I turn toward him, I see hesitation in his face. Caleb licks his lips and squeezes my gloved hand, and my heart stutters as I realize he's nervous. Does he worry I won't like this?

"That sounds fun," I assure him.

Despite my general dislike and fear of the shifters, I have to admit they're fascinating. This is a perfect opportunity to learn more about their strengths, too. Maybe even their weaknesses.

It's about ten minutes of walking before we reach the bonfire. My legs and feet are cold, but I refuse to admit that to Caleb. I can tell he's picked up on my subtle shivering by the way he hurries me toward the flames.

"Are you too cold?" he asks. "I'm happy to get your pants and shoes from the car."

"I'm fine," I say. "The fire is warm."

It's a shame Caleb doesn't show this level of care and concern toward the thousands of humans the shifters murder each year.

A few people are sitting around the fire, and they shoot Caleb and me quick, friendly smiles before returning to their conversations.

Caleb wipes the light dusting of snow off the empty chair closest to the fire and plops down, pulling me onto his lap. I try hard not to think about the wolves watching us from between the trees as he wraps his arms around me.

A man approaches from our right. He's holding two plastic cups.

"I got you something to drink," he says, handing the cups to Caleb and me.

My face heats as I realize he's naked, but I'm not sure what else I expected. Clothes don't exactly survive the transition between man and animal. Caleb tightens his grip on me, his chest vibrating with laughter.

"Thank you," Caleb says.

When the man leaves, I sip my drink. It's alcohol. Thank the fucking heavens. This has been the most stressful two weeks of my life, and I need a drink. It's never occurred to me to ask Caleb for alcohol. Maybe I should. It would help pass the time and, hopefully, make the thought of killing him hurt less.

Two wolves slam into one another opposite the fire. They snarl before lunging again, and I can only watch the grace and speed at which they move in horror. I've seen videos of wolves fighting, but I've never witnessed it firsthand. It only illuminates the biological advantage they have over humans. We stand no chance against them in a hand-to-hand fight. They'd rip through us with ease.

We have weapons, but they *are* weapons.

Caleb chuckles. "They're showing off for you." He flicks his fingers at them, shooing them away. "Stop trying to impress my mate."

They ignore him, continuing to fight, but they eventually vanish back into the forest. The sun is quickly setting, making their eyes glow. I'm not a fan.

"Do you not participate?" I ask Caleb.

"I used to, but not anymore." He sips his drink. "Most of the wolves you see fighting are unmated. Once we find our other halves, we discover other ways to release our pent-up energy."

He's talking about sex. Mated wolves choose to have sex instead. I don't blame them.

I mentally curse HPAW for the extent of my injuries. If it weren't for my ribs, I have a feeling Caleb would've bedded me long ago. He probably would've done it that first night.

"I asked for them to stay out of sight tonight, though," Caleb continues. "I didn't want to overwhelm you."

"Hold up." I raise a hand. "You mean to say they have sex *here*? In the woods?"

Caleb's responding chuckle doesn't ease my shock. "Of course. We may look like humans, but we are still part animal. It's —I've been told it's quite exciting to fuck your mate under the stars, and many shifter men feel a sense of dominance in fucking their mate where others can see."

Well, fuck me. I wouldn't have guessed.

"But..." I shake my head. "Shifters are prudes, are they not?"

Caleb snorts, digging his fingers into my sides. "Be careful what you say out here, Ev. Talk enough shit and you just might provoke a mated pair into giving you a show."

"I have no interest in watching animals have sex." I pause, thinking through my following words, before continuing. "Do you want to have sex with me out here? Do you...Does your wolf want to fuck me?"

Caleb kisses the sensitive spot behind my ear. "I admit the thought of fucking you out here does have a certain appeal. And, no, my wolf doesn't want to fuck you. I've never had much interest in having sex in my animal form. I suppose I should've taken that as a clue that my mate would be human."

A woman standing near the fire begins to strip. She's wearing a loose dress, and I flush as she rips it over her head, revealing she's wearing nothing underneath. I hate myself for the way I subtly shift, blocking Caleb's view.

He kisses my cheek, his lips warm, before making a big show out of turning away from the woman. I understand that nudity is natural among the shifters, but I don't like the idea of Caleb seeing others.

"It's not funny," I whisper.

Caleb's budding smile falls. "Of course not. You're the only woman I lust after, Ev." He grabs my chin, urging me to look at him. "Although I must admit I like seeing this jealousy in you. Shifters are protective of their mates. I like your possessiveness."

His smile returns, and I just know I'm not going to like his next few words.

"Maybe I should put myself in more positions like this."

I elbow him hard in the side.

Caleb blinks, then flings us out of the chair with a dramatic shout. What the fuck? I land in a heap on top of him, a bit disoriented as I wait for pain to erupt from my ribcage. It doesn't come, though, which I quickly realize is due to Caleb.

He holds my hips, preventing me from slamming against him. There's a twinge upon impact, but nothing more. Our spilled drinks lie beside the chair, long forgotten, as Caleb rolls over on top of me and yanks my hat over my eyes.

"Caleb!" I shriek, smacking blindly at his hands. "Release me!"

Caleb pulls my hat just above my eyes. He's beaming. "No." The hat is pulled back down.

I flail, pushing at his torso with all my strength. I hate the way I'm laughing, too, unable to stop myself from enjoying this. It's stupid and childish.

Caleb finally lets up, and I huff as I fix my hat, returning it to the top of my head.

"You're a jerk," I snap.

He rolls me on top, encouraging me to straddle him. I feel dumb for how hard I'm smiling. My cheeks are beginning to hurt.

Caleb touches my cheek. "I love you."

I blink, my smile falling. "No, you don't."

"Pretty sure I do."

Caleb's looking at me with an expression much too soft, and I hate it. He's not supposed to love me. He can't love me. We've only known one another for two weeks. That's hardly enough time to fall in love. He doesn't even know me.

Everything I've told him about me is a lie, and I haven't done anything to earn his affection. We spend every day together, sure, but his workdays are long and filled with meetings. We get home just in time for bed, and I sleep like a fucking log.

Then we wake up and do it again.

He hasn't fallen in love with me.

"I'm not expecting you to return the sentiment, Ev," Caleb says, brushing a strand of hair from my face. He tucks it into my hat. "I'm only telling you how I feel. There are no strings attached."

Are the wolves eavesdropping on us? I glance around, spotting several pairs of glowing eyes peering at me from between the trees. Why would Caleb say this to me in such a public setting? Warmth floods my face, and I fight back tears as I scramble to my feet.

Caleb follows. He's silent, and I avoid eye contact.

"I'm sorry, Ev," he says. "I didn't mean to upset you. I won't say it again."

God. He's only making things worse. I wish he'd stop speaking.

"Let's go home," I say. "I'm getting cold."

Caleb shifts his weight from foot to foot, then awkwardly picks up our spilled drinks and tosses them into a trash can nearby. The shifters standing near the fire are silent, all pointedly avoiding looking in our direction. This is uncomfortable.

The walk back to the car is silent. The drive back to the house is silent.

We take turns showering and readying for bed, all without words. I'm not sure what to say, and Caleb has already said too much. We're tense as we lie beside one another in bed, our arms brushing. Guilt gnaws at my insides, but I don't regret my response to Caleb's confession.

I feel bad enough about what I'm doing, and having his love is only going to make it harder. I just can't let that happen.

Chapter Fifteen

Caleb's pretending that last night never happened. I appreciate that, and I play along as we get ready for the day.

"Hungry for anything specific?" he asks.

"Not really."

He cooks breakfast for me every morning, usually something with eggs or yogurt. He's a good cook, and I can tell he takes pride in feeding me. His chest puffs up whenever I compliment his dishes, the man practically imitating a peacock.

I hop in the shower while he heads downstairs, and I refuse to let myself think too deeply about last night as I clean myself, dress, and meet him in the kitchen. A plate is set out on the counter, but Caleb is nowhere to be seen.

Wherever he's wandered off to, I'm sure he'll be back soon.

I begin eating, and sure enough, he saunters into the kitchen just as I'm finishing up. He's wearing a navy-blue sweater, the fabric thicker than usual.

"Are you about ready?" he asks, eyeing my empty plate.

I nod. "Yep."

We don't speak much as I clean up and head to the door, and that doesn't change during the short drive into town. I'm sure we're both feeling awkward after last night, but I fear bringing it up will only make things worse.

Rosy rises from her desk as we step into the building.

"Morning, Alphas," she says, greeting us as she does every morning.

Caleb smiles. "Good morning, Rosy."

He seems just as cheery as usual as he breezes past her and heads upstairs. He doesn't carry me up them anymore, and I hand Rosy my coat and hat before following after Caleb. He holds open his door for me, and I make myself comfortable on the couch underneath the large window.

"I want..." Caleb sighs, running his fingers through his hair as he sits at his desk. "I've been worrying all morning about what to say to you, but I need to rip off the bandage. I'm sorry for telling you I love you last night. You've been through a lot these past few weeks, and I shouldn't rush you. I understand why my words make you uncomfortable. I imagine I would feel the same way if I were in your position."

He's apologizing for telling me he loves me. I squeeze my eyes shut, unable to keep this up. I can't do it. I just can't. Caleb isn't a bad person. He's the opposite, and I can't lie to him any longer. It isn't right.

I'm not a killer. I've never done it, and I don't know how HPAW thought all that training would make me capable.

Maybe Caleb and I can work together to fix relations with the humans. I'm a human, so surely, Caleb will understand why I want peace between our kinds. I'm willing to bet he'd be agreeable to it. I think he'd do it for me.

I'm letting down the humans, but Caleb isn't the evil man HPAW is making him out to be. He's kind and genuine, and so are the other shifters I've met. Everybody here has been so fucking kind to me. They don't treat me differently because I'm a human. My race doesn't matter to them at all.

Caleb clears his throat, his gaze darting toward his computer. "The Aubert and Allard packs have been fighting. Land disputes," he says, changing the subject. "I've received a formal request to step in and settle things."

I lick my lips. Is Caleb actually telling me about his work? Why?

"Why are you telling me this?" I ask.

Caleb taps his fingers against his desk. "I've been thinking that perhaps you might like to work with me. You seem to enjoy accompanying me to the office, and I can tell you're interested in my meetings. Would working fulfill you?"

"I don't know anything about shifter politics."

"I'll teach you."

He makes it sound so easy. Maybe to him, it is. Will he still let me work when he knows the truth? I highly doubt it. My affiliation with HPAW will destroy our trust.

Caleb stalks toward me, his eyes soft as he kneels beside the couch and grabs my hands. "I want you to be happy, Ev. I can tell you're holding back from me. From all of us, really. Tell me what you want, and I'll make it happen."

"I—" I start. I need to tell him.

Caleb releases me and turns, facing the door. Somebody's coming. My confidence crumbles as two hard knocks vibrate through the room.

"Come in," Caleb orders.

He doesn't move, continuing to kneel beside me as the door is opened to reveal Caleb's second-in-command, Logan. I haven't seen him since Caleb sent him away, but I recognize his thick facial hair and muscular, borderline-bulky frame. My gaze dips to his marked hand.

His design is cool. Two harsh, flame-like lines travel from his knuckles to his wrist. It's a crisp white. Just like Sash's. Just like Caleb's.

Logan's gaze darts between Caleb and me. "Good morning, you two." His gaze settles on Caleb. "There's a shipment out back. Do you want to take a look?"

Caleb hums, feigning indifference, but I know better. I'm no fool, and I know damn well there's no shipment out back. That's a horrible code phrase.

I watch through my lashes as Caleb rises. What's he hiding from me?

"I'm coming," Caleb tells Logan. He turns toward me. "I'll be right back. Stay here."

Stay here? He's never asked that of me before. Even when he leaves to attend his meetings, he doesn't ask me to stay put.

Years of training allow me to remain outwardly calm. Daniel would be proud of me.

Caleb leaves. I count to thirty, giving him time, before sneaking out of his office. I'm not sure where he went, but I assume he's not conducting this business out on the main street.

I slink across the building, heading toward his father's old office. It's filled with boxes, but it overlooks the back of the building.

I crouch as I approach the window, peering through the very bottom corner in search of Caleb. I find him immediately. He's standing beside a freight truck. There are two wolves beside him, Logan and another man I don't recognize. They speak hurriedly to one another before Caleb gestures for them to open the doors of the truck.

Maybe Logan wasn't lying about the shipment.

I'd try to open the window if I thought I could get away with it, but the shifters have impeccable hearing. Caleb would undoubtedly notice.

The truck doors open and Logan steps inside.

I slap a hand over my mouth, in absolute disbelief as he drags out five human men. No, not men. Boys. They can't be much older than eighteen, twenty at the max. The one on the left is covered in acne, and the one beside him has braces. Fucking braces.

They look terrified, and I can tell they're pleading as they're pushed to their knees. The boy with braces drops his forehead to the ground, openly sobbing.

The shifter with Caleb and Logan laughs. I can only watch in horror as Caleb approaches the boy with acne. He crouches, grabbing the back of the boy's head.

I flinch, disgust roiling through me as he forces the boy's head upward and spits in his face. The boy is now sobbing, his shoulders trembling as my mate's saliva trails down his eye and cheek.

Caleb twists his head to the side, effortlessly breaking his neck. I gag. The human's limp body is dropped, and Caleb moves down the line. He kills them all.

When Logan begins tossing the limp bodies into the truck, I hurry back into Caleb's office. Adrenaline courses through me as my training kicks into place. My heart is pounding—that tends to happen when you watch five people be executed, and I need an excuse for it.

I open Caleb's computer and type in a random password. I repeat this until it locks me out. Caleb will notice, and he'll assume my accelerated heart rate is due to my failure to gain access to his computer.

When Caleb returns, I'm lounging on the couch. His brows furrow, but he doesn't say anything as he sits behind his desk. He opens his computer. I chew at my bottom lip.

Then he laughs. "Evelyn!" He peers at me over the top of the device. "You've locked me out."

I shrug, feigning innocence. "I don't know what you're talking about."

"I'm beginning to worry about your solitaire addiction." He abandons his computer, shutting the lid and giving me his full attention. "I meant what I said earlier."

I cock my head. "What's that?"

I hardly remember. Our earlier conversation has been overshadowed by the sight of him snapping the necks of five humans. Is he going to tell me about them? That's wishful thinking. I don't bother getting my hopes up.

Caleb clasps his fingers together. "Tell me what will make you happy. You're holding yourself back. There's no need to answer now, but think about it. I want you to thrive here."

Caleb is a good mate. He's a good leader, too, but I don't give a fuck about the shifters. I care about the humans. It's time to leave.

I haven't learned everything there is to know about the wolves, but I've learned enough to give the humans an advantage. I need to kill Caleb before I soften toward him any further. My feelings are compromising things. I can't let that happen.

I'll kill him tonight.

Chapter Sixteen

Perhaps I'll wait a few more days. I have more to learn, and I shouldn't rush things.

Besides, it's supposed to storm tonight. Well, not really a storm. There will be some snowfall, but it's probably not in my best interests to kill Caleb and attempt driving to the American border when the weather is poor.

I sit opposite Caleb, prodding silently at the food on my plate. Caleb made pork chops for dinner. They're delicious, but everything he cooks is.

"It should be a quick meeting," Caleb continues. "King and Everett are always arguing. It isn't anything I haven't dealt with before."

"Can I join?" I ask.

Caleb quirks a brow. "You want to? Sitting in a room with three alphas isn't anybody's idea of a good time."

It's mine. If I'm going to linger, I might as well make my time worthwhile. It makes me feel better about procrastinating. I can make as many excuses for myself as I want, but that's what I'm doing. Procrastinating. I don't want to kill Caleb. The thought makes me nauseous. Seeing him kill those humans isn't making it any easier, either.

I'm sure there's something useful to learn during that meeting. Besides, I'm eager to meet another alpha. Are they as large and intimidating as Caleb? I've overheard a few whispers about King and Everett, but nothing that'll be exceptionally useful to HPAW.

"Why are you in charge of mediating?" I ask.

Caleb swallows around a mouthful of food. "I have the most dominant wolf. If they're going to listen to anybody, it's going to be me."

I hum, thinking that over. "Why don't they kill you?" I ask. Caleb blinks. I continue. "You have sway over them, and I'm sure they don't like that. Shouldn't they want to kill you? It would bring them closer to the top."

"That's an interesting question," Caleb admits. He rubs his chin, thinking it over. "That's just not how shifters operate. My wolf's dominance qualifies me to be the alpha, but the title doesn't mean anything if I don't have the respect of my people. If my pack lost faith in me, they'd tear me apart."

Caleb sips his water, then continues. "If another alpha attacked me, I don't imagine they'd make it far before my pack tracks and hunts them down. Besides"—Caleb stabs his meat with his fork—"my pack has already decided who the alpha after me will be. Killing me wouldn't benefit King or Everett. It would only anger the Knox pack's next alpha."

"Would it still be called 'the Knox pack'?"

"Full of questions today, are we?"

"Humor me."

Caleb chuckles. "No. My pack would take the new alpha's name."

"And who would the new alpha be?"

Caleb slips a piece of meat between his teeth.

"You're not going to tell me?" I ask.

Caleb chews.

"Fine." I huff. "Tell me more about your wolf, then."

Caleb swallows. "What do you want to know?"

"You said you don't have two streams of consciousness, but you share a mind with your wolf. How does that work?"

Caleb takes a minute to think. I'm soaking in everything, all of this vital information HPAW will salivate over.

"Having a wolf is like having an extra set of feelings you can't control, but they're simple creatures." Caleb smiles, dragging a hand through his hair. "They have basic desires. They enjoy fighting, fucking, eating—anything you would expect an animal in the wild to enjoy. As long as we're fulfilling those needs, they don't really make much of a fuss."

"What makes your wolf angry?" I ask, pushing for the dark secrets I'm certain he's hiding.

Caleb blows out a breath. "Angry? Not much, honestly. He doesn't like feeling challenged by other shifters, which is a given. He doesn't like loud noises. He doesn't like it when other men are near you. Basic things, really."

Caleb isn't going to tell me anything interesting. I knew that was coming.

I change the subject. "So can I join your meeting with King and Everett tomorrow?"

Caleb's budding smile falls. I know what that means. "We're meeting in the Lockstone pack. I'm leaving tomorrow morning, likely before you wake, and I won't be back until late into the evening."

Of fucking course. I force a smile, not wanting Caleb to see how annoyed I am. I suppose this isn't a complete bust, though. This gives me time to look through Caleb's things. There hasn't been a good opportunity, and I'm eager to get into the files in the office upstairs.

The bed is empty when I wake the next morning. I fly out of bed, sprinting downstairs to make sure Caleb's truly gone. I'm disappointed to miss the meeting with the alphas, but I'm choosing to look at the bright side of things. This is my first time alone inside Caleb's house, and he's guaranteed to be absent the entire day.

I'm going to search every inch of his space, and hopefully find a weapon. HPAW didn't exactly provide me with one.

I skid to a stop as I step into the living room, my gaze landing on the freckled woman sitting on the couch. What the fuck is Sash doing here?

She smiles, clasping her hands together as she rises. "Good morning. I'm sorry for intruding on you without warning, but Caleb said it would be all right for me to come over. I didn't expect you to be asleep, but you were and I didn't really want to run all the way back home or wait outside, so I decided to come in. I'm sorry if that makes you uncomfortable."

I swallow.

Sash continues. "We didn't exactly get off on the best foot, and I was hoping to remedy that. With Caleb gone for the day, I thought this would be the perfect opportunity to get to know you better."

You've got to be kidding me. My one damned day of freedom, and Sash is here to ruin it. I rock back on my heels, trying and failing to find a way out of this. The only excuse I can think of to give is menstrual or pain-related, but each comes with a unique set of drawbacks.

It hasn't been confirmed, but I'm reasonably certain that shifters can smell menstrual blood. Sash would know I'm lying. If I say my injuries are bothering me, Caleb will be on my ass. He's finally stopped treating me like a broken, delicate flower, and I'd rather not return to that.

Sash clears her throat. "We're family, after all."

"Sorry, I'm slow to wake. I'm still a little groggy." I curl my lips, forcing them into a rigid smile. "I'd love that. Thank you."

Sash's shoulders relax. She brushes her hands down her pants before stepping around the coffee table. "Would you like a tour of the pack? Caleb explicitly told me not to overwhelm you, but the pack agrees that he's being overly protective. Our pack is beautiful, and you should see more than the inside of his home and office."

His home and office are the only places I care to know, but I keep that particular thought to myself. I should be eager to learn more about the pack.

"That sounds amazing." I glance down at myself. "Just let me get dressed."

I retreat upstairs, cursing out the gods the entire way. I should've just fucking killed Caleb last night and been done with it. Caleb's sister seems nice, but I really don't want to get to know her. What if I like her? It'll only make things more complicated.

I peek out the window. There's no snow. I could've left.

I take my time showering and dressing, a small part of me hoping Sash will be gone when I head back downstairs. She isn't.

Caleb left the car here, and she takes the initiative to drive me into town. She brings me to a small diner. I try not to look too amazed as we take our seats, not wanting her to realize I've never been to a restaurant before. I told the shifters I once worked in one, so I should be familiar.

"Don't think I didn't notice you didn't eat breakfast." She chuckles. "Order whatever you want. It's my treat."

It turns out I like Sash. Her smile is infectious, and she enjoys chatting. I'm pretty sure she could hold a conversation with a brick wall, which is ideal. She spends the entire meal telling me about the members of the pack, at least those who live nearby. I don't know these people and don't recognize their names, but Sash doesn't seem to care.

She pays for our meal, then drags me down the main strip. We pass the coffee shop I went to the other day, and Sash points out the grocery store, library, bank, elementary and middle schools, and even a hairdresser. It's so...normal.

If it weren't for the occasional shifter running about in their wolf form, I'd think this is a regular human town. A father is heading toward us, a small boy sitting on his shoulders. Behind them is the mother, her hand clasped tightly around another boy's hand. The boys look identical. Twins.

They smile at Sash and me as they pass by.

"So..." I clear my throat. "You and Logan are mates."

Sash bobs her head. "That we are. He's originally from the Lockstone pack, and we met at a mixer when I was fourteen." She pauses, laughing. "He's four years older than me. You should've seen his face when he realized his mate was only fourteen. Absolutely horrified. It took a couple of years"—Sash shoots me a sideways smile—"but I eventually won him over."

Up ahead is a group of women. They look around my age, maybe a bit younger. They're laughing with one another, big smiles lighting up their faces as they round a corner and head down a side street.

I wonder what it's like to have friends. Daniel is the closest thing I'd consider to a friend, but it's very literally his job to keep me safe.

"I'm happy Caleb found you," Sash continues.

"Really?" I can't help but take the bait. "You're not disappointed in me being a human?"

Sash takes a moment to respond, thinking carefully about her following words. "I'm not disappointed, but you being a human does come with a set of challenges."

"The pack and other alphas losing respect for him?" I guess.

"No." Sash shakes her head. "Shifters tend to move quickly, especially when they meet during adulthood. Humans are more cautious in relationships. I heard about what happened at the bonfire the other night. I don't blame you, but my heart goes out to Caleb. He trusts in the mate bond, and I imagine it's painful to be paired with a human who doesn't experience it the same way he does."

I don't know what to say to that, so I choose not to say anything. I'm upset with Caleb for telling me he loved me, especially in such a public setting. He was setting us up for failure. I would've been uncomfortable with the confession even if I hadn't been here on behalf of HPAW.

"Is Grace okay?" I ask, shifting the topic. "Was she disappointed when Caleb called off the engagement?"

I'm not above prying.

Sash shoots me a sideways glance, her eyebrow quirked. "Grace is fine. She didn't have any particularly strong feelings toward Caleb. She only agreed because..." Sash trails off, grimacing. "Grace wants children, and there aren't many shifter men willing to donate their sperm. Their mates would never allow it. Pairing up with an unmated man was her best option."

I chew on my bottom lip. I never considered that.

"I assume there are other unmated men for her to pair up with, though?" I ask.

Sash makes a non-committal noise. "Many men feel it's a betrayal to their mate, even if she's dead. Caleb was only considering it to make the pack happy."

"Why would the pack care? I thought the alpha title wasn't passed through the bloodline?"

"It's not," Sash agrees. "But shifters are a family people. They want to see themselves in their alpha, and a perpetual bachelor would make the pack uncomfortable. They want to know that he honors their values."

Sash clears her throat, then spins to step in front of me. Her eyes are wide in panic. "Please don't take this to mean that we expect you to have children with Caleb. The pack does hope for them *eventually*, but they aren't rushing you."

A mental image of Caleb with children flashes through my mind. Would he be a good father? Probably, but we'll never know. Caleb will be dead before a child is even a possibility. I'll make sure of that.

It's dark by the time Sash brings me home. I don't know when to expect Caleb to return, so I decide against searching through his things. I don't need him catching me, and I especially don't need the onslaught of questions that would surely follow.

Chapter Seventeen

Caleb's back. At least, I hope that's him slipping into bed behind me.

I huff. His chuckle confirms his identity.

"Sorry, mate." He kisses my cheek. "I didn't mean to wake you."

He smells clean. I roll over, eyeing his wet hair and bare torso. I'm surprised I didn't hear him come in. I've never been a heavy sleeper, and I assumed the shower turning on would wake me. I guess not.

I blame the thick, terribly warm bedsheets. They're unbearably comfortable, and they almost always put me to sleep within minutes. I'll miss these when I'm gone.

"What time is it?" I ask. I sit up, rubbing the sleep out of my eyes. "How did the meeting go?"

Caleb groans, flopping onto his back. "It was long, but Everett has agreed to back off while King deals with HPAW. It's a tentative truce. The two don't agree on much, except for the fact that they hate HPAW more than one another."

I hope that isn't true. If HPAW can convince them to break their truce, doors will be opened for us. We'll have hope.

"Did you have a fun day with Sash?" Caleb asks. "Sorry I

didn't warn you about her stopping by. She caught me as I was on my way out of the pack."

"I had a good time," I admit. A better time than I wanted to have, if I'm honest with myself. "She gave me a tour."

Caleb grunts. "That's *my* job."

"One you failed to do." I trail a finger down the center of Caleb's chest, unable to help myself. He's painfully distracting, and I'm all too aware that we haven't had sex. I'm feeling better. There's no reason to continue postponing.

"I missed you..." I whisper. It's not entirely a lie.

Caleb raises a brow, his eyes growing heavy. I know he wants me.

"Did you miss me?" I ask.

Caleb nods. "More than you know. Today was torturous."

I don't allow myself to overthink as I swing a leg over his hips. Caleb's hands fly to my hips, holding them tight as I straddle him. I'm wearing only his T-shirt, which I'm certain turns him on.

He licks his lips, peering between my thighs. "Are you already wet for me, baby?"

Yes.

"You're going to have to work harder than that," I say instead. "I'm not a faucet, Caleb."

Caleb shoots me a look, then slides the hem of his shirt up my thighs. His fingers tickle my sensitive skin, and I have to swallow down a moan. I want him so badly, especially after spending the day apart from him. I wasn't lying when I said I missed him. I've grown familiar with the damned man, and I didn't enjoy being away from him.

"Are you sure about that?" Caleb challenges. "Are you sure your cunt isn't soaking for me right now?"

I'm not wearing underwear, and I see the moment Caleb realizes. His eyes widen just slightly before he levels his expression, trying to hide the flash of excitement I already saw.

He drags his thumb over my clit. "This feels wet to me, Ev."

"Do you think it's wet enough for a cock to slip in?"

Caleb releases a shaky breath. "It's wet enough for *my* cock to slip in."

He shoves two fingers into me to prove his point, curling them upward. I shut my eyes, struggling to collect myself. I'm supposed to be torturing him, not the other way around.

"I'm not going to fuck you tonight," he says.

My eyes spring open, and I shoot Caleb the dirtiest glare I can muster while he's fucking me with his fingers. "And why the hell not?"

He eases his fingers in and out, the drag and thickness of them making my thighs shake. I whimper when he pulls them out. Why does he insist on doing this to me? He wants to fuck me. I can feel the proof of that beneath me. He's hard, straining against the thin material of his underwear.

"What kind of mate would I be if I fucked my mate before tasting her?" Caleb asks. "I'm going to make you cum every way possible before letting myself have you."

His hands return to my hips, and I scramble to grab the bed's headboard as he yanks me forward. My sex drags against his chest before landing on his tongue. I'm sitting on his face.

Caleb wastes no time.

The first exploratory swipe of his tongue has me shivering, my hands flying to his head. What Caleb lacks in experience, he makes up for in pure excitement. It doesn't take long for him to have me rocking against his tongue, desperately chasing my own high.

I try my best not to hear the sounds he's making. Caleb is noisy, slurping and sucking and moaning with abandon. My orgasm is so fucking close, and I throw my head back as I grind against his mouth.

When he eases two fingers inside me, I shatter. Caleb licks me through it, and only once I drop my forehead onto the headboard does he release me. I scoot back, sitting on his chest.

"Did you like that?" he asks.

I groan. "Shut up."

He's making fun of me. He knows I liked it. The way he's purring beneath me only proves it.

Caleb rolls to the side. I fall onto the bed, facing him. He looks calm as he pulls the blankets above us and tangles our legs together, but he's still hard.

"Are you going to fuck me now?" I ask.

I know the answer even before he shakes his head. "Not yet."

"What're you waiting for?" I pry, growing genuinely exasperated.

Caleb ignores me, choosing instead to pull my thigh over his hips. He continues adjusting, pulling down his underwear and easing his thick cock between my thighs. I sigh, clenching as he drags the head of his cock through my folds.

Should I offer to put my mouth on him? I've never given a man oral. I might enjoy it with Caleb.

"I want to be inside you so badly," Caleb admits. "My wolf is practically screaming at me to push inside." He notches himself against my entrance but doesn't go any farther. I could cry, I'm so desperate for it. "I bet I'd slip right in. Your cunt is practically begging for me."

That's not much of a secret.

Caleb strokes himself, his fist flying over his length. His hips are twitching, and I know he's fighting every instinct to push forward. I arch my back, angling my hips so it would be easy for him, but he doesn't take the bait.

"Are you going to wear my cum tomorrow?" he asks. "I want every shifter you come across to know you're mine."

Caleb grunts, his jaw clenching as he spills between my thighs. He coats me, covering every inch of my slit with his release.

He jumps out of bed the second he's finished.

"Don't move!" he orders.

I frown. "I'd be more inclined to listen to you if you fucked me."

Despite my snarky remark, I don't move. Caleb steps into our closet, returning a minute later with a pair of my underwear. He pulls back the covers and slips them up my legs, a lethal smirk covering his face as he secures them around my hips.

"Perfect," he says, pressing the flat of his palm against my sex. His release smears against me and soaks the fabric. "I like knowing my mate is covered in my cum."

I lick my lips, fighting back a smile.

"You're quite a filthy virgin," I tease.

Caleb shrugs, not the least bit offended, and flops onto the bed beside me. "There are worse things to be."

That there are.

I wake alone in bed. The sheets beside me are cold, and I can't help but feel disappointed as I head into the bathroom. Where did Caleb venture off to?

I spend several minutes in the bathroom, using the toilet and brushing my teeth, before heading downstairs. I find my shifter in the kitchen, leaning over the counter and sipping his morning coffee.

He's looking out the back window. I follow his gaze. It finally snowed last night. Several inches cover the ground, which isn't ideal. The roads in the shifter lands aren't cared for, nor are they salted. I need to get out of here before they become undrivable.

"What does your wolf look like?" I ask. I caught a glimpse of it that first day, but I hardly remember. I was in so much pain, and he transformed into his skin form almost immediately.

"You want to see my wolf?" Caleb asks. Why does he sound so surprised?

"Of course." I shrug. "Why wouldn't I?"

Caleb straightens up. "I thought you'd be scared. My wolf is large."

"I trust you."

The look Caleb gives me is so fucking soft, I have to turn away. I push open the back door, distracting myself with anything that isn't Caleb's heart eyes. We haven't discussed his confession of love the other day, but it's heavy on my mind.

Does he really love me? How does he know? I want to know everything about his feelings toward me, but I don't want to encourage him by showing too much interest. I can't tell him I love him, not when I'm planning to murder him. It's too cruel.

"Well?" I gesture to the back door. "I want to see."

HPAW will want to know. They've captured several shifters in the years I was under their care, but the shifters they managed to get into their possession are almost always women or weak, older men. The strong, virile men are never captured alive.

They fight until death.

Caleb saunters around the kitchen island and out the back door, his arm brushing against mine. I resist the urge to physically react. My skin is still so sensitive to his touch. It's not nearly as all-consuming as it once was, but it's still intense.

I watch through the window as Caleb strips off his clothing. The transformation is gruesome. His body twists and contorts in ways that would kill a human, and his mass grows until the man is replaced with a giant wolf. His fur is the same dark brown as his hair, and even on all fours, he's almost as tall as me.

My heart races as he enters the house, my adrenaline spiking. I wasn't lying when I told Caleb I trust him, but being around such a large, deadly animal is still terrifying. There's no way around that.

His watchful brown eyes track my every movement, the intense expression odd to see on an animal. This isn't just an animal, though. This is a shifter.

"You're large," I say.

The wolf's head bobs.

The fur on the back of his right paw is discolored. It's white, just like the mark on his skin form. I instinctively glance at my own dark mark before returning my attention to the wolf.

I'm not sure how I'm supposed to interact with Caleb in this form, and after a moment's hesitation, I touch his torso. His fur is coarse, and his ribcage expands as he draws in breath. He's so fucking muscular.

A low hum pours from his throat as I trail my hand down his spine, essentially petting him. The shifters don't enjoy being likened to dogs, but it's hard not to draw comparisons. They're both four-legged, furry creatures with slightly pointed ears and fluffy tails.

When I reach for Caleb's tail, he flicks it away with a quiet grumble.

"No touching the tail," I say. "Got it."

I take another minute evaluating him. He has no visible weakness. He has the body of a predator, but the intelligence of a human. It's an intimidating combination.

I crouch, peering between his thighs. He remains still, allowing me to eye his penis. It's transformed with the rest of him, and I can't help but grimace. Not only is it too large to reasonably take, but it's covered in fur and, honestly, pretty ugly.

"I'm relieved you have no interest in having sex in this form."

Caleb makes an odd, gasping choking sound that I'm pretty sure is a laugh. Then he wiggles his head against my crotch. I shove him away, painfully aware that I'm still wearing the underwear he put on me last night. I must reek of him.

"Fuck off, Caleb," I hiss.

He makes that gasping, choking sound again.

I straighten up and circle him, slowly growing comfortable. This is far from an HPAW-level evaluation, but it's the best I can do at this time. I lift each of Caleb's limbs, testing his range of motion and feeling his musculature. If I had to guess, I'd say he weighs almost five hundred pounds.

I touch his ears, running them between my thumb and pointer finger. They're softer than I expected.

Caleb seems happy with my exploration. His quiet humming turns into a straight purr the more I touch him.

"I like your purring," I admit.

The purring stops. I snort. "Sorry, I forgot. You call it a *murmur*."

I shift my focus to his head. He fights me as I try to pry open his jaw. Despite him being unable to talk in this form, his narrowed eyes and tense jaw tell me everything he wants to say. I ignore him, continuing to pull at his mouth until he gives in and opens up.

His teeth are sharp, and his canines are as long as my pointer finger. He's a born killer.

"How many humans have you killed?" I ask.

I regret the question the second it slips from my lips. Caleb goes still, his body tightening before he pulls his jaw from my grasp and slinks back outside. *Fuck*. I shouldn't have asked. I'm not sure why I did. Maybe it's because I'm desperate for Caleb to tell me the truth. I want him to take the initiative to tell me about the humans he murdered. I want to know about the shipment.

I want it to be a misunderstanding. I need him to prove that HPAW is wrong about him and his people.

Caleb shifts into his skin form. He openly stares at me as he tugs his clothing back on, and I take this moment to collect myself. Is this it? Is he going to tell me the truth? I've given him the perfect opportunity. I *want* him to take it.

My heart pounds as he enters the house.

"Why'd you ask me that?" He's quick to the point.

I swallow. "I don't know. You *have* killed humans, haven't you?"

Caleb closes the distance between us. It's impossible to read his expression, but he doesn't seem angry as he nudges my chin, urging me to look up.

"Yes, I have."

"How many? Who? When was the last time?"

Caleb cups my cheeks with both hands, burying his fingers in my hair and brushing his thumbs across my cheekbones. I recognize the relief that flashes in his eyes. He was expecting me to panic, to look at him differently.

"This isn't something you should concern yourself with."

I frown, the disappointment crushing. "Caleb..."

"We should get going," he says, changing the subject. "We're running late, and I have early meetings today."

"But—"

"I'm not discussing this with you, Evelyn."

He's not going to tell me. I shouldn't be as hurt as I am.

"I'd like to stay home today," I say. "I didn't sleep well last night. I should rest." When I can tell Caleb's about to argue, to insist I can relax on his office couch, I continue. "I slept on my ribs wrong, and they're hurting."

My ribs feel fine. They occasionally ache if I move in just the right way or if I overexert myself, but most of the time, I forget they were ever injured. Doctor Greg says I'm healing splendidly.

"Of course," Caleb says, giving in. "You should rest."

I've made up my mind. I gave Caleb the opportunity to tell me the truth, and he chose not to. I can no longer put this off. I'll use today to prepare, to find and hide a weapon he isn't going to notice is missing. This is happening.

I jump into action the second Caleb's out the door.

My lips tingle from the curt goodbye kiss he gave me, and I resist the urge to touch them as I head into the kitchen in search of a knife. I have to slit his throat while he's sleeping. It's the only way to successfully kill him.

Caleb does a fair bit of cooking, and I fear he keeps a close tab on his knives. I don't know if he suspects me of anything, but if he does, he'll undoubtedly notice if one is missing.

I hum a children's lullaby. I have faint memories of my mother singing it, but I don't recall most of the words. I don't have many memories of my parents, just a few flashes. The song is a good distraction, just enough to keep my mind from running.

I don't want to think too deeply about what I'm doing.

How much does Caleb suspect? Surely, more than he lets on. He's never outright asked about my lies, but I know he's picked up on a few of them. Caleb trusts me, or at least pretends to, but he's no fool. The more time we spend together, the more I've come to realize that. He's smarter than I gave him credit for.

It's only a matter of time before he sees through me fully.

I pull open the kitchen drawers, searching for a forgotten, unused knife. Even a switchblade will work. I have high hopes for the junk drawer, but there's nothing more than a few batteries and a tiny pocketknife.

I flick it open, but I already know it won't work.

Caleb is fast, and I won't have time to hack away at him with a tiny blade. I don't particularly want to, either. I want this to be a one-and-done, so I'll need a blade that is both large and sharp enough to cut his jugular.

I scan every nook and cranny of the first level of Caleb's home, but I find nothing of use. I'm not as disappointed in that as I should be, and I tug my hair out of my face as I head upstairs and into the spare bedroom Caleb uses as a home office.

The walls are bare, and a wooden desk and an uncomfortable-looking office chair sit in the center of the room. I peek inside the desk drawers. Empty. I try the filing cabinets next. They aren't locked, but they're also empty. Just my fucking luck.

The rest of my search is just as useless. I don't even find an extra pair of scissors, and Caleb would surely notice if the main kitchen ones went missing. I'll have to use one of the nice kitchen knives, but I'll have to sneak it the same day I plan to kill him. Am I really going to do this? *Yes.* I inspect his knives, eventually picking out the one I'll use.

I replay the memory of Caleb spitting in that human boy's face before breaking his neck. He executed five humans without a moment's hesitation, then returned to me as if nothing had happened. There was no remorse, no regret. Nothing.

If I didn't know any better, I'd say he actively enjoyed killing those men. If he can do it, I can do it, too.

I check the time, shocked to see several hours have passed. I was thorough in my search, and I'm sure I left my scent in every corner of the house. Caleb will smell it, but I don't think he'll say anything. He's caught me looking through his things before, and he doesn't seem to mind.

I finally meander to the bathroom to clean up, scrubbing the dried cum off myself before changing into a fresh pair of underwear. I begin planning my escape route as I do so.

HPAW had me memorize a historical map of Canada. It's important that I know the road system, but it's been weeks since I last saw a map. My memory is fuzzy, but I estimate it'll be about a six-hour drive. It was several to the cabin, and Caleb's pack is even further in.

I'll need to stop for gas within the shifter lands, which isn't ideal. The stations are long abandoned, and I doubt many of them still have gas in their underground tanks.

If I make a wrong turn and end up stranded, I'm as good as dead. The wolves will come after me once they realize their alpha is dead, and I doubt they'll be forgiving.

Caleb returns home while the sun is still out. "You're home early," I say from the kitchen.

He steps into the room with a laugh. "Eager to be rid of me?"

He's so fucking beautiful, and I find myself momentarily forgetting how to breathe as he pulls me into his arms. I replay the mental image of him spitting on and killing that boy. It has become an effective way for me to manage my emotions.

"How was your day?" I ask, pulling out of his arms.

"Boring." He clears his throat. "Sash and Logan invited us to a small get-together tonight. It's a last-minute thing. Would you like to go?"

Not really. "Do *you* want to go?" I ask, avoiding answering.

Caleb shrugs. "Yes. Wolves are social creatures, y'know?" Caleb shifts his weight from one foot to the other. "Grace will probably be there, though."

Wonderful.

I'm not upset about that anymore. Jealousy burned through me like wildfire the first few days after discovering Caleb's particular relationship with the woman, but it's since settled. I don't blame Caleb for choosing her, nor do I blame her for accepting. It's not like I have much room to be jealous, either.

I have a long, intimate history with men.

If I were serious about my relationship with Caleb, I'd want to go. I'd want to get to know the members of his pack. I haven't made much of an effort to do so these past several weeks, but it was easy to blame my injuries. But I'm feeling better than ever now, and Caleb knows that.

I resist the urge to sigh. "I'd love to go," I lie. "It would be nice to get to know Sash and Logan better."

Caleb's responding smile is breathtaking. It's a shame everything I say is a lie.

Chapter Eighteen

Caleb's hand is warm in mine, and I instinctively lean against his side as the cool, wintry air hits my cheeks and whips my hair around my head. A strand finds its way into my mouth, and I curse before spitting it out.

Did Caleb see that? He's not looking in my direction, but he's fighting back a smile. He saw.

My nerves ratchet as we approach Sash's house. It's a brick cottage with white trim and vines growing up the sides. Caleb gives my fingers a gentle squeeze before pushing open the iron gate that leads up a cobblestone walkway.

It's a beautiful, quaint house. I'm sure the human who once lived here loved it. They were probably devastated as the wolves drove them away.

The lights are on inside, and several silhouettes are visible beyond the thin curtains. This isn't a small get together. This is a full-on party.

Caleb spins toward me as we reach the front door. I have a millisecond to respond before his lips are on mine and his hands are sliding underneath my traffic-cone inspired winter jacket. Despite the temperature, Caleb's hands are warm.

"There are more people here than I expected," he whispers against my lips. "Would you like to go home?"

"We're already here..."

"I don't care." Caleb brushes his thumbs across my cheeks, the touch settling my racing emotions. This damned bond. "I only care about you, Ev. If you're not comfortable, we'll leave. No questions asked."

I want to scream. Instead, I smile.

"I'm okay," I say. "Let's go inside."

Caleb doesn't look like he entirely believes me, but he doesn't embarrass me by questioning my lie. I'm sure the shifters can hear us through the door, and they're nosy people.

"I'll be by your side all night," he says. "I promise."

Caleb pushes open Sash's front door, welcoming himself inside. She's on us the moment my coat and hat are removed, her beaming smile the first thing I notice before a drink is placed in my hand and my forearm is grabbed.

I shoot Caleb a panicked look as his sister drags me away, but he only shrugs.

What happened to being by my side all night? Dirty, fucking liar.

Sash takes it upon herself to introduce me to everybody here, even the few people I've already met. I try not to flush too deeply as she loudly announces over and over again that I'm Caleb's mate. I spot the occasional glance at my marked hand, but nobody outright stares.

Still, the glances are almost always followed by a scrunched nose and pursed lips. They don't approve of the color. I'm sure they all have their own suspicions about how it came to be so dark. They're probably right.

I stick my hand in the front pocket of the giant sweatshirt Caleb forced over my head earlier. I hated that he was putting me in what is essentially a sack, but now I'm glad to have a place to hide my hand.

I'm embarrassed by my marking. I always have been, but now

it's for an entirely different reason. It's so fucking dark. I used to detest the fact that I had a mark, but now I hate that I've ruined it.

Deep down, I wish mine were light like everybody else's. Mine is a beacon, signaling to everybody all the horrible things I've done to my bond with Caleb. I shouldn't care as much as I do, but I can't help it.

I occasionally catch sight of Caleb as Sash drags me around. He's the tallest man in the room, making it easy to spot him. Every time, without fail, he's already looking at me.

He's ready to come over at the first sign of my discomfort.

The realization makes my cheeks warm, and I clear my throat before turning back to the shifters surrounding me. Well, I'm trying to. I'm only half-listening to their conversation, my gaze continually darting toward Caleb. He's standing with a group of three men, and he's laughing.

He looks so at ease. This must be second nature to him. He wasn't lying when he said shifters were social creatures.

I catch sight of Grace. She approaches Caleb's group, easily slipping into their conversation. I find my legs carrying me in that direction before I permit them to do so.

I hate looking like a jealous woman, but the mate bond doesn't seem to have the same reservations as it urges me to approach Caleb and tuck myself against his side. It actually encourages me to do more than that, but it'll be a cold day in hell before I bend over and ask him to fuck me in front of these people.

"There you are!" Caleb smiles, wrapping his arm around my shoulders. He turns toward the group. "This is my mate, Evelyn."

The way he says *mate* makes me flush. His tone is so full of pride, so full of excitement. It physically hurts. I'm no mate to him.

Now that I'm here, I realize Grace isn't exactly in the same small group as Caleb. He turned his body away from hers before my approach, subtly dividing the group into two. He further divides us as he steps back, removing us entirely.

"Are you having fun?" he whispers, tucking a strand of hair behind my ear. "My pack loves you. I've heard nothing but praise this evening."

His gaze drops to my lips. I know where this is going, and I tilt my face upward as he brings his mouth to mine. I'm expecting a quick kiss like when we were outside, but instead, he tilts his head to the side and slips his tongue between my lips.

Oh. Heat pools in my abdomen as he wraps an arm around my waist and presses me entirely against him. It feels good, and I set my empty cup down before curling my fingers into the fabric of his shirt.

Caleb moans into my mouth, the noise louder than it should be, considering we're in a room full of shifters with impeccable hearing.

He shifts, pressing himself further against me. I wouldn't say I'm shy, but Caleb's comfort in showing physical affection is hard to match. Our bond pulsates as he slips his fingers underneath the hem of my shirt, letting his bare skin graze against the small of my waist.

Then he brings his cheek to mine, gently rubbing me with his prickly skin.

The room around us quiets. It's hard not to notice the sudden hush.

Caleb doesn't seem to care as he continues rubbing his cheek against mine. He once told me this was an apology between mates, but I'm starting to fear he left some details out. He underplayed what this means.

When Sash and Grace did this with me, Caleb said it was a symbolic way to place me above them. Is that what he's doing now? *Fucking Caleb.* This isn't at all a casual gesture, and it sure isn't an apology. Hierarchy is important to shifters.

Caleb looks awfully pleased with himself when he finally pulls away. The chatter in the room returns.

"Are you having fun?" Caleb asks.

"Yes."

In all honesty, I am. The shifters are friendly, and if it weren't for the fact that I'm about to murder their alpha and spill their secrets to HPAW, there are a few I'd consider wanting to be friends with.

I've never had friends—at least, not real ones. HPAW promised I can live a normal life once my work with the shifters is finished. I'm looking forward to it.

I doubt the education HPAW insisted I receive will translate to much in the real world, but I'm resourceful. Besides, I'm not looking for much. I want an easy, low-stress life. I want to hunker down in a small town, the kind where everybody knows everybody.

I want to feel safe and secure.

I used to dream of finding a handsome human man to have a handful of children with, but that particular facet of my dream no longer sounds exciting. Caleb, despite his secrets and shifter status, has ruined all other men for me.

I'll be a spinster instead.

"Do you promise?" Caleb asks. "If you aren't enjoying yourself, we can leave."

I blow out a breath. "I'm having a great time, Caleb. I promise."

He nods happily to himself, then takes my hand, grabs my empty cup, and pulls me into Sash's kitchen. I lean against the counter as he makes me another drink. He doesn't make one for himself.

"You don't drink much," I observe.

Caleb nods, handing over my cup. "I'll have a drink or two on special occasions, but I like to remain in control of myself. If there's ever an emergency, I want to tackle it with a clear head."

He's a good leader.

I take a sip. He's also a bad influence. He may not drink, but he made mine strong enough to make my eyes water.

I splutter. "Are you trying to get me drunk?"

Caleb only winks. It's playful, and I find myself at a momentary loss for words as I come to the realization that he's actually fun.

Caleb is attractive. He's large and muscular, and he has a jawline sharp enough to cut glass. He's intelligent, hardworking, and a damned alpha. We've spent almost every minute together these past few weeks, but they've been either at his work or in his home. I haven't really seen Caleb interact with others.

I suppose we went to the bonfire together, but we didn't stay for long.

I sip my drink, wincing at the burn, before letting him guide me back into the living room. He doesn't let Sash steal me away this time, and when she eventually convinces me to play a drinking game, Caleb follows me like a lost puppy.

Grace wanders over to watch, but she keeps her distance. I know I have no reason to dislike her. She's been nothing but polite to me, and Caleb only chose her because they're family friends and her mate is dead.

It makes sense. I know that.

Still, I find myself possessively leaning against Caleb every chance I get. He seems happy with my dramatic display, the man practically preening whenever we touch.

We play a game I've never heard of before. It involves a small ping-pong ball and a deck of cards, and I lose comically fast. Within minutes, Logan and a man I don't know very well are the last ones playing.

I take this opportunity to size up Logan. Caleb hasn't outright confirmed it, but I highly suspect Logan is his second-in-command. He's not as large as Caleb, nor does he exude the same level of dominance, but the shifters clearly respect him.

HPAW will be pissed when they realize the two shifters they spent months watching at that cabin were Caleb's sister and second-in-command. If they'd known, they would've killed the pair when they had the opportunity.

I'm glad HPAW didn't realize. I like Sash, and I'm happy she wasn't killed. She'll become a target once Caleb is dead and

Logan steps into his role, but maybe I can convince HPAW to spare her.

They don't want to kill all the shifters. They just want to dismantle and remove them from power.

Caleb stands behind me, absentmindedly rubbing my hips. Well, I *think* it's absentminded until he presses himself against my back. His fingers tighten around my waist, and his warm breath tickles my ear a second later.

"Are you ready to go?" he asks.

I glance around the room. "We haven't been here for long."

Caleb takes my empty cup and hands it to a random passerby. The shifter shoots Caleb a dirty look, but it lacks any real malice. I watch the interaction, again reminded that the shifters love Caleb. He's their alpha, but he's also found a way to be their friend. I imagine that's a hard line to draw, but he's managed it.

I suspect Caleb can manage anything he puts his mind to. He's too smart not to.

"Would you like to go home with me?" Caleb asks.

I snort. "We haven't been here for very long."

He kisses the sensitive skin beneath my ear. "You've been rubbing against me all night, mate. I smell like you. You smell like me." His voice grows quiet. "We haven't had sex, and I'm getting possessive. I'm having trouble controlling my urges, probably because this is such a casual setting, and if we don't leave, I fear I'm going to start a fight."

A fight? The idea of Caleb fighting over me is more intriguing than I'd care to admit. Would he fight in his skin or wolf form? Both are appealing in their own ways. His wolf form is deadly, but I'd love to see his skin slick with sweat as he—

Caleb groans, the noise too loud for the impeccable hearing within this room. "I can smell you, Ev." His following words are practically growled. "*Everybody* can smell you. If you're not willing to bend over the couch, then we need to leave immediately."

Bend over the couch? Is he serious? We're in his sister's home.

I'm scooped up into Caleb's arms. He doesn't bother putting me in my coat and hat as he rips them out of the entryway closet and carries me out of the house. Whistles, hollers, and teasing follow us outside.

"Caleb!" I try to sound angry, maybe even affronted, but my laughter ruins it.

"I warned you." He shoots me a beaming smile, then tosses me into the passenger seat of the car. "I need to take a cold shower and change into something that doesn't smell like your arousal before I lose my fucking mind."

The car door slams shut, and I use my hands to try to physically stop myself from smiling like a giddy child. It doesn't work.

Chapter Nineteen

Caleb's chest rises and falls with deep, even breaths.

I roll onto my side, watching. His fingertips rest against my thigh, the shifter wanting to touch me even in sleep. If I move, he'll adjust to remain in contact with me.

My gaze travels to his neck. He shaved this morning, but dark, coarse stubble already covers the spot where I intend to slit his throat. Humans die within seconds when their jugular is cut, and I suspect shifters are the same. They're generally harder to kill, and they heal at a rate humans can only dream of, but they aren't invincible.

They bleed out. Caleb will die.

I'm going to stay with him until it's complete. He'll realize what's happening in those final moments and hate me for it, but I can't stomach the thought of leaving him to die alone.

The mate bond has taken a firm hold of me. I tried my best to fight it, but it won. I care for Caleb. I might even love him.

It's a crazy thought, especially when I've seen firsthand the way he treats humans. We're nothing to him, but even that knowledge isn't enough to entirely deter me.

Caleb crinkles his nose, his lips twitching with sleep. It's much cuter than it has any right to be. What's he dreaming about? Me?

I selfishly like the sound of that. I want Caleb to dream of me.

This entire situation is fucked up. I don't want to do any of this. I don't want this responsibility. I want to curl into Caleb's arms and forget that humans even exist. I want to turn against my kind.

I won't. I can't put my desires before the millions of humans HPAW protects.

I watch Caleb draw another breath before placing my lips on his throat. I need to see his reaction time.

Caleb stirs, then tilts his head back. He trusts me, exposing his neck without a second thought. I suppose that's good. I feared he'd jolt awake the moment his neck was touched.

It's a vulnerable spot, and Caleb has quick reflexes. His instinct isn't to defend himself when he's sharing a bed with me, though. That will probably change when it's a knife touching his throat and not my lips, but I can't exactly test that theory without raising alarms.

Well, maybe I can. Knives aren't the only threat I can bring to his neck.

Caleb lets out a sleepy moan. I sink my teeth into his throat, biting hard.

Before I can register what's happening, I'm on my back and Caleb is hovering above me. His eyes are wide open, suddenly alert. If he wakes this quickly when I attack him, he'll have time to pin me down and kill me before blood loss makes him weak.

Caleb blinks, his eyebrows furrowed. "What are you doing?"

A strand of hair falls over his eye. I push it back. It's time for a trim.

"Biting you," I say.

Caleb continues staring at me, his eyes wide and mouth slightly open, before he shakes his head and flops onto my torso. He's heavy, but I don't complain about his weight as he burrows his face against my shoulder and breathes in my scent.

"Why?" he mumbles into my skin.

I shrug. "I thought shifters liked that. I'm marking you."

Shifters don't mark, but it's a common rumor spread among the humans. There are communities that practically worship the shifters. They don't care about the damage and pain the wolves inflict. All they see are toned muscles and pretty faces.

They've romanticized the idea of mate bonds. Before coming here, I thought they were idiotic fools. Now, I'm not so sure. I hate to say it, but I see the allure. Caleb is beautiful, and I swear my heart skips a beat whenever he smiles.

Caleb shuts his eyes and shakes his head, but a smile is tugging at the corners of his lips. He finds this endearing. I'm going to use this to my advantage.

"I had a dream that you were killed," I lie, "and I once heard somebody say that if shifter mates bite one another, they can feel one another's emotions. If I bite you, I'll know you're safe."

"I wish that were true, mate." Caleb cups my cheeks. I'm spewing straight nonsense, but he's not laughing. He's taking my concerns seriously, which is more than I expected. "The bond does share some things, but it's nothing you need to worry about."

I sit up. This is news to me. "What does it share?"

Caleb grimaces, not immediately responding.

"Well?" I urge.

"If we were ever to be..." he hesitates. "Well, if either of us were to be unfaithful, the other would feel it."

"How so?"

"The partner of an unfaithful mate feels pain during the act."

I take a moment to think that through. If I were to have sex with another, *Caleb* would feel pain? There's no way.

"So, if I were to cheat on you, *you'd* be the one in pain?" I ask, clarifying. Caleb nods. I frown, not sure I want the answer to my next question. "Have you...Was there..." I trail off, unable to find the words.

Caleb shakes his head. "It's only felt *after* meeting. I wasn't in any pain...before."

I bob my head, so damned relieved to hear that.

I won't share this particular piece of information with HPAW. I don't necessarily agree with their interrogation methods, and I won't give them ammunition to do something horrid to the occasional shifter they capture. I'd like to believe they're above rape, but I can't guarantee it. Desperate people do desperate things.

"Shifters don't bite," Caleb says, returning to our earlier topic. He urges me to lie back down, then pulls my thigh over his waist. "If we did, don't you think I'd have sunk my teeth into you by now?"

I shrug. "No. We haven't even had sex."

Caleb trails his fingers up my bare thigh. I'm not sure why he hasn't tried to have sex with me. I know that, at first, it was because I was injured. That made sense, but I've been feeling better for a while now. I haven't taken a single painkiller in weeks, and Doctor Greg has given me the all-clear to resume regular activity.

It's not as if Caleb has been avoiding all intimate touch. He's put his mouth and fingers on me, and he seems to love fucking my thighs, but it never goes further than that. I don't understand why, and if I'm honest with myself, I'm a little annoyed.

"I don't want you to think I'm only interested in you for sex..." Caleb eventually admits.

I resist the urge to laugh. "Trust me, I don't think that."

"It's more than that." Caleb blows out a breath. "I've waited twenty-nine years to have sex, and I want our first time to be meaningful. I don't want to just fuck you, Evelyn. I want to make love to you."

I'm going to gouge out my fucking eyes. Caleb looks so earnest, so fucking open and raw and exposed. He looks at me like I've hung the damn moon.

I speak without thinking. "I do love you, Caleb. I want to make love to you, too."

Caleb is pure elation. His eyes widen, and his mouth pops open before his lips curl into an absolutely breathtaking smile. It's an image I want to remember forever. It's an image that's going to haunt me.

Caleb looks so happy, and a piece of my heart cracks as he rolls over me, pinning me with his hips.

"Truly?" he asks. "You truly mean it?"

My hands shake as I cup either side of his face, holding him steady. "Of course I mean it."

It's a piece of honesty I didn't intend to share. I'm not entirely sure what love is supposed to feel like, but what I feel for Caleb isn't casual. He's weaseled himself into my heart, slithering through the cracks of the carefully crafted mental wall I built between us. No amount of training and preparation has kept him away.

He has me questioning everything I've ever believed. If that's not love, then I don't know what is.

"I love you too, Ev," Caleb whispers.

He slots himself between my thighs. I'm hardly surprised to feel his hard cock pressing against me, incessant and needy. The way he looks at me physically hurts, so I avoid making eye contact. I stare at where we're touching instead, pleased Caleb decided to sleep in only his underwear tonight.

His abs flex as he sits back on his heels, his hands sliding up my thighs in the process. He's taking off my shirt a moment later, silently stripping me. I let him, unable to stomach the thought of asking him to stop. I want this. It's wrong and a thousand shades of fucked up, but I can't help it.

I need Caleb.

He tosses my shirt aside, leaving me bare from the waist up. I lift my hips, helping him remove my bottoms. He groans when I'm finally naked beneath him, and I hook my fingers into the waistband of his underwear.

"Take them off," I order.

Caleb smirks, the picture of confidence as he removes them.

He looks good, and he knows it. He must know how badly I want him, too. I'm slick between my thighs, wet and ready to take him. I'm sure he's noticed.

"Fuck." Caleb grunts, gripping himself. "You'll tell me if anything hurts?"

"You're not going to hurt me."

Caleb shoots me a sharp look. "You'll tell me if anything hurts."

"Yes."

Caleb finally closes the distance between us, running the tip of himself against my slit. I so badly want him inside, and I'd be tempted to roll my hips and hurry things along if I didn't already know he'd stop me. Caleb likes to take things slowly. He likes to savor me.

He's a damned tease.

"You're perfect, Ev. So fucking perfect."

I wish HPAW had never found me. I ran away from home, traveling to the shifter lands in search of Caleb. I probably would've found my way to him. I would've been brought here and raised among the shifters, and I wouldn't have known anything about the conflict between them and the humans.

Despite everything, I want to be Caleb's mate. I want to pop out his stupid fucking children and live an ignorant, happy life.

Knowledge has ruined that for me.

Caleb notches himself against my entrance. "I'm so honored to have you as my mate." He pushes inside, stretching me to my limits as he guides his cock deep into me. I've taken men before—too many to count—but Caleb is easily the largest.

He watches my every movement, pausing when he's halfway inside.

I whine. "Don't stop."

"I'm hurting you."

I slide my hands down his back, feeling every flexed muscle, before grabbing his ass and yanking him in. Caleb could stop me

—it would be easy for him—but he lets me pull him. His hips slam against mine, his length filling me to the brim.

I can practically feel him in my throat.

"*Shit*." Caleb drops his forehead against mine. "You're so... You're so fucking warm."

He pulls out halfway, then eases back inside, quickly settling into a smooth rhythm. A small part of me was expecting Caleb's movements to be jerky, but that was a silly assumption. The shifters are too graceful to be anything but excellent lovers.

Caleb rolls his hips, hitting all the right spots. I'm not going to last long, especially not when Caleb begins rubbing my clit. He's learned exactly how I like to be touched, and I curse as an orgasm begins coiling in my belly.

Caleb kisses me, sloppy and messy, before trailing wet kisses down my throat. "Do you like knowing you're the only woman I'll ever touch? That your cunt is the only one I'll ever experience? Only you."

I do. I honestly fucking love it.

"Are you mine?" I ask.

Caleb grits his teeth, his body hot and cheeks flushed. "Yes."

He's close. I can tell by the way his smooth, calculated thrusts are turning desperate. His hips slam against my ass with every thrust, and I can hear just how wet I am. Our fucking is obscene.

Caleb peers down at me, everything in his gaze screaming *possessive* and *wild*. He looks every bit the shifter he is.

"And you're mine," he hisses. "All." *Thrust.* "Fucking." *Thrust.* "Mine." *Thrust.*

I shatter, my back arching and thighs clamping around his waist as my orgasm absolutely wrecks me. I've never felt anything like this, and I'm pretty sure the noises I'm making are inhuman.

Caleb squeezes his eyes shut, his movements quickening. He's truly fucking me now, all concern about hurting me forgotten as he chases his own high. He pants into the space between us, the noise drowned out by the sound of our slapping skin.

"Cum in me," I beg. I shouldn't ask. It's cruel, but I can't stop myself. I'm not in the fertile part of my cycle, but I'm close enough for this to be risky. Caleb knows that.

His eyes spring open. "Are you sure?"

"Yes!" I want to give Caleb this experience. "Please. I love you. Please."

Caleb's fingers curl around my thighs, squeezing the flesh as he fucks into me. His moans are filthy, and I imprint them to memory.

"I'm going to cum in you." Caleb hisses. "I'm going to cum deep inside you, Ev. Are you ready for it?"

He shoves deep inside, his jaw tightening as he stills and finds his release. He's twitching inside me, filling me with cum that leaks down my thigh when he pulls out a second later.

I'd love the feeling if it weren't a lie. Caleb thinks he's getting me pregnant and starting our family. I'm giving him a good experience before I kill him.

He pulls me into his chest, holding me tight. His heart is pounding.

"I love you," I say again.

I hate myself for meaning it. I hate the situation we've found ourselves in. I hate the decision I'm being forced to make. I want to choose Caleb so badly, but I can't.

I can't put this off any longer. It's killing me, and at this rate, I'll lose the confidence to act. I will kill Caleb tomorrow. No more procrastinating.

Chapter Twenty

Caleb isn't sneaky in his glances, but I don't mind. I like it when he looks at me.

I readjust my position on the couch, shifting so I'm facing Caleb. He cocks his head to the side, a smile beginning to emerge as I shove my toes underneath his thigh. He's wearing a pair of dangerously short exercise shorts, and I'm taking full advantage of the exposed thighs.

They're warm, and they act as the perfect weighted blanket for my feet.

"Are you still sore?"

I ignore the question. I thought Caleb would be horrified to learn I'm sore and tender after last night's activities, but the asshole enjoys it. The knowledge has stroked some part of his absurd male ego.

Caleb huffs, then turns back to his television. We rarely spend time in the living room, and we *never* watch TV, but Caleb insisted we leave work early to watch a sports game. It seems, despite the shifters' hatred of our kind, they enjoy our athletics. I don't understand it.

The TV announcer drones on, but I'm not paying attention. I don't care for sports, especially American football.

I fight back laughter as Caleb leans forward, fully engrossed in the screen. I'd go as far as to say he looks nervous. It's a close game, and Caleb is rooting for the losing team. He mumbles quietly to himself as the men line up on the field. I enjoy watching Caleb watch TV. It's so mundane.

My laughter bursts free when Caleb groans and throws himself against the back of the couch. The announcer is droning on about an interception. Caleb looks about ready to yell at the screen, his eyes narrowed and lips pursed.

"Have you always been interested in watching grown men wrestle?" I tease.

The glare Caleb shoots me is frosty. "Why do you insist on bullying me today?"

It's a distraction. If I'm not focused on Caleb and his every movement, then I'm thinking about the sharp kitchen knife I hid underneath my pillow while Caleb was showering this morning.

The game resumes. I eye my marking. The dark-red color remains unchanged, which is a good thing. Caleb would suspect something was wrong if it were to darken.

I'm sure it'll change after I slit his throat.

It still shocks me how little he seems to care about the current color. If I were Caleb, I'd be livid. I'd be demanding to know precisely what he did to cause his mark to darken. I'd want names, dates, and addresses. Everything.

Caleb is too good for me.

I shift, cuddling up against him. He shivers as I slide my hand underneath his shirt, resting my palm against his chest. Our bond seems to hum between us, pleased with our physical contact.

"I'd crawl into your skin if I could," I whisper.

Caleb doesn't miss a beat. "That's a really weird thing to say, Ev."

I shrug. Caleb's warmth seeps into me, the man practically a furnace. I'm going to kill him tonight. His warm body is going to grow stiff and cold. I'll never feel his soft touch or hear his gravelly voice again.

"Did you know that most professional sports players before the exodus were shifters?" Caleb asks.

I didn't know that, but it's not surprising. Shifters are more athletic than humans, and it makes sense that they'd use that to their advantage.

"How did packs work when you lived among the humans?" I ask.

Caleb takes a moment to answer. "From what I know, it wasn't too hard. Most of us lived deep in the country, and those in populated areas disguised their packs as exclusive, invitation-only clubs."

"It's just so hard to believe you lived among us for so long and we had no idea you existed."

"Many humans knew about us," Caleb admits. "The general population didn't, but anybody in power was aware of our existence. There were...conflicts between us, and ultimately, we decided it was best to separate."

"Why not just expose yourselves? Why leave?"

"We didn't want the conflict," Caleb says. "It was a complicated situation."

We finish the game in silence, and I hold back tears as we head upstairs.

We shower together, and I milk every second of it. I take my time washing Caleb, memorizing every muscle and curve of his naked body. I even convince him to let me wash his hair, and I bite my tongue so hard, it bleeds as I work my fingers through the thick strands.

I'm wide awake when we finally crawl into bed, and I stare at the ceiling while waiting for Caleb to fall asleep. The hours pass by at an agonizing pace.

Am I really going to do this? I have to.

This is bigger than Caleb and me. I need to protect the human population as a whole, and if I fail, so will they. I'm not doing this for me. I'm doing this for the millions of young human children who deserve to grow up in a world not plagued by the constant threat of death.

We don't stand a chance against the wolves, and we need to fight back while we still can. It's our only hope. *I'm our only hope.*

Caleb's fingers twitch against my thigh. I roll onto my side, facing him.

His chest rises and falls in a slow, even rhythm, and his pupils dart behind his eyelids. He's asleep.

I reach into my pillowcase, confirming my knife is where I placed it earlier. It is. I drag my finger along the point, hesitating, before pulling it out. The knife is lightweight, and I readjust when my palm grows sweaty.

I have to do this.

Despite my best attempts to remain calm, my heart pounds as I glance at the clock and realize it's three in the morning. The sun will be rising in a few short hours. I'm out of time.

I slide out of bed, careful not to wake Caleb. His reflexes are too quick, and I should keep as much distance between us as possible. I can't let him grab me.

Tears blur my vision, and I roughly wipe them away as I stare at Caleb's sleeping form. His dark eyelashes cast a shadow on the tops of his cheeks, and his full lips are open just the tiniest bit. I want to kiss him and feel his lips on mine one last time, but I won't take the risk.

My movements are slow and calculated as I plant a knee onto the bed and lean just close enough to reach his throat. I make sure his pupils are still fluttering behind his eyelids, confirming he's asleep, before bringing the knife to his neck.

I'm sorry.

The blade reflects the small amount of light coming in through the window. Is it coincidental that the hand I'm using to kill Caleb is the same one that holds my mark? The color appears black in the dark, but maybe that's just how it looks now.

I imagine killing your mate is enough to have it turn as black as night. It'll be a permanent reminder of what I've done. Every day, I'll look at it and remember Caleb, and every day, I'll remember how it felt to drag a knife across his throat and watch the life vanish from his eyes.

The humans will paint me a hero.

I watch Caleb, admiring his jawline. It's strong, and I can't count the number of times I've run my tongue along it. It's one of my favorite things to do, especially when he's just shaved and the skin is still smooth.

I bring the knife to his throat, suck in a slow breath, and slice.

I might as well be watching myself through a movie screen. My hand feels disconnected from my body as the tip of the sharp blade drags across Caleb's skin like butter. I apply more pressure, needing to make sure I cut entirely through his jugular, but a hand clamps around my wrist before I can completely slice through the vein.

Caleb's eyes fly open. He makes a choked noise as he rips my hand away from his throat.

My knife cuts his shoulder, and I manage to yank my hand from his grip and scamper backward before he gets a better hold on me. My back slams against the doorframe, sending a hot spike of pain up my ribcage.

I ignore it.

The knife is still in my fist, and blood seeps from Caleb's neck and into the sheets below. His mouth is open, but no words emerge as he slams his palm over his throat and struggles to sit up. He's significantly more alert than I anticipated. *God fucking dammit.*

I dart out of the room. There's no banging of footsteps behind me, but I'm not taking any risks. Caleb is awake, and I'm not entirely sure if he's going to live or die. Either way, I need to get out of here.

The car keys are sitting on the entryway table, and I scoop them up before running barefoot to the car. In my planned scenario, I killed Caleb and had time to get dressed before leaving.

Snow sticks to my bare feet, painful but easy to ignore. Music blares as I turn on the car, but I don't bother adjusting any settings as I back out of the driveway and turn onto the road.

The engine gives a little whine before bursting into life, and I white-knuckle the steering wheel as I make my escape. If Caleb isn't dead, there's a good chance he'll send his pack after me within the hour. I suspect they can travel faster than this shitty vehicle. It doesn't help that they aren't limited to the roads, either.

I turn off the radio, needing silence.

My toes burn as the snow on my feet and legs melts, and I pull my eyes off the road for a moment to adjust the heat. I'd like to make it to the HPAW meeting point without hypothermia.

Caleb's blood covers my hands, the crimson moisture smeared across the wheel and gearshift. I hate having it all over the place, but I don't have anything to wipe it off with. I'm only wearing his shirt, and I don't want to stain it with his blood. I plan to keep it as some sick, twisted memento.

The roads are empty, which I expected, but the snow makes them hard to drive on. At least there's no ice. It'd be humiliating if I went through all this work, only to crash into a tree and die.

Despite my attempts to keep my tears from escaping, my eyes have other plans. Wetness streams down my cheeks and drips down my neck. I wipe it away, angry with myself. I always knew how this would end.

I don't get to cry about it now.

Is Caleb dead? No human would survive that injury, but Caleb's no human. Shifters have exceptional healing. Can he heal from such a traumatic injury, though? There's no way. Questions continue to swarm my mind, all blending until I can't possibly make sense of them.

Are the shifter borders guarded? If they are, I'm in for a world of trouble. It's too late to change course and adjust my plan. HPAW gave me a meeting point, and I'll do everything in my power to get there.

My eyes continually dart toward the forest on either side of the road. Are the shifters coming after me? They're fast, and they can cut through the forest while I'm forced to drive on the road.

Caleb is most likely dead.

The realization steals my breath.

Did he follow me downstairs? Were his final moments spent desperately trying to get to me, only to watch as I ran away? I wanted to stay with him until it was finished, but I was startled when he grabbed my hand.

He was too alert.

He still had the advantage.

Did he understand that I betrayed him? Did he have time to put the pieces together?

Hours pass, and the sky is a haze of pinks and blues when I'm forced to pull over at an abandoned gas station. I'm on empty, and I really fucking hope there's still gas here. There has to be. Shifters might not use vehicles recreationally, but surely they do for shipping and other industrial needs.

The station door creaks as it swings open. The place is untouched, and if I didn't know any better, I'd think it was still in use. The humans left in such a hurry when the wolves took over.

I find a hat, thick socks, and a pair of slip-on rubber shoes in a small clothing aisle. I don't hesitate to shove them on. I'm freezing.

There's a manual gas pump in the back room. It's small but surprisingly heavy, and my arms burn as I drag it outside. There should be a small maintenance hole cover, and I kick around the snow until I find it.

When I finally pry it open, I'm met with the pungent smell of gasoline. Thank the fucking heavens.

I hope I don't blow myself up.

HPAW trained me on this, and I follow their instructions as I set up the manual pump and begin pulling up the gas. It takes several minutes for gas to start pouring out, and I secure the hose into the car's gas tank the moment it does.

There's no way to know how much is in the tank, so I pump until my arms burn, then remove the hose and start the engine. The gas gauge displays halfway, and I shut off the car to resume pumping. I need a full tank.

My arms are going to be sore.

My annoying tears resume as I work on pulling up the gas, the stress of today bubbling over at the worst time possible. I'm tired and cold and hungry, and I just killed the man I love. Those aren't the makings of a great day.

Or year. Or even life.

I continue pumping until the damn thing jams. It won't fucking budge, and I resist the urge to scream as I place all my weight on it. It still doesn't move.

Piece of fucking trash.

I check the gas gauge again. It's three-quarters full, which I suppose I'll have to make do with. I'm meeting HPAW in a small, abandoned town just beyond the shifter border. It was evacuated a little over thirty years ago, making it a good, private spot for HPAW to wait for me.

I should be able to make it there on three-quarters of a tank. I'll be cutting it close, but I'll be transported to an HPAW vehicle once arriving.

Caleb consumes my thoughts as I drive. I fluctuate between bone-deep regret and grudging resolve.

I had no choice.

I did this for the millions of innocent humans HPAW protects. Killing Caleb was my only option.

Except it wasn't.

I shake my head, refusing to let myself indulge that thought as I drive down a now-empty highway.

I avoid driving through the once-populated Canadian cities, sticking to the abandoned highways that go around them. I never learned the exact locations of Caleb's pack members, and I'd rather not run into a pocket of them.

My gas tank is teetering on empty when I finally pull up to

HPAW's meeting point. This place is a ghost town, and my gaze flickers toward the rooftops as I drive down the main road.

There's a gunman on the roof of one of the buildings, the man impossible to spot unless you know what you're looking for.

That's where I need to be.

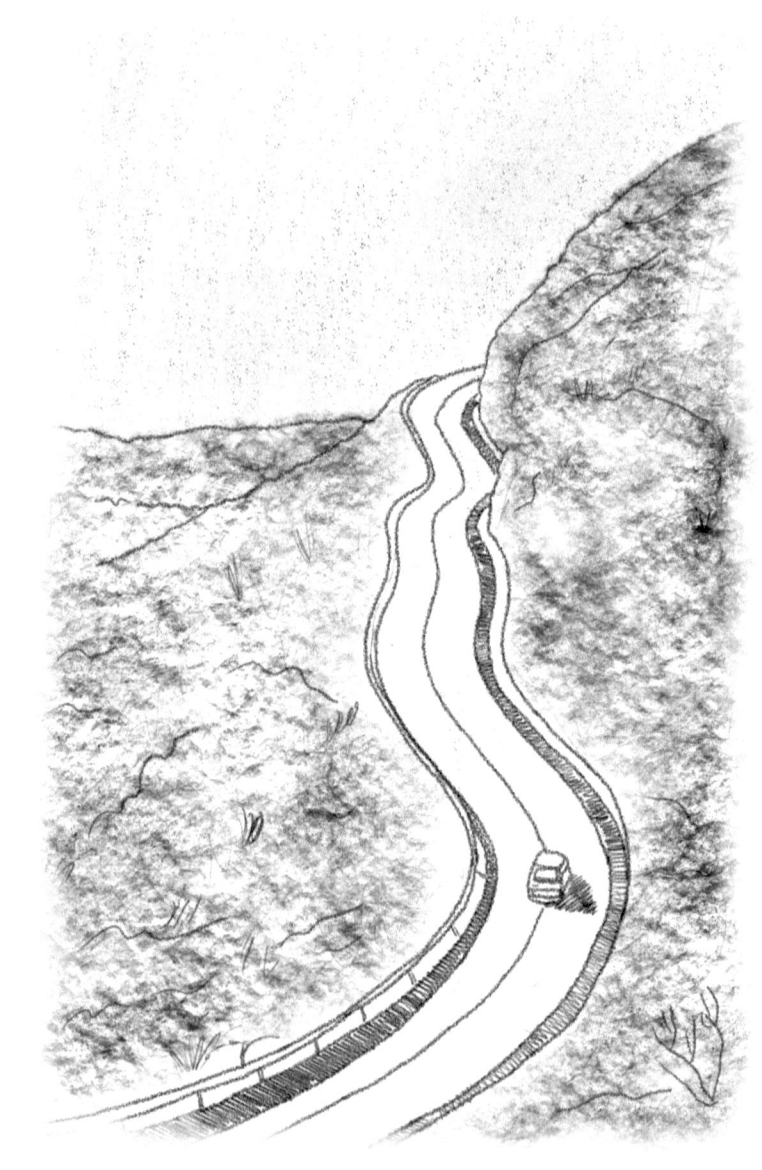

Chapter Twenty-One

A man in full HPAW tactical gear greets me as I step out of my vehicle. He's younger than me, maybe in his early twenties, with bright blue eyes and black hair cropped closely to his head. His last name is printed on his chest. *Anderson*.

Four additional men step out of the crumbling building I parked in front of. I glance between them, hoping to find a familiar face, but I don't recognize any of these men. They're all as young as Anderson. Fresh HPAW meat. Waiting indefinitely in some long-abandoned city isn't a job for the valuable soldiers.

I was hoping Daniel would be here.

"Looking for someone?" Anderson asks. I shake my head. He continues. "Were you followed?"

"Not that I know of."

"Is Alpha Knox dead?"

I hold back a wince. "I believe so."

Anderson's lips flatten into a thin line. "You *believe* so? How can you not be certain?"

"Alpha Knox was severely injured when I left, but I didn't stick around to ensure he died," I admit. "I couldn't without risking my own life."

Anderson glances behind him, making eye contact with the four other men. They're having a silent conversation, one I'm reasonably certain is about me. Whatever. They have no idea what I've been through or how hard it is to kill a shifter.

I'm willing to bet HPAW's simulations are the closest they've ever gotten to real combat. They're in no position to judge me.

After several seconds, Anderson turns back to me. I don't appreciate the way he's looking at me—almost as if *I'm* the enemy. I thought the soldiers would be happier to see me.

"Call in reinforcements," Anderson says to the others. "Let them know that the marked dove has returned." He shakes his head. "And let them know that she failed to kill Alpha Knox."

Asshole. I bite the inside of my cheek, remaining silent. It isn't easy.

I've grown comfortable with speaking my mind these past few weeks, but HPAW doesn't tolerate it the way Caleb did. In fact, I'd go as far as to say that Caleb enjoyed it. He valued my thoughts and opinions.

I'll likely never experience that again.

I press my lips together, taking a moment to collect myself, before speaking. "Do you—"

Anderson interrupts me. "Are you compromised?"

"Excuse me?"

"Strip her," he orders his men. "Make sure she's clean, and bring her inside once you've cleared her."

Clean? Compromised? What the fuck is he talking about? I step back, blood rushing through my ears as the four men form a circle around me. Who the fuck do they think they are to strip me? I've done nothing wrong, and I won't be treated as the enemy.

The men continue their approach. I spin around, keeping tabs on their position. I won't win in a fight against four men, but I'm confident I can land a solid hit or two before they take me down. I'll aim for knees and nuts.

The men attack at once. Two go for my arms, and another for

my legs. The fourth stands back, silently observing. I lash out, my dominant fist crushing the nearest nose before being captured. I don't get the opportunity to swing with my other arm, but the man at my legs is fumbling.

I kick, satisfied as my foot slams against the tender flesh between his thighs. He groans, snapping his knees together with a pained curse. My ankle is trapped between his legs, and when I try to pull it free, he grabs and pins my calves together.

My arms are pulled behind my back, the angle so painful I'm worried about my shoulders dislocating.

"She broke my fucking nose," the man behind me whines. He sounds nasally. Good.

I throw my head back, satisfied when my hard skull smashes against something. There's a crack, and the man with the broken nose cries out again.

"Fucking *bitch*," he whines. "Leave me alone."

"You leave *me* alone!" I hiss. "Let me go!"

My hair is grabbed, preventing me from throwing my head back again. *Shame.* I was planning to do so. This wasn't a fair fight, but I'm glad I managed to inflict some damage. Not as much as I hoped, but enough to feel good about myself. Daniel would be proud of me.

The fourth man finally steps forward, tugging at my shirt. I squirm, trying and failing to break free as the fabric is pulled away from my chest. There's a flash of a knife. He intends to cut my shirt off.

I'm almost relieved when an ear-splitting snarl emerges from behind us.

There's a sudden commotion, and the men begin dragging me forward. They're bringing me to the building Anderson went into. It looks to be the only one around still habitable. The elements have gotten to the others.

Bullets spray around us, the *pops* loud and startling. The soldier on the rooftop is firing.

Is there only one shifter? Is it Caleb? Is he still alive? Hope blooms. I shove it down.

A scream rips from my throat as my left shoulder is pulled, and the man who was holding me flies through the air. He lands with a sickening crunch several feet away, his head twisted at an odd angle, and there's a blur of brown fur as a shifter darts past me. I can't bring myself to look away as the wolf descends on the man, ripping him apart within seconds.

The other soldiers release me, abandoning me in the street as they run for the building.

I don't move. There's no point.

I'd recognize this shifter anywhere, and Caleb isn't going to let me escape.

Bullets sink into his torso. He hardly seems to notice. The man he's on is already dead. He was probably dead before he hit the ground.

Caleb springs off him, his muscular form launching him into the air and through the closed doorway of the building HPAW has made their own. The thick oak door doesn't stand much of a chance against a full-grown shifter male—especially not one as large as Caleb. It splinters beneath his weight.

There are screams from inside. Loud, masculine ones filled with terror. More bullets. More screams.

I stare at my feet. My hands are shaking, and I clasp them together as I wait. Caleb is either going to die inside that building or murder every HPAW soldier. He won't let himself be captured, and my interference won't make a difference.

I'll wait here.

The screaming stops, and the low snarl that vibrates through the open doorway confirms that Caleb is indeed still alive. There's a shout from the rooftop, another few *pops*, then silence.

I don't look up as something heavy falls from above, landing with a loud thump on the cement about a hundred feet away. It's a body, one covered in clothing. Not Caleb.

Several seconds pass before Caleb emerges from the building, stalking forward in his animal form. It takes all my courage to meet his gaze. He's already looking at me, nothing but pure hatred in his eyes.

That hatred remains as he transforms out of his animal form. Is this the part where he kills me? I can't say it's entirely undeserved.

He's covered in blood. I can't tell which is his. He has several active wounds, some bleeding more heavily than others. My stomach roils as he reaches into a wound on his abdomen, his muscles bunching as he wordlessly rips out a bullet.

"You're lucky that human had shit aim," Caleb says. He drops the bullet, letting it bounce away, then points to my stolen vehicle. "Get in the car, Evelyn."

There's dried blood all along his neck and chest. The wound I inflicted on him has healed, but the evidence remains. An emotion that feels an awful lot like relief washes over me. I didn't want to kill Caleb, not really. Maybe I subconsciously failed on purpose.

Caleb brushes past me and rips open the passenger seat door. "Get in the fucking car."

He's never spoken to me in this tone. I flinch, glancing around. I have nowhere to go.

"Are you alone?" I ask.

"Why?" Caleb raises a brow. "Planning another assassination attempt?"

He blinks, his gaze quickly traveling from my head to my toes before lingering on my shoulder. I'm cradling my arm, but I drop it as soon as he draws attention to it. The soldier overextended it when Caleb attacked him. I'm pretty sure I pulled a muscle.

Caleb doesn't ask if I'm okay.

He looks away, his upper lip curling.

I take a moment to collect myself, mentally accepting the fact that I've failed. I won't beg for mercy. I won't beg Caleb to spare my life. I accept this.

Chapter Twenty-Two

Caleb picks another bullet out of his thigh.

"How many times were you shot?" I ask.

I spot at least four bullet holes. Three on his torso and one on his thigh.

Caleb ignores my question as he straightens up, rising to his full height, and steps forward. I take two steps back, my gaze flashing toward the driver's-side door. Can he outrun a vehicle going at full speed?

"Don't even think about it," he snaps. He points to the passenger seat. "Get in. I won't ask again."

I have no choice. I clasp my hands behind my back, a sad attempt to hide their tremors, before climbing into the passenger seat of the car. Caleb is behind the wheel a heartbeat later, and he pointedly avoids looking in my direction as he turns the car around and begins driving back the way we came.

"HPAW was thoughtless to give you a meeting point so close to the shifter border." Caleb scoffs. "I've been trailing you for hours. It's given me time to think—to put together the pieces the mate bond had me foolishly ignoring."

I bite at the skin on my bottom lip, not stopping even when I taste blood.

"I knew you were hesitant about my kind," Caleb continues. "Most humans are, but I was a fool not to realize just how deep your hatred was. It never occurred to me that you were working for HPAW. Kudos to you, I suppose."

Caleb lets out a dry laugh. "I believed you loved me." His laughter grows, borderline hysterical. "I found the fucking knife. Did you think I wouldn't notice a knife hidden underneath our pillows? I found it and told myself you were just being cautious. Surely, my mate wouldn't want to hurt me. She's just skittish, maybe a little nervous to be living in the middle of a shifter pack. She was recently abducted and tortured, after all. She wants to feel safe. I can't fault her for that."

I stare out the front windshield. I have nothing to say, and even if I did, I doubt Caleb wants to hear it.

Caleb adjusts the air vents, blasting me with warm air.

"I hope you aren't pregnant."

His words sting. They shouldn't, not after everything I've done, but they still do. Is that why he hasn't killed me? It makes sense. He doesn't want to risk killing his unborn child. He'll wait until he has confirmation that I'm not pregnant before taking my life.

Caleb sighs. "Why'd you do it?"

I take a moment to respond. "I'm protecting humankind. I had no choice." The answer isn't what he wants to hear, but it's the truth.

"You had a choice." Caleb taps his pointer fingers against the steering wheel. "It seems I have a choice to make now, too." He slams on the brakes, and the seatbelt digs into my throat as the car jerks to an abrupt stop. Caleb spins in my direction. "What should I choose, Evelyn?"

I shove my hands underneath my thighs, sitting on them. They won't stop shaking, and I don't want Caleb to see. I open my mouth, shut it, and open it again. I don't know what to say. Is Caleb looking for me to beg for my life? Beg him to let me live?

"I don't want to die," I eventually say.

"I don't know many people who do."

I refused to show Caleb mercy, so I can't very well expect him to show *me* any. If I'm honest with myself, he's probably well within his rights to kill me. If I were an outsider watching this, I wouldn't blame him.

Caleb tuts. "You really think I'm going to kill you?" He shakes his head and resumes driving. "How disappointing. HPAW will kill you if you return to them. Once you've given them the sad scraps of information I've shared with you, you'll no longer be useful. If anything, you'll be a liability."

I lick my lips, unsure. He sounds so confident.

Daniel practically raised me. He may not be a warm, glowing father figure, but he would never let anybody hurt me. If he thought there was a possibility of HPAW killing me, he'd warn me. I know he would.

"I no longer want you as a mate," Caleb continues. "But I'm not going to hand you over to HPAW to be tortured for information and murdered. I'll tell my people you were unfaithful. It will explain your dead mark. You'll be permitted to remain within the pack lands, but I want nothing to do with you. If I hear even a *whisper* of you conspiring against us, I'll have your throat torn out, ex-mate or not."

My dead mark?

I rip my hands out from underneath my thighs.

My mark is black as night, not a hint of color left. The once-sharp edges are now fuzzy and blown out, the design distorted and almost unrecognizable. I swallow, my throat dry. Our bond is dead.

"I saw you kill those men," I whisper. "Your *shipment*. You spit in that human boy's face, then snapped his neck. You killed all of them. I saw it."

Caleb nods. "I did. Those men kidnapped, tortured, and murdered a twelve-year-old girl."

What? I open my mouth, then snap it shut. Is that true?

"Would you like to read the autopsy report?" Caleb continues. "We also have video footage, if the report isn't enough for you. Human men love to harm young female shifters. Prepubescent shifters are weak, and humans take advantage of that. We had been looking for those men for months."

I squeeze my eyes shut, a headache forming at my temples. Even if what Caleb says is true, it doesn't change anything. This is only one example of many.

"The shifters claimed the entirety of fucking Canada during the exodus," I tell him, "displacing millions of humans. You *continue* taking land, pushing farther and farther south. You wish to enslave us."

Caleb blinks, cocking his head to the side. Then he laughs. "Is that what the American government is telling you now? It can't be said that you people aren't creative."

"What's that supposed to mean?"

"Why should I bother trying to explain anything to you?" Caleb asks. "You've made your judgement, and you won't believe a word I say. I won't waste my time."

I stare at my mark for a moment longer, then tuck my hands back underneath my thighs. I don't care to see it.

"Explain it to me," I say. "You're suggesting that HPAW is lying, so tell me the truth."

I'm eager to see how Caleb defends generations of murder and abuse. I've seen the photographs and read the reports. Men, women, and children torn to shreds in their homes. They had been innocent, murdered solely because they'd had the misfortune of living too close to the border.

Caleb twists his fists around the steering wheel, his knuckles turning white. "We didn't displace millions of humans, Evelyn. Most of Canada was already shifter territory. We just legitimized it. The shifters who happened to be living outside the borders chose to come, and it was pure coincidence that so many came from the States. It wasn't some orchestrated attack, and we didn't force anybody out of their homes."

"Millions of Canadian human refugees came to the States

after the shifters took over. There were massacres. You killed the humans who were too slow to leave."

Caleb shoots me a sideways glance. "I don't know how to respond to that. That's simply not true. Several million humans were living within Canada when we legitimized ourselves, and most chose to stay."

"Where are they now?"

"Gone." Caleb shrugs. "Shifters are loyal to their mates, and most humans born without a marking choose to leave. They aspire to have families, which they can't do here."

What Caleb is saying is wildly different from HPAW's teachings. Somebody is lying to me. If Caleb is to be believed, that means HPAW has entirely rewritten history. How is that even possible to do at such a large scale? The people who were alive during that time would have shared their stories. People would notice the discrepancies. There would be questions.

"Your government doesn't like us because we're stronger than they are," Caleb says. "Most of your intelligent, influential leaders were shifters, and we took a great deal of information and power with us. HPAW is terrified we'll use it against them."

"Do you plan to?"

"No." Caleb shakes his head. "We have no interest in taking your land or killing your people. Honestly, we just want to be left the fuck alone."

"Humans who live near the border are frequently murdered," I say. "I've seen the images and read the reports."

Caleb shrugs. "It's not us. Either the images and reports are fake, or the human government is committing the murders and blaming us."

"Why would they do that?" They would never. It's a horrifying thought.

"Because humans are selfish, irrational, and fearful creatures." He looks into my eyes as he spits his insults, making me painfully aware that they're also aimed at me. "Shifters maintain good relations with other countries. We have extensive and robust trade agreements, as well as powerful alliances. America hates that. They thought themselves on top of the political food chain before the exodus, and they can't handle the loss of power."

Caleb pinches the bridge of his nose. "Do you think HPAW truly gives a shit if you live or die? They look at you and see a means to an end—a way to finally get their revenge and prove they're big and scary."

I don't know what to say. I don't even know if I believe him. I'm not sure if I *want* to.

If Caleb's telling the truth, it means my entire life, and everything I've ever been told, is a lie. HPAW insists the shifters terrorize the borders, forcing themselves onto our land in violent attempts to take us over. They say the shifters intend to enslave us, to take over our government and use us for cheap labor.

"A black mark frees me from the burden of you," Caleb says, changing the subject. "I'll tell the pack that I caught you in bed with another man. An American human. It'll explain why you snuck out of the shifter lands. They'll understand why I can't send you back. You know too much, and the humans will torture you for information. I suggest you keep quiet about having tried to murder me."

With a flick of his wrist, the radio is turned on.

I open my mouth to speak. Caleb turns the radio louder. It must be hurting his ears. My heart thumps, and I slowly shut my mouth before directing my attention out the windshield.

Chapter Twenty-Three

The remainder of the ride is spent in silence. I try several times to speak, but Caleb turns the volume up before any words find their way out of my mouth. By the time we pull into the winding driveway leading to his home, the music is so loud, my teeth are vibrating.

Sash is sitting on the front porch in nothing more than an oversized T-shirt and a pair of men's socks. Upon closer inspection, I realize both items belong to Caleb. She must have run here in her wolf form, and my clothes are too small for her.

She jumps to her feet as we make our way up the driveway, and Logan steps out of the doorway behind her. He's also wearing Caleb's clothing.

I pull my hands out from underneath my thighs, taking another glance at my mark. What am I supposed to do now? I failed HPAW, and Caleb is done with me. I was raised to believe my purpose in life was to infiltrate the shifter pack and kill Caleb.

I have no education, no hobbies, nothing to fall back on. I don't even have a family.

"I—" I ignore Caleb's death glare as I turn down the music. "HPAW told me that shifters killed my parents. I was an orphan, and they said they were going to protect me from you." My voice cracks. I clear my throat, then continue. "Is that not true?"

Caleb parks the car in the usual spot. He taps his fingers against the wheel, seemingly contemplating my question. My heart is pounding, which I'm sure he can hear.

"I'll look into it," he finally says. "You can consider this my final kindness. Don't ask me for anything else."

He steps out of the car, the door slamming shut behind him.

Sash runs to him, her body a blur until she crashes into his chest. Her mouth is moving, her eyebrows furrowed and lips pursed. Caleb says something to her, and her sharp gaze cuts in my direction. Pure hatred shines in her brown eyes, but it shifts into pain as she turns back to Caleb.

He shakes his head at something she says, then jerks his head toward the road.

She hesitates, but then she and Logan silently pull off their clothes, transform into their wolf forms, and disappear. Caleb walks inside his house, not once looking back at the car.

I remain where I am. The car gradually grows cold, and eventually, I have no choice but to follow Caleb inside. He's nowhere to be seen, but I hear him stomping around upstairs.

I clench and unclench my fists, hesitating, before tiptoeing up the stairs. They're splattered with blood.

The primary bedroom door is open. I rock back on my heels as I stare at a bloodied handprint wrapping around the door frame, then continue moving. There's so much blood. There's no way Sash and Logan will fall for the cheating lie, not if they saw this.

The bedsheets are soaked through, and the floor is covered. I wrap my arms around my waist, hugging myself as I notice the handprint on the end table. It's smeared, dragging toward the wall.

Caleb was struggling to stand.

He's now beside the closet door, his chest heaving as he stares at the bloody bedsheets. He refuses to look in my direction.

"I'm sorry," I whisper.

His entire body stiffens. "You aren't."

He rips open the closet door and begins grabbing my things. I step aside, moving out of his way as he carries them into the guest bedroom down the hall.

"I'll have an apartment in town prepared for you," he says as he returns, barely sparing me a glance. "You'll stay in the guest room until it's ready."

I clear my throat. "Okay."

It takes Caleb several trips to empty my side of the closet, and almost three for him to bring my toiletries and bathroom luxuries to the hallway bathroom.

He doesn't need to tell me that's the one I'll be using from now on.

I've gotten the hint.

I wring my hands before realizing the movement makes the dried blood on my palms flake. Disgusting. My lip curls as I look down, watching blood specks fall onto the floor.

Caleb rips the sheets off the bed.

He grunts. "You can leave now."

His eyes are dark and void of emotion. Still, I search his expression for something—anything. I find nothing, and after a tense few seconds, I leave. The door slams shut behind me.

I choke up as I step into the spare bedroom, but I refuse to let things go any further than that. I don't cry. My things have been thrown haphazardly on the unmade bed, forming a large, messy pile. I collapse into the chair beside the dresser.

What am I supposed to do now?

I lick my thumb and wipe at my mark, secretly hoping it only looks so dark because there's dirt on my hand. The dirt wipes away. The mark remains the same. Panic floods my system, and I start using my nail instead.

I scratch my skin until it's red and raw. The hazy blackness never changes.

The guest bedroom door bursts open just as my skin begins to bleed. Caleb is freshly cleaned and dressed, his hair still wet. How long have I been sitting here? His gaze travels to my hand, to where I'm frantically scratching at my mark.

"I recommend having the skin removed at the hospital," he says. "Your method will only introduce bacteria. I'd rather you not die of an infection on my watch."

I shake my head. "I'm not trying to remove my mark. I'm—"

"I don't really care," he says, interrupting. "I'm leaving, and I recommend you be on your best behavior while I'm gone. The house is being monitored, and I assume Sash has been efficient in my order to inform the shifters of your infidelity and our dead bond."

What about the blood she clearly saw? She and Logan were wearing Caleb's clothing, so they must have come up here. Caleb probably told her the truth. She's his sister, after all.

Caleb licks his lips, aimlessly glancing around the room. He's acting as if this conversation bores him, as if he's so completely done with me that he can't even be bothered to be in the same room with me.

It's a lie. I know it's a lie.

"The shifters have been alerted that you're a flight risk. If you step foot outside of this house, they have orders to bring you back with whatever means necessary. I wouldn't expect them to be gentle."

I snort. "I wasn't."

Caleb raises a brow, finally giving me his full attention. "What's that supposed to mean?"

"I've seen the way you treat one another."

"Explain."

I shrug. "That first time you brought me to your office. We drove past those two wolves attacking that young man. He was in his skin form, and they were circling him and biting his legs. They tore out his calf."

"Are you talking about the Dawson brothers?" Caleb barks out a laugh. "They were playing, Evelyn. The Dawson brothers are adolescents, still new to their wolf forms. The one in his skin form has trouble shifting. The other two were trying to provoke his wolf side to emerge."

"They tore out his fucking calf," I repeat.

"Of course they did. Shifters heal quickly." Caleb gestures to his throat, showing his already healed skin. "Pain is what draws out his wolf. If a shifter doesn't learn how to transition at will, he'll lose himself. He'll spend his entire life feeling trapped in his own body. His brothers love him. They're willing to do what it takes to help."

I fall silent.

"Why didn't you tell me?" I ask.

"Why would I?" Caleb runs his hands through his hair. "I don't know what you do and don't know about shifters, and I wasn't going to treat my mate as if she were stupid. I figured if you didn't understand something, you'd trust me enough to ask. *Clearly,* I was wrong."

Caleb leaves. His heavy footsteps fade as he heads downstairs, and the front door slams shut a minute later. Where is he going? Probably to work.

I suppose I should shower.

My movements are mechanical as I grab a change of clothes and head into the hallway bathroom. It's smaller than the one Caleb and I shared, but I refuse to torture myself by dwelling on the change. I strip out of Caleb's shirt.

Will he ask for it back? Probably not.

What should I do about HPAW? What should I do about myself? I doubt I'll be given another chance to escape, and even if I am, I'm not sure I want to take it. What are the odds that Caleb is telling me the truth? If HPAW has been lying this entire time, there's no telling where their limits are.

What if *he's* lying, though? Would he lie about that? Would HPAW? My mind is reeling, and I don't know who to believe. I'm just a pawn. I've always been just a pawn.

The shower is scalding, and I stand underneath the spray until my skin loses feeling. The burn doesn't make me feel any better, and I mindlessly clean myself before getting out and getting dressed.

I need to talk to Caleb. I need to understand.

If what he says is true… I can't fathom that thought. What if he is truly good? What if he truly trusted and loved me, and I destroyed it all for a lie? Have I just betrayed the only person who has ever been truthful to me?

I clutch at my chest.

Should I expect to live within the Knox pack until I grow old and die? What will Caleb do? Will he return to his original plan to marry Grace? My lungs constrict. Will I be forced to watch them grow a family? Will I see their children running around town?

That sounds like perfect torture—forced to watch Caleb grow his family and live a long, fulfilling life while I wither away in some sad apartment. I doubt I'll ever even make a friend. The shifters will hate me when they're told I was unfaithful to Caleb.

They treasure their bonds, and their alpha. They'll never forgive me.

I eye my blackened mark. Can a mark lighten? If what Caleb says is true and I can prove I'm loyal by lightening my mark, will he be open to forgiving me? I doubt it. I slit his fucking throat.

I head downstairs, painfully aware the house is being monitored. The car keys are missing, and when I peek out the front door, a wolf I don't recognize is lying on the porch. It straightens up, its brown eyes narrowing as it shifts into a threatening crouch.

I retreat inside.

There's another wolf in the backyard.

Unsure of what else to do and desperate for some sense of normalcy, I start cleaning. Tidying is mindless, and it offers the distraction I'm craving. It takes hours to clean all the blood, and my arms ache from the scrubbing, but I don't stop.

HPAW threatens to fill my mind, but I push those thoughts aside. I don't have the mental capacity to process all that's happened today.

Caleb doesn't come home at his usual time. Eventually, the sky grows dark and I can't find anything left to clean. I sit on the couch, staring blankly at the front door.

I was convinced that either I would kill Caleb or I would die. There was no alternative where we both survive, and there especially wasn't an alternative where he discovers I'm a part of HPAW and decides to keep me captive in his pack. Why didn't he just kill me?

It's probably the mate bond. Caleb may not want to be with me, but that doesn't necessarily mean he wants me dead. I suppose that should make me feel good, but it doesn't.

I've always had a concrete goal to structure my life toward, and I'm useless without one.

I jolt as the front door bursts open. Caleb stumbles inside, unsteady on his feet as he barrels into the foyer. Sash and Logan are behind him, each one holding an arm.

Is Caleb drunk? He can barely stand, and he laughs maniacally as Logan practically carries him up the stairs. Caleb doesn't once look at me.

Sash lingers at the bottom of the stairs, watching the two ascend. She's on me the minute they're out of sight. My head snaps to the side, her slap so intense, my teeth rattle and an immediate headache blooms in my temples.

"You're a fucking cunt, Evelyn," she hisses, "and if I had my way, you'd be dead."

My mouth is open, but I have nothing to say. My head aches, and it takes everything in me not to cradle my burning cheek. I deserved that slap, and I wonder if she did it because she believes I cheated on Caleb or because she knows I tried to kill him.

"I hope you enjoy the pain you'll feel when my brother fucks his new mate," she continues.

I take a step back. What is she talking about?

Sash must recognize my confusion as she smiles, her face alight with glee. "You don't know, do you?" Her smile grows. "You killed the bond, so Caleb is free to take a wife." She grabs my hand, ripping it toward her. I flinch as she trails her finger over my blackened mark. "Your side is dead, so he won't feel anything, but Caleb has been faithful to you. His mark remains white, so you'll feel *everything*."

"Let her go." Logan descends the stairs, taking two at a time as he eyes my contact with Sash. His gaze travels to my cheek, lingering on the burning skin where Sash struck me. "Knox gave you explicit orders not to harm her. Did you hit her?"

Sash releases me, stepping back. "No, of course not." Her stern gaze settles on me. "Did I hit you, Evelyn?"

I swallow, my throat dry, before shaking my head. "No, you didn't."

"See?"

Logan hums, grabbing Sash by the elbow and pulling her outside. The front door slams shut behind them, and I sink to the floor. I'm exhausted.

Chapter Twenty-Four

Caleb is clanking around upstairs. He's loud in his steps and, I'm assuming, stumbles.

I rub my burning cheek, resisting the urge to slam my head against the wall behind me. What the fuck has my life become? I didn't sign up for this.

A particularly loud bang has me clambering to my feet and heading upstairs, worry lacing my movements. I've never seen Caleb drink, not to the excess he has tonight. I'm surprised Sash and Logan chose to leave him alone with me in his current state, but I suppose they don't consider me to be much of a threat.

Caleb won't allow himself to be vulnerable around me ever again, and I don't realistically stand a chance in a fight against him. Even drunk, he could kill me with ease.

There's another loud *thud*, the sound followed up almost immediately by a low groan. I quicken my pace. Did Caleb fall? How much did he have to drink?

"Evelyn!"

My movements falter as he calls out my name. Why?

"Come here!"

He sounds excited, which I'm not going to take as a good sign. Occasionally, on holidays and during special celebrations, the younger HPAW soldiers would find their way to my bedroom after too many drinks.

I'm the only marked woman—at least, the only one I know of—who lives within the facility, and men occasionally took that to mean I'd be an easy lay. I turned most of them away.

I never felt guilty for the ones I welcomed into my room, though. If anything, I enjoyed it. I liked knowing I was giving away something the shifters valued. I didn't know Caleb, but I was eager to hurt him. I never considered that Caleb would be a virgin, but I did expect his experience to be limited.

Should I tell him I wasn't lying when I said I loved him? Probably not. He won't believe me. I don't really blame him. I wouldn't believe me, either.

Caleb is swaying in the hallway beside his office door. He leans against the wall for balance, his fingers curling around the wooden door frame.

His mark is still white. Will it change now that I've destroyed our bond? Will it disappear? I could ask, but it would be a waste of breath. He isn't going to answer.

Sash's words seep into my mind. Is Caleb really going to take a new mate? Will he fuck her? He assured me he had no plans of doing so with Grace, but that decision had been made out of respect for the mate he'd never met. The situations aren't the same.

The thought of Caleb with another woman makes my stomach churn. I hate it.

"Come on, now." Caleb jerks his chin toward his office. "I want to show you something."

He's smiling, but it lacks emotion. His eyes are empty, void of the mirth and glint of excitement they usually reflect. I don't trust it, but I follow his direction and walk into his office.

He leads me to his desk, forcing me to sit in the chair.

Then he stands behind me, leaning over my shoulder. His breath reeks of whiskey, and I grimace as he turns on his computer and begins sifting through his files. I've never been given the password to his home computer, and my eyes flicker over the hundreds of files stored here.

Caleb opens a folder. There's a video and a text file inside.

"You're welcome to watch the video, but I don't recommend it," he says.

"What is it?"

I can feel the weight of Caleb's gaze on the side of my head. "Those men you saw me kill, it's a video recording they took of them torturing and murdering the little girl they kidnapped. It's graphic. I needed to search the video for clues, and it took me hours to get through." He pauses, then clears his throat. "There have been several over the years, but this is the worst. I should have taken the time to torture those men as they did Emilie, but..." He blows out a breath, whiskey hitting my face. "I don't know why I didn't. I just wanted it to be over."

Caleb shakes his head, then opens the text file. "This is the case file. Read it." He's sauntering out of the room a moment later. As he exits, he raises a hand and smacks the top of the doorway. He's still drunk. "Let me know when you're done. I have more to show you."

I swallow, then begin reading the file. It's worse than I imagined. Caleb noted in detail the torture those men inflicted on the young shifter girl. They were experimenting on her, trying to test her shifter capabilities and limits.

There are a few rumors surrounding HPAW's treatment of the occasional shifter they manage to obtain. I've never seen them torture anybody firsthand, but I'm sure their methods aren't friendly. Still, I know with absolute certainty that they'd never do this to a child. There's no way the American government would sanction it.

My eyes are burning as I finish the report. My deep-seated distrust has me clicking on the video next. I make it less than two minutes in before frantically clicking out. Caleb wasn't lying.

I wipe at my eyes as he returns to the room, lingering in the doorway.

"Would you have let those humans live?" he asks. "Granted them mercy?"

I shake my head. "No."

Caleb pulls up another video. His hand falls to my shoulder, but he quickly removes it.

"One of my men was sent to the HPAW headquarters on a diplomatic mission three years ago," Caleb says. "He was a messenger. Nothing more. He never returned, and this is what I received two weeks later."

He begins the video and strolls out of the room. I shift my focus to the screen. My heart stops. I recognize this shifter.

It was brief. Daniel was escorting me back to my room, but I convinced him to let us take a detour to the second-floor cafeteria. It's a heavily restricted floor where the medical team works, but this particular cafeteria has the chocolate-chip cookies I enjoy.

Several soldiers were bringing a shifter to the medical team for testing. It had been years since HPAW had last captured a shifter, and even longer since that shifter had been brought to our particular facility.

Daniel tried to usher me away the moment he realized what was happening, but it was too late. I caught a glimpse of the shifter. He was heavily drugged and strapped to a metal gurney. His hair was freshly buzzed, and his lower half was covered in a thin, white sheet. I distinctly remember thinking he didn't look *that* frightening. He was so tall that his ankles dangled off the end of the gurney, and his upper body was covered in rippling muscle, but he was limp and unconscious.

Daniel later told me that the shifter had been captured during an attack on one of our smaller towns near the border. He said the wolves had infiltrated our lands in the middle of the night and struck in the early hours of the morning. Hundreds of humans had been murdered—innocent families torn to shreds.

It was all over the news. I saw the images and heard stories from the few survivors. Did HPAW make it up? How? A lie at that scale would be impossible to cover. Surely, somebody would speak out about the inaccuracies.

Did Daniel know? Was he lying to me, or did he believe the stories he was being told?

Our medical team put the shifter under and used him for testing. We needed to gain a better understanding of shifter anatomy and their physical tolerances.

This man on the screen is not under anesthesia. He's wide awake, and he screams and writhes as he tries to break free of his restraints. They're metal and cemented into the ground. He's not going anywhere.

The medical team remove the sheet covering his lower half.

They begin with simple slices, their voices quiet as they give out numbers and figures for recording. They monitor how long it takes him to heal before inflicting more wounds. Things progressively get worse. I look away when they start testing regeneration.

"Watch," Caleb orders.

He's standing in the doorway, silently monitoring my movements. I didn't notice his approach.

I shake my head. "I don't want to."

He's on me in a second, his fingers pinching my chin and forcing me to look. The medical team saws off the shifter's leg.

"I didn't know," I say, trying to break free from Caleb's rough, borderline-painful grip. "Please, I'm sorry. I didn't know."

Caleb refuses to release me. He holds my head steady as the man in the video continues to scream and plead. He says that he has a family. He says his mate and children are waiting for him at home. He says he's a good man and doesn't mean any harm. He's here on a diplomatic mission. The shifters want to find common ground.

The medical team ignores him. Some even laugh. Only one woman looks hesitant, her gaze filled with guilt as she glances between her hands and the shifter. It's noticed, and she's excused from the procedure.

"I was sent this video, along with three others," Caleb says. "They kept him alive for weeks."

Word spread when the shifter died. The medical team wanted to determine how quickly shifters recover from mercury injections. Something about their kidneys. One of the doctors injected too much, and the shifter died instantly. The doctor lost her job.

I wonder now if it was a mercy kill.

Caleb pulls away from the video, then opens another file. "We don't correspond much with the American government, but here's everything dating back ten years. We've tried to find common ground with HPAW, but they refuse to accept any terms—even those most favorable to them. They want us to submit entirely and reacclimate into your society and government. They want to control us."

I drag a hand down my face. "Why didn't you tell me this before?"

Caleb barks out a laugh. "Why didn't I tell my nervous human mate how atrocious her kind are? How much we fucking hate Americans? I wanted you to acclimate, Evelyn. I wanted you to feel comfortable around us. I wasn't going to insult your kind or speak poorly about them. I would never lie, but I wasn't going to say anything unless you explicitly asked. I figured you would eventually. It's called having patience."

Caleb scratches at his chin. He shaves daily, but he didn't this morning. I assume that slitting his throat threw a wrench into his daily ritual.

It's hard to believe that was just this morning.

I look through the files Caleb pulled up, reading about every bit of contact the shifters and HPAW have had within the last decade. There isn't much, and what I see has my blood boiling. Caleb isn't lying—not about a single damned thing.

Caleb stands behind me, silently reading over my shoulder.

The silence grows deafening, and every report adds to the weight in my chest. I gnaw at my bottom lip, continuing even when it hurts. What have I done? There's no fixing this. I've thrown away everything over lies.

"I'm so sorry," I whisper. "I had no idea. I thought... I didn't know."

Caleb takes a moment to respond. He absentmindedly slides his thumb over the faint scar on his neck. "You asked me to cum inside you."

I look at my hands.

"You took everything I held special. You took it knowing how much it meant to me and how little it meant to you," he continues. "You're selfish, and now I have nothing. If you're pregnant..." Caleb pauses. I can practically *feel* the tension oozing off him. "If you'd succeeded in killing me and everything went according to your plan, what would you have done with my baby?"

I dip my chin, too ashamed to answer. I wasn't thinking clearly.

"Answer me," he demands.

"I wouldn't have kept it."

"Adoption?"

I shake my head, my breath hitching. HPAW would never let me give birth to a shifter, especially not one fathered by Alpha Knox. It would be a liability.

"Say it."

"I don't want to."

"Say it, Evelyn."

"I would've had an abortion."

Caleb storms from the room, slamming the door shut behind him. I drop my head into my hands, my thoughts splintering. What the fuck am I doing?

Chapter Twenty-Five

I can't move.

My feet are bound, and my arms are tied behind my back. Rope bites into my skin, drawing blood. I wiggle my wrists, testing my range of motion. There's not much.

Laughter surrounds me, but I can't see who it comes from. The room is too dark.

A hand wraps around my ankle. I scream.

More laughter. "She's a fighter, isn't she?"

My body grows cold. I know that voice. I know that line.

There are five men. No amount of screaming and begging makes them stop. When they begin tugging off my clothes, I'm suddenly blinded by a bright light.

The masked faces of HPAW's doctors loom above me. Three of them stand beside my naked body, and a fourth tightens metal restraints around my wrists. Where am I? What are they doing?

They bring a scalpel to my skin. I scream again. Why are they doing this to me? Every cut is pure agony, and tears stream down my cheeks as they speak to a camera about my healing rate.

They joke amongst themselves, but they never once look directly at me.

I don't heal. I'm not a shifter. The doctors don't seem to notice *or care as they bring out larger and larger blades. Two grab my thigh, holding it steady. Then I notice the saw.*

No. No. No.

I scream and slap at the hands on my shoulders, desperate to get away. They're going to cut off my leg. The room is dark, limiting my sight, but I don't let it stop me as I crane my neck and bite at the person holding me down.

They move before I make contact.

"Evelyn!"

"No!"

A lamp is turned on. I realize I'm in the guest room bedroom, the sheets tangled around my ankles and the oversized shirt I threw on before bed twisted around my torso.

Caleb is above me, still holding my shoulders. He releases me as the fight leaves my body, my mind finally coming to terms with reality. It was just a dream. I was dreaming about the videos of the young girl and the man the shifters sent to speak with HPAW.

"Fucking hell, Evelyn."

Caleb runs his hands through his hair. His eyes are bloodshot, no longer holding the glaze of alcohol. They rake down my frame, a quick scan, before returning to my face. He drops into the chair pushed against the wall.

I sit up, taking notice of his current state of undress. He's naked. I must've been making noises in my sleep, enough to cause alarm. He probably ran in here the moment he woke up and heard me.

"I shouldn't have made you watch those videos," Caleb says, breaking the silence. "I'm sorry."

I glance at the bedside clock. It's two in the morning.

"I wouldn't have believed it if I didn't see it for myself," I admit.

A small part of me would've always doubted. It's hard to

accept that everything you've been raised to believe is a lie. I'm still processing, but I believe what Caleb says is true.

I was a fool to believe HPAW. I've been living among the shifters for weeks, and I saw how kind they were to one another. I never allowed myself to consider the possibility that the shifters were truly good people, and I over-anchored on the few confusing encounters I saw. I was searching for reasons to distrust Caleb.

"Are you okay?" Caleb asks.

I nod instinctively, then decide to be truthful and shake my head. Keeping secrets hasn't gotten me very far.

"I'm far from okay, Caleb," I admit.

He snorts. "You and me both."

We make eye contact. It feels…tentative.

"Can we work through this?" My voice cracks. "If I could take it all back, I would. I don't… Can we start over?"

Caleb shakes his head. "No, Evelyn. It's too late."

I refuse to believe it. I climb out of bed, an intoxicating mixture of adrenaline and desperation coursing through my system. Caleb watches through his lashes as I drop to my knees before him, but he doesn't brush me away as I plant my hands on his thighs and slot myself between them.

"Please," I plead. "Give me a chance to fix this."

I don't beg, but I'll do it a thousand times over for Caleb. I'm in the wrong, and I fully acknowledge that. He's been nothing but good to me. He's been a loving mate who's never asked for more than I was willing to give. I responded by refusing to give him the benefit of the doubt and slitting his throat.

Caleb's breath smells of mint, the whiskey gone.

"Please," I repeat.

I slide my hands up Caleb's thighs, the muscle tensing beneath my palms. He looks to be in pain, the skin between his eyebrows crinkled and his lips flattened into a straight line. His eyes squeeze shut as I rub my cheek against his thigh.

I doubt he'll let me rub my cheek against his, and I hope he understands what I'm trying to do. I'm apologizing in the way I know is most meaningful to his kind.

Caleb doesn't respond the way I'm expecting.

He's naked, and my face is admittedly close to his privates, but this isn't an attempt at seduction. Still, his body responds.

I hesitate, my emotions torn. Caleb feels used, and I don't want to aggravate that further, but he's aroused about two inches from my face. I make eye contact with Caleb, giving him ample time to stop me, before taking hold of him.

He hisses, his hips jerking.

"I've never had a man in my mouth," I admit.

It's not something I've ever had much interest in. I'm not actively against giving a man oral, but I have a weak gag reflex and I don't like how submissive the action feels. Caleb peers down at me, his gaze heavy, before gently wrapping a hand around the back of my head.

"You own my mouth, Caleb," I say. "Take from me. Be selfish. Please."

Caleb exhales a quiet curse. "Fuck, Evelyn." He rubs a thumb underneath my eyes, wiping away a stray tear, before sliding the digit to my lips. I open my mouth, letting him ease his thumb between my teeth. He presses down on my tongue.

I breathe evenly through my nose, willing myself not to gag.

Thankfully, Caleb's thumb tastes like nothing more than clean skin. He must have showered before bed.

"I'm not going to make love to you," he warns.

My words are muffled as I speak around his thumb. "I don't expect you to."

His throat bobs, his expression darkening as he replaces his thumb with his cock. My eyes spring open as he feeds me his length, inch after inch sliding into my mouth.

I gag almost immediately. Caleb doesn't stop.

He continues until he hits the back of my throat. I try my best to breathe through it, wanting to make this good for him. Judging by his possessive, heady stare, it is. He cups the back of my head again, guiding me up and down.

I dig my fingers into his thighs, trying to take him deeper. I want to make this as good as possible, continuing even when my jaw grows sore and drool begins to run down my chin.

"You're such a fucking whore for me." Caleb grunts, pulling out of my mouth. "Say it."

My face is blazing red as I stare at him with swollen, spit-covered lips. "I'm your whore."

Caleb shakes his head, his nose crinkling. "You're not *my* whore. You're *a* whore, for me."

"I'm both."

Caleb's cock twitches, his physical reaction to my words speaking volumes. He can say whatever he wants, but he likes my insistence on being his.

"I've imagined how it would feel to have your mouth on me," he says, his hips jerking. I gasp, choking as he hits the back of my throat. "I just always thought you'd be doing it as my mate."

His words sting, but I suspect he meant them to.

Caleb's angry, and I can't blame him. He curls his fingers into the hair at the base of my neck, holding me captive. My jaw muscles burn, and tears leak from the corners of my eyes as he fucks my mouth.

He finishes with a low moan, his cum filling my mouth in spurts. I swallow around him, taking as much as I can. I feared I wouldn't like the taste, but it's not bad.

Caleb releases me, and I wipe my mouth as I sit back on my heels.

"Was that okay?" I ask. My voice is hoarse.

Caleb's hands twitch by his sides, his fingers tapping rapidly against his thighs.

"Caleb?" I repeat.

His entire body seems to deflate. "I'm tired," he whispers. He steps away from me, his movements uncharacteristically clunky. "This doesn't change anything, Evelyn. You're not my mate, and you're still moving out tomorrow. I made the arrangements today. I'll cover your rent and expenses until you're back on your feet."

I'm still processing his words as he leaves, the bedroom door clicking shut quietly behind him. An apartment. Tomorrow. He told me he was planning this, but there was so much else happening that I didn't have time to really sit with the information.

I'm sure sitting with it now. It rests on my tongue, bitter and impossible to spit out.

Chapter Twenty-Six

My eyes are swollen when I wake the next morning. I spend several minutes staring at the ceiling, working up the courage to climb out of bed. I'm not sure what time it is, but I can tell it's early.

Caleb moves about the house. He's silent, but an occasional floorboard creaks and gives away his movements. His feet thump against the wooden steps as he heads downstairs.

I've been brainwashed.

I doubt the shifters were responsible for my parents' deaths, if they're even dead. Maybe HPAW killed them, or maybe they lied to me about everything. Caleb said he'd look into it, and I hope he finds answers. I don't remember my family much, but I want to know what happened to them. Were they punished for hiding a marked child? They must've known who my mate was. The image of Caleb's mark was plastered everywhere.

I force myself out of bed and into a fresh change of clothes, then follow Caleb downstairs. He's sitting at the kitchen counter, a steaming mug clutched within his palms. He doesn't look up as I enter the room, but his body tenses just slightly.

"HPAW found me when I was seven," I start. "They're all I've ever known."

Caleb said his piece, but now it's my turn. I'll never forgive myself if I don't tell him the entire truth. It's humiliating to admit I was fooled, but I'm willing to sacrifice my pride if it means finding common ground with Caleb.

"I saw the photograph of your mark and knew I was your mate. I snuck out of my home, hopped on a bus, and traveled into the shifter lands. The borders weren't well patrolled back then..." I clear my throat, then continue. "I thought the idea of having a mate was romantic, and I went searching for you. I thought if I ran into a shifter and showed them my mark, they'd direct me to you."

Caleb straightens up. "They likely would have."

"I ran into HPAW's border control instead."

If Caleb is going to leave me, he's going to do so having all the facts.

"They brought me to their headquarters and questioned me," I continue. "It went on for hours, and eventually, they came in and told me that my parents went into the shifter lands searching for me. They said my parents were mauled to death and I was now an orphan."

I can't help but laugh. Saying it now, it all sounds so stupid. They were manipulating me, but I was a child. As I grew older, I became so entrenched in their beliefs that it never occurred to me to question them.

I draw in a breath. "I lived in an HPAW facility for over fifteen years. I was exposed to the content and education they approved. I was told so many gruesome, horrific things about you and the shifters, and I truly believed the only way to save my people was to kill you."

Caleb stares into his mug, silent.

"You'd sacrifice me if it meant saving the shifters, wouldn't you?" I ask. Caleb doesn't answer, so I continue. "You would. You'd have no choice. You're the alpha, and we both know you couldn't spare my life at the detriment of theirs. It wouldn't be right."

Caleb still doesn't look up.

"I thought I was saving the humans, Caleb. I love you. That wasn't a lie, but I was doing what I thought I had to do. This was never about what I wanted. This was about duty. I had a duty to the humans, and I couldn't let one person stand in the way of that."

"You didn't ask," Caleb says after a drawn-out silence. "All you had to do was ask, Evelyn. If you truly loved me, you would've asked. You would've given me the benefit of the doubt. You would've at least let yourself consider the possibility that I wasn't the monster HPAW made me out to be."

"But..."

"Besides," Caleb continues. He gestures to my blackened, fuzzy mark. "It's too late. Our bond is dead."

I can't believe this. "What's your plan, then? You pick another woman? You fuck and have a family with her while I'm forced to sit back and watch?"

"I won't deny you a good life," Caleb says, shrugging. "I've spread word that you were unfaithful. It will take the shifters a while to see past that, but they will with time. Males who have lost their mate will approach you, and I won't stand in their way."

His frown deepens. "I'd send you to live with another pack, but I can't in good faith do that, given your history with HPAW. I'd have to inform the other alpha, and I can't guarantee that they'd keep the information secret, or that they'd even accept you into their pack. Our children are vulnerable..."

He fears I'd hurt the children. I would *never*.

"It will take a while for my mark to blacken as yours has," Caleb says. "But it will with time. A dead bond can't be sustained. Once mine has blackened, we'll be entirely free of one another."

I resist the urge to scoff. "We'll never be free of one another, Caleb. I'm drawn to you. Every molecule of my body is tied to yours. I know you feel the pull, too."

Caleb cocks his head to the side. "I don't feel it. When your mark turned black, your end of the bond died. The sparks are gone. The pull to you is gone. You're no longer my mate."

No. That's simply not true.

"I don't want anybody else," I admit. "I can lighten my mark, can't I? If it can grow darker, surely, it can also grow lighter." I drag my hands down my face. "I want you to tell the truth about me. Tell your pack that I was a member of HPAW and tried to kill you. I'll earn their trust. I'll earn yours, too."

Caleb throws back the remainder of his drink, then rounds the table and crouches before me, bringing us eye level with one another.

"I don't want to be with you, Evelyn," he says. "I understand you were lied to, and I don't hold that against you, but that doesn't change things for me. I don't want to be with a woman who tried to kill me. I don't want to be with a woman who so greedily and selfishly took from me." Caleb brushes my hair out of my face, tucking a strand behind my ear. "You knowingly took everything I held dear and ruined it."

I step back, sinking into a dining chair.

"I'm doing you a kindness by lying about the true reason for our split," Caleb continues. "Many have lost loved ones to HPAW, and I won't subject you to that level of hatred."

He leaves for work, not casting me another glance or sparing me a single word. I remain in the dining room, still reeling from our conversation. I can't entirely blame him. I wouldn't want to be with a man who tried to murder me, or who slept with me knowing full well it meant different things to us both.

Several hours pass before the front door opens and Caleb returns. Two men are with him, Logan and another I don't recognize. He's young and slim, maybe in his late teens, but he looks like a carbon copy of Logan.

Are they related?

Neither of them looks in my direction as they head upstairs. Caleb hesitates in the doorway before making his way to me.

"Your apartment is in the center of town, near my office," he says. "It's a walkable location, so you should be able to get to everything you need."

My gaze travels to his hand, my heart pounding as I take in its new state. The crisp, white lines are now a light pink, the change subtle but most definitely there. Mine took years to darken, and I assumed Caleb's would be the same.

"How long will it take for it to turn black?" I ask.

Caleb shrugs. "A few months, maybe. I'm not sure. This isn't common among shifters."

I'm not surprised to hear that. They cherish their mates.

"And you'll take a new mate right away?" I'm asking questions I know will only hurt me, but I can't stop. I'm a glutton for punishment.

Caleb shifts his weight from one foot to the other. He looks uncomfortable with the topic. "I'll take a wife, not a mate," he finally says. "Shifters are only given one mate, and I'd never dishonor the sanctity of the mate bond by giving any other woman that title."

He still hasn't answered my question.

"And how long will you wait to take a wife?"

"I don't know." Caleb frowns. "I haven't thought about it. It's hard for shifters to conceive outside the mate bond, so I don't have the luxury of waiting. My children will likely have dominant wolves. It's not within the pack's best interest for me to postpone."

So, he'll be taking a wife immediately. I debate offering to carry his children, to serve his needs so he doesn't have to take a wife, but I refuse to stoop to that level. I may not have much dignity, but I have some.

Logan and the young shifter come downstairs with my clothes. They leave the front door open, and I watch as they throw everything into the back of Caleb's car. They're back a minute later, heading upstairs to get the remainder of my things.

"Come on." Caleb gestures for me to follow him.

I do without pause, my fight gone. I aimlessly slip on my

bright-orange coat and yank my hat over my head, then follow him onto the frigid front porch.

Caleb pulls a card out of his wallet. "Here." He hands it over. "Use this for whatever you need. Groceries. Furniture. It doesn't matter."

My hand shakes as I accept the credit card.

Logan and the shifter return with the last of my items.

"Do you want me to take her?" Logan asks Caleb.

Logan doesn't look in my direction, pointedly ignoring my existence. I'm sure he's not feeling any soft emotions toward me right now. He probably wants to rip my throat out, just as Sash does.

"I'll take her," Caleb says.

Logan frowns, his gaze briefly flashing toward me. He makes no attempts to hide his disgust as he looks me over, his lip curling and back stiffening. Caleb straightens up, and Logan silently averts his gaze.

"Are you sure?" Logan asks.

Caleb nods. "Yes."

Tension mounts between them before Logan submissively dips his chin and leaves, transforming into his wolf form and disappearing into the woods.

The walk to Caleb's car is painful, and the short drive to the apartment is even worse. It's indeed in the center of town, only two blocks over from his office.

The brick building looks cozy from the outside, three stories tall and covered in overgrown vines. The first floor houses a cute pottery studio, and Caleb leads me to a black-painted door to the right of the entrance. There's one small step leading to the door and a buzzer on the wall. I scan the names listed in the glass box until I find mine.

It's in Caleb's handwriting, and it looks like he wrote 'Ev' before changing his mind and writing out the full 'Evelyn.' The 'Ev' is centered and large, and the remainder of my name is small and squished.

I'm Apartment 3B.

Caleb pulls out a small keychain. It holds a fob and two individual keys.

"The smaller one is for the mailbox," he explains, waving the fob in front of the scanner above the door handle.

The door clicks as it unlocks, and warm air smacks me in the face as Caleb pushes the door open. It leads to a narrow hallway, with a staircase at the end. I wrap my arms around myself as I step inside.

Mailboxes are built into the wall on the right.

"There are four units in this building," Caleb says. "I've signed you up for a year lease and prepaid, so you shouldn't have to worry about rent. I figure a year is enough time for you to get yourself sorted."

Caleb follows me up the staircase. I'm winded by the time I reach the third floor. There are two doors, the one on the left labeled 3A and the one on the right 3B. Caleb unlocks my door and pushes it open.

I step inside.

The apartment is beautiful, an open-concept space with giant windows and hardwood floors. The kitchen is modern, and a sizable island opens to the main living area. It's already furnished. An oversized gray couch sits in the center of the living room facing a fireplace, complete with end tables and lamps.

A TV is mounted on the wall opposite the couch, with pictures strategically hanging around it. I step onto the plush rug covering most of the living room floor. The place is beautifully decorated, but I don't want to be here. I want to stay home with Caleb and pretend none of this ever happened. I want to go back to how things were.

There's a short hallway just past the kitchen. A door on the left opens to a bathroom, and I scan the walk-in shower and stocked shelves before turning and pushing open the door on the other side. It's a laundry room.

The bedroom is last. It's practically a duplicate of the room I shared with Caleb, the green bedding almost identical. A dresser and mirror sit across from the bed, and a set of doors leads to a small walk-in closet.

"I'll bring your things up," Caleb says.

"I'll help you."

He waves me away, rejecting the offer before retreating down the hallway and out the front door. I listen to it slam shut, and the second I know I'm alone, I sink to the ground. This isn't what I want.

I allow myself only ten seconds to wallow in self-pity before walking into the bathroom and splashing water on my face. My reflection in the mirror above the sink taunts me. I look like shit, my hair a mess and my cheeks splotchy. Logan probably got a kick out of seeing me look so pathetic.

Caleb returns with an armful of my belongings. He sets them on the floor just inside the apartment before disappearing again. I struggle not to panic when he makes his final trek.

"This phone works." He points to a landline hanging on the kitchen wall. There's a pad of paper on the counter beside it. "I've written my phone number there. Call if you're pregnant."

I wince.

Caleb continues. "I'm going to leave now."

I nod. "Okay." A brief pause, then, "I'm not the woman you think I am. I was selfish, but that's not who I am. There's more to me than you think."

I sound crazy—obsessive, even. I don't care. Shifters are territorial and possessive. They like crazy. Besides, I mean what I say. Caleb saw the worst possible side of me, but that's not who I am. I was playing a role, pretending to be somebody I'm not, and I'm going to prove that to him.

Caleb sighs. "All right, Evelyn."

He doesn't believe me, but I don't care. I refuse to be reduced to the role of HPAW's puppet. There's more to me than that. There has to be.

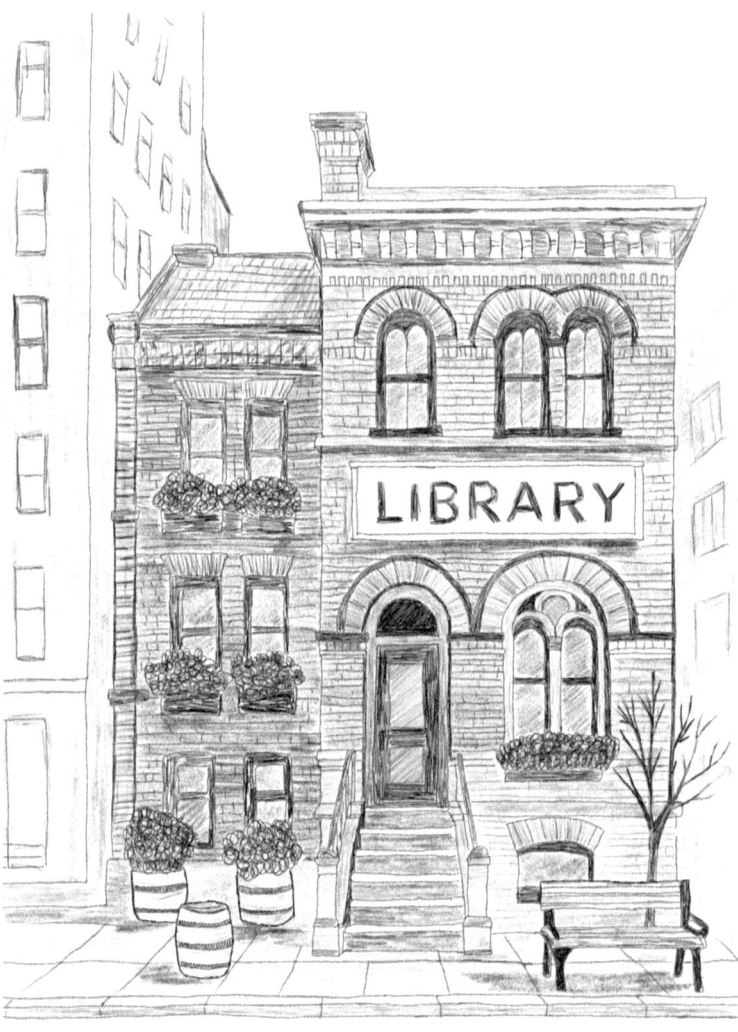

Chapter Twenty-Seven

Getting out of bed is a challenge. I lie in a ball under my sheets, unsure what to do with myself. I have no mission, nothing to do, and no fucking friends.

Caleb kept me busy, but without his distraction, I'm painfully aimless. HPAW made a fool of me. I made a fool of myself. There were so many times when I thought about telling Caleb the truth, about giving him the benefit of the doubt, and I regret never finding the courage to do so.

I drag my fingertips over my scarred knees. Had Caleb asked me about this scar, I would've told him it was earned while learning how to ride a bike. I don't even know how to ride a fucking bike. I got this scar when I was fourteen. I was sparring with a soldier—a blonde-haired, skinny boy who couldn't have been any older than nineteen. I landed a good hit, and he got angry. He shoved me to the ground from behind, and my bare knees took the brunt of the impact.

My fingers trail up my thighs. So many scars. So many lies.

I'm tired of lying. I'm tired of pretending to be somebody I'm not.

There's a public library in town. Caleb briefly mentioned it once, and Sash pointed it out when she gave me a tour. I'm sure there are books about shifters there—books that haven't been written by humans. It seems like a good place to start.

I was eager to learn about the shifters while with Caleb, but only in the context of what would be helpful for HPAW. I didn't waste my energy learning anything else, and I should've. It's not too late to do so. I might as well learn about the people I'm going to be spending the rest of my life around.

I force myself out of bed and into the kitchen. The pad of paper still sits beside the landline, Caleb's number scratched into the top sheet. My palms grow damp, and I wipe them on my pants before making the call.

Caleb answers on the third ring. "What?"

"I'd like to go to the library and read about shifters—about your culture and whatnot."

My request is met with silence.

I clear my throat. "Is that okay?"

"I don't care what you do," Caleb eventually says. "You don't need my permission to leave your apartment."

"I don't want you thinking I'm still working for HPAW," I admit.

Caleb huffs. "I don't care if you are. You're not getting anywhere near our borders. Learn all you want. It won't do you any good."

I'm not going to argue with him. Daniel used to use this expression, something about beating a dead horse. He refused to do it. I have no interest in it, either. Caleb doesn't trust me and begging him to isn't going to fix anything.

I draw in a breath, hold, and slowly release. *Be calm, Evelyn.*

"Okay. I won't bother you—"

Caleb interrupts me. "How do you plan to get there?"

"To the library?"

"Obviously."

"I'll walk."

"No," Caleb says. "I'll stop by and drop off my car. I have no use for it anymore." He only ever used it with me. "I'll have a tracker placed on it. If you veer off path, I'll know."

I bite my tongue. "I understand."

"I'll be there in an hour."

The line goes dead. I slam the phone back into its base, frustrated by the conversation. It's going to take a long time to earn Caleb's trust. I can't rush it.

I'm showered, dressed, and fed by the time Caleb arrives. I open the door for him, quickly clasping my hands behind my back when his gaze darts toward my right hand. I don't want him to see my blackened marking.

He grunts. "I parked out front."

He looks better today. Refreshed. He's freshly shaven, and the dark bags underneath his eyes have vanished. The same can't be said about myself. I've been avoiding looking in the mirror.

He clears his throat. "I looked into your family..."

I perk up. "And?"

"They're dead." The blunt words steal the breath from my lungs. I deflate. "It wasn't shifters, but I can't find any details about their cause of death. It doesn't appear that you have any other surviving relatives, either. Sorry."

"Okay."

I figured as much, and I already knew I didn't have any relatives. My parents were both only children, and both sets of my grandparents had died before I was born. I never had an extended family.

Caleb smacks his tongue against the roof of his mouth. "I'm sorry I don't have good news for you."

I lift and drop one shoulder. "It's fine."

"Whatever you say." Caleb hands me the car keys. "Don't make me regret this."

A warm gust of air hits me as I push open the library doors. Today's wind is brutal. Winter is quickly settling in here, and it's fucking frigid.

I pull my coat tighter around myself as I look around.

The library is old, but it's well-maintained. Floor-to-ceiling wooden bookshelves span the left and right sides of the building. In the center is a wide walkway filled with round tables and the occasional leather couch. This building is cozy, quaint.

Several shifters mill about, many flipping through books but a few clustered together in groups.

Directly in front of the doors is the reception desk. The woman behind it is already looking at me, her lips twisted in a sour frown.

She's older than me but still young. Maybe in her early thirties. Her bright-red sweater draws attention, as do the large snowman earrings she's paired with it. Ignoring her scowl, she looks cheerful—just not toward me.

I assume she's heard the rumor about my cheating.

I force myself to smile as I approach her. "Afternoon," I say, desperate to seem friendly. "Are there any books about shifters here?"

The woman's gaze travels to my exposed hands. I want to hide them behind my back or in the pockets of my coat, but I resist the urge. It's no secret what happened to our bond, and I'd rather she take her fill of my blackened marking now than continually try to sneak glimpses.

Her face twists into disgust.

"Yes," she finally says. "I just got off the phone with Alpha Knox, and I've set aside some books for you." She turns, gesturing for me to follow her. "Come."

Am I supposed to use Caleb's title now? That's how most shifters refer to him, but mates don't use titles with one another. I'm officially no longer recognized as his mate, though.

The woman leads me down the center walkway, past the bookshelves. I peer down the rows, amazed by the sheer number of books here. I've never seen anything like this. Are most libraries this large? It's incredible.

"What's your name?" I ask.

"Mary."

The few shifters here are watching us, their brown eyes locked on to my every movement. I stare at Mary's heels, trying to avoid meeting their pointed glares. I drew a lot of attention at the HPAW facility, but it was never quite this hostile.

Mary leads me to one of the round tables. There's a stack of seven books sitting in the center, and Mary points to the chair on the left. It's in direct view of the reception desk, which I doubt is a coincidence. Mary intends to keep a close eye on me.

"Why does Alpha Knox want to pre-approve your reading material?" she asks.

I pause, scrambling for an answer. The shifters don't know I worked for HPAW. They think I cheated on Caleb. They probably think it's odd that he wishes to keep shifter information from me.

Mary taps her foot against the ground, waiting for my answer. I'm sure the nearby shifters are tuned into our conversation, too. Why wouldn't they be? They're probably wondering the same things.

How am I supposed to answer her? Caleb lied about my betrayal because he thinks my relationship with HPAW will make me irredeemable in the eyes of his pack. They'll never forgive me. But I don't want to be a liar. I've done enough of that, and if I'm going to prove that I'm not the person Caleb thinks I am, I need to begin with the truth.

"I didn't cheat on Caleb," I admit. "I was—"

Mary sneers. "It's *Alpha Knox* to you."

"Okay. I didn't cheat on *Alpha Knox*. I came here as an undercover member of HPAW. My mission was to earn your alpha's affection, learn vital information about the shifters, and eventually kill Alpha Knox. I attempted to kill him and return to HPAW two days ago."

I'm not going to disclose just how close I came to killing Caleb, but that's for his benefit, not mine. Caleb has a reputation to uphold, and I don't want to risk the pack thinking less of him because a human woman almost bested him. I'll leave the details of my betrayal up to him to share.

The quiet chatter in the room falls silent. All eyes are on me, and I clear my throat before pulling out my seat and slinking into it. Sweat trickles down my inner arms as I shrug off my coat, and it takes all my courage to look up and meet Mary's gaze. I did this, and I intend to take responsibility for it.

I lick my lips. "I've since learned that the things HPAW told me are untrue, and I want to make amends. I'm not a bad person, and I intend to prove that."

Mary's pupils dilate and her shoulders jerk, anger pushing her wolf features to the surface. Is she fighting back a shift? Is she going to kill me? It sure fucking seems like it.

I refuse to break eye contact. Despite my training, I don't realistically think I can win in a fight against a shifter. Still, I'm not going to cower. I did what I did, and I'm prepared to own up to it.

Somebody approaches on our left, placing a hand on Mary's shoulder. It's Logan.

"Leave," he orders. Mary brushes him away. Logan spins, placing himself between us. "Leave now, Mary. You heard Knox's orders. Nobody is to touch Evelyn."

Mary scoffs, pure hatred behind her pretty, brown eyes. "HPAW is responsible for my grandfather's death. They fucking skinned him, and this—"

Logan shifts, his muscles tensing. "Leave it alone, Mary. Knox has made his decision to allow Evelyn to remain in the pack, and you *will* respect that." He cocks his head to the side. "Shall I tell him that you've disobeyed his direct order?"

Mary grinds her teeth, stepping away. I can tell it physically pains her to do so, and I realize Caleb might've been onto something. Maybe it is best that the pack believes I cheated on him. Too late now, I suppose.

Logan fills the seat opposite me. Did Caleb order him to monitor me? He says nothing as he pulls out his phone and begins tapping away. He's probably telling Caleb about my conversation with Mary. Very well.

I hang my coat over the back of my chair and pull the top book off the stack. It's a memoir. I read the title, my throat dry. It's written by the alpha responsible for the exodus.

Logan remains at the table, never once looking away from his phone as I read. I fly through the memoir, flipping the pages with rapt focus. It's precisely as Caleb said. The alpha responsible for the exodus was a high-ranking government official. He spoke with the human American government on behalf of the shifters, but things went south when the humans decided to push the shifters to undergo genetic testing.

Bile rises up my throat. They wanted to breed the shifters. I had no idea. That isn't the story we've been told.

The shifters rebelled, obviously. It was the last straw, and they decided to announce themselves to the public and isolate themselves in Canada. The country was mostly shifter populated, anyway. The American shifters retreated to Canada, joining the newly established packs.

I drag my fingers through my hair. My hands are shaking, as is my breath. Logan glances up, then returns his attention to his phone. I grab the next book. It's about markings and mate bonds. A small part of me wants to brush it aside. My bond is dead, and even if I do find a way to fix it, Caleb doesn't want anything to do with me.

It doesn't hurt to flip through it.

The first section is about markings. It discusses how the designs are unique to mated pairs and how the color represents the purity of the bond. It's all things I already know. The next section explains what the specific design reveals about the bond between a mated pair. It's fascinating, but I can't bring myself to read it—not here.

Logan sets his phone down, practically tossing it onto the table. I spare him a glance, but I don't linger. He's glaring at me.

"Everything okay?" I ask.

"Peachy."

The following section covers the coloring of a marking. I read it in great detail. Infidelity, abuse, and abandonment all cause a mark to darken. That's expected, but there are a few other causes I wasn't expecting. Drug use, unapproved masturbation, and misuse of shared resources have all been reported to cause discoloration.

There's no information on how to reverse the darkening. Caleb wasn't exaggerating when he said a mark fully blackening isn't something that happens to the shifters. A bond rarely gets to this point of ruin, and it's even rarer that the pair then decides to try to repair what's been broken. From what I've read, they're usually ecstatic to finally be free of one another and go their separate ways.

The book does briefly mention that marks lighten over time. The text says its natural state is white, and most will gradually transition back. It says it takes months, maybe even years.

I don't have years—or even months. Caleb's mark is darkening by the day. I drop my forehead to the table, the tiny shred of hope I was foolishly holding on to dying.

"Are you almost done?" Logan asks. "I have things I need to get to."

I peer up at him. "You don't need to stay here with me."

"I do, actually." He rises, bundling my books in his arms. I resist the urge to snatch them out of his hands. "Take these home with you. I'll clear it with Mary."

He shoves the books into my chest. They're surprisingly heavy.

"Did you know?" I ask. "About Caleb and me?"

Logan nods. "Of course. Sash and I saw the blood."

I wince without meaning to. There was so much of it.

I don't say anything as I set down my books, pull on my coat, and pick them back up. I didn't think I'd be allowed to take these with me. I'm tempted to thank Logan, but I doubt he'll appreciate it.

My training is the only thing that keeps me from trembling as I walk out of the library, Logan hot on my heels. The shifter won't see me cry.

Chapter Twenty-Eight

My brain is fried. No, it's beyond fried. It's burnt to a tiny, black crisp, and it's useless. My books are scattered around me, and the scrap paper I've been using for notes is a blur of half-sentences and bullet points.

I straighten my spine, stretching my back. It provides momentary relief, but the pain returns as soon as I relax. I've spent an entire day holed up in my apartment, hunched over these books. It's been insightful.

I rub my eyes, trying to remove the blur.

I should take a break, but I'm not sure what else to do with myself. Caleb kept me busy. We spent most days in his office, and evenings were spent cuddling on the couch. I don't have any other hobbies.

I touch my cheek, remembering Sash's slap.

Perhaps I'll go for a run. HPAW provided me with an expansive indoor gym, and I always enjoyed running. I haven't partaken since meeting Caleb, primarily because of my injuries, but it might help burn some of my pent-up energy.

Doctor Greg hasn't cleared me for that level of exercise, but he can fuck off. I'm losing my mind here. Besides, with the rapidly cooling temperatures, it won't be long before the sidewalks are covered in snow and running is no longer an option.

I dig through my closet, searching for clothing suitable for running. I don't have many options, but I find a pair of loose pants and a long-sleeved shirt that will work. It's not the best material, but it'll have to do.

The streets are mostly empty, and I avoid making eye contact with the few shifters outside. I focus on running. Daniel was big on form. He was always shouting corrections whenever I was unlucky enough to be in the gym at the same time as him.

I replay them in my head, not wanting to make an ass of myself in front of the shifters. They're naturally athletic, and I care too much about what they think of me. I used to run upward of ten miles a day back at the facility, but I grow winded after only a few minutes.

Still, it feels good. My mind is empty for the first time in days.

I cut right once I reach the end of the street, purposefully heading away from the town's center. It's a cowardly move, but one I refuse to feel bad about. I'll find the courage to face the shifters soon, just not today.

I run until I'm pretty sure I'm about to die, then turn and take the same path back.

Left foot. Right foot.

I'm panting, my breath visible in the frigid air. This was a mistake. I'm going to die, and my ribcage is pulsating with every beat of my heart. Not to mention that my hands have gone numb.

I shake them out as I round the final corner leading to my apartment building, too distracted to notice the shifter exiting the pottery studio. It's a teenage girl, and she clutches a paper bag to her chest as she easily maneuvers around me. My reflexes aren't quite as quick, especially after my run, and I let out a quiet squeak as I dart around her.

She continues past me, and I awkwardly turn toward the front door of my apartment. I'm looking over my shoulder, watching the girl walk away, when I realize I've miscalculated the single step leading to the door. My toe slams into it, and I'm pivoting forward before I can rightsize myself. My knees and palms hit the concrete, and my forehead bounces off the exterior door.

Fucking dammit.

I scramble up, my face flushed as I slam the fob against the door and shove my way inside. Only once I'm safely out of sight do I touch my stinging forehead. There's a bit of blood, but it's nothing concerning.

I feel like a fucking idiot.

I hold the sleeve of my shirt against the small gash, willing it to clot as I head up the stairs. My hand falls to my side as I unlock and step inside my apartment. Caleb's inside, pacing the length of my kitchen.

He takes one look at me, his nostrils flaring, before closing the distance between us. I hardly have time to react as his hands find my head, tilting it back so he can examine the cut. He doesn't touch the wound, but he flicks my sweaty baby hairs aside so he can get an unobstructed view.

"What happened?"

I shrug. "I went for a run and ate shit, obviously."

Caleb's frown deepens. "You haven't been cleared to run."

"I needed to get out of the apartment. Doctor Greg says fresh air is good for me."

"He also said you should avoid high-intensity exercise." Caleb grabs my arm, tugging me into the bathroom. He points to the toilet. "Sit."

His hands clench and unclench at his sides before he pulls out a first-aid kit. I sit obediently on the toilet, confused by his care. Why's he even here? We haven't spoken since he dropped off the car keys, which is intentional.

I'm giving him space.

If I'm honest with myself, I need space too. I went from being HPAW's pawn to Caleb's mate, and I suppose it would be good for me to figure out who I am beyond them. I should discover myself, or whatever the expression is that people always say.

Caleb pokes and prods at my forehead, his nose crinkling and nostrils flaring. "I didn't realize I'd need to supply you with a helmet. I'm taking you to the hospital."

I rise, ignoring his helmet comment as I nudge him aside and look in the mirror above the sink. I'm fine. It's a minor scrape, and it hardly hurts.

"It looks worse than it feels," I say. "Head wounds always bleed."

"I wasn't asking."

I meet Caleb's gaze in the mirror reflection. "Why do you even care?"

My attention shifts to his mark. The color continues to darken, and it's now a fleshy pink. The edges aren't smudged as mine now are, but I figure it's only a matter of time. Our bond is dying before our very eyes.

Caleb already considers it dead, but I'm holding out hope. I shouldn't. He's made it abundantly clear that he doesn't want me, but I've always been persistent.

"You may have a concussion," Caleb insists. He glances at his phone. "I don't have time for this today."

"Great," I snark, "because I don't have a concussion. What do you know about them, anyway?"

Shifters heal too quickly to suffer from concussions, at least ones with prolonged side effects. It must be nice.

"I've been meeting with Greg these past few weeks," Caleb says, digging through the first aid kit. "He was teaching me about human anatomy and health. I know all about concussions, Evelyn."

My heart thumps. He was meeting with Doctor Greg? I had no idea. Why did he never mention anything to me?

"I don't have a concussion," I assure him. "What are you doing here, anyway?"

Caleb shakes his head. "I thought I'd check in and see how

you're doing after you took it upon yourself to announce to my entire pack that you were a member of HPAW."

He sounds annoyed, his words sharp, but I don't regret my decision.

"I've decided I no longer wish to live a lie," I say.

"Good for you. Why was your apartment door unlocked?"

His topic changes are giving me whiplash. "There are only four units in this building," I say. "And you need a fob to get in the building. I figured it was safe to leave the door unlocked for thirty minutes."

"It's not." Caleb slaps a bandage on my forehead. "Don't do it again."

I expect this to be the end of it, but then he's dragging me out of my apartment and down the stairs. Frigid air smacks me in the face as he shoves open the exterior door.

"What're you—" I groan as he unlocks the car and forces me into the passenger seat. "I don't need to go to the hospital, Caleb. I'm fine!"

He doesn't listen, and fifteen minutes later, he's storming through the double doors of the hospital's main entrance. I follow behind him, not bothering to hide my anger. I'm trying to prove that I'm capable of caring for myself, and he's undermining my work.

"We're almost there," Caleb says, sparing me a glance over his shoulder.

I hum. "Great."

Doctor Greg meets us at the reception desk. He's wearing his usual attire, black slacks and a button-down shirt with a white coat thrown over it. He shoves his hands in his pockets, his gaze darting between Caleb and me.

"Everything all right?" he asks.

"Evelyn fell." Caleb jerks a thumb in my direction. "And now she has a concussion."

"I scraped my forehead," I correct Caleb. "I'm perfectly fine."

The corners of Doctor Greg's lips twitch upward. I can't help but notice that he's not looking at me with outward hostility. Even the receptionist sitting nearby remains neutral. If anything, she looks bored, her chin propped into her hand as she taps aimlessly at her computer.

"How'd you fall?" Doctor Greg asks.

I hesitate.

Caleb takes this as his cue to answer. "She went for a run, and she fell."

Doctor Greg's budding smile falls. "I told you no high-intensity exercise."

I throw my hands into the air, but I don't bother defending myself. I went for a run and got a small scrape on my forehead. It's not the end of the world. My ribcage feels fine, and I hardly feel the cut on my head. If anything, the small hairs caught underneath the bandage hurt more. They tug when I move my eyebrows.

"Let's take a look," Doctor Greg says.

He leads me to a private room down the hallway. Caleb follows, practically clipping my heels with every step. For a man who insists on being done with me, he's sure showing a lot of concern.

Will people think I've done this on purpose to get Caleb's attention? Will Caleb think that? I wish I had. It'd be much less embarrassing.

Doctor Greg examines my head first, then checks for signs of a concussion. "You're fine," he eventually says. "It's just a scrape."

I let out a quiet sigh. "Shocker."

Caleb enters my line of sight, interrupting the conversation. "And her ribs?"

"Also fine. Humans are surprisingly durable, Alpha. Your mate isn't going to perish from a small head wound."

We both stiffen at Doctor Greg's use of the word *mate*. I wait for Caleb to correct him, I fully expect him to, but he doesn't. It's definitely awkward, though.

Doctor Greg excuses himself, and Caleb and I make our way

outside. We're silent the entire way back to my apartment, and I don't question Caleb as he walks with me to my unit. Is he planning to stay? I don't need a babysitter, and I don't want his pity. I want Caleb to be around me because he wants to be, not because he feels obligated to.

He follows me inside my apartment.

"You don't need to stay," I assure him.

Caleb hums, flicking through my scrap paper on the kitchen island. He takes time to read over my notes, his expression unreadable. I wish I knew what he was thinking.

"You're thorough," he eventually says.

"The subject is important to me."

Caleb reaches the bottom sheet, the one on mate bonds. I told myself not to read the books. It's a waste of time. Caleb made his decision, and I should respect that. Still, I couldn't resist the temptation. I scanned every page in the two books I was given, and I took more notes than I'd care to admit.

Caleb shuts his eyes. For a brief moment, he looks exhausted, like the weight of the world is on his shoulders.

"Have you found anything?" he asks.

He doesn't outright ask, but I know what he means. "Not really," I admit. "Markings are finicky. There isn't a lot of information on reversing the darkening of one. Mate bonds are annoying."

Caleb laughs, the noise loud and throaty, before he dips his chin in agreement. "I've never heard somebody call mate bonds annoying."

He continues scanning my notes, pausing when he reaches one of the last pages. "What's this?"

I shift, peering over his shoulder. "It's a list of things you like."

"I've gathered that. Why?"

Blood rushes to my cheeks. I wasn't expecting him to come over, let alone read my notes. Self-preservation has me wanting to lie, but that goes against my recent decision to be truthful.

"I figured if bad things darken the mark," I start, "then maybe good things will lighten it. I made a list of things you enjoy."

"Why?"

"As inspiration for ways to win you over."

Caleb's gaze flickers down the list. He reads it twice. "You're persistent," he finally says. "I'll give you that."

"I prefer to say *determined*."

Caleb hums. "I'm sure you do."

He sets the list down. I chew on my bottom lip, not letting him see how disappointed I am by his reaction. I was hoping for more—either positive or negative. He's giving me nothing more than complete indifference.

I tap my fingers against the counter, drumming them along the surface. "I might have some helpful information on HPAW."

Caleb quirks a brow. "You're my mate, Evelyn. They wouldn't have exposed you to anything they didn't want me knowing."

I cross my arms over my chest. He doesn't know what I know. I spent years in the facility. I'm sure I have *some* helpful information.

"They're always running experiments. I'm not allowed inside the lab, but they have impressive technology. Microphones that can pick up sound from a quarter mile away. Chips, but not the kind you eat. Lights that can't be picked up by—"

"Enough, Evelyn."

"I know where the facilities are," I try.

"As do I." Caleb steps away, putting space between us. "I don't care to discuss HPAW with you."

He pulls his phone out of his pocket. It's vibrating, and he declines the call. Two seconds later, it begins vibrating again. Caleb declines the call once more, then storms to my front door, ripping it open to reveal Logan.

"What do you want?" Caleb asks.

"You to not wander off without telling anybody where you're going," Logan snaps. He lowers his voice. "We've heard back from..." He shoots me a look. "Our contacts have gotten back to us. We should discuss."

Caleb's quick to dismiss him. "Not now."

"Alpha...." Logan's voice is tight. "This is important."

Caleb rolls his shoulders, pure aggression oozing from him. Logan looks down, breaking eye contact. It's shocking to see. I'm aware that Caleb's title was earned through the dominance of his wolf, but he's friendly with Logan. They're family.

Caleb turns to me. "Refrain from injuring yourself again."

I try not to let my disappointment show as he leaves, but the emotion is there. Something is happening with HPAW. It's been building for weeks. It's making me anxious.

Chapter Twenty-Nine

My palms are damp, and I wipe them on my pants before pushing open the library doors. I'm going to get a job. I'm twenty-four years old, and I've never had one. It's about time that changes.

I hold my chin high as I approach Mary, not wanting her to sense my weakness. She's wearing a dark-red sweater. That's nice. It won't get stained with my blood when she rips me to shreds.

She looks up, and the tiny thread of hope I was holding vanishes as she releases a visible sigh. I haven't even spoken, and she's already annoyed by me. We're not off to a great start.

"Good morning," I greet her.

Mary blinks, looking entirely unamused, as a low hum emerges from the back of her throat. "What do you want?"

I eye the books piled up on the side of her desk. She's placing plastic sleeves around the front covers. *I can do that.* It doesn't look too complicated.

"Are you hiring?" I ask, refusing to let myself shrivel under her sharp glare.

Mary raises a brow, her lips flattening. A clock behind me ticks as the seconds pass, and I find myself holding my breath as the awkward silence between us stretches.

"I'm a fast learner, and I—"

Mary lifts her hand to stop me. My jaw snaps shut with a quiet click.

"I'm not hiring."

I knew she'd say that. "I don't need much pay, and I'm available whenever—"

Mary scoffs. "Don't beg, Evelyn. The answer is no."

I glance to the right. People are looking, watching my embarrassing interaction with Mary. They're soaking this up, probably enjoying every second of it.

"Well..." I clear my throat, the words thick on my tongue. "Please let me know if anything changes."

Mary only stares, her face void of emotion. She isn't going to respond. I spin on my heel, retreating before I make even more of an ass of myself. The coffee shop is next. The barista there was friendly that one time I went, and I know they're hiring.

It's only a five-minute walk there, and I'm relieved when I see the hiring sign is still taped to the front door. I give it a quick scan before stepping inside, a bell above the door chiming as I do so. *Confidence, Evelyn. People like confidence.*

The place is busy, and I don't recognize the woman behind the counter. She has the typical brown hair and brown eyes all shifters share, but she's surprisingly short. I'm average height for a human woman, maybe even a bit on the tall side, and the barista only makes it to my chin.

She spares me a glance, then turns away as if she didn't see me. She ignores me completely as I reach the counter.

I read the name tag pinned to her chest. "Good morning, Clover!"

She continues cleaning the coffee machine. I rock back on my heels, waiting for her to finish wiping the nozzles with her wet rag. She takes her sweet time, probably on purpose. I'm patient. Once Clover is finished with the nozzles, she begins cleaning the counters.

How long should I wait? It's clear she has no intention of serving me.

The chime above the door sounds as someone enters behind me. Clover frowns, unable to continue avoiding me. I'm the only one in line, and I'm in front. She'll have to serve me before the other customer.

Clover finally looks at me. "What can I get you?" Her voice is flat, but I'll take it. It's better than her completely ignoring my existence.

"Are you still hiring?" I gesture to the sign. "I'd like to apply."

Clover blinks, glances behind me, and blinks again. I shift my weight from one foot to the other, then begin counting. If I reach ten and she still hasn't responded, I'll leave. There's only so much disrespect I can endure in a single day.

The shifter behind me clears his throat.

Clover shakes her head. "We don't need your help."

Figures. I dip my chin. "That's unfortunate. Well, thanks for your time."

Clover raises a brow, probably expecting me to throw a tantrum or storm out of here in tears. I refuse to give her the reaction she wants. I'm not the horrible, spoiled person they think me to be.

Clover shifts her focus to the person behind me. "What can I get for you?"

I turn, locking eyes with Doctor Greg. He smiles, the only shifter willing to be friendly with me. I appreciate it.

"You're looking for a job?" he asks.

"Unsuccessfully, but yes."

"The hospital needs a custodian." He licks his lips. "It's not glamorous, but it's a job. If you're interested, you're welcome to stop by tonight. Around six."

Is he serious? I don't care if the job involves cleaning out bedpans and washing bloody sheets. It's clear nobody else is going to hire me, and I need to keep busy before I lose my mind.

"I appreciate that." I drag my hands down my face. "I'll be there."

I hurry out of the coffee shop before he changes his mind. I don't know how to clean, but I'm a quick learner. I'll figure it out.

The hospital is beginning to feel like a second home.

I shield my eyes, blocking the setting sun's glare as I walk through the empty lobby. Quiet instrumental music plays from the speakers installed in the room's ceiling, and I tap my fingers against the empty front desk as I wait for the receptionist to return. I'm anxious.

It feels like hours before somebody finally emerges from the back area. It's a woman I've seen before. Michelle. She's young, and she offers me a bright smile as she sinks into her chair.

"Evelyn," she says. She taps on her keyboard, lighting up the computer screen. "You're here for Doctor Greg, yeah? About the custodian position?"

"Yes." I purse my lips. "Can you let him know I'm here?"

Michelle clicks her tongue against the roof of her mouth. "He already knows." She points to a row of empty seats. "Take a seat. He's finishing up a consult and will be out shortly."

The quiet tapping of her keyboard is oddly soothing, and I focus on it in a sad attempt to keep my mind from wandering. I've been having disturbing daydreams, most of them about HPAW torturing me as they did that shifter.

They cut open my flesh, torturing me under the guise of testing my physical limitations. The fears have begun infiltrating my dreams, too, the thought seeping into my mind whenever I'm still for too long. I'm hoping this job helps with that. It'll give me a purpose, something to break up the monotony of my new life.

"Evelyn!" Doctor Greg bursts into the lobby with a wide smile. "I'm glad to see you."

Should I shake his hand? That's what people do during interviews, right? Doctor Greg spins away before I decide on the matter. He gestures for me to follow him into the back.

"We've been short-staffed since HPAW's attack last week," Doctor Greg says. "Two of my apprentices were called away for training. It's been a hassle."

My movements falter. "Training for what?"

"Nothing." Doctor Greg cuts left down another hallway, and I scramble to do the same. "Forget I said anything."

That's easier said than done. Are the shifters planning an attack? Does this have to do with the hushed emergency Logan came to Caleb with yesterday?

Doctor Greg turns down another hallway without warning. The shifters are fast and smooth in their movements. I feel like a baby deer just learning to walk.

He brings me into what looks to be a break room.

A nurse is sitting on the small, beige couch in the center of the room. I recognize her. Nurse June. She was there that day in the woods, when Logan and Sash found me in the cabin.

Her black hair is tied back, and when she flicks a loose strand out of her eye, I can't help but notice her mark. It stands out against her dark skin, the floral pattern similar to mine. Well, it's similar to what mine *used* to look like.

She drops her hand as she notices my gaze, her frown turning into an outright snarl.

"Don't fucking look at it."

I jolt, not expecting that. "Sorry."

Doctor Greg sighs. "Be nice, June. She doesn't know."

Know what?

"Her mate passed away when they were children," he explains. "It's considered rude to stare at the mark of a relict." Greg leads me into a connecting room. Inside are shelves full of cleaning supplies, a sink, and a washing machine.

Doctor Greg gives me a moment to look around. "The job shouldn't be too challenging," he says. "The floors need to be cleaned daily, and you'll need to restock the rooms after each patient." He points to the laundry bin beside the washing machine. "The nurses will place dirty scrubs and linens in here. You need to wash and fold them."

That sounds easy enough. The hospital isn't huge, and it doesn't seem that busy. Doctor Greg is the only doctor in the area, and I've only ever met a handful of nurses. I doubt shifters often require medical help, not with their advanced healing capabilities.

"Pay is every two weeks," Doctor Greg continues. "Are you free to start tomorrow?"

That soon? I don't see why not.

"Yes. I am."

Doctor Greg beams. "Great!"

We step out of the cleaning room, and Doctor Greg digs some paperwork out of a cabinet. It looks official, and I chew at my bottom lip as he slides it between us.

"You'll just need to fill this out by tomorrow. I know you've had a..." He hesitates before continuing. "You have a *unique* past, so feel free to skip over any sections you aren't sure about. I'm sure Alpha Knox won't mind if I skip a few technicalities."

I flip through the paperwork, reading some of the things I need to fill out. It wants to know my date of birth, which I'm unaware of. In fact, I don't know most of this information.

"Why are you doing this?" I ask.

Doctor Greg shrugs. "You're a nice kid. I have better things to do than hate you for something out of your control."

Slitting Caleb's throat wasn't exactly out of my control, but I keep that comment to myself. Doctor Greg is the only person in this pack willing to engage with me, and I'm not going to bite the hand that feeds me. I'm desperate for companionship.

Chapter Thirty

Caleb is standing outside my apartment door. He's wearing a brown sweater I love. It's a thick knit, and I've always appreciated how it stretches across his muscular shoulders.

"I locked the door this time," I say.

The corner of his lip twitches upward. "I noticed."

He moves aside, waiting for me to unlock my door. I'm surprised he doesn't have an extra set of keys, but I don't question it as we step into my kitchen.

"What're you doing here?" I ask. I set the paperwork Doctor Greg gave me on the counter.

"I—" Caleb pauses. "You were spotted at the hospital."

I nod. "Yeah. I got a job there."

"A job?"

"Yes." I lean against the counter. "If I'm to live in this pack, I need to find a way to support myself. I only have a year, remember?"

Caleb licks his lips. "I just didn't think you'd move so quickly."

"What else am I to do?" I gesture around the apartment. "Sit here and wallow in self-pity? My entire life has been dictated for me. It's about time I do something for myself."

"And that something is to become a custodian at the local hospital?"

I cock my head to the side. "I didn't tell you what my job is."

Caleb falls silent. I try not to stare at him, but it's hard. Things between us have flipped so suddenly, but that doesn't mean my emotions have vanished. I still want him. Mate bond or not, I want to be with Caleb.

Things could have been so good.

"Why are you here, Caleb?" I repeat.

He throws his head back, staring at the ceiling. "We've had some recent complications with HPAW."

"Complications?"

Caleb bobs his head, then begins flipping through my notes. I haven't made any additional progress since he was last here, but that doesn't deter him. He reads through everything with startling intensity, his eyes darting over every word. His throat bobs as he reads my list of things he enjoys.

"Caleb?" I ask. "What complications?"

He purses his lips, pinning them shut.

I wait.

"They've been pushing at the borders," he finally says. "It's been happening for weeks, but it's picked up these past few days. I can't continue to ignore it."

"Then don't."

I have no love for HPAW—no loyalty. Let Caleb and the other shifters rip them apart. They deserve it.

Caleb stares at me. "Humans will die." He groans, planting his hands on the counter. "I shouldn't care what you think about me. I should let my pack rip apart the HPAW soldiers. I should let them make your precious human men scream." His eyes meet mine. "But then I think about you, and I can't pull the fucking trigger."

"Why?"

"It would start a war."

"And why is that a problem?" After all I've seen and read, HPAW deserves it. The people have been lied to, but the government is corrupt. I wouldn't blame the shifters for finally taking action, and I'm honestly surprised they haven't done so sooner.

Caleb steps around the counter, closing the distance between us. I ignore the pounding in my chest as I look up at him. I want to hope, but his rejections have been explicit. I won't beg for a man who doesn't want me. I can't let myself stoop to that level.

My eyes flutter shut as Caleb leans in, brushing his nose against my shoulder. He trails it toward my neck, so slowly and so gently. I shiver and tilt my head back, giving him more room.

"What if my children are hybrids?" he whispers. "What will they think when they learn I was the alpha who started a war between the shifters and humans?"

My throat is dry. I swallow. "You would have to have children with a human woman to create hybrids..."

"I'm aware."

"Am I pregnant?"

He burrows his face in my neck, inhaling. "No."

I can't help but feel relieved. Children sound nice *someday*, but not now. I would hate to bring a child into this mess.

"Do you...?" I pause, hesitant to voice my question. At what point is Caleb going to pull away? His rejection stings, even when I'm expecting it. "Do you still see yourself having children with me?"

His breath warms my throat. "I haven't completely ruled it out."

Hope blooms. I shove it down. "I thought our bond was dead?"

"It is, but my wolf still finds himself enamored with you."

His wolf. Not him. That should be enough to deter me, but I'm a glutton for punishment. I can't help it. I'm grasping at straws.

I throw caution to the wind. "Do you still love me?"

Caleb stiffens. I've pushed too far. He pulls away, removing himself from me entirely. I could drive forward, throw myself at him in a desperate display for attention. It would be easy, and a tiny part of me thinks it would work. I don't want that, though. I want Caleb to come to me of his own volition.

I push my hair out of my face. "Can I see your marking?"

Caleb silently extends his hand. The color is darker. Always fucking darker.

"Would you consider accepting me back even if our bond dies?" I ask.

Caleb shrugs. The moment is over. "Can't promise anything," he says.

He retreats to the other side of the counter, his movements clearly intentional. He wants a physical object between us. It's probably for the best. I don't want to do something that either of us would regret. There are already too many regrets between us—most of which are on my end.

Caleb eyes the paperwork Doctor Greg gave me. "You'll need to open a bank account if you want direct deposit." What the fuck does that mean? "Have them call me if there are any issues."

He's gone before I have the chance to ask what the hell a 'direct deposit' is.

This shouldn't be too hard. Everybody has a bank account.

There's only one bank in the area, and I drive there the moment it opens. I'm not sure what to expect as I enter the building, and I hold my hands to my chest as I look around. The building is rustic, covered in muted browns and old leather furniture. There's a small seating area to the left, with two empty cubicles beside it. Directly across from the door is a short line of people waiting to speak with an employee.

The man is standing behind a tall counter, looking bored as he waves the next person in line over. I join the back, patiently waiting for my turn. It takes almost forty-five minutes to reach the front of the line.

"I'm here to open an account," I say as I approach the employee.

He huffs. "You need to wait over there." He points to the empty seating area on the left. "Somebody will come by to help you open a new account."

What? I just waited in this line for nothing? I bite my tongue, reining in my anger as I head to the seating area. *This is bullshit.*

The leather chairs are uncomfortable, and it takes almost an hour for somebody to come out to help me. It's a middle-aged man with slicked-back hair and a bored expression. He lazily looks me over before flicking his fingers, rudely ordering me to follow him into one of the cubicles.

"What can I help you with today?" he asks, sighing midway through his sentence.

I suck in a breath, count to three, and release. "I'd like to open a bank account."

"All right." He starts up his computer, then proceeds to print out a thousand and one forms. I'm getting really tired of paperwork. If this is what being an independent adult consists of, I'm not sure I'm cut out for it.

He slides the paperwork in my direction. "Fill these out."

I do my best, but there are several things I don't have answers for. I also don't have the required documentation. One call to Caleb clears everything up, though. It's brief, and the man is red in the face as he hangs up the phone.

By the time I have everything squared away, I've been given a thick welcome packet and a whole bunch of bank information I'm not sure I'll ever use. All I need are my account numbers and my debit card. The man said that would be enough to set up direct deposit, which is when my paychecks are deposited directly into my account. What a fun concept.

I toss everything onto my kitchen counter when I finally get back to my apartment. The welcome packet hits my teetering pile of books, sending everything to the ground.

I groan. "Shit."

I didn't realize just how frustrating this would be, and I miss how easy things were with Caleb. Life was simple, and I wasn't given death glares everywhere I went. I wipe my nose with my sleeve. I refuse to cry.

There's a knock on the door. Caleb? I pick up my books and run my hands over my hair, trying to smooth the messed-up strands. The knocking continues, growing in volume and intensity. What the hell is going on?

I open the door to see a man I don't know on the other side. He's tall and muscular, unsurprising for a shifter, and he's wearing a ratty, black T-shirt with loose sweatpants. His hair is messy too, like he just rolled out of bed.

"Yes?" I ask.

He looks me head to toe, openly judging. "Can you keep it down?" *Keep it down?* The man isn't done. "I might as well be living next to a bull, and I'm tired of hearing you sob. Get it together."

I recoil. "Excuse me? I'm not loud." I take a moment to collect myself, then continue. "And I don't sob. My occasional crying is very much average."

"Well, I live *here*." He points to the only other apartment on the floor. 3A. "And I can hear it through the walls. I understand that Knox left you and that's hard to deal with, but bitching and moaning isn't going to bring him back."

My blood boils, and the last bit of patience I had evaporates. "Close your fucking ears, then."

I slam the door shut before letting out an exaggerated groan, hoping he hears it through the door. Fuck him. Fuck everything.

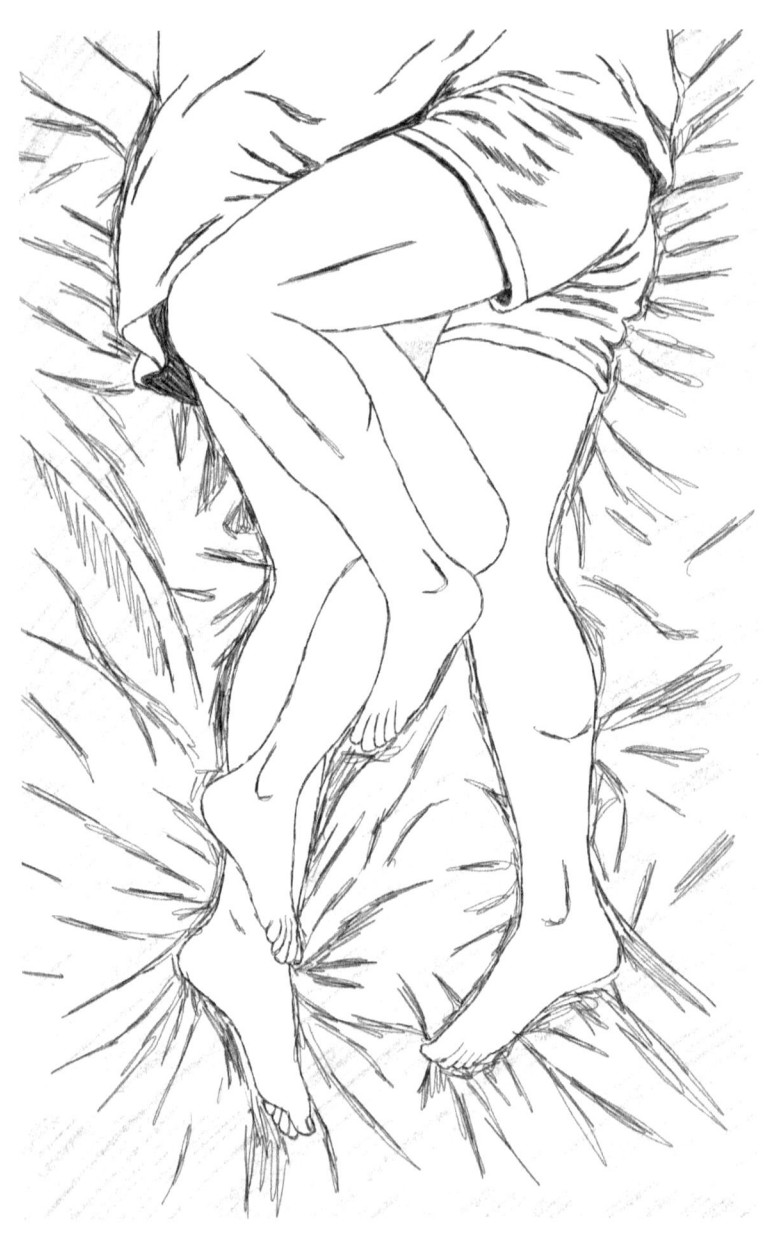

Chapter Thirty-One

Working isn't as fun as I imagined. I thought it would be glamorous. Maybe not the work itself, but definitely the independence. I'm not having a great time.

My shoulder and back muscles are sore from cleaning, and I fight back a wince as I stick my mop in the water bucket. I need to refill it soon, the water a murky gray, but I want to finish this hallway first. How long has it been since the floors were last mopped? Too long, I'd say.

Voices travel up the hallway, and I shiver as I recognize the one belonging to June. She hates me. She hasn't outwardly done or said anything, but she never misses an opportunity to give me a dirty look or cutting glare.

I finish the area I'm working on, thankfully without encountering June, and wrap up my last few tasks for the day. The hospital doesn't see much traffic. A total of six shifters came in today, four of whom were children in need of routine physicals. The fifth was a young man with mysterious injuries I'm not privy to the details of.

Something is going on with the shifters. Caleb has admitted to trouble with HPAW, and I suspect this was related to it. Doctor Greg ushered the man into the back before I could get a good look at him, and the nurse assigned to him has been tight-lipped. I went as far as to eavesdrop on her conversation with June, but she didn't spill any details.

The fifth visitor was a pregnant female in need of an ultrasound.

I tried not to make eye contact with her. Caleb has confirmed that I'm not pregnant, and seeing that woman had shame filling every pore and crevice of my person. I was wrong to do what I did, and I don't think I'll ever be able to forgive myself for it.

I doubt Caleb will ever forgive me, either. I don't blame him.

Frigid air whips my hair around my head the second I leave the building. I hate the weather here. I thought I knew cold, but this is ridiculous. I'm surprised there isn't snow covering the ground, but I assume we're only a few weeks away—if not days.

A particularly large gust of wind has my teeth chattering, and I yank my coat tighter around myself as I climb inside Caleb's car. I start the engine, but I don't move. I worry my hands around the steering wheel instead, procrastinating.

I don't want to go home.

My apartment is lonely, and I'm tired of being alone. Doctor Greg is the only shifter who is nice, but I doubt he wants to spend his free time with me. He's a middle-aged man with a mate and a gaggle of children. He has better things to do with his time.

I should return home. My stack of books is calling to me, specifically the two on marks. I shouldn't let yesterday's tender moment with Caleb affect me, but it has. The sad truth is I want to fix our bond. I'm desperate for it.

Caleb's mark is darkening with each passing day, and I don't have the luxury of time.

The drive to my apartment is borderline painful. I chew at my bottom lip, continuing even as I taste blood. I bite harder as I turn onto the street, but instead of parking in one of the empty spots in front of the building, I turn right and make my way down a road I most definitely shouldn't.

This is a bad idea.

I continue down the road, making turns I memorized long ago, until I pull into Caleb's winding driveway. There's a light on inside, but I can't see through the sheer cream curtains covering the windows.

Caleb is home.

My hands tremble as I park and make the short walk to the front door, but I don't dare to knock. I lift my arm but quickly drop it back by my side. This is a mistake. I step back, my shoulders sagging.

Caleb pulls open the door.

He's wearing only a pair of loose sleep pants, and he hardly seems affected by the cold as he steps onto his porch and looks around. His gaze flickers from me to the car, then back to me.

I'm expecting questions.

"I know you hate me," I start. "I just..." I pause, my voice trailing off.

Caleb steps aside and jerks his chin toward the doorway. "Come on."

He follows me inside, silent as I tug off my coat and shoes. He wordlessly hangs my jacket inside the closet, an action he's done dozens of times, but I never took much notice of it until now.

We stare at one another, and I cross my arms as I debate my next move. I didn't think this through. Caleb cocks his head to the side, his nostrils flaring. I'm sure I smell like the hospital's cleaner and dirty mop water.

"Are you alone?" I ask. I can't see anybody from where I stand, but I'm not looking to humiliate myself in front of anybody but Caleb.

He shrugs. "Why does it matter?"

Coming here was a mistake. I begin to turn, fully intending to leave, but Caleb halts me with a firm grip on my bicep. His brown eyes are boring holes into the sides of my face, impossible to ignore.

"I'm alone," he admits. "And if this is your subtle way of

seeing if I'm entertaining other women, the answer is no. There's nobody else."

I ignore how happy that makes me. "Can we pretend?" I ask.

Caleb frowns. "Pretend?"

I nod. "Just for tonight? Please."

Caleb rolls his shoulders. Despite his unruly hair and wrinkled clothing, he looks good. It's those damn shifter genes. I can't say the same for myself. My face is breaking out, from stress or hormones, I can't tell, and the center of my bottom lip is split.

He gestures upstairs. "Go on, then."

It's not a warm invitation, but I'm just desperate enough to take it. My limbs are heavy, and I hug my arms around myself as I head upstairs and into his bedroom. Caleb follows, but his silence speaks volumes.

I curl my fingers into the skin of my biceps as I step inside. It physically hurts to be in here after what I did, and the memory of his blood pooling on the floor and soaking into the wood flooring haunts me.

"You have new sheets," I say.

I snap my jaw shut. Of course he has new sheets. His were stained with blood.

Caleb lingers in the doorway. "Shower," he orders. "You reek."

My cheeks flush. He's never spoken to me like this. I may have made mistakes, but I have *some* semblance of dignity. I didn't come here to be insulted.

"Why do you come in so much contact with Greg?"

I pause. "What?"

"His scent is practically oozing off you," Caleb continues. "Did you fucking full-body rub up against him or something?"

It takes a moment for his words to register. When he says I reek, is he referring to Doctor Greg's scent?

"I—" I turn, facing Caleb. "I suppose I brush up against him occasionally while we're working. He lingers in doorways, and some of the hallways are narrow. It's not intentional."

Caleb's frown deepens. "Don't come to me smelling of another man again. You won't be welcomed inside." He licks his lips. "Now go shower."

He's jealous. It's the last thing I expected from him, and I fight back a smile as I escape into his bathroom. Caleb can pretend to hate me all he wants, but these little moments are telling. I'll take my victories where I can get them.

I stare in the bathroom mirror for a long while after showering. Caleb snuck inside and placed a change of clothing on the sink. They're his, and they swallow me. I fiddle with the hem of his shirt before stepping out of the bathroom.

Caleb's sitting on the edge of the bed, his head in his hands.

I rock back on my heels as he runs his fingers through his hair and straightens up. His breath hitches at the sight of me in his clothing, and he doesn't bother hiding his stare as he flicks off the bedroom light and slides into bed.

I settle beside him, my heart pounding.

"Why did you come here, Evelyn?"

"I miss you."

We lie side by side, staring at the ceiling. Will Caleb push me away if I try cuddling? I shift, adjusting the shirt riding up my hips, before rolling onto my side with my back facing Caleb. He doesn't react, and I scoot back until my butt brushes his arm. It's a clear invitation.

He doesn't take it.

"Ten women went missing from a smaller pack last year," he whispers instead. "We now suspect HPAW abducted those women." He drapes a heavy arm over my waist and hugs me against his chest. "I suspect they..."

His voice trails off. I wait, but he doesn't continue.

"You suspect what?" I push.

Caleb gives me a tight squeeze but otherwise doesn't respond. He slides his hand up the front of my shirt until his palm rests over my heart. He's holding me so tightly, I'm at risk of suffocation, but it's exactly what I need.

"Why do you think they took those women?" I ask. "For more testing?"

"It doesn't matter. Go to sleep, Evelyn."

Why won't he tell me? Does he still think I'm going to run to HPAW with the information he shares, or is he just doing this to punish me? It's frustrating either way.

Caleb's body heat seeps through my clothing, warming me to the core. It lulls me right to sleep.

Chapter Thirty-Two

The bed is empty when I wake, but it hasn't been that way for long. I'm doused in sweat, and the spot next to me is still warm.

I shove the sheets down to my waist and roll onto my back. Last night was the best I've slept in weeks, and I stretch my arms above my head before turning toward the bathroom. The door is closed, but the shower is running.

Should I leave? I don't want to overstay my welcome. It's not like we had sex, but the way Caleb held me felt intimate.

The shower shuts off. I climb out of bed and fix the sheets, waiting for him to leave the bathroom. He does so after a few minutes, a cloud of steam billowing out around his fully dressed form.

He looks good. He's dressed for work, in dark-brown trousers and a thick, cream sweater.

"Thank you for last night," I say, quick to break the silence.

Caleb flexes his marked hand before subtly moving it behind his back. It's too late. I've already noticed how dark it's gotten. Almost black.

"What's happening with HPAW?" I ask. "Are we in danger?"

Caleb quirks a brow. "That's none of your concern."

So, he's back to acting like an asshole. Nice to know.

"I have the right to know," I argue. "Everybody else does."

Caleb shuts down before my very eyes. His gaze grows distant as it sweeps through the room, lingering just a moment on the bed before settling on the door. I'd kill to know what he's thinking right now.

He used to be so open with me. Now it's like trying to rip out teeth. I suppose I don't blame him. I did try to kill him and run to his enemy to share all his secrets.

"I'm not discussing this with you," he finally says.

He leaves the room, heading downstairs. I don't bother saying goodbye as I retreat to my car and drive back to my apartment. I shouldn't have come here last night. It was a mistake.

Caleb's sweatpants threaten to slide down my waist as I check my empty mailbox and storm up the stairs of my apartment building. Even tied and rolled at the waist, they're still comically loose. I'm sure Caleb got a kick out of seeing me in them.

I make eye contact with my rude neighbor as I round the top of the stairs. He's standing in front of his door with his back to me, and he peers at me over his shoulder as I near. His body quickly follows his head, and I tighten my grip on the stair railing as he faces me directly.

He's holding several pieces of mail, and he tucks them under his arm as he looks me up and down. I don't appreciate it. His gaze feels condescending, and I just know he's judging. He takes his sweet time looking over my baggy shirt and poorly fitting sweatpants.

Then he lets in a dramatic inhale. Can he smell Caleb? I hope not.

I'm not ready for anybody to know I spent the night with him. Everything is so awkward and tense between us, and I'd like to figure things out with him privately before rumors spread. This guy looks like one to spread rumors.

"What?" I snap, losing my patience.

He snorts. "Nice outfit. Real classy."

He's laughing at me. I ball my hands into fists. I don't know what this guy's problem is, but I'm not in the mood to deal with it.

"Do you have a name?" I ask.

He nods, shooting me a cocky smile. I want to smack it off his face as I tap my foot against the ground, waiting for him to elaborate. He doesn't, and I shut my eyes and count to ten. "...And it is?"

"Adam."

"Well, Adam," I snap, "you're a dick."

He quirks a brow, the corners of his mouth twitching upward into a mocking smile as I brush past him, retreating into my apartment. Guilt hits me the second I shut the door, but I have no reason to feel guilty. Adam has been nothing but rude, but I don't want to stoop to his level.

I'm better than that. I *want* to be better than that.

I'll make amends later.

I have a few hours to kill before I need to be at the hospital, and I haven't eaten since lunchtime yesterday. Would Caleb have made me something had I told him about my lack of dinner? He used to love cooking for me, and he took care to ensure I was always well fed.

Feeding myself has never been something I've concerned myself with. Excluding the times HPAW explicitly decided to starve me, they prepared and brought me three square meals a day. Caleb took over that responsibility.

It's been a learning curve. I don't think about food until I'm starving, and planning my meals ahead of time is challenging. But I'm trying, and I'm proud of the progress I've made. It's slow, but it's consistent.

Were my parents good cooks? I can visualize our dinner table if I concentrate hard enough, but I have no memory of eating at it. Maybe they preferred to eat in the living room. I'll never know.

I throw some dethawed chicken and a handful of cut-up vegetables on a baking tray. I've watched Caleb make dozens of variations of this meal several times, and I feel a sense of accomplishment as I stick everything in the oven.

After much internal debate, I also stick a dozen cookies in the oven. The dough is premade, but I enjoy it. I can't stomach the thought of verbally apologizing to Adam, so the cookies will have to do.

I spend the remainder of my time skimming my books on shifter culture and mate bonds.

This morning's interaction with Adam lingers at the back of my mind, and I stop by his apartment before leaving for work. The mere sight of his door pisses me off, and I spend a long minute glaring at it before knocking.

He opens it within seconds, and I force myself to smile as I thrust a plate of cookies in his direction.

"For you," I hiss through my teeth.

Adam blinks, his eyes narrowing as he peers at the plate. His throat bobs and his nostrils flare. The fucker likes cookies.

"Why?" he asks. "Have you poisoned them?"

Despite his distrust, he doesn't hesitate to snatch the plate out of my hands.

"I'm sure you'd be able to smell if I poisoned them," I say.

Adam shrugs, not arguing my point, before shoving a cookie into his mouth. He hums as he chews, which I take as a good sign.

He swallows. "I don't have anything for you."

"I don't expect you to."

"Good."

Adam steps back into his apartment, then slams his door in my face. I jolt, startled by the sudden movement. Well, fuck him too.

Chapter Thirty-Three

Mary ignores my very existence as I slink into the library. It's the best response I could have asked for, and I keep my head low to avoid the gazes of the other wolves.

I'm not sure what I'm looking for as I slink down the first aisle on the left, and I quickly find myself in the fiction section. I find a spine that looks interesting, and my heart pound as I tuck it under my arm.

What are the odds that Mary refuses to let me read this? Will she take it away? There's a small sitting area in the back corner of the library. I take refuge in it.

I tuck my knees against my chest and yank my shirt over them, bundling myself into a tight ball. I'm probably stretching out the fabric of my shirt, but I can buy myself a new one when I get paid through my direct deposit.

Working at the hospital is tiresome—more so than I imagined—but it's worth it. For the first time in my life, I feel independent. I get paid next week. I'll have worked for something. It feels good.

I find myself engrossed in my book within minutes, and I gnaw mindlessly at the inside of my cheek as I flip page after page.

"What are you doing?"

The sharp voice startles me. A bitter metallic taste fills my mouth as I accidentally bite my tongue, and I swallow around it as I meet Mary's curious expression. She stands only a few feet away, her arms crossed over her chest.

I clear my throat. "What do you mean?"

Mary gestures to my huddled-up form. "Why are you reading here?"

I take my legs out of my shirt. "...You want to know why I read in the library?"

"Yes."

"Because I like books?"

My answer comes out as a question, my confusion only growing. What else am I supposed to do in a library if not read?

"Obviously." Mary sighs. "But why don't you check them out?"

Check them out? What the fuck is she talking about? I'm not following.

Mary cocks her head to the side. "You do know that you can check out books and take them home with you, yeah? You can keep them for up to three weeks."

Is that true? I had no idea. When Logan said he would take care of things with Mary, I took that to mean I wasn't typically allowed to take the books home. I thought he was breaking the rules so he wouldn't have to sit with me at that table any longer.

Mary's chest expands, and I can practically *see* the annoyance radiating off her.

"How many books can I check out?" I ask.

"Ten at a time."

I squeak. Ten? She must be lying.

"I have five at home," I say.

Mary nods. "I'm aware, and I'm counting them toward your limit."

Her pinched expression softens before quickly returning. She gestures for me to stand with a flick of her two fingers. "Come."

I follow her to the front desk, trying hard not to look too

visibly excited. This feels too good to be true, and I'm prepared for the moment my high crashes. There's a catch. I know it's coming.

"Do humans no longer have libraries?" Mary glances at me over her shoulder. "Are they different now?"

It's a good question, one I don't have an answer to. I know *what* libraries are, but I've never had the opportunity to learn how, exactly, they operate. This is the first one I've been to.

"I'm not sure," I admit. "HPAW found me when I was seven. I was never permitted to leave the facility, so I've never been to a human library."

Mary's pace slows. It gives me time to catch up with her.

"Seven?" she asks.

"Yes."

"And you never left the facility?"

"No."

Mary frowns. "What about your parents?"

"HPAW told me they were killed by shifters," I say. I hesitate, my throat tight, before forcing myself to continue. "Caleb... *Alpha Knox* looked into it for me. They're indeed dead, but he believes it was HPAW's doing."

I believe him. I imagine HPAW didn't want to deal with the trouble that came with kidnapping me, and the easiest way to prevent it was to kill the only people who would raise questions.

"What about school?" Mary asks.

I can't help but laugh. "That wasn't a luxury I was afforded. I had tutors, I suppose, but attending an actual school was out of the question."

Mary steps behind her desk, quiet as she begins tapping at her computer. I shift my weight from one foot to the other, waiting and following her lead. Is she going to ask me questions? I'm not sure I'll have the answers.

Several minutes pass before the computer beeps and a machine beside it begins making noises. It's an unpleasant grinding sound, and it continues until a small card falls out of the front slot and lands in a basket.

"Give me your book," Mary orders.

I clutch it to my chest. Why does she need my book?

For the first time, Mary cracks a smile. "I'm not going to take the book from you, Evelyn."

She sounds genuine. I'm not sure if I believe it, but I don't want to make a scene. I slide the book across the desk, my pulse racing as she scans the barcode on the back.

"Here." She returns it to the desk, then sets the card she created on top of it. "That's your card. You need it to check out books. You have three weeks, and you'll be charged for each day you're late. I'm not above putting the balance on Alpha Knox's account and putting a hold on yours if you don't pay."

I stare at her, dumbfounded. "It's this easy?"

Mary nods. "Yeah. Try not to fuck it up."

I eye the sprawling rows of shelves in disbelief. Any of these books can be mine, for free, for three whole weeks?

Mary clears her throat, demanding my attention. "What did HPAW tell you about us?"

I wince. "Not very kind things."

"Like what?"

Why does she care? "They said shifters are cruel, violent people who take pleasure in torturing and killing humans. I believed that by killing Caleb, I'd be saving the entire human population."

My cheeks redden. I feel foolish saying it out loud, and even more so for having believed it so wholeheartedly.

Mary frowns, leaning back in her chair. For once, she doesn't correct my improper use of Caleb's name. "That's a lot to put on a seven-year-old child."

I shrug. She's not wrong.

Multiple heads are turned toward me, the few shifters here not bothering to pretend they aren't listening. They know I was a member of HPAW and tried to kill Caleb, but they have no idea why.

I want to explain myself. I was an impressionable child with no family, and I was lied to by grown adults who knew precisely how to manipulate me. I shouldn't have done what I did, but there's more to it than meets the eye.

My hatred of wolves was ingrained in me for years. HPAW made me believe that the entire human population depended on me, and I was just trying to do what I thought was right.

"Do you still think those things?" Mary asks.

"No," I'm quick to say. "I don't."

Mary stares blankly at me, and I tap my fingers against the back cover of my book before nervously clearing my throat and gesturing to the door.

"I should get going."

Mary doesn't stop me. She doesn't say anything as I leave, but I can feel her heavy stare on my back. What does she think? Does it change anything? Probably not, but it still feels good to have had the opportunity to explain myself.

Chapter Thirty-Four

Coffee burns my tongue. I hiss, running my tongue along the roof of my mouth. *Damn.*

I glance at the clock, surprised to see how little time has passed since I last checked it. I don't work today, and I don't know what to do with myself.

My gaze shifts to the pile of books sitting on my coffee table. I finished the one Mary helped me check out yesterday, and I didn't waste time picking out several more. I'm going to spend the day reading them.

I reach for one, but my black marking steals my attention. Well, it threatens to. I refuse to look at it. The smudged lines hover at the edge of my vision, and I last only two seconds before looking at them. Black. Smudged. Dead.

I turn, burying my face into one of my couch cushions, then scream. It's cathartic. I continue until my chest is heaving and my vocal cords hurt. That feels better. Kind of.

I shove my hair out of my face and pick up my book. Mary held back laughter as she checked it out, but she didn't outright mock me for my genre choice. It wouldn't have bothered me. I'm not ashamed of my desire for romance.

Mary was oddly tame with me. I wouldn't go as far as to say she was helpful or friendly, but her dirty glares were softer and she didn't snap at me when I forgot to use Caleb's Alpha title.

I open to where I left off, skimming mindlessly over the words. This book isn't capturing my attention as much as I hoped, but I'm over halfway finished and determined to see it through.

My eyes grow droopy about fifty pages in, and I stick a bookmark between the pages before rolling onto my side and letting my eyes slip shut. Sleep hovers at the edges of my mind, threatening to pull me under, before abruptly vanishing as somebody bangs on my door.

I jerk upright, annoyed and disoriented as I scramble to my feet and make my way to the door. The banging continues, growing louder with each passing second. What the fuck is going on? Caleb would never knock like this, not unless it were an emergency. Is it an emergency? I hurry, ripping open the door.

My shoulders fall when I lock eyes with Adam.

I frown. "What do you want?"

My infuriating neighbor frowns and steps back. He looks me up and down, openly judging my clothing. I'm wearing Caleb's shirt, the one Adam caught me in after I spent the night at Caleb's house. I cross my arms over my chest.

The corner of Adam's lip twitches. He's laughing at me.

It's not like he's in a much better state of dress. His sweatpants hang loosely off his hips, and his shirt looks to be at least twenty years old. The once-dark color has faded to a dingy gray, and I'm pretty sure I spot a hole near his armpit.

"Well?" I prompt.

Adam sighs, already annoyed. I don't understand why. He's the one bothering me. He works his jaw from side to side before shoving a piece of paper against my chest.

I scramble to catch it. "What the fuck?"

"Everybody is talking about how you didn't know what a library card was."

Okay? What am I supposed to do with that information? I assume everything I do is spoken about among the shifters. I seem to be a fun topic of discussion.

The paper Adam shoved at me is folded up, and I exhale as I unfold it. There's a handwritten list of bullet points inside. I read through it, beyond confused. What is this supposed to be?

1. The coffee shop you frequent has a reward program. Ask them for a punch card the next time you go in. Every tenth coffee is free.

2. If a shifter asks you to play catch, say no. You are the object to catch, and they will chase you.

3. Stay away from shifter toddlers. They bite.

4. Your mate has been frequenting the bonfires to burn his extra energy. Mateless shifter women have been all over him, hoping to catch his attention. It's embarrassing that you haven't shown up to put them in their place.

5. I'm an elementary school teacher. Third grade. You once ran past the elementary school. Don't do that again. The children ran to the windows and mocked your form.

6. You have poor running form. Push your shoulders back and shorten your strides. You look like you're about to topple over. It's unattractive.

7. Your apartment smells stale. Open your windows.

What the fuck is this? I reread the list, skipping over the fourth item. I don't care to read about Caleb's interactions with other women, especially not while Adam is here to see my every reaction. He'll take sick pleasure in my discomfort.

I also skip over his insults on my running. I have excellent form. Daniel made sure of that.

"What's the point of this?" I ask. Is he trying to help or humiliate me? I can't tell.

Adam scratches the stubble on his jaw. "You made me cookies. I don't want to owe you." He rocks back on his heels, then jerks his chin toward the list. "Did you see what I wrote about Knox and the mateless women?"

"Yes." I shove the note into my pocket. "Why are you telling me this?"

"Word is spreading about your upbringing. There's been a lot of speculation about your relationship with HPAW..." Adam trails off, grimacing, before continuing. "I work with children. I see how vulnerable they are—how vulnerable *you* must have been. I don't really like you, but you don't deserve all the hate you're getting."

I suck my cheeks into my mouth, my eyes narrowing.

"I tried to kill your alpha..." I point out.

Adam nods. "Yeah, and he's lying to you about your mate bond." He points to my hand. "His is no longer darkening. The color stopped changing days ago. Knox is prolonging the inevitable, and with HPAW's recent attacks, we don't need the uncertainty. I'm taking it upon myself to speed things along."

Caleb's marking is no longer darkening? I need to sit. My head swims as I retreat to my couch, dropping onto the cushion nearest the door. Adam welcomes himself inside my apartment, shutting the door behind him.

"Do you want a drink?" he asks.

I don't answer. Adam doesn't even seem to notice as he looks around, taking in my space. Under normal circumstances, I'd wonder what he thinks of it, but I genuinely don't give a fuck right now. Caleb's marking is no longer darkening? Why hasn't he said anything?

"He told me his mark would blacken and our bond would die," I say. "He said that once both of ours were black, he'd be free to take a wife."

Adam hums. "That's true." He crosses my apartment and pushes open two of my windows. "Two blackened marks equal a dead bond." He makes his way to my stack of books, flicking through them. He doesn't comment on the genre as he shifts his focus to my old notes.

"Your notes are unorganized..." he mumbles. "Knox should enroll you in higher education."

I ignore his snobby insults. "Why do you think his mark stopped darkening?"

"I'll have Mary direct you to the grammar books the next time you visit the library," he continues. "They'll be better for your brain than this..." He taps his fingers against the top book in my stack. "This erotica."

He picks it up and reads the back, his eyebrows raising. "I might have to borrow this once you're finished."

"How do you know his mark stopped darkening?" I'm running out of patience.

Adam sets my book down. "I'm not sure Knox will be pleased to learn his mate is reading porn."

"I'm sure he'll be even less pleased to learn there's a male in my home making comments about my porn," I snap.

Adam barks out a laugh. "Fair point." He extends his hand, showing me his marking. His is floral like mine, but while mine is covered in intricate details, his is simpler. Thin vines travel up his thumb and pointer finger before joining together on top of his hand and wrapping around his wrist. It's a light pink, close to the crisp, white color of an untainted mark, but not quite.

"It got pretty dark while I was attending university," Adam admits. "I struggled with the fidelity aspect of having a bonded mate. Why should I save myself for a woman I don't know? I let women put their mouths on me."

"I'm surprised to learn shifter women were willing to touch a man who isn't their mate."

"I attended a human university in America." He waves his hand, casually dismissing the direction of our conversation, as if he didn't just drop a giant bomb.

He attended an American university? How many shifters are doing that? How long has this been going on? I assume the universities are unaware. I also assume that's not where the infiltration ends. How many facets of human life do the shifters still have access to? Are they in our government? Are there shifters in disguise as HPAW members?

"I've yet to meet my mate," Adam continues. "But I'm excited for her. I've matured since university, and I treat my bond with the respect it deserves. My mark has lightened over the years. I'm hoping it will be white by the time we meet. I won't lie to her about my past, and my mark will prove that my intentions are pure." Adam flexes his hand. "Not every shifter is lucky enough to lighten their mark. It's rare, but it happens. You're doing something the bond likes."

I can't imagine what that would be. Other than my one moment of weakness the other day, the one that led me to his bed, I've been successfully avoiding Caleb. He's been doing the same to me, too.

"You should really stake your claim on him soon," Adam continues. "We need our alphas united. It's how packs operate, and you two are fucking everything up. It's selfish."

I don't know what to think of any of this.

Adam gestures to my hand. "Your mark was deep red when you joined the pack. Why?"

"HPAW encouraged me to do things they knew would harm my bond with Caleb."

"Like what?"

I smack my tongue against the roof of my mouth. "Have sex, primarily."

Adam's eyebrows furrow. "I was with two to three women a

night for several years, and my mark didn't come even *close* to being as dark as yours. You must've had a lot of sex."

I hide my hands behind my back.

"You were captured when you were seven..." Adam trails off, looking for confirmation. I give it with a curt nod. "How old were you when they started encouraging you to have sex?"

I turn away, staring at the wall beside his head. That's none of his fucking business.

"Well?" Adam urges.

"I'm not sure," I spit out. "I was thirteen, maybe."

Adam whispers a hushed curse, then paces the length of my living room. I remain where I am, watching his long legs carry him from one side of my apartment to the other. What's his problem?

"They brought you other thirteen-year-olds?" he eventually asks.

I scoff. "Of course not. The facility was swarming with soldiers. I'd pick from them."

"And how old were those soldiers?" Adam asks.

I bite my bottom lip, refusing to answer. They were adults. He knows that. I know that. It doesn't need to be said out loud.

"Evelyn... I'm so sorry."

"You should go," I say, interrupting. "You've given me a lot to think about, and I'd like to be left alone now."

Adam looks like he wants to argue, his mouth opening and shutting, before he turns and leaves. I lock the door behind him, then retreat to my couch. I lie face down, letting everything I just learned absorb. Caleb's mark is no longer darkening, which he very conveniently hasn't mentioned.

I'm no fool. He's going to those bonfires, letting unmated women throw themselves at him. I'm sure there are a few who are excited at the prospect of being chosen as his wife. He's letting it happen, and it's apparently so egregious that my asshole neighbor has taken pity and told me.

Jealousy colors my vision red. I'm done trying, done making a fool of myself.

I made mistakes, but I'm a victim, too. Caleb insists on ignoring that, blaming me for everything that's gone wrong between us. It's exhausting, and I'm done.

Chapter Thirty-Five

I step out of the bathroom, my hair dripping wet and a damp towel wrapped tightly around my torso, only to lock eyes with a flushed Caleb.

His clothes are disheveled, the collar of his shirt messed up and his pants full of crinkles. There's a wet spot on his thigh. Upon closer inspection, I realize it's drool. He must've run here in his wolf form, his clothes held in his mouth. I allow myself only a second to wonder if he redressed in public or inside my apartment lobby before telling myself I don't care.

His nostrils flare. "Why does your apartment smell like Adam?"

"Probably because he came by earlier."

He's probably also listening to my conversation with Caleb. He made it abundantly clear that he can hear everything that goes on within my apartment, and I doubt he respects my private conversations.

Caleb hums. "I was under the impression you two didn't get along." He glances at the wall separating our apartments. "I've received multiple angry visits from him these past few days. It seems you make quite a bit of noise."

Adam is so fucking annoying.

"I didn't realize you two were such good friends," I say.

"I'm friendly with everybody," Caleb says. He pauses, thinking over his following words. "We were roommates for a brief period during university."

I dip my chin. "I see."

How are the shifters getting into American colleges? The shifters may have found ways to hide their marks when they lived among the humans, but we now know what to look for. People are on high alert. Even without the markings on their hands, both Caleb and Adam are fucking huge. There's no way they would've gone unnoticed.

People surely would've suspected.

If I were still working for HPAW, I'd pry for details. Is Caleb expecting me to? I bite my tongue, refusing to take the bait.

"Were you getting blowjobs, too?" I ask instead.

Spite and anger have the question erupting out of me. I'm pretty sure I already know the answer, but Caleb clearly has no issues lying to me. I resist the urge to look at his hand. Adam says his mark is no longer darkening, and I want to see the proof for myself.

Caleb's gaze flickers in the direction of Adam's apartment, his eyes narrowing. "No, I was not. Adam and I had differing views on what saving ourselves for our mates means." A moment of tense silence passes before Caleb continues. "Why was Adam here?"

I wrap my towel tighter around myself. "That's none of your concern."

Caleb blinks. Blinks again. Blinks for a third time.

"Not my concern?" His gaze darkens, and that odd glaze comes over his eyes. His wolf is interested in this conversation, too. "I can assure you it very well fucking is, Evelyn."

I can only imagine the emotions his wolf is feeling. From what I understand, the animal part of him acts purely on emotion. It must be pissed that another man was alone with me in my apartment. That's too damn bad.

I go to step into my bedroom. Caleb stops me. He moves quickly, standing in the living room one second and blocking my bedroom door in the next.

I glare up at him. "Move."

"No." Caleb meets my glare. "Why was Adam here?"

My hands curl into fists. "Because we were fucking, of course."

Caleb runs his tongue along his top teeth. At the same moment, something hard smacks against the wall Adam and I share. It's Adam, probably hitting the wall in anger. I ignore it.

Caleb looks about ready to burst. The little vein in his forehead is pulsating, and I can practically *feel* the angry heat emanating from his torso.

"That's not funny." He speaks slowly, enunciating every word.

I shrug. "I'm not joking."

"Adam has *not* touched you."

"Maybe he has."

Caleb doesn't get to care. He's openly flirting with other women. Besides, he once told me he hopes I make a life for myself in his pack. He sure intends to, so why shouldn't I? He promised me that he would wait until his marking blackened and our bond was dead. That was a lie.

"Adam has a big cock," I say. Another pound on the wall, this one louder than the last. I'm taking this too far. I don't care. "And his tongue... *Fuck*... It's just so—"

"I should've accepted those blowjobs," Caleb spits, cutting my sentence short. "I wish I had fucked those women who threw themselves at me. You should've *seen* the way they looked at me. There was one woman. A sexy, little redhead. Her name was—"

I shove Caleb's chest. "Fuck you!"

He doesn't move, and his chest rumbles with mocking laughter. "Haven't you gotten the hint by now? I don't want to."

I stop breathing. Caleb snaps his mouth shut with an audible click. He closes his eyes, his cheeks rounding as he exhales. His muscles relax as he calms, but I've never been so stiff.

"Why are we arguing, Evelyn?" he asks. "Why are you upset with me?"

"You tell me."

Caleb drags a hand through his hair. "What did Adam tell you?"

"Show me your mark."

When Caleb hesitates, I take the initiative to grab his wrist. He doesn't fight me as I pull his hand between us. His marking is now a deep red, almost as dark as mine was when I came here.

"When did it stop darkening?" I ask. Caleb doesn't answer. I continue. "Do you truly detest me that much? I was a *victim*, Caleb." I swallow, refusing to let myself cry. "I was a child, and I didn't know any better. You don't get to judge me for that."

I was lied to and abused by the adults who were meant to protect me. I understand why Caleb is mad at me. I tried to kill him, for fuck's sake. I fully understand his anger, but it doesn't change the fact that this is a complicated situation. Things aren't nearly as black and white as he wants them to be.

Caleb shakes his head. "You don't understand, Evelyn."

"Then tell me." My voice cracks. I ignore it. "Tell me, Caleb."

"HPAW's weapons now emit a high-frequency noise that overwhelms us in our wolf forms," he says. "We can't shift, and it leaves us vulnerable to their bullets. They attacked a small border pack last week. We weren't prepared. It was a slaughter. Men. Women. Children. All fucking dead."

My heart pounds, and I clutch the edges of my towel as I wait for Caleb to elaborate. HPAW is continually developing new weapons and strategies, but they're rarely successful. Shifters are hard to kill, and they're skilled at adapting to the changes HPAW implements.

"One shifter survived," Caleb continues.

"With a message, I presume."

Caleb nods. "Yes. They threatened you..."

"I don't understand what this has to do with you denying our mate bond."

"It has *everything* to do with it." Caleb presses his forehead against mine, then runs his thumbs across my cheekbones. His touch is soft, borderline reverent. "If people believe our bond is dead, you're not so much of a target. You lose importance." Caleb swallows. "I need HPAW to believe you're unimportant to me, at least until we know how to defend ourselves against their new weapons."

I grind my teeth. This isn't how I anticipated this conversation going. I thought we'd argue. I thought Caleb would break my heart. He's exceptionally good at that.

"What're you going to do?" I ask. "With HPAW?"

Caleb hesitates. I lower my gaze. He doesn't want to tell me. Our bond might be healing, but he still doesn't trust me. I'm not sure what else I can do to prove myself. At this point, it's on him. I've done all I can.

"We're going to kill them."

My head snaps up. Caleb blinks, waiting for my reaction. Is he expecting me to panic? To beg him to spare HPAW?

I straighten my spine, holding eye contact. "As you should."

Caleb has gone out of his way to avoid war with the humans. He's made a genuine effort, but he has to prioritize his pack. I might have once argued with him, maybe even *pleaded* with him to show mercy, but I'm done with that.

Fuck HPAW. They lied to me. They abused me. They raped me. I have no love for them.

"And where does this leave us?" I ask.

It takes Caleb a long minute to answer. "I don't know."

Of course he doesn't. I'm not going to figure it out for him, either.

I sigh. "You should leave."

Caleb licks his lips. "You don't understand, Ev. If I reclaim you as my mate, I'm not letting you out of my sight. That job you're so proud of? Gone. Your impromptu trips to the library?

Gone. I will be by your side every minute of every day. You will not leave my sight."

He takes my wrist, sliding his fingers up my arm. I swallow, my throat dry as his fingertips travel up the side of my neck. "Is that what you want? The game has changed. HPAW has proven to be a credible threat, and being my mate puts a target on your back."

I open my mouth, then clamp it shut. I wouldn't be able to work or visit the library? Caleb threw me to the wolves, literally, but I've adapted. I've found pleasure in my independence. It's hard—and oftentimes lonely—but there's a sense of pride that comes with it.

Caleb tucks a strand of hair behind my ear. "Think about it, Ev."

He's brushing past me a moment later. I stare at my bedroom door, not moving even as my apartment door opens and shuts. There's a quiet click as my front door is locked from the outside. So Caleb does have keys, after all. I figured as much.

Chapter Thirty-Six

Adam is standing in front of my door when I return from work the next day, his arms crossed over his chest and a deep-set frown marring his features.

"Why did you tell Knox that we were intimate?"

"Because I wanted to make him angry." I gesture for Adam to step aside, then unlock my front door. "And because I don't like you."

Adam follows me inside. "I gave you valuable information, and you betrayed me."

I kick off my shoes and retreat into my living room. Adam makes himself comfortable in my apartment, pulling out a kitchen barstool and plopping down on it. For as much as he's whining about the way I used him to taunt Caleb, he clearly isn't intimidated.

Caleb knew I was lying, anyway.

"I don't appreciate you going to Caleb with our disputes," I say.

"I wouldn't feel the need to if you were a respectful neighbor."

"It's no wonder this apartment was available on such short

notice," I say. "You're annoying. Nobody wants to live beside you."

Adam shakes his head, pulling open my fridge. "This apartment wasn't empty. Your mate offered the previous tenants an excessive amount of money to break their lease and move out. This building has a great security system, and it's only a few minutes' run from Knox's office." Adam shuts the fridge, evidently not finding anything of his liking inside. "Your mate tried making me move out, too, so he could tear down our connecting wall and turn the entire floor into one unit."

"You should've accepted his offer."

Adam nods. "You're telling me. I didn't realize just how miserable living beside you would be."

I'm not offended by his insults. He can talk about hating me all he wants, but he's the one sauntering around my apartment like he owns the damned place. I don't understand why.

"Isn't there somebody else for you to bother?" I ask.

"No." Adam pushes open one of my windows. "My friends have all found their mates and started popping out babies. I need a break from them."

"Where's your mate?"

Adam shrugs. "Your guess is as good as mine. I haven't met her yet."

"Maybe she's dead."

"And maybe you should shut the fuck up."

I raise my eyebrows but don't respond. Adam leans over my windowsill, letting the chilly, winter air blow his hair out of his face. He stares blankly out of it, his face slack. Can't he do this in his own apartment? I'm sure he has windows, too.

"Can I borrow one of your books?" he finally asks.

"Of course not," I say. "I don't trust you with it. You can check it out of the library once I'm finished."

The corners of Adam's lips twitch, almost curling into a smile. "I like you, Evelyn."

I can't fathom why.

"There's a bonfire tonight," he continues. "We're going."

Adam surely thinks highly of himself if he believes I'll willingly go anywhere with him. I trust him about as far as I could throw him and, judging by his sheer size and the amount of muscle he keeps hidden under his ratty clothing, I doubt I could so much as lift him off the floor.

"I'm not going anywhere with you," I say.

An icy gust of wind comes through my open window, hitting me square in the face. I wince, stepping out of the way.

Adam pulls the window shut. "Well, that's just not true because you're coming to the bonfire with me tonight."

"And why would I do that?"

Adam shrugs. "Because this thing happening between you and Knox has gone on too long. Knox told you what was happening with HPAW, and it's caused a lot of uncertainty and fear. We need stability. You, Miss Evelyn, will provide said stability."

"Caleb is a grown man," I argue. "And he's been leading the pack without a mate by his side for years. I'm sure he's perfectly capable."

Adam grabs my jacket and shoes. "He's a shifter with a broken bond. Your mate is an incredible leader, but he's distracted. You're a distraction." He shoves my things into my hands. "You will go to the bonfire tonight, and you'll stake your claim. You will clarify for everybody your position within this pack and within our alpha's life."

"How do you even know Caleb will be there tonight?" I ask.

I'm not agreeing to anything. Caleb gave me a lot to think about yesterday, and I don't yet have my answer. If he had come to me with his proposal two weeks ago, I would've accepted it without a second thought. I wanted nothing more than for things to go back to the way they used to be.

But now I have a job with direct deposit and a library card I'm making good use of. I'm sure Caleb will still find time to take me to the library, but it won't be at my leisure. And I'll have to quit my job. There's no way around that.

The truth is that I don't want to give those things up. I'm independent for the first time in my life, and it feels incredible.

Besides, what if Caleb and I aren't able to work? There's so much bad blood between us, and I'm scared it has permanently altered our relationship. He'll never fully trust me again.

Adam groans. "Look, I overheard your conversation last night—I appreciate your compliments on my cock, by the way—and I get that you're dealing with a lot, but let's be honest with ourselves here. You're going to choose Knox. We both know that, and all you're doing is prolonging the inevitable."

"I—"

"Yeah, yeah, yeah," Adam continues. "You don't want to give up your independence and freedom and all that, but it's not like you're losing it forever. Your mate wants you to stick by him for a few weeks, maybe for a few months, until everything with HPAW is smoothed over. You'll be bored, but you'll survive."

I glare at Adam but don't argue. I don't like how much he overhears. He knows too much about my personal relationships, and it's not appreciated.

Adam quirks a brow. "Every day that you procrastinate is another day that unmated women are rubbing up against your mate. They can tell how...frustrated he is. They run alongside him, nipping at his ankles and trying to start a fight. They want to play with him."

I clench my fists but otherwise don't give Adam the satisfaction of a reaction. That doesn't seem to bother him in the slightest.

"He can't exactly tell them off without sharing it's because you two have decided to patch things up," Adam continues. "They're on him every fucking night."

Anger has my face flushing. "Shut up."

"Don't be a coward, Evelyn."

I'm not a fucking coward.

Chapter Thirty-Seven

I glare at the back of Adam's head as he leads me into the woods, his pace just a little too fast to be comfortable. I should slit *his* throat next.

Wolves blur as they run around us, darting in and out of sight with unnatural ease. Nobody attacks me, which I count as a personal victory. Maybe Adam wasn't lying when he said the pack is eager for Caleb and me to find common ground.

I don't understand why. I was a member of HPAW. They should hate me. Maybe my less-than-stellar upbringing has earned me some pity. I don't love that, but I'll take what I can get.

Three wolves run up on us. They're intimidatingly massive up close. Why did HPAW even bother teaching me how to fight? There was no point. Maybe it was about discipline, or their attempt to turn me into a killer.

The wolves circle Adam, nipping at his ankles. He grunts, kicking out his foot. "Fuck off. I'll join you later." He jerks his chin toward me. "I have precious cargo."

The wolf he kicked whines before darting forward, sinking its teeth deep into Adam's calf. It draws blood, and Adam spins and fully kicks it in the arm.

"Fucking asshole. You'll pay for that."

The wolf yips, sounding almost excited by the threat, before darting away. I try to follow its movements, but it's too fast. Do they know how to fight in their skin forms? As far as I'm aware, they almost always transform into their animal forms when dealing with HPAW soldiers. If HPAW found a way to prevent the shifters from transforming... that's not good.

Adam continues walking, speeding up once the flickers of a flame appear between the trees. I recognize the area. Several shifters are standing by the fire, and they look over as Adam and I approach. They seem confused, their gazes darting between Adam and me.

"Where is he?" Adam asks.

A woman opposite the fire lifts her arm, gesturing to the left. Despite the cold weather, she's in a practically sheer dress. I assume it's easy to slip on and remove when shifting between animal and skin forms.

"He's taking a lap," she says. "He left a while ago. Should be back soon."

Adam hums, pulling out a chair. "Sit," he orders me.

I should tell him to fuck off. Instead, I scoot the chair closer to the fire and plop down. It's freezing tonight, and the fire is the only source of warmth. I'm not going to turn it down out of spite.

"What are—" I turn toward Adam, my voice dying in my throat.

He's already undressing, his shirt coming up over his head and his pants quick to follow. I turn away, uninterested in seeing anything else. I was under the impression that he'd be sticking by my side, but when he transforms into his animal form and takes off into the woods, I realize I'm on my own.

I'm a lone human surrounded by agitated shifters. This is wonderful.

I wait, impatient to get out of here. I don't know the way out of the woods, so I'm stuck here until either Adam or Caleb returns. I suppose I could ask one of the other shifters here for help, but I don't.

A small part of me wants to see Caleb. Is Adam telling the truth about my mate being surrounded by unmated women, or is he exaggerating to make me mad?

Several minutes pass before Caleb appears. I recognize him immediately. His size gives him away. He's larger than the other wolves, and he draws attention. It's hard *not* to notice him.

Caleb runs into the clearing, his paws pounding into the damp ground and kicking up mud. He's practically covered in it, and it flies in all directions as he lunges at a shifter on his right.

They both topple over, a pile of snarls and sharp claws as two other shifters join in. I know they're only playing, but seeing three shifters attacking Caleb is a terrifying sight. They're vicious, drawing blood without care.

Caleb holds his own, fighting with strength and speed I didn't realize he possessed. It's incredible, and I find myself leaning forward to watch. Several shifters take turns attacking Caleb, circling him before darting forward to take a bite.

One buries its teeth into Caleb's hind leg. It's a hard bite, and when he pulls away, a chunk of leg is missing. I wince, gulping. Caleb limps back a step, then pivots and sinks his teeth into the shifter's throat.

He could kill the shifter if he bit down, but he doesn't. He holds the shifter captive, forcing it to roll over onto its back.

Then it transforms. My heart stops.

A naked woman lies on the ground beneath Caleb, her long dark hair splayed around her shoulders as she laughs and tries to roll away. My hands curl into fists, but I otherwise don't react. I'm giving Caleb the benefit of the doubt, something I should've done a long time ago.

"Okay, okay!" The woman snorts, her fingers curling around Caleb's paw. "You win!"

Caleb releases her and steps back. Only once they're no longer touching can I breathe again, and I draw in a deep inhale as the woman sits up. Caleb gives his back to her, facing another shifter.

The woman finally takes notice of me. She stills as we make eye contact, and then she fucking smiles. It's vindictive, and I lose all semblance of control as she turns back to Caleb.

I'm tired of this fucking shit.

Caleb still hasn't noticed me, and he doesn't see the woman lunging for his back.

I'm out of my chair in a heartbeat, blood rushing through my ears as I storm toward the wolves. Is it a good idea to throw myself into the middle of a shifter fight? Nope. They're only playing, but it's still dangerous.

One wrong move and I'll be split in two.

This woman isn't in her animal form, though. She throws herself onto Caleb's back, her thin arms wrapping around his neck and her legs around his waist. Caleb rears back, standing tall on his hind legs, before trying to shake her off.

They don't notice me approaching from behind. I use that to my advantage as I reach up, grab a handful of the woman's hair, and rip. She releases Caleb with a cry, and I find a sick satisfaction in the way she falls. I release her before she lands, watching as her back smashes against the hard ground. Her head is quick to follow.

Caleb transforms out of his animal form, but I pay him no mind. I'm focused on the woman, adrenaline coursing through my system as she flips around and jumps to her feet. I'm expecting to be met with anger, but her gaze is filled with unnerving excitement as she lunges for me.

Ah, fuck. I step back, barely processing what's happening as the naked woman descends on me in an attack of gangly limbs and wild laughter. What the hell is happening? She has a natural advantage, but I realize almost immediately that she has no skill.

I hook my leg around her thigh, then roll her underneath me. Her hips buck as I sit on her, but I'm not going anywhere. She'll have to try harder than that to get me off.

She smashes her palm into my mouth, trying to push me away. I bite. Hard enough to draw blood.

Something in her expression shifts. She's realizing what I already know to be true. I'm a better fighter, at least in this form. I'm going to win.

Arms loop beneath my armpits and hoist me into the air, effortlessly removing me from the woman.

"Alright," Caleb's low voice rumbles in my ear. "That's enough of that."

He marches me away, only stopping once we're on the other side of the bonfire. I'm panting, my harsh breaths loud as he finally sets me on my feet. I'm livid, maybe even a little embarrassed, as I glare up at him.

"Why are you starting fights with my pack members?" he asks.

I scoff. "Why are you rolling around in the dirt with naked women?"

"I would hardly say that's what's happening." Caleb rolls his shoulders, then continues. His voice is noticeably softer. "Danielle is a happily mated woman. We weren't—"

I interrupt. "Adam told me that you're letting unmated women rub up against you. He said you're playing with them. Every night."

Caleb cocks his head to the side, two lines forming between his eyebrows. He looks genuinely confused, and I curse as the pieces fall into place. I fucking hate Adam.

"Danielle is a schoolteacher," Caleb eventually says. "She works closely with Adam."

It seems he's coming to the same conclusion. Adam lied to me. He spewed straight shit to get me out here, and he probably convinced Danielle to provoke me into taking action.

I scuff my foot against the muddy ground, no doubt dirtying my shoes. I regret coming here. Women aren't swarming Caleb, and I just made an absolute fool of myself for no reason. Fucking idiot.

Caleb clears his throat. "Look at me."

"I'd rather not."

He frowns, cupping my cheek. "Look at me, Evelyn."

"Do you still love me?" I finally give in and look at him. I'm tired of us skirting around one another. "Despite everything, do you still love me?"

I clasp my hands together, running my fingers over my blackened mark. The color hasn't changed, but I'm hopeful. Caleb's marking has stopped darkening, so we must be doing something right.

Caleb chews on his bottom lip, hesitating. "It's not that simple," he finally says.

"Yes, it is. Do you still love me? Yes or no."

Caleb lifts his head, scanning the area. I grab his face, stopping him. "Don't look at them. Look at me." I tighten my grip, letting my fingertips dig into the hollow of his cheeks.

Out of the corner of my eye, a shifter approaches. It's a man I've seen once or twice before. He works closely with Caleb.

"Alpha…" he starts.

Caleb's eyes never stray from mine. "Leave us."

"The other alphas are—"

"Walk away."

The shifter huffs, then retreats.

"Do you still love me?" I repeat.

Caleb gulps. "I told you I loved you the last time we were here, and you humiliated me."

"I know. I'm sorry."

Caleb shrugs, then draws in a shaky breath. "I still love you."

Warmth erupts in my chest. I was really hoping this would be his answer, but I wasn't certain. I betrayed Caleb, and I wouldn't blame him for holding reservations.

"Then I'm willing to be your mate, whatever that entails," I say. "I'll quit my job, and I won't leave your side until things with HPAW have settled. I'll let you do whatever you feel you need to do to keep me safe, but only if you take me back as your mate."

Caleb blinks. "And when things with HPAW have settled... what then?"

"Then you'll teach me everything I need to know about being the female alpha. We'll find a place for me in your pack." I gulp. "You will fuck your children into me. You will be mine, and only mine."

Caleb pants into the air between us, his breath warm. He's practically *vibrating* with energy, hopefully positive.

"You don't know what you're asking for."

I spread my arms out wide. "I absolutely do." We're drawing a crowd. Shifters are closing in on us, their eyes shining in the dark. Caleb ignores them. I do the same.

"Danielle could have killed you," he says. He sucks on his teeth and moves in closer, towering over me. It's an intimidating position, but I refuse to back down. "Shifters fight dirty. You had her pinned, and she was seconds away from transforming."

I shrug. "I didn't like the way she threw herself at you."

Caleb licks his lips, his gaze turning heady. He likes that I fought for him.

"Shifters take public claims very seriously," he murmurs. "You fought another woman for me. Do you know what that means?" His hands find my hips. "You've claimed me, Evelyn."

He spins me around, then pushes me down. My knees land on the cold, mushy ground, and my upper body quickly follows. I just barely catch myself, digging my palms into the ground.

"Does this go both ways?" Caleb asks. "You pretended to be mine, but you chose HPAW."

I drop my head, ashamed, then peer at Caleb over my shoulder. His eyes are shining, his wolf watching our every interaction. I know what it wants. Caleb has told me about mated pairs fucking in these woods. He wants to prove to his pack that I belong to him.

"I'm yours," I promise. "I belong to you. I swear it."

His tight grip on my hips is the only thing keeping me

upright. I know where this is going, and a full-body shiver runs through me as he tugs my pants and underwear down over my ass.

"Do you want this?" he asks.

I arch my back and push up my ass, presenting myself to Caleb. His responding moan tells me he enjoys it.

"Yes."

He shoves his hand between my thighs, dragging his fingers through my folds before plunging two inside. I jolt, clenching around him.

"Always so fucking wet." He groans. "Such a whore for my cock."

I meet his gaze over my shoulder. "Just as a good mate should be."

Caleb bares his teeth, his arms flexing as he frees his cock and shoves into me. He's not gentle, and he doesn't give me any time to adjust as he pulls back out and drives back in. His fucking is hard, just the way it needs to be.

I don't care if everybody hates me. I don't care if they think I'm an undeserving mate. Caleb is mine, and I refuse to let that be confused. Even without our bond, he's still my mate. He's chosen me, and I won't let there be any confusion about my place in his life.

Caleb grunts, his upper body pressing against my back with every thrust. The sound of his hips slapping against my ass is obscene, but I don't care.

"I'm the only woman who will ever feel this," I tell him. "Promise it."

Caleb buries his face against my neck, breathing in my scent. "Only you." His voice is thick with need, and I hope everybody here hears it.

I look up, finding and locking eyes with Danielle. She's still by the fire, now wearing a thin dress as she stands beside a man. He's looking at her with a mildly annoyed expression, one she ignores.

That cocky smirk from before reemerges as she lifts her cup, silently acknowledging my gaze.

Caleb grabs the back of my head, forcing me to look away.

"Don't you fucking dare," he hisses. "You will look at nobody but me while I'm inside you."

He's about to finish. His moans grow clipped, and he can't keep his hands still. They slide from my hips to my waist, dragging over my ass before returning to my waist. He pulls out at the last minute, curses, then shoves back inside.

I pant, my head hanging between my shoulders as he finishes inside me.

Caleb groans, dropping his forehead against my back as he pulls my pants back up, covering me. I glance around, relieved to see only a few shifters looking in our direction.

"Don't worry," Caleb says. "I didn't make a spectacle of you. Wolves are territorial, alphas specifically. Watching is a risk most don't care to take."

Did Adam see? I sure hope not. I doubt Caleb would let him, either, not after I tried using him to make Caleb jealous.

"Let me see your hand," Caleb orders. "Your marked one."

I shift, rolling to the side so I'm sitting on my butt. Caleb has already sorted himself, his pants up and secured at his waist. He's holding open the coat I removed earlier, and I let him slide it up my shoulders.

Then I give him my hand, but I don't look.

"It's changed," he says.

"What?"

I look, my jaw slack. My marking is still black, but the lines are no longer smudged. They're crisp, just the way they were before. I flex my fingers, in disbelief.

"Do you feel it?" My voice cracks. I shake my head. "Do you feel our bond again?"

Caleb dips his chin. "I thought I felt it when I pushed inside you, but it's slight. It's been flickering in and out." He shoves a strand of hair out of his eye. "I thought maybe I was imagining it."

"Well, there's no getting rid of me now." I force out a laugh.

"If I knew sex would've fixed our bond, I would've jumped your bones ages ago."

Caleb snorts, then helps me stand.

"You're cold." He turns, shouting into the forest. "Adam!"

I love seeing Adam summoned like a little bitch. I hope it hurts his ego.

Caleb strokes my cheek, drawing my attention. "I have an important meeting in an hour that I can't miss," he says. "I need to travel there in my wolf form, so I can't bring you with me. Adam will take you to your apartment. I'll be by shortly, I promise."

He's leaving? I bite my cheek, then nod. We can talk later.

Chapter Thirty-Eight

Adam helps himself to my half-eaten bag of chips. I glare at the side of his head.

"I can handle it from here," I say. "You can leave."

"Love the confidence, but I've been given strict orders to stick with you until Knox returns."

I don't understand why Caleb ordered Adam to babysit me. He clearly doesn't like Adam, and I don't, either. I'm willing to admit my neighbor has been helpful here and there, but he's a nuisance. He's a dirty fucking liar, too.

"Did you see Caleb and me have sex?"

"No. Gross."

He shoves another handful of chips into his mouth. I turn away, disgusted at the sight. Adam has no manners, and I feel bad for the mate he ends up with. She's in for a rude awakening when she realizes her mate is an intrusive slob.

Adam drops onto the couch beside me. I scoot away, my irritation rising as he picks up my book. He flicks through the pages, then picks up one I haven't gotten to. If he notices the half-naked man on the cover, he doesn't acknowledge it. He reads the back cover, his lips pursed.

"When do most shifters find their mates?" I ask.

Adam spares me a glance. "In their teens, but almost always by early adulthood. I'm particularly unlucky."

That's one way of putting it. Adam is in his late twenties, and that's a long time to be alone. How long will he wait for his mate? Will he eventually give up and pair up with an unmated woman?

"Are you lonely?" I ask.

"Yes." He grabs another one of my books, his lips twitching as he reads the back cover. "I hope my mate doesn't take this much of an interest in porn."

I scoff. "It's romance." A brief pause, then, "And there's nothing wrong with enjoying it."

I snatch the book out of his hand and move the others out of his reach. I don't care for his unsolicited opinion.

We sit in silence until Caleb steps through my front door. About damned time.

Adam finally takes his leave, slamming my apartment door shut behind him. A second later, I hear the muffled slam of his own door shutting.

"He insulted my books," I say.

Caleb kicks off his shoes. "Do I need to beat him up for you?"

"That would be nice."

There's a bang on the wall. I resist the urge to throw a book at it in retaliation. Adam is a child. An overgrown, dirty child.

Caleb pushes the sleeves of his sweater up his forearms as he walks into my apartment. His mark remains unchanged, the color still a deep red. How long will it take to begin lightening? Days? Weeks? Months? What if it takes years? I suppose it doesn't matter too much as long as it doesn't keep darkening.

"I hate when your apartment smells of other men," Caleb admits. He pushes my window open, letting the cold air in. "I'm going to sleep here tonight. Tomorrow, we'll stop by the hospital for a check-up and for you to give Greg your resignation."

"I don't need check-ups anymore."

Caleb raises a brow. "Humor me."

"Okay."

Things fall silent. What now?

"You didn't orgasm earlier," Caleb finally says.

"Was I supposed to?"

"Not really." Caleb steps behind me. His breath hits the back of my neck, and I can't suppress my shiver as he slides his hands down my arms. "But I don't want to leave you hanging."

"Are—" I pause, clearing my throat as Caleb's mouth meets my shoulder. He sucks on the skin, no doubt leaving a mark. "Do you think this is a good idea? After everything...maybe we should wait."

Caleb spins me around.

I press my hand against his chest, stopping him. "Not right now."

He immediately backs away. "Okay."

More silence.

I look around, smacking my tongue against the back of my teeth. Caleb clears his throat no fewer than fifteen times.

"Do you want to talk to me about your experience with HPAW?" Caleb finally asks. "I'm sorry I didn't listen to you before. I understand they didn't treat you well, and if there's anything you'd like to share, I'm here to listen."

I shrug. "I don't really want to talk about it."

It's the truth. I don't want to dwell on my experience with HPAW. I want to move forward, and I don't feel I can if I'm constantly revisiting my time in the facility. It sucked. I was abused. That's all the attention I'm willing to give it, at least right now.

"I'm sorry I tried to kill you." I gesture toward Caleb's neck. "I feel terrible about it."

Caleb hums, brushing his fingers over the faint scar. "You aren't the first person to try to kill me, and I doubt you'll be the last. It comes with the alpha title."

The silence resumes. Should I try to bring up a mundane conversation, maybe some small talk? I've never been very good at either.

"I'd like to stay close to the office over these next few days," Caleb says. "In case you're wondering why I had Adam bring you here instead of to our home." *Our home.* "There's a meeting of the alphas tomorrow afternoon. They just arrived, and they're staying nearby. I was welcoming them into the pack earlier. That's where I went and why Adam brought you to the apartment."

"You're meeting about HPAW, I assume?"

Caleb nods. "Yes." He pauses, blows out a breath, then continues. "I'd like you to come tomorrow. If we're going to do this, we're going to do it right. No more secrets."

Caleb rolls on top of me. I groan, burying my face in his armpit. He smells like home.

There's a faint vibrating on my left. Caleb's phone. Who is calling him this early? Caleb lets out a muffled curse as he reaches for it. I'm expecting him to ignore the call, but he rolls off me and brings the device to his ear once he sees who's calling.

"What?" Caleb's voice is thick with sleep. I shiver.

A feminine voice comes through the line. I recognize it immediately. Sash. I haven't seen her since she hit me, and I'm in no hurry to encounter her again. My ears still ring from the force of her slap, and I'm not entirely certain she won't kill me the next time she sees me.

"I don't know what you're talking about," Caleb grumbles. He throws an arm over his eyes. "I wasn't at the bonfire last night."

Sash is yelling. I can't make out the words, but they sure aren't happy.

Caleb hums. "Did she try to kill me? I'd almost forgotten about *having my fucking throat slit open*, Sasha. I appreciate the reminder."

More yelling.

"Look." Caleb sits up, interrupting whatever Sash is saying. "I appreciate your concern, I really do, but you're overstepping. My relationship with Evelyn is my business, and it's not up for discussion. If you don't have anything of value to say, then this conversation is over."

I chew on my bottom lip. Sash was never anything but kind and welcoming toward me before all of this. She accepted me into her pack and family with open arms, and I can't really fault her for being protective of Caleb. Their parents are dead. They're the only family they have left.

Caleb hangs up his phone and tosses it aside.

We lie beside one another in silence. It's tense. I'm the first to break it.

"What now?" I ask.

"With you or with HPAW?"

"Both."

Caleb throws his head back, dragging his hands down his pinched face. "With us, I don't honestly know. My mark is no longer darkening, and yours has decided to resurrect itself. It's convenient timing. The pack will accept you back into the fold with time. It's already begun, and your healing mark only further proves your honesty."

I'm relieved to hear that.

"We still have a lot to work through, obviously," Caleb continues. "But my focus has to be on HPAW right now."

Caleb turns his head, watching my reaction. I'm not offended. Our bond isn't going anywhere, and it's not the priority right now. We'll have time to work on it once things have stabilized.

"I understand," I say.

Caleb nods, letting out a relieved sigh.

"And with HPAW?" I pry.

"Plans will be cemented tonight." Caleb clears his throat. "The alphas from almost every pack will be in attendance. Many of them have aggressive ideas. I've been dismissing them for years, but after the recent attacks..."

Caleb trails off.

I brush my thumb over his forehead, smoothing out the skin. "You don't need to explain yourself to me. I trust you."

"Humans will die."

"HPAW brought it upon itself."

Caleb stares into my eyes, a small smile tugging at the corners of his lips. "You're not fragile. I appreciate that about you."

Maybe, had my life shaped out differently, I would have been. Perhaps the thought of war and death would have filled me with horror. I've been lied to too much for that. HPAW wasn't kind to me, and I have no compassion for them. They made their bed, and I'm more than comfortable making them lie in it. I trust Caleb not to mindlessly target humans. The shifters have proven that's not who they are. They're good people.

I touch Caleb's chest, then slide my fingers up the column of his neck, enjoying the way his pulse beats against me. His throat bobs as he gulps, and I circle his Adam's apple before continuing upward. His stubble tickles my fingertips. He's due for a shave.

I cup his cheek, leaning in for a kiss. Caleb meets me halfway, his lips soft as they press against mine. It's a short kiss, but it says everything we aren't in a position to verbally share.

Caleb's brown eyes flutter open as I back away. He looks tired. Merely discussing HPAW is exhausting, and I can't imagine how stressful these past weeks have been for Caleb. It's no wonder Adam was so determined to force us together.

I'd thank him if he weren't such an annoying asshole.

"I hate to rush you, but we have a busy day today..." Caleb admits.

I snort, shoving down the covers and sliding out of bed. What a nice way of telling me it's time to get my lazy ass out of bed. I'm mindful not to dillydally as I dress, and I step out of my bedroom in a better mood than I've been in since my attempted murder.

Caleb is in the kitchen, tapping on his phone with one hand and cooking with the other. The sight of him cooking for me stops me in my tracks, and I draw in a trembling breath as a wave of emotion rushes through me.

"Evelyn." Caleb frowns, his eyes narrowed. "What's wrong?"

I shake my head. "Nothing. I'm just feeling very happy today."

Caleb hums, clearly not believing me, as he sets out two plates and dishes out a simple breakfast of eggs, toast, and beans. It's not his most elaborate dish, but I love it all the same.

"Do you think your sister will ever forgive me?" I ask.

Caleb shrugs. "Beats me. I've never asked her to befriend somebody who tried killing me." He meets my gaze, a smile tugging at the corners of his lips. I relax as I realize he's only teasing. "She'll forgive you. She saw the aftermath of *everything*, and it scared her. There was a lot of blood, and I was nowhere to be found. She thought I was dead. She just needs a little more time."

I suppose I can't fault her for that.

Doctor Greg hardly looks surprised to see Caleb and me enter the hospital together. He meets us in the lobby.

"Does this mark the end of your employment?" he guesses.

I nod. "Unfortunately."

"We'd also like a check-up," Caleb butts in. "Her ribs and her head, primarily."

I touch the spot on my forehead. I forgot I ever cut it. It's so minor, it's not even a thought in my mind. It definitely doesn't need to be examined.

Doctor Greg shakes his head. "No more check-ups. Evelyn is fine."

He's gone before Caleb has the chance to argue, disappearing into the back with a shake of his head. I could kiss that man. When Caleb shifts, clearly preparing to follow the doctor into the back, I grab his arm and yank him back.

"Please stop fretting over me," I beg. "I'm fine."

Caleb grumbles.

"I'll let you know if I'm ever in pain," I continue. "Besides, don't you need to prepare for your meeting with the alphas?"

That's the right thing to say. Caleb stops glaring at the door through which Doctor Greg disappeared. I worry he'll find some excuse to bring me back sooner rather than later, but I'll deal with that when the time comes.

Hopefully, it's after we meet the other alphas. I've heard a lot about them, and I can't say I'm not nervous. What will they be like? Are they like Caleb? I suppose I'm going to find out.

Chapter Thirty-Nine

Caleb dresses up for the meeting. His black suit hugs his muscular frame, fitting snugly yet not inappropriately so. It must be custom. He's wearing a crisp, white button-down underneath. It's his tie that captures my attention, though.

I laugh, stepping closer to get a better look. The light-blue fabric is covered in tiny animals.

"Wolves?" I ask.

"Of course." Caleb smirks, straightening out his tie as he gives me a quick scan.

I'm wearing black slacks. Caleb bought them for me shortly after we met, but I've never had a reason to wear them. I tucked a fitted, white button-down into them. It's the nicest top I own, the fabric silky and expensive.

"We match," I say, gesturing between us. "Are you sure I shouldn't wear something more, I don't know, feminine?"

Caleb shakes his head. "I'm introducing you as my female alpha, and we're discussing war. You're expected to wear something practical."

I look down at my black shoes. They're shiny and flat, and they have a good grip. Quite practical.

Caleb leads me outside and into my car. It's nice not to drive. Caleb always handled that when we were together, and while I thought driving was fun and exciting at first, it's grown tedious. I quickly realize we're heading in the opposite direction from his office.

"Where are we going?"

Caleb sighs. "Everett is avoiding finding his mate. It's a long story, but he refuses to meet in public spaces. There's a small building about an hour outside the city. It's the only place he's willing to meet."

I nod. "Will only alphas and their mates be there?"

"No," Caleb says. "Some have chosen to bring their high-ranking wolves with them, and Maverick has chosen to bring the two children viable to become the future alpha of his pack."

I'm strangely calm when Caleb finally pulls up to the building. It's a small spot, clearly once used as an office building. It's thankfully right off what was once a busy road, sparing me a long walk from the car to the entrance.

There's a car dealership on the left, but the lot is empty.

"How innocuous," I say as Caleb pulls into the parking lot.

Caleb shrugs. "Blame Everett."

"Every shifter in there is going to know that I was a member of HPAW and tried to kill you," I say.

Caleb hums, considering my words. "Yes. They'll also know that HPAW has been systematically abusing you since you were a child. Some will be skeptical, but most will understand the position you were put in. Plus, your marking is healing. There's no denying that our bond remains and you're my rightful mate. They'll show you respect."

"And if they don't?"

"I'll see to it that they do." Caleb grabs my hand, bringing it to his mouth. He kisses my darkened mark, his lips lingering. "You can do this."

I force myself to take several calming breaths before unbuckling my seatbelt and stepping out of the car. Caleb is by my side in an instant, his arm wrapped tightly around my waist. It's comforting, and I hold my chin high as we walk toward the building.

Caleb doesn't hesitate to push open the front door, barging his way inside.

Ah, fuck. There are more people here than I expected. At least forty shifters are present, and most of them are arguing. The alphas are easy to pick out. They stand a head taller than the others, and they seem to be the loudest.

The alpha closest to us draws my attention. He's also dressed up, donning black dress pants and a tucked-in button-up shirt, but the shirt is at least two sizes too small. His broad shoulders are tugging against the fabric, threatening to rip the seams.

Behind him are two teenage boys, one about sixteen and the other several years younger. Maybe twelve. It's hard to tell. Both are taller and bulkier than human boys, making it nearly impossible to guess their ages.

They stand stiffly behind the large alpha. This must be Maverick, and the two children behind him are the ones who may someday take over his pack. When will they know for certain who will take over? A question to ask Caleb at a later date.

Maverick turns toward Caleb and me, and then he's in front of us. He stands toe to toe with Caleb, but he's smiling. I can't tell if they like one another or not.

"You're late," Maverick grunts.

Then he turns to me, an odd glint in his eye as he looks me up and down. I sneak a peek at his marking—crisp white and full of jagged lines like Sash's and Logan's.

"You must be Evelyn," he says.

Caleb wraps his arm around my waist, holding me close. He's making a statement. "Yes. This is my *mate*, Evelyn Johnson."

Maverick quirks a brow. "I'm pleased to hear it." His slight smile falls. "I need to speak with you, Knox. Privately."

Caleb's answer is immediate. "No." He looks around the room. "There isn't time."

"It's important."

Caleb tightens his grip on my waist. I spot a familiar face in the back of the room. *What the hell is Adam doing here?* He's standing by himself, not partaking in the several arguments surrounding him. If anything, he looks bored.

He looks good, though. I've only ever seen him in ratty clothing, but he looks clean in his black dress pants and crisp, white shirt. His clothing even looks ironed. He owns an iron? I doubt it. He probably snuck into my apartment and stole mine.

"If there's something you wish to say to me, you may say it in front of my mate," Caleb insists.

Maverick's face screws up. He clearly doesn't wish to speak in front of me. I step aside, pulling out of Caleb's grasp.

"Adam's over there." I point to the wallflower. "I'm going to go say *hi*."

I'm politely excusing myself, and Caleb better take the fucking opening. I'm not interested in this room witnessing a pissing contest between Maverick and Caleb, especially over whether or not I should be privy to a private conversation. I'll earn the other alphas' trust with time.

Caleb shoots me a pained glance. I grab and squeeze his hand, trying to silently convey that I'm not upset.

"I'll be quick," he promises. Then he turns and practically shouts Adam's name, capturing the attention of the entire damned room. I wish to wither away as Caleb points to me, his eyebrows raised.

Adam places a hand in front of his mouth, hiding a laugh as he nods at whatever Caleb is silently saying to him.

I force the stiffness out of my joints as I walk toward Adam. I'm going to kill Caleb later.

"You don't look like shit for once," I say by way of greeting.

Adam shrugs. "I can clean up when the situation calls for it."

There's a stack of chairs and a folded-up table pushed up against the wall behind him. He moves for one but freezes when he takes notice of my frosty glare.

"I can stand," I snap.

Adam raises his hands, palms outward. "Okay. No need to get your panties in a twist."

"What're you doing here?" I ask. "What have you—"

An ear-piercing noise cuts off my words, and before I can even try to figure out what it is, Adam's tackling me to the ground. He's obscenely heavy, and I land on the floor with a hard *thump* just as the wall nearest us implodes.

Adam takes the brunt of the explosion, and the table leaning against the wall flips over the top of us.

He grunts as it cuts through his back, pressing him further into me. What the hell? Adam curls his arms around my head, tucking my face into the front of his shirt as the room around us bursts into chaos.

The high-pitched noise only seems to grow in volume. Adam cries out, burrowing his ear against the ground.

This is HPAW.

I cup my hands over Adam's ears, hopefully dulling the noise, as gunfire explodes within the room. Where is Caleb?

I attempt to wiggle free from Adam, but another loud explosion causes him to tighten his grip, preventing my escape. I press my hands harder against his ears as the incessant high-pitched screech grows louder.

It makes my head hurt, but it doesn't affect me nearly as much as it does the shifters.

Adam cups his hands over mine, pressing them harder against his ears, before lifting his head and looking around. His eyes are wide as he scans the room, flickering from person to person. I do the same, unable to comprehend what I'm seeing.

Humans in masks and full tactical gear storm in through the blown-out exterior wall. Wolves lunge for them, but it's clear they're struggling by the way they shake their heads and press their usually pointy ears flat against their heads.

The soldiers fire at the wolves, most landing at least a few hits before they're taken down and torn apart. The shifters who are hit cry out, the pained whines that pour from their throats like a stab to the heart.

I find Caleb.

He's in his wolf form at the front of the carnage, but his eyes are on me. His entire body is angled so he never loses sight of me, despite the vulnerable position it puts him in.

"I need to get you out of here," Adam shouts. It's hard to hear him over the carnage. "Don't fucking fight me, Evelyn, and don't let go."

I continue cupping his ears as he curls a hand under my butt, urging me to wrap my legs around his waist. I do so, holding him tightly as he prepares to jump up and run. Caleb continues to watch us, and he makes brief eye contact with Adam before dipping his chin and lunging at a soldier who gets too close.

Bile rises up my throat. What is happening? How did HPAW know about this meeting, and how did they get this far onto shifter land without being detected?

Adam jumps to his feet and takes off in the opposite direction from the fighting. He runs inhumanely fast, despite carrying me, and I tuck my face against his chest and squeeze the sides of his head for dear life as he pivots left, jumps over a knocked-over chair, and nears an emergency exit.

Not many wolves are attempting to flee. Judging by the sheer number of torn pieces of clothing on the floor, most have shifted.

Caleb told me the noise prevents shifters from transforming into their animal forms, but this wasn't a room full of regular shifters. These were the alphas and leaders, the men and women with the most dominant wolves.

We make it only a few feet from the door when another explosion rattles my teeth. It's from where we're headed, and I make eye contact with a flying piece of metal just moments before it smashes into my skull.

Chapter Forty

My head hangs, my chin pressing against my chest as my bare feet slide along cold metal. I'm sitting on a hard surface, faintly aware that my hands are tied above my head. The sharp bite of metal digs into my wrists, and I jerk sideways as the room around me spins.

The air smells like sweat. There's a slight whirring, too, but I can't tell if the sound is coming from inside my head. It feels like my skull has been split open—it probably has—but I push past the pain and force my eyes open.

Adam is the first thing I see. He's chained up across from me, maybe dead. He's slumped sideways, his handcuffed wrists the only thing keeping his body upright.

We're in a metal box—steel, maybe. A storage container, or perhaps the back of a truck. The whirring is the outside air hitting the frame.

How long have I been unconscious? How did HPAW manage to get this deep into the shifter lands without being spotted? Were they driving this truck?

My head lolls forward, and something drips into my eye. Blood, I assume.

I'm sure my head is fucked up.

Adam is the only other person here. Did HPAW not capture any other wolves?

Where is Caleb? I faintly remember him fighting alongside the shifters, his bright-brown eyes locked on me. I lost sight of him when Adam began running for the back exit, though. Did he see us getting taken?

Adam groans. So, he's alive. That's nice.

The pounding in my head makes it hard to focus, and it's only a matter of time before I pass out. Blood is steadily pouring down my face, dripping over my eye before trailing down my cheek and dripping off the tip of my chin.

My head isn't the only thing injured. My right shoulder is screaming, dislocated, and the entire right side of my chest is a ball of flame. Is my nipple gone? *Fuck.* Air hits my bare skin, so I know my shirt is torn open. I try to look, but I can't see that far down.

"Evelyn?"

I meet Adam's gaze. He licks his lips and tugs at the handcuffs chaining his wrists to the wall above his head. They don't budge.

I let out a dry laugh. "I believe we've been captured."

My words end in a pitiful cough. Pathetic.

Adam tugs on his restraints again, but with no success. The handcuffs aren't budging.

"I can't feel the lower half of my body," he quietly admits. "Everything is fuzzy."

I'm not surprised. He's only chained by his wrists, and HPAW would've locked up every inch of his body if they were concerned about him breaking free.

"I assume they've drugged you," I say. "A high dosage of xylazine is an effective, short-term way to paralyze a wolf and prevent them from shifting."

Adam throws his head back, resting it against the metal wall. "What's xylazine?"

I crack a smile. "Horse tranquilizer. It lowers your blood pressure and heart rate, and at very high doses, it causes shifters to lose feeling in their limbs."

Xylazine is frequently used by HPAW doctors when they have a captured shifter they want to question. The drug doesn't affect the mind, but it renders shifters immobile. Ideal for interrogation.

"How long have I been unconscious?" Adam asks. "I don't remember anything after the wall exploded."

"Neither do I." I shrug. "I only just woke up."

The vehicle jerks, and I cry out as my shoulder pulls. Adam looks me over, his gaze lingering on my chest.

"My nipple's gone, isn't it?" I ask.

He shakes his head. "Your nipple is fine, but a giant piece of metal is sticking out of your chest directly above it."

Well, that's not good.

"Is it going to kill me?"

Adam grimaces. "Maybe if it got pulled out. I think you'll be fine as long as it remains. It's plugging you up."

"Wonderful." My voice wavers. "Do you have any life-threatening injuries I should know about?"

"Not that I know of." Adam tugs again at his restraints, still with no success. He flexes his fingers and tries to wiggle his wrists through the metal, but that also doesn't work.

Even if he manages to free his arms, he can't fight. I doubt the man has enough strength in his legs to stand, let alone defend himself. HPAW will chain him back up and inject more xylazine.

I search for cameras. None to be found.

Adam continues to fight with his restraints. I busy myself with trying not to bleed out and die.

Is Caleb still alive? I imagine he's on a rampage right about now. The pack is probably in chaos, and I hope not too many shifters were killed in the attack. I faintly recall seeing a few wolves shot down, but maybe the wounds weren't lethal.

Doctor Greg is going to have a busy night.

I doubt Adam and I were unconscious for long, maybe five to ten minutes, and I count to keep track of the time. Shifters are fast, and I'm confident Caleb is on his way to us. It's only a matter of time before we're rescued.

I count.

And count.

And count.

Enough time passes that I'm certain we're out of shifter lands. Caleb's sure taking his sweet time getting to us.

Adam makes a pained noise. I look up, watching through blurry vision as he tries to stand. The xylazine must be wearing off.

His legs shake, his knees knocking together. I'm surprised he doesn't crumble as he turns toward his marked hand. His forearm is covered in dried blood from where his handcuffs have torn open his skin. He brings his marking to his face.

"Adam?" I ask.

Is he going to try gnawing his way through the metal? He presses his lips to his mark instead, kissing the white design. I tilt my head, confused, before recoiling in horror as he opens his mouth and bites into his flesh.

A loud, pained whine slips from Adam's throat as he sinks his teeth into his mark, ripping it clean off. Blood spews as he bites straight through muscle and ligament, the sight nauseating.

Adam roughly chews and spits the skin onto the floor. It lands with a splat between us.

I heave, staring at the mangled flesh as Adam's knees give out. He collapses, blood continuing to pour from his hand. Adam is losing it. He's been in this truck for a few hours and is losing his fucking mind.

"What..." I pause, unable to comprehend what the hell I just saw.

Adam stares at the ceiling, his breathing ragged.

"I don't want them knowing who my mate is," he says. "They'll hurt her to get to me. I won't let that happen."

I swallow, my throat dry. "Will it heal?"

Adam clenches his jaw, then shrugs. "Probably not."

"You'll still feel the mate bond, though? Right?" My voice is laced with desperation, but I don't think I could hide it even if I tried. I'm too exhausted, too injured, to hide my emotions.

Caleb said he couldn't feel the bond once my mark went black, but that's different than one being bitten off. It has to be. Adam has waited so long for his mate, and I know how badly he wants one.

"You still have a mate, don't you?"

"I don't know."

I open my mouth, then snap it shut.

"Caleb is on his way," I finally say. "He's just waiting for the right moment."

Adam licks his lips and spits out a mouthful of blood, several emotions flashing across his face. Doubt is the most prominent. He doesn't believe me, but I don't need him to. He'll see I'm right when Caleb saves us.

"Do you really think Knox would wait to save you? That he'd sit around and wait for the perfect opportunity to strike?" Adam's voice is unnaturally soft, but I refuse to believe what he's saying. "You're dying, Ev. If he were able, he'd have torn apart this vehicle and every HPAW soldier the first moment he could."

I turn away. "That's not true."

Adam doesn't know what he's talking about. I resume counting.

The vehicle eventually slows to a stop. I shoot Adam a look as the back doors are pulled open, ready for wolves to pour inside.

Three humans jump inside instead. They're HPAW soldiers, decked out head to toe in tactical gear. They pay me no mind as they approach Adam, and the one in front pulls a needle out of his vest pocket.

Adam kicks at the man's leg, his arms still uselessly handcuffed above his head, but the man easily sidesteps Adam and plunges the needle into Adam's neck.

The drug takes only seconds to take effect. Adam falls limp, and the soldiers turn toward me. I make eye contact with the nearest one. His blond hair is greasy, and he pushes a stray strand out of his face as I flatten myself against the wall.

He caps the needle and returns it to his vest, then pulls another out of a separate pocket.

I groan. "No."

The man grabs my chin, his calloused fingers rough as he sticks me in the neck. There's a sharp pinch followed by a burn, but it's nothing compared to the pain in my shoulder and chest. I'm sure it's a tranquilizer, probably a fraction of the strength of the one Adam was given, and I glare into the soldier's dull, blue eyes with as much hatred as I can muster.

Fuck him.

"We're almost there," he says, his words clipped. "Try not to die before then."

I'd spit on him if I could find the strength to move my lips.

My eyes flutter shut as the men retreat, jumping out of the back of the truck with near-silent movements. Gravel crunches underneath feet before the doors are slammed shut. Then there's some metal clanging, probably a padlock being slid into place.

Well, shit.

Completed Works

THE FEMALE SERIES

The Female is a why choose demon romance with a dark dystopian setting, declining fertility rates, captured women, and three irresistible men.

The Female | Her Males | Their War

Chev's Mate

Queens

THE CURSED KINGDOM SERIES

The Cursed Kingdom is a slow burning, why choose romance with a mystical faerie realm, two infuriatingly attractive princes, and high conflict between the faerie and shifter kingdoms.

The Cursed Kingdom

The Shattered Kingdom

LAND OF WOLVES DUOLOGY

Land of Wolves is a high intensity shifter romance with fated mates, government indoctrination that leads to painful betrayal, and impending war between the shifters and humans.

Land of Wolves: Revelations

Land of Wolves: Retribution (Coming June 2026)

STANDALONES

The Nanny | A Nanny/Single Father Romance

Lord of Dread | An Arranged Marriage Historical Romance

Aine | A Dark Shifter Romance

Upcoming Works

STANDALONES

His Assignment | A Bodyguard Mafia Romance (Release Date TBD)

The Dragon's Agreement | A Dragon Fantasy Romance (Release Date TBD)

ONGOING SERIES

Fates | Book Six of *The Female* Series (Release Date TBD)

The Hidden Kingdom | Book Three of *The Cursed Kingdom* Series (Release date TBD)

TRIGGER WARNINGS CAN BE FOUND ON:

inviwright.com

Stay Connected

SOCIAL MEDIA

Follow Invi Wright on social media to stay up to date on her newest releases, listen to her gab about romance & fantasy books, get regular book recs, and join a fun community of romance lovers!

TikTok & Instagram: @inviwright

EXCLUSIVE CONTENT & CHARACTER ART

Subscribe to **@inviwright** on Patreon for:

- Exclusive access to ongoing novellas
- Exclusive audio chapters
- SFW and NSFW character art
- Partake in polls (help decide what book she'll write next!)
- A free ebook copy of every book she publishes

www.ingramcontent.com/pod-product-compliance
Lightning Source LLC
LaVergne TN
LVHW040037080526
838202LV00045B/3381